THE CONTRACT

Brett Hoffmann has spent much of his career at an international consulting firm. *The Contract* is his first novel.

THE CONTRACT

BRETT HOFFMANN

MICHAEL JOSEPH
an imprint of
PENGUIN BOOKS

This is a work of fiction. Characters, institutions and organisations mentioned in this novel are either the product of the author's imagination or, if real, used fictitiously without any intent to describe actual conduct.

MICHAEL JOSEPH

Published by the Penguin Group
Penguin Group (Australia)
250 Camberwell Road, Camberwell, Victoria 3124, Australia
(a division of Pearson Australia Group Pty Ltd)
Penguin Group (USA) Inc.
375 Hudson Street, New York, New York 10014, USA
Penguin Group (Canada)
90 Eglinton Avenue East, Suite 700, Toronto, Canada ON M4P 2Y3
(a division of Pearson Penguin Canada Inc.)
Penguin Books Ltd
80 Strand, London, WC2R 0RL, England
Penguin Ireland
25 St Stephen's Green, Dublin 2, Ireland
(a division of Penguin Books Ltd)
Penguin Books India Pvt Ltd
11 Community Centre, Panchsheel Park, New Delhi – 110 017, India
Penguin Group (NZ)
67 Apollo Drive, Rosedale, North Shore 0632, New Zealand
(a division of Pearson New Zealand Ltd)
Penguin Books (South Africa) (Pty) Ltd
24 Sturdee Avenue, Rosebank, Johannesburg 2196, South Africa

Penguin Books Ltd, Registered Offices: 80 Strand, London WC2R 0RL, England

First published by Penguin Group (Australia), 2009

10 9 8 7 6 5 4 3 2 1

Cover design by Cameron Midson © Penguin Group (Australia)
Text design by Claire Wilson © Penguin Group (Australia)
Cover image: man by Kelvin Murray / Getty Images, tunnel by Bjanka Kadic / Millenium Images, UK
Typeset in Fairfield Light by Post Pre-Press Group, Brisbane, Queensland
Printed and bound in Australia by McPherson's Printing Group, Maryborough, Victoria

National Library of Australia
Cataloguing-in-Publication data:
Hoffmann, Brett

The contract / Brett Hoffmann
9781921518119 (pbk.)
Murder – fiction. Corporations – corrupt practices – fiction. New York (N. Y.) – fiction.
A823.4

penguin.com.au

For Julia, Dax and Odo
More than you know

November 1967, Atlantic Ocean

Campbell Reeves mopped the sweat from his brow with a sodden handkerchief as he contemplated the endless ocean. The old liner's air conditioning was totally inadequate for the heat and humidity of the equator and he was on the sundeck at the top of the ship, in the shadow cast by a lifeboat, having abandoned the stuffy interior.

The captain had announced they'd soon be crossing that invisible line dividing north from south and many passengers had joined Campbell on deck to be a part of it. Of course, all they could see was an endless expanse of water, which cared not one whit whether it was known as the North Atlantic or the South Atlantic Ocean, and Campbell soon bored of the spectacle.

Making his way down to the promenade deck – which was at least covered, though still open to the elements at the sides – Campbell noted once more the years of constant service beginning to show on the old girl. The remarkable range of beautiful woods and veneers that had been used to line the ship were, in places, badly worn. Doors squeaked, the paintwork was peeling, the carpet was threadbare in spots. Just like me, Campbell mused. At the end of my useful working life. Soon to be pushed into retirement and replaced by a younger model.

He ran a finger around the collar of his shirt. The tie felt tight. Many of the other male passengers sported open-necked, even short-sleeved, shirts but such informal dress wasn't for Campbell Reeves. He was a traditionalist. Travelling first class meant dressing appropriately – meaning appropriate for your status and the exclusive setting of the ship's premier mode of travel, rather than appropriate for the weather. He wasn't wearing a jacket, but he would be when it came time for dinner. At least the restaurant's air conditioning seemed to cope, particularly after sunset.

I need a drink, Campbell decided after looking at his watch. It was a little early, perhaps, but how could it matter when you're at sea and still days away from port, where the hours mattered more? He set out to find his travelling companion.

Campbell Reeves was sixty-seven years old, the same age as the century, and he wasn't used to change. He'd lived in Peoria, Illinois, all his life, born the son of a Caterpillar Tractor Company executive. He'd only ever worked for one company, the president of which was his oldest and dearest friend, Gilbert Collins.

The only significant change in the routine of Campbell's life came when he married his wife, Elizabeth. Just when everybody thought he'd spend the rest of his life as a contented bachelor, Campbell met Beth, not in Peoria – where every eligible young lady had been paraded and rejected – but in New York, just after the end of the war in '45. Young, vibrant and passionate, Beth had completed the puzzle for Campbell. With her, he had everything he'd ever wanted, and he was content.

I wish she was here, Campbell thought, not for the first time. This trip was too long to be away from her. As much as he normally loved travel on the great ships, the length of this journey, and the heat and discomfort, had taken the shine away. But Gilbert had been so excited and so insistent, and Campbell wasn't about to let his old friend and boss down.

The trip had been presented to Gilbert Collins by the board of the company, in recognition of his service as president and chairman for thirty-five years. Like Campbell, Gilbert would soon be put out to pasture and the cruise seemed like the perfect way to start winding down. But Gilbert had no intention of making the journey alone; his own wife had been dead six years already. He needed a travelling companion and the choice was obvious. Cam Reeves was his closest buddy. They'd been inseparable since they were young men, caught up in the thrill and horror of World War I. Cam had been too young to see action, but Gilbert was two years older and served briefly in France towards the end of the conflict. He'd returned a man, with enough experience of both battle and leadership to develop his father's simple company into a burgeoning enterprise.

He cast a long shadow, but his younger friend felt comfortable building a life in that shadow. When the family firm needed to improve its accounting and finance functions, Cam took the college courses Gil nominated for him, before returning to Peoria to join the only business he would ever work for. Together they represented the new breed of college-educated, dynamic, modern-thinking executives waiting in the wings for the previous generation to die out or shuffle away. Gilbert had to wait until 1932 to take over the helm of CMS, but since then he and Campbell Reeves had been living out their destiny. It had been fun.

Now, in 1967, they were the dinosaurs. A newer breed of executives – with even better college degrees and faster and more modern ideas – were hovering, desperate to take over. Gilbert's son Ewan was the leader of the pack. Around him, he'd gathered a small group of high-fliers, hungry to prove themselves. And they had. In the past few years, the young guns had brought home a deal which laid a foundation for the company's continued success for the rest of the century and beyond. It was an amazing coup for Ewan, achieved without assistance from his father. The writing was on the wall. The old guys had outlived their usefulness. For Gilbert, the prospect was clearly daunting, but Campbell had much to look forward to. By marrying such a young woman, he knew he stood an excellent chance of enjoying her companionship until his time was up.

Campbell licked his lips in anticipation of the drink to come as he hunted for his friend. The boat was huge. Almost five city blocks long and twelve decks high, it stretched out of sight in both directions. There were countless places Gilbert Collins might be, but Campbell knew there were just a few where he was likely to be.

First he went forward to the observation lounge and cocktail bar, which curved its way around the front of the promenade deck and afforded a splendid view out to the bow of the ship. The art deco gaudiness of the place still appealed to Campbell, even if the younger set found it old-fashioned. Give me fine woods and steel over plastic any day, he thought to himself as he toured the room, entering on the port side and exiting through the starboard door. No sign of Gilbert.

Back out on the sheltered promenade, Campbell nodded politely to other passengers braving the tropical heat and strolled the length of the ship, patting his face and neck dry with a handkerchief as he went. At the far end of the deck was the first-class smoking room, one of Gil's favourite spots on the ship.

Two decks high, the room was illuminated by skylights and lined with rich English oak. Gil Collins, an inveterate Anglophile, had always loved the idea of the Gentlemen's Club, where men could escape to swap bawdy stories over cigars and brandy. The smoker's lounge fit the image perfectly with its secretive alcoves,

4

leather armchairs and little tables. Of course, the average clubby Englishman would have disagreed entirely. The room was far too modern and decorative to be regarded as kin to the great London clubs of the Victorian era. But it was elegant and comfortable and the Americans loved it.

Gilbert sat staring into the empty fireplace. He'd been aboard during winter voyages when a real coal fire was set there, adding even more Edwardian charm to the room. Now the air was muggy and uncomfortable and he was bored with the book he'd been reading. He turned instead to contemplating an even more boring future.

His son was about to take over the company. His main role in life was coming to an end. And, unlike his old buddy Cam Reeves, Gil had no one to go home to. His wife was gone. His son was young and impatient, focused only on the business, as he should be. That left Gilbert completely alone.

Well, alone apart from his daughters and his grandchildren. And his charity work and his board appointments and his mansion and his staff. And his collection of fine automobiles. And good friends like Campbell and Beth Reeves, of course. He started to feel a little better. Then he saw Cam coming in from the deck, sweating like a pig, as usual, and looking thirsty.

'Come over here and cheer me up, you old sea dog.' Gil waved cheerfully. 'This heat's getting to me, making me all melancholy.'

'We're a bit like the ship, aren't we?' Campbell sat down heavily in a leather armchair. 'At the end of our useful service.'

Gil stood up to stretch the lethargy out of his body. 'Why the heck are we so maudlin today? We've been at sea nearly two weeks already. Why the sudden mood change?'

'Maybe 'cause we've crossed the equator. It's the symbolic halfway point in our journey.'

'We've got more than halfway to go,' Gil said, sitting down again. 'We'll be crossing the equator again before journey's end.'

'Maybe it's the heat. How would I know?'

'A drink, then. To replace some fluids and to celebrate the crossing of the equator. Not too many people can say they've done that on this tub, right?' Gil looked around for a waiter.

'Danny O'Hanlon did it. During the war. Sailed to Australia when she was a troopship. He said they had bunks stacked seven high in the swimming pool.'

'And I'll bet they couldn't order whisky sours from the steward,' Gil said, with a smile, using hand signals to attract a man in a white coat. 'By the way, I've signed us up to play bridge later, with Max Horner and his wife.'

Campbell groaned but knew better than to complain. He didn't really like bridge and he liked the Horners even less. They were from Detroit – he was a VP at General Motors – and they'd been allocated seats at the same dining table as the two men from Peoria. Cam could do without extra time in their company. But Gil called the shots, had done for more than forty years, and Cam wasn't about to try changing that now. So he nodded and lit a cigarette while they waited for the cocktails to arrive. Gil sucked happily on his pipe and they settled into the silence of comfortable friendship.

A few nights later, as the lights of Rio de Janeiro faded into the distance behind the ship, Campbell and Gilbert were again ensconced in the smoking lounge. A boozy lunch ashore, a session of whisky sours before a wine-soaked dinner and the brandies on the table in front of them had rendered them mellow, and a little introspective.

Uncharacteristically, Gil had been rambling on for thirty minutes, praising Cam for his friendship and loyalty, and Campbell was embarrassed. He wasn't used to hearing this kind of praise from his friend. We've spent too much time together, he thought, and now we've run out of things to say. He tried steering the conversation back to neutral subjects, like sports or the ship.

But Gilbert would have none of it. He was looking inwards and he didn't like what he saw. 'You know, when they gave me this trip, I thought I was history. Finished.' His voice was heavy with booze and misery.

In contrast, each day of the cruise had rendered Campbell more comfortable with the idea of retirement. Thinking ahead to timeless days spent with Beth, just pottering about in their beautiful garden, was increasingly satisfying. He realised he really wanted his boss to get comfortable with the idea too. 'Hey, Gil, we're both history, right? Like the ship. It's time to hand over to the next generation.'

'Not finished like that!' Gil sounded annoyed. 'I mean finished, finished. Dead. I mean dead.'

Campbell looked at his friend, trying to understand what he really meant. Gil looks old, he thought, worn out. With a full head of white hair and a lean body borne of regular exercise, Gil had always been the better looking of the two. But in the yellow light of the lounge, the lines on his face appeared to be deeply etched. His eyes hung low with dark bags, and his mouth seemed to fold down at the edges. Cam wondered if that was how old he looked.

'What the hell are you talking about, Gil?'

'I'm serious. They don't want me to get back to the States. I thought they were going to do it on board, then nobody but you showed up.'

'Hey, buddy, you're not making any sense. And I think you've had enough of this.'

Campbell leaned over to push his friend's brandy balloon out of reach. Gilbert smacked his hand away like a naughty child and picked up the glass as if nothing had happened. 'You're the only one I can trust, Cam. They'll get me eventually; they might even get you.' He gave his pal a sad look. 'You're already too close to me. They know they can't trust you.'

Reeves sat back in his chair, wanting to make sense of the rambling. 'Who is "they"? And why can't they trust me?'

'They can't trust you because you're a decent man, Cam. They don't trust decent men.'

Campbell shook his head in confusion. 'Are you talking about the firm? The next generation? Of course they're gonna want to do things their own way, but we have to let go. It's their company now. You remember what it was like when we took over? Your dad wouldn't have been happy either, if he'd still been alive.'

'You're missing the point, my friend.' Suddenly Gilbert didn't sound inebriated at all. The look on his face was deadly serious. 'They can have the damn company. They've got the damn company. It's the loose ends I'm worried about. They're going to want to tidy up the loose ends. And we,' he indicated each of them in turn with an index finger, 'are the loose ends.'

Campbell took a swig of brandy. 'What do you mean, "tidy up"? And why are we the loose ends? What the hell are you talking about?'

Gil pointed to himself. 'I'm a loose end because I know too much.' The finger swapped back to point vaguely in Cam's direction. 'You're a loose end 'cause they think I tell you everything. I thought that if you didn't know, you'd be safe, but now I realise they'll just assume I told you anyway.'

'Told me what?'

'You'll know the whole thing before this trip is over. You need to know, maybe you should even write it all down. You're good at writing, Cam, better than me. But not tonight, okay? I'm too hammered and we have plenty of time now to —'

Gilbert stopped talking. His mouth remained open. The blood drained away from his face. His eyes were fixed on a point somewhere over Cam's left shoulder, towards the centre of the room. Campbell twisted around in his chair and gasped in surprise. Three young men in modern lounge suits were standing there. He knew two of them well.

'Jesus Christ!' Gil muttered. 'We're dead!'

1

October 2002, New York City

Jack stared at the blinking red lights on the telephone. On, off, on, off. The damn things never seemed to stop. Not so very long ago he'd been in love with those blinking red lights. They meant another client was on the line, or another deal, or another offer. And, as always, voicemail would be populated with neatly packaged opportunities – to buy, sell, list, issue or participate. They represented money and success, those blinking red lights. If you're a trader, and your lights don't blink, you won't be a trader for long.

But he'd grown to despise the red lights. Maybe they did represent success, but he was growing to despise that too. For Jack, success had gone from primary motivation, to status symbol and, finally, to little more than a millstone. The burden of a brilliant reputation was something he had never anticipated when he set out to conquer the great money markets of the world. Everybody wanted a piece of him now. Everybody wanted him to just keep doing what he'd always been doing – making them richer.

Trouble was, Jack was over it. Trying to stay ahead of a market in turmoil was exhausting. The outrageous acts of both terrorists and internet entrepreneurs had combined to make it a hellish year for the market. Finding the motivation to keep the machine cranking over was increasingly tough and the thought of doing it forever was truly depressing.

He glanced around the trading floor, looking in vain for Matt McCormick. Then, unenthusiastically, he picked up the telephone handset and pushed a button. One of the red lights stopped blinking.

'Jack Rogers,' he said.

'Jack, it's Dean Loftus, from Hamilton's in London. Congrats on the Singapore deal. It's all over the financial pages here. Listen, I know you're busy, but I think I have an opportunity for you . . .'

Jack suppressed a sigh and looked across the sea of computer screens, telephones and fellow dealmakers once more. He spotted Matt across the other side of the room, and stood up, gesturing angrily with one hand. He knew it was unfair. McCormick was probably the hardest-working guy on the floor. His breaks were never longer than half the time he was entitled to. But there was a price to pay for being protégé to Jack Rogers.

Matt hurried over, not a hint of resentment in his eyes. He took his seat, at the desk abutting Jack's, and automatically picked up the phone. Another flashing red light disappeared. Jack sat back down and idly consulted one of his computer screens, manipulating his mouse with the left hand while he made sketchy notes with a Mont Blanc pen in his right. He made noncommittal grunts to the banker in London through the handset tucked under his chin, while he absorbed the latest market data from the screen. Then he disconnected the call abruptly and, ignoring the renewed flashing light of line one, he punched the voicemail button and listened to messages. More scribbled notes, which he pushed over to Matt's desk for action.

Only one message was vaguely interesting. Margaret Bland had called to remind him of the presentation ceremony at 11 a.m. Each quarter, a bonus pool was divvied up among Sutton Brothers' best performers. The boss liked to hand out the cheques personally, with a little ceremony and a well-worn set of platitudes. During his eight years at the bank, Jack had been a regular in the line-up and had heard Frank Spiteri's speech a few too many times. But he liked Frank and always worked hard to hide his cynicism.

Working for Frank Spiteri – now that would be more fun. In addition to running the New York office of Sutton Brothers, Spiteri headed the bank's mergers and acquisitions division. Jack had wanted in to M&A very badly, and even bullied the bank into funding an MBA at Columbia to improve his credentials. But, even with the Masters under his belt, Spiteri had been immovable on the subject. 'We're downsizing, Jack,' he'd said. 'Mergers are out of fashion right now. It wouldn't be a good career move for you, anyway. The money's not as good and there's even more time away from home.'

Jack didn't care about any of that, but Spiteri had just given him a good-natured pat on the back and said, cheerfully, 'Besides, my boy, I don't think the bank could afford to lose your contribution to the bottom line. Play to your strengths, eh?'

It was a little after 10.40. Jack stood up and stretched. A few of the young women on the trading floor exchanged glances and watched him, some more discreetly than others. Jack was just over six feet tall and in the best shape of his life, having resorted to exercise in an effort to ease the tedium of his average work day. His wardrobe reflected his spending power, his dark brown hair was regularly maintained and his nails neatly manicured. His schoolmates back at state high school in suburban Sydney would be hard pressed to recognise him these days. Twelve long years he'd been away from Australia, having said farewell just after his twenty-fourth birthday. Four years in the City of London, eight in Manhattan. He'd left Sydney slightly rough around the edges and he'd emerged as a sophisticated Wall Street player, technically one of the most eligible bachelors in the city.

Only technically. He'd been living with Peta Fitzsimmons for seven of those eight years in New York, but they weren't married. Until they were, Peta refused to adopt the title of 'wife'. Didn't like being called 'girlfriend' either. So they referred to each other as 'my partner'. Jack would have preferred 'husband' and 'wife'. After all, if he got the promotion he was expecting soon, he'd be made a partner in the bank, and would be surrounded with 'partners'. And Peta already had two partners of her own, co-owners of her fashion line and string of boutiques.

But there was a problem. Jack wanted the titles, not the wedding. Marriage, they'd always agreed, would only be necessary as a prelude to starting a family. Peta's free-thinking, Florida-based parents never pressured her on any issue, and for Jack, ignoring his family's disapproval was relatively easy when they were thousands of miles away. But lately, the pressure had been coming from closer to home. Peta was ready for the next step. Jack wasn't. In truth, he didn't really mind the marriage part, but he was seriously uncomfortable with the baby part that would follow.

Watching the clock, Jack took two more calls before signalling to Matt that he was heading upstairs. The younger man nodded stoically as his hands flew from the phones to the computers to the papers on his desk.

Jack took the stairs up to the main lobby of the building, one floor above the bank's trading room. There, he poked at the button for an elevator that would take him to the uppermost floors.

The twenty-eighth floor of this particular tower on Broad Street was where Sutton Brothers kept the most senior partners of the New

York office on display. And that's just what it looked like – a series of large glass cages, all basically the same but each organised or decorated individually, to reflect the character and personality of the specimen residing there. The sense of visiting big cats at the zoo was reinforced by the fact that many of the cages appeared empty, but somehow occupied, suggesting the inhabitants were hiding in among the natural cover created by furniture, office equipment, plants and documents. Other big cats paced back and forth, talking into the telephone, or lazing in their recliner chairs, staring at a computer screen. In some cages, Jack could see pairs or trios gathered around small tables covered in papers and coffee mugs.

Large offices and meeting rooms swept around the outside of the floor, bathed in natural light and monopolising the best views. In the centre of the floor there was a large reception area for clients, together with more meeting rooms and cubicles for the partners' assistants. Sleek, modern design and expensive artwork proclaimed the bank's recently acquired image of vitality and success in a modern age. No more the rich woods and dark colours of the secure and stolid past – Sutton Brothers wanted to be seen as a go-getter in the new century.

At the far end of the floor, Frank Spiteri occupied the biggest cage of all. His status was emphasised by the slim, silver blinds hanging over the glass walls of his enclosure so that, with a twist, the office could be made private. He liked to keep the blinds open to observe all activity on the floor. But when those blinds were shut, all four floors of Sutton Brothers were soon electrified by wild rumour.

As Jack walked towards the office he could see a small group of immaculately presented fellow bankers gathered at Margaret Bland's desk. Margaret – whose family name, sadly, perfectly reflected her personality – had been Frank's assistant since long before Jack joined the team. She was arranging the young stars into a line in the large space outside Spiteri's office, according to some predetermined order of her own devising. As Jack arrived, she gave him a brief but, for her, sincere smile and ushered him to the head of the line.

'How you doing, Margaret?' Jack said, paying scant attention to the other bonus recipients. Although only thirty-six, Jack was older than most of them.

'Fine, thank you, Jack,' she said crisply and moved back to her desk to collect a small pile of envelopes. Then she hurried to her boss's door to usher him out. The clock was about to strike the hour.

As soon as Frank emerged from his office, Jack could tell something was wrong. His dark, handsome looks were stiffened by a grim set to his jaw and creases of concern around his eyes. The perpetual tan on his face seemed paler than normal and the silk designer tie around his neck was very slightly, but very uncharacteristically, askew.

Radiating tension, he whipped the envelopes out of Margaret's hand and marched directly to the spot in front of Jack. A peek at the envelope, then a quick glance into Jack's eyes, then he stuck out his hand. Instinctively, Jack shook it firmly.

'Congratulations once again, Jack.'

'Thanks, Frank,' Jack said, trying to hide his surprise.

Spiteri stepped to the right and looked at the next name on his list. Congratulations. Handshake. No speech. No personalised praise or words of encouragement for the next quarter. None of the usual stuff about the Sutton Brothers team. He just moved down the line quickly, clearly distracted.

Jack looked at Margaret's face and saw concern and curiosity. Spiteri was a man of habit. He was also a man of massive personality. Even when their largest client suddenly went belly-up two years earlier, Frank had remained cheerful and unconcerned, his smile and charm undiminished by the shocking news. His booming voice broadcast words of optimism and promise, just as they had done after 9/11, brilliantly shoring up office morale. But, today, he wasn't sending out the usual signals. Today was very different.

When the last envelope was presented, Spiteri turned away and walked back towards his office with no further comment, one hand thrust deeply into his trouser pocket.

The bonus winners hurried away to the elevators, some expectantly opening the envelopes and all eager to get back to doing it all over again. Jack stayed back, tucking the envelope inside his suit jacket.

'What's up with Frank, Margaret?' he asked.

'I don't know.' She was still looking concerned. 'He's been like that most of the morning.'

'Maybe he got a call from the Ferrari people telling him how much his service is going to cost.'

Margaret didn't smile. She didn't appreciate jokes at her boss's expense. 'He certainly got a call from someone,' she said. 'On his private line. Whoever it was, they sure upset him.'

Jack pondered the possibilities. Wife asking for divorce; kid expelled from school; doctor calling to say he's got cancer. It would have to be something major to faze Frank Spiteri.

'Well, don't let him take it out on you,' Jack advised, as he moved away, eliciting a disapproving look from the loyal assistant.

Jack pulled the unsealed envelope from his jacket pocket as he walked, and looked at the cheque inside. The bonus was bigger than he'd expected after a tough quarter and his mind turned at once to the prospect of some retail therapy. The last bonus had gone on the plasma screen and surround sound system for his den. This time it was Peta's turn. Could he trust himself to pick out some delicious piece of jewellery to suit her offbeat taste? Maybe they could take a trip to Tiffany's together but no doubt she'd have something more radical in mind.

He made his way slowly back along the corridor to the elevators. Everything on this floor is so quiet, he thought. And so light. The trading room was completely cut off from natural light – like a casino gaming room, designed to remove any perception of day or night. Keeping the players at the machines longer. And the noise down there wasn't dissimilar to a casino either, with phones and shouted conversations and bells to mark the time. It turned out the people with whom he had the most in common, in terms of his working environment, were the dealers of Las Vegas.

A sharp shout pushed the image from his head. Margaret Bland's thin frame was hurrying down the corridor towards him. As she drew closer, she said, 'Got a minute, Jack? Frank needs to speak to you urgently.'

Excellent, Jack thought, another distraction.

'Only because it's you asking, Margaret,' he said, and turned to follow her back to Spiteri's office.

Once he'd been ushered inside and the door was closed, Spiteri pointed to one of the low, leather armchairs arranged around a coffee table in front of the glass wall. Again, Jack noticed the signs of stress on the managing partner's face as he sat in an adjacent seat. And when he spoke, Frank's voice was quieter and more serious than Jack had ever heard before, his accent more apparent.

'I want to talk to you about Stella Sartori,' he said.

2

At that moment Stella Sartori was watching the sun rise over luminous blue water, a gentle breeze playing with her perfectly straight, shoulder-length hair. The sand on the beach below glowed faintly orange. Joggers in skimpy gear tracked along the hard-packed sand close to the water's edge. Her mother and sister were still asleep inside, but it had been five long nights since Stella had enjoyed the idea of sleep. She was out on their tiny balcony, twelve storeys up, long before the sun bothered showing up.

Her state of mind was dampening the holiday fun for her family, and she felt bad about that. They'd all been looking forward to this for a long time. But where else could she have gone? And how could she pretend nothing was wrong? She couldn't act as if last week never happened.

If Freda, her doting mother, knew the full story, things would be even worse. And Angie, sweet and kind older sister that she was, couldn't be trusted with a secret. She'd never been reliable in that department. So Stella had only her own counsel to work through the shock and the dire implications of what had happened.

Little wonder she was distracted.

She sat up on the sunlounge and reached for Angie's packet of cigarettes next to the ashtray on the table. She was normally a packet-a-year person, succumbing to temptation only at boozy parties or after the adrenalin rush of unexpected success. But this would be her third of the day, and it was not yet 7 a.m. As she sucked smoke into her lungs she felt a rawness in her throat.

The sliding glass door behind her grated open, giving Stella a start. Angie stumbled onto the balcony, dressed in a light, white nightdress, pushing hair from her half-closed eyes. She squinted at the view and then looked at Stella.

'Whatcha doing?' she asked, hardly moving her mouth.

'Watching the sun come up. Checking out the hot bods on the beach. You know.'

'Right,' Angie said, skeptical. She closed the door behind her then gestured with her hand. 'Give us a puff.'

Stella passed her the cigarette and Angie took three long draughts, virtually burning down the whole stick, before handing it back. Stella took a single, half-hearted puff and then stubbed the butt in the ashtray. Her mouth felt foul and she longed for a mint to suck on. She looked out to sea, but could feel Angie's eyes still watching her.

'You know, I think Lizzy's going to be as gorgeous as you, sis. She's only eight, but she's already turning heads. She's the spitting image, I reckon.'

Stella smiled at the memory of her feisty little niece who'd always shared her olive skin, dark green eyes and brown-black hair. It had been nearly two years since she'd seen Elizabeth and her brother. And one of her own two brothers had a new baby, whom she'd never laid eyes on. She felt a sudden urge to go home. To get even further away from the difficulties and dangers threatening her career, maybe even her life. The thought of Australia, so far from everything, was almost irresistible. But she knew she had to overcome the urge to run and hide. She had to go back and finish what she had started.

'Well, she has a beautiful mother,' Stella said quietly.

'I don't know,' Angie said, sitting clumsily on the end of Stella's sunlounge and grabbing a small roll of fat through the cotton of her nightdress. 'I'm still putting on weight. Never lost it after the babies. But we were a couple of spunks once, weren't we, Stell? Of course, you still are.'

Stella just gave Angie a small smile and turned her head to look away. Now that Angie had distracted her from reliving the assault, a wave of tiredness swept over her. She closed her eyes and began to drift.

'Is everything all right with David?' Angie asked tentatively.

Without opening her eyes, Stella nodded once. 'Same old David,' she said.

'He's not, you know, causing trouble again?'

'No more than usual. He doesn't have access to my bank account any more.'

'I bet he was pissed off about our chicks' holiday. Barry sure was, 'specially when he heard about the golf course. "What the hell are *you* gunna do on a golf course?" he says. "Play with a few balls," says I. Then I show him this skimpy bikini I bought. It cost me ten bucks at a discount warehouse and I wouldn't be seen dead in it, even if I could get into it, but it was worth it just for the look on Barry's face.'

Stella's smile broadened and she was, for once, glad of her sister's ability to talk incessantly about nothing at all. Now she was jabbering on about the girls at work and how everybody was jealous of their big beach vacation. Stella's mind floated towards the promise of a dreamless sleep.

A prod on the arm startled her. 'Ooh, sorry, sis,' Angie was saying, 'were you asleep? I can't see your eyes behind those sunnies.'

'No. Sorry. Just drifted off a bit. Sorry.'

'That's okay, doll. God knows you could use it. You've been a wreck since you arrived. Are you sure we can't help? 'Cos if it's a marriage thing, or even a divorce thing, you know we're here for you, right?'

'Thanks, Ange. I know that. I do have some issues with David, but when the time comes, I reckon I can handle divorcing him on my own. But that's not what's been on my mind at all. It's a work thing, honestly.'

Angie looked slightly annoyed. 'Well, can't you put it aside for a little while then? We've come all this way to have a fun-in-the-sun, super-hot, girls-only vacation, Stella. You think you can get with the program a little?'

Stella opened her eyes and took off her dark glasses. 'Look,' she said, 'I wasn't supposed to be here for this part of the trip. You and Mum wanted to get some shopping in, remember? I need a bit of space to sort something out, okay? Just give me a couple of days. I'll be fine. You and Mum just do what you were going to do anyway. I'll sort it out, I promise.'

'We're moving on soon,' Angie said, hurt. 'To the fancy resort.'

'I know, I know. I promise to be the life of the party for part two, okay?'

Angie grunted doubtfully as she stood up and moved back to the glass door. As she went back inside, she said, 'I'm going to get a bit more sleep before breakfast. You try to get some too, sis. Try not to think about it.'

Try not to think about it. Excellent idea, Stella thought ruefully. If only it was that easy. She closed her eyes once more and felt her body crying out for some downtime. Her mind, however, refused to cooperate. The annoyingly persistent memory of an innocuous hotel room in Peoria, Illinois, jumped back into her head.

*

The knock at the door waking her from a restless nap. Here to check the minibar, a voice says and, when she looks through the spyhole, she sees a dark-haired man with a broken-looking nose wearing what looks like a uniform. Fumbling with the chain – not wanting to inconvenience anyone and happy for the distraction – she opens the door. She is shoved back with overwhelming force. A huge man has her in a bear hug, pushing the air from her lungs. He rushes her across the room until her legs hit the bed and she falls backwards, his massive bulk crashing down on top of her.

He repositions himself, his knees on her chest and shoulders, the crotch of his black pants thrust directly in her face. She kicks her legs wildly. She goes to scream, but a rough, pudgy hand presses hard over her mouth, its smell distinctive and disgusting. Looking up she sees the big chin of a pale, heavy-set man with red hair and freckles and a slit for a mouth. Looking back are two pinpricks of eyes, glazed and dispassionate.

Then, out of the corner of her left eye, a shiny object comes into view. Terror ripples though her body. A knife. An enormous knife with a long, wide blade, serrated on one side. It flashes in the light from the nightstand as it moves closer to her face.

She goes stiff with shock and stops struggling. She registers the dark-haired man moving in the room. She stares up at the double chin, desperate to understand what's going on. The chin jiggles. He says, 'Don't move and don't make a sound,' and he waves the knife in her face again. Then he eases back a little on her mouth, and breathing is easier. An involuntary grunt escapes from her throat. He says, 'No noise, or I'll stick you right now, understand?' and she tries to nod her head.

She feels a sense of relief when he shifts his weight off her and removes his hand from her face, but then he moves the knife to his left hand and lets it rest on her chest, pointing directly at her throat. He sits on the bed beside her, his bulk pushing against her body.

'You shouldna got on the wrong side of Mr Cross, bitch.'

The mention of Cross sends a jolt through her. Her client had ordered this? It was inconceivable.

'Shut the fuck up, ass wipe!' a deep voice says and the whale sitting beside her screws up his face and leers at her. She hears the other guy working his way around the room, rifling through everything. She hears her small suitcase being emptied onto the floor.

The redhead doesn't watch his buddy. He just looks her up and down. She is wearing thin trackpants and a tight T-shirt. She clenches her fists in disgust, her nails digging into her palms, as the man moves his hand across her chest. Still holding the knife, his fingers knead one breast, then the other. His eyes move to her crotch, then back to her face and his thin lips curl in triumph.

He lowers his head and his foul-smelling mouth close to her left ear and whispers, 'Soon as we find it, we're gonna go have us a little fun. We gonna make your last night alive very special, honey.' He giggles and squeezes her breast harder. Her heart beats like a metronome on crack. She looks at the knife and wants to grab it. Stab him or die. Better than being his sex doll. She tries to swallow the fear in her throat as she readies herself to fight.

The dark-haired guy comes closer and says, 'Later, man,' and the big oaf stops groping her, but the knife isn't moved away.

The dark-haired guy continues, 'Can't find nothin' that looks like it don't belong to her. There are no papers here. You sure he didn't say nothin' else?'

And the whale says, 'He just said she's got some paper belongs to him.'

He looks right in her face and says, 'He said he didn't care if she was dead as long as he got his paper back. Matter of fact, he said if she vanishes and the paper vanishes too, that would be just dandy. I say we just take everything she's got and get outta here. It's time to party, man.' He rubs his pants with his right hand and blows her a kiss. She tastes vomit rising in her gullet.

Then, Ben Fisher saves her life. Loud, incessant knocking on the door. Threats to call the manager. The redhead stands up, next to the bed, keeping the knife close to her side. The dark-haired guy moves over to the door and pulls something out of his pocket. She thinks it's a gun. She wants to warn Ben but the redhead has one finger to his lips. Ben keeps knocking and calling her name. Then she hears Jodie's voice saying she's off to get security.

Now she feels some of her power coming back. She sees indecision on the face of the dark-haired one. She says, 'Go, before security gets here. Get out now!' Redhead scowls at her and Ben calls out 'Stella? Is that you?' The dark guy glares. He nods and says, 'Let's go,' but the redhead doesn't move. He is staring at her with pure hatred. The other guy says, 'Let's go!' again, a little louder, but she doesn't relax, even when the big bastard moves away.

Stella opened her eyes. The vision of that dark afternoon was instantly replaced by a shimmering view of gently swaying palm trees and early morning beachgoers, seen through the bars of the balcony railing. Her body still held some tension, as if her attackers had only just left, but this time was better than the last. With each reliving of those terrifying memories, she felt slightly more in control of her fear and anger. She had survived. And she still had a chance to make Daniel Cross pay. So what if it was one woman pitted against all the resources of two multi-million-dollar enterprises and all their friends on Wall Street? So what if she couldn't think of a single person to help her? And so what if her career and reputation were already in ruins?

Only one thing was absolutely clear. She had to try.

3

'How well do you know Stella?' Frank Spiteri asked.

'Not particularly well. We've been on two courses together,' Jack said. 'I liked her.'

Spiteri sat close to Jack, their knees almost touching, and he kept his voice soft. 'I like her too. She's one of my best employees. Maybe the very best.'

Jack noted a sadness in the deep voice, as if something good had been lost forever. Spiteri was fidgeting with his pen, spinning it around in his fingers restlessly – and his eyes darted about, instead of maintaining their usual intelligent focus. It was the first time Jac had seen the managing partner nervous, and he found the conditi dangerously infectious.

'What's going on, Frank? What can I do to help?'

Spiteri's eyes stopped moving and fixed on Jack. He held pause, as if deciding where to start. Finally he said, 'You k sort of work we do in Mergers and Acquisitions, Jack? W saying? Of course you do. You were looking to get into weren't you?'

'Yes,' Jack said, sensing an opportunity. 'I'd love to work with you guys. Helping companies find the right targets to buy, formulating the deal, setting the price, looking at the structuring, identifying risks, doing due diligence, all of it.'

'So you understand due diligence.'

'I think so. We send in a team to examine the operations of the target company, looking for risks and opportunities and making sure the price is right. That sort of thing.'

Spiteri nodded. 'It's one of our best businesses. We're good at it and we make a lot of money from it. And our best due diligence team leader was . . . is, Stella Sartori. In the few years she's been with the bank she's earned herself quite a reputation on Wall Street. She has a knack for finding things nobody else uncovers and, on occasions, her work alone has saved our clients millions of dollars. I've worked with her personally on a number of deals and I've never had any reason to distrust her.'

Jack sensed real sincerity in Spiteri's face and in his voice. The face was deeply lined, but dark and masculine, an easy face to look at. The voice hinted at Mediterranean origins – Malta, according to the office grapevine. Just into his sixties, and a resident of the US more than forty years, Frank Spiteri had long ago stopped thinking of himself as a foreigner, unlike Jack who still did after a mere eight years.

'So, what's Stella done?' Jack was intrigued.

'Well, she's got herself caught up in something,' Spiteri said. 'It's complicated but it has the potential to be very damaging to the firm.'

Ah, Jack thought, the cardinal sin. Thou shalt not damage the good name of Sutton Brothers.

'I'm sure I don't need to say it, Jack,' Spiteri continued, 'but it's bviously highly confidential. Like any merger deal, the client stuff is very sensitive, but in this case we also have the problem of protecting our professional standing. Stella's done some things that don't look good on first inspection. I'm sure she had her reasons, but at the moment we have a very unhappy client and a runaway employee and a company board waiting for a report to tell them to go ahead with a major deal. You must only discuss this with me, understand?'

'Of course, Frank, but what do you mean by "runaway employee"?'

'Stella,' Spiteri said, with disbelief, 'has disappeared!'

'Disappeared?'

'And she's stolen some very sensitive material from the target company.'

'Are you sure? That doesn't sound like the Stella Sartori you've just described.'

'I know, I know. But that's what I'm hearing. I need to find out more, of course, and I need to find Stella as quickly as possible. That's where I think you can help.'

Jack sat back in his chair, curious but cautious. 'What can I do?' he asked.

Frank gave him a long, searching look. 'I'd better start at the beginning,' he said. 'Ever heard of Kradel Electronics?'

'European company, listed in Frankfurt and London,' Jack said quickly. 'In the defence sector. Their stock's been doing well lately. They won a big contract to make parts for the Joint Strike Fighter, as I recall. They produce electronic gadgets for military aircraft, that sort of thing.'

The boss was impressed. 'Very good, Jack, you really know your stuff. You know who the CEO is?'

Jack racked his brain. 'Last I knew, and it would be a few months back now, I guess, the position was vacant after the sudden death of . . . now, what was his name?'

'Rudy Hartschorn,' Spiteri offered. 'His replacement was Daniel Cross.'

'Ah, Daniel Cross.'

'You know him?'

'Only by reputation. We did a private bond issue for his firm a few years back. I wasn't directly involved but I heard he was pretty, ah, aggressive. What was the name of that company?'

'CMS,' Frank said. 'Collins Military Systems. Daniel was president for twenty years until his recent move to Kradel. They're one of my best clients. I've worked with Daniel on many, many deals over the years. I have a great deal of respect for him but, I agree, he can come across a little forceful at times.'

'Brute of a client', was how Jack remembered the scuttlebutt, but he was glad to have chosen a more diplomatic description. Cross and Spiteri were obviously old buddies.

'So,' Frank resumed, 'Dan Cross is the recently appointed head of Kradel. It's a European conglomerate headquartered in London. That's where Daniel has been based these past four months. As I said, before that he headed up CMS, which is still majority-owned by members of the Collins family, although Daniel has a fair chunk of it, I'd say, after so long in the top job.

'In the early days of his leadership, CMS grew rapidly. Back then, I helped him buy out some competitors and absorb smaller companies to add technical expertise. Business went a bit flat after the end of the Cold War, but they've done okay, and they have excellent research and development facilities.

'Anyway, one of Daniel's first acts at Kradel was to convince the board to buy CMS. There are obvious synergies between the two companies and a subsidiary operating in the US would provide Kradel with greater access to the biggest buyers of military hardware in the world. Also, the Collins family has lost interest in running the firm.'

Spiteri looked up to see if Jack was following. 'I was asked by Daniel and the board of Kradel to send a team into CMS for a quick due diligence exercise. Daniel's influence with the Collins family and his knowledge of the company means the deal is a friendly one, but our role is to facilitate it and help fix a fair price after preparing a pretty standard report outlining the risks and opportunities. It's not a huge job, but it's a very important one for us if we want to continue getting work from Kradel, which is a major opportunity.'

Shifting in his seat, Frank gave the ceiling a long gaze before going on. 'Maybe Stella was too senior for the job,' he said, turning his eyes back to Jack's, 'but she was available, and I knew she had some vacation plans starting later this week. This was just a small job, one she could get out of the way before she left for Australia or wherever it is she's headed.'

'Why do you say she was too senior?' Jack asked. 'You just said the job was really important.'

'Yes, yes, but I'm managing the high-level stuff. Stella's used to leading teams where she has direct contact with the client board or CEO. And she likes to get into the strategic side of the deal. All we needed here was a team to go in, gather data, complete a bunch of checklists and do the number-crunching in a hurry. We couldn't find an available human resources expert so Stella was asked to lead the team and do the HR review as well. She said she was happy to do it, but I know reviewing pension plan liabilities and executive contracts isn't really her thing.'

'What happened?'

Spiteri gave an exasperated sigh. 'I don't really know, Jack. All I know is the whole job was scheduled to take less than two weeks, including delivery of the report. We're now at the beginning of the second week and Stella appears to have decided to sabotage the whole operation.'

He heaved another sigh – and his voice dropped in both tone and volume. 'Like I said, Jack, she's stolen some sensitive documents, including information that could be highly damaging to CMS and Daniel Cross. And she's disappeared with the lot.'

'Why would she do that?'

'I'm not sure, but last Wednesday morning I got an irate phone call from Daniel Cross. He'd just arrived in Peoria after a long flight from London and when he got to the CMS plant he discovered that a critically important file was missing. It was last in Stella's possession – our own people have admitted that – although nobody's clear on why she wanted it in the first place. And then she disappeared. Not just from the plant, but from the hotel, seemingly from Peoria altogether. Daniel's had the authorities and his own people out looking for her.'

'What do you know about the file?'

'It relates to highly sensitive contractual arrangements with the Pentagon. It's a top-secret file, Jack, and Stella may have breached some federal law by taking it.'

'Why would she do it? And what could have motivated her to take off?'

'Well,' Spiteri said, looking slightly uncomfortable, 'she says she was attacked and her life was threatened. The details are pretty vague.'

Jack was shocked. 'Attacked? You mean physically? Where? On the client's premises? Is she okay?'

Spiteri shook his head. 'At her hotel. I can't even be sure it was connected to her work. And she's okay, Jack, don't worry about that. Physically, anyway. I can't be sure what's going on in her head.'

'But —'

'Jack, I've already told you how highly I think of Stella. Of course her safety is my first priority. Her career is also important to me, as is the reputation of this firm. I'm hoping we can resolve this quickly and quietly and all get back to business with reputations intact, but her games are making it increasingly hard.'

A tanned hand was placed reassuringly on Jack's forearm. 'Daniel Cross had a telephone conversation with Stella after her departure from Peoria. I also spoke to her just before she took off. She'd had a run-in with a couple of over-zealous security guards, but she was fine and the danger, such as it was, had passed.'

Jack's forehead creased into a quizzical frown. 'You've spoken to her?'

Spiteri leaned back in his chair and crossed his arms defensively. 'I suppose you could call it speaking. It was more like shouting, I guess. I'm afraid I didn't handle it very well, but I'd just had Daniel chew my ass for sending a thief and a blackmailer into his company and he wanted answers from Stella. When she rang I demanded to know what she'd done with the file but she refused to tell me. She was extremely upset about being assaulted and she accused Daniel of being behind it. I told her not to be so stupid and stubborn and she hung up. I said the wrong thing, I know that now.'

Regret creased his face. 'When she spoke to Daniel the next day, she wouldn't tell him what she'd done with the file either and, according to him, she used the call to interrogate him instead of explaining her own actions. He's convinced she's setting out to damage him personally or blackmail him or try to embarrass one of the companies, or all of the above. He's a very unhappy man at the moment. He's on his way here now. By the time he arrives I will need to have a strategy in place to fix this. I just hope he's in a better mood than he was when I was in Peoria last week.'

'You went out there?'

'I was in Peoria Thursday and some of Friday. Daniel wanted me to come down hard on the rest of the team, but I knew they weren't going to tell me anything Stella didn't want me to know. They're very loyal to her, as you will see.'

Jack tried to keep a startled look from his face. 'I will?'

'I want you to go out there, Jack,' Spiteri said, his eyes showing sincerity and concern. 'We have to find out where Stella went and we have to open a dialogue with her as soon as we can. I can hold Daniel off a few days but he has every right to sack us on the spot and refuse to pay for the time we've spent so far. It's only because of my long relationship with him that he hasn't advised the board of Kradel to can us already.'

He gently touched Jack's arm again. 'I've promised we'll put this right, and quick. He's agreed to let me send someone out there to trace Stella's footsteps and have another go at the team. To try to find out what motivated her to steal the file and take off the way she did. Maybe then we'll know what this is all about. Daniel insisted I send someone from outside the mergers division but I talked him around. I had someone in mind. I thought only someone who knew the team would be able to gain their trust. But when I saw you this morning, it occurred to me you'd be perfect.'

'Why?'

'Well, you're a fellow Aussie for a start, so Stella might be more open to trusting you, if you find her. Daniel will be pleased I found someone independent, someone who isn't already too close to her and the others. And you're senior, you're trustworthy and you're smart. I know I can rely on you to handle Daniel delicately, keeping him happy while you get what you can from the team. I can introduce you to him this afternoon.'

'What makes you think the team will talk to me? Like you said, surely someone who knows them —'

'Oh, Jack, give yourself some credit,' Frank interrupted, with a knowing smile. 'You're one of the best schmoozers in the business.

Why else would your clients keep writing me to say how much they love you?'

Jack winced at the exaggerated praise. A few clients, maybe, had written over the years, but it was the money they really loved, not Jack. He just helped them get it. Besides, flattery wasn't required to get him on board. This was change, this was intriguing. This wasn't the windowless trading floor. Whether or not he could get his colleagues to open up was incidental – Jack wanted to know how Stella's saga was going to play out.

He said nothing at first. His instincts told him there was more to be gained from Frank Spiteri's desperate desire for a quick solution. So he sat back in the chair and looked thoughtful, as if weighing the pros and cons. He could see Frank searching his face, looking for some indication that the ego-stroking had worked. When Jack saw a flicker of doubt in those brown eyes, he said, 'I don't know, Frank, I'm a bit uncomfortable about spying on my colleagues. And if they're not telling you anything I don't see why they'd talk to me. On the other hand, I can see you need to do something and I'd like to help. Then again, I have a lot on my plate already. It'd be a lot of work to cover all my deals, just for a couple of days in the mergers business . . .'

'How 'bout we make it more than just a coupla days?' Frank said quickly, on the crest of a brainwave. 'We could make your move to mergers a permanent one! That's what you've wanted to do, isn't it, ever since you finished the MBA?'

Jack's eyes narrowed with suspicion. This was a better deal than even he'd been fishing for. Perhaps he hadn't appreciated the full measure of Frank's desperation. That was worrying, but the thrill of a dream being fulfilled overwhelmed any doubt.

'That would be fantastic, Frank,' he said. 'Can you really make that happen?'

'Of course,' said Spiteri, a brief smile signalling his relief. 'I can make it happen in a heartbeat, but you may need more time to get things sorted out downstairs.'

Less time than you think, Jack thought ruefully. The line of traders willing and able to take over his portfolio would form quickly and enthusiastically. A big move by a senior player created opportunities for rapid advancement in both prestige and wealth among the hungry junior traders. Like officers promoted in the heat of battle after the death of a general, Jack's departure would be seen by most as a chance for glory, not as a loss. The loss would be felt later, when unhappy clients grumbled about the unavailability of their favourite market guru and voted with their funds under management. But, Jack concluded, all that would be somebody else's problem. It was some other guy's turn to try and tap dance his way to profits in a crazy market.

Frank Spiteri sounded a note of caution. 'Of course, some would say it's a risky time to be joining the mergers team at Sutton Brothers, Jack. If we don't sort out this mess and save our good reputation we may find business a little lean for a while.'

'I'll take that chance,' Jack said.

'And of course, the money usually isn't as good. It's okay, but it's nothing like you've been used to in the markets. How about we pay you what you earned last year for the first twelve months? After that I'll fit you into an appropriate senior pay scale.'

'That's very generous, Frank, thanks. I'm sure you'll do what's fair.'

'Great,' Spiteri said, rubbing his hands together and looking happier than he had all day. 'Let's get down to the details.'

4

It had been a balmy afternoon in late spring, about six months ago, when Jack first spoke to Stella Sartori. He'd seen her before, not knowing who she was or even that she worked for Sutton Brothers – at the nearby Starbucks, in the elevator, on the street outside the building. Stella was a woman not forgotten quickly. Then he went to Tarrytown in upstate New York to attend a course for star performers on track for partnership. And there she was. Not just a fellow employee of the bank but a member of the same elite group.

The setting had been impressive. Proud old trees and manicured lawns surrounding a grand, nineteenth-century mansion once the summer playground of some New York dynasty, but now converted to convention and training facilities. The grounds sloped away to the edge of the Hudson River, which was sparkling that day as it flowed gently towards the city. Manhattan seemed like a figment of the imagination, though it was barely two dozen miles down the river from this idyllic spot. And against the backdrop of this impressive vista, Jack remembered the tall, slender form of a woman walking towards him, wearing a white blouse and linen pants, dark hair pulled back from a finely sculpted face, with high cheekbones and large eyes. Confidence and poise, he recalled. Almost intimidating.

'Hi there, Jack,' she'd said, white teeth flashing in a smile as she extended a hand. 'I wanted to introduce myself. My name's Stella Sartori. They tell me you're from Oz, too.'

The image flew from Jack's mind as he registered the return of Spiteri, who'd been outside talking to Margaret for a few minutes. He sat down in the chair next to Jack's and picked up the conversation as if never interrupted.

'So you're saying I just need to call Kevin Fields.'

Jack nodded.

'And he decides who takes over what?'

Jack nodded again. 'Tell him I'll meet with him later to share out the portfolio. I have some other obligations – meetings with clients and a marketing lunch I'm supposed to speak at – but Kev can do those.'

Spiteri was satisfied and leaned forward to the speakerphone on the shin-high coffee table in front of them. Jack enjoyed watching the master manipulator at work, as Frank – using only his smooth voice and the power of the English language – deftly played Kevin Fields, fellow partner and Jack's immediate boss on the trading floor. By the end of the short conversation, Frank almost had Fields believing that Jack's sudden move to Mergers and Acquisitions was all his own idea.

Spiteri returned to more pressing matters. He briefed Jack on the members of the Sutton Brothers team who were still working at the CMS plant in Peoria.

'Truth is they probably could have come back at the end of last week,' he said. 'They've finished all the on-site data collection, but I asked the senior people to stay a couple extra days. I think it'd look better if we've still got a team there when Stella resurfaces, don't you?'

Jack shrugged, unsure of Spiteri's logic.

'Anyway, if you're going to track Stella's movements and activities it'll be easier to put it all in context if they're still there. Also, I figure you'll have a better chance of getting them to talk there than you would if they were back here in their comfort zone. A couple of them were pretty pissed about spending the weekend in the boonies, they'll probably do anything to get back to the city!'

A brief smile from Jack acknowledged the joke, but his colleagues weren't his main concern.

'Frank, you said you saw Daniel Cross in Peoria last week. What's his status out there? Aren't there some ethical issues here, given that he's the CEO of the company looking to buy CMS?'

Spiteri nodded sagely. 'Reasonable question, Jack, very reasonable.' He took a deep breath before responding. 'Daniel Cross is a brilliant man with a very strong personality. He can be quick to anger but he's usually quick to forgive and forget, too. A pragmatic man. As a businessman he's one of the best I know. He could have had much greater wealth and prestige if he'd been prepared to move to a big, listed company earlier in his career. He had the opportunities and the offers, I know that for a fact, but he chose to stay with CMS, mostly out of loyalty to the Collins family. Without him the company wouldn't have survived this long and it won't last much longer without Kradel taking over. Okay, maybe he shouldn't be playing such an active role at CMS right now, but one of the Collins family members was put in the top job when Daniel left and it didn't work out. Believe me, Daniel's leadership is in the best interests of the stockholders and, ultimately, in the best interests of Kradel too, if we can just get the deal sorted out.'

Jack was not entirely convinced, but Frank was determined to move on. He handed Jack two thick files in blue cardboard covers. 'These are the standard files we prepare for a proposed merger; a file on each of the companies. They are individually numbered and it's the responsibility of each member of the team to keep their copy secure.'

He stabbed a finger towards the files. 'These,' he said with a hint of disapproval, 'are Stella's copies. She left them behind when she took off. I doubt they'll help you find her, 'cause there's nothing in them that's different to what the rest of us have. Still, you may find it interesting to see how we pull together information on merging businesses.'

Jack felt the weight of the files in his hands and experienced a surge of satisfaction. He was a strategic business consultant, not just a hotshot trader.

'You'll have to go to Peoria tomorrow, Jack, so work with Margaret on the travel arrangements. Daniel Cross will be here after lunch today. I'll tell him about you and if he agrees to your involvement I'll call you up to meet him, okay?'

'Sounds good,' Jack said as he stood up. He smiled and held out his right hand. 'Thanks for the opportunity, Frank. You've made my day.'

The boss shook his hand warmly and patted him on the back as they walked to the office door. 'See you this afternoon. Good luck with Kevin.'

As he waited for the elevator Jack's elation began to bubble to the surface. The prospect of endless days of tedium was suddenly and completely gone. He'd come upstairs for a bonus he barely appreciated and was returning with a new career path.

'G'day!' he said, with a wide grin, to the two people exiting the elevator. They almost recoiled, startled by such uncharacteristic cheerfulness.

He had to consciously wipe the grin off his face when he arrived at the entrance to the trading floor. He was met by Kevin Fields, who was eager to take credit for getting Jack the transfer he'd been wanting so badly. He insisted they talk through the portfolio immediately and come up with transition plans for all clients and positions in the market. Jack knew these things had to be done, but already this felt like part of his distant past and he found it hard to muster the necessary enthusiasm. He wanted to go somewhere quiet and look at the blue files.

Young Matt was the big winner. In the interests of time Jack talked up the skills and experience of his protégé, arguing that Matt could handle most of his deals and relationships. It would either make or break the kid and Jack made a mental note to wish him well. It took more time to brief the strangely nervous Kevin on the client meetings and the presentations Jack was locked into. Fields appeared agitated by the prospect of taking on these tasks personally and sought suggestions for alternatives. By the time they were done, Jack's stomach was growling and the clock was showing 2 p.m. They wrapped up the discussion and Jack agreed to cast his eye over a transition plan and schedule later that day.

Across the room he saw McCormick desperately trying to look unflustered. Jack felt both sympathy and triumph. Only one more afternoon looking like that, he thought. Hopefully Matt's love of the game will last longer than mine.

Cutting diagonally through the rows of desks and chairs, studiously ignoring the wild gestures Matt was making at him, Jack left the floor and ran up the stairs. He passed through the security gates and the sliding glass doors at the entrance. On the nearby corner he spotted one of his favourite New York sights — a hot-dog vendor. Within a few minutes he was back inside the building.

At his workstation Matt was still talking into a headpiece slung over his left ear. Jack dropped two hot dogs with the lot, a soft pretzel and a can of Coke on Matt's desk and smiled at the look of exaggerated relief on his face. Back at his desk, Jack leaned forward to protect his shirt and tie and munched his way through two dogs while listening to voicemail messages, trying unsuccessfully to avoid dropping ketchup on the phone.

Between calls Matt dubbed him slack for being AWOL for three hours and wanted to know what the big pow-wow with Kevin Fields was all about. Jack ignored the gibes and deflected the questions. The whole 'Stella Sartori' deal was still subject to Daniel Cross's approval. No point in getting Matt's hopes up yet.

He placed a telephone handset to his ear and pretended to be listening. Matt shoved lists of proposed transactions under his nose and he initialled those he liked the sound of but only part of Jack's brain was on the trading floor. The rest was in Tarrytown remembering the tall, slender woman with olive skin and dark green eyes. And, he recalled, a sensuous mouth from which issued a rich, intelligent voice with an accent that was both comfortably familiar and oddly out of place.

His sharpest memory was in a lounge, long after the evening meal. Little more than black shapes on a black background could be seen through the large windows circling the room. Inside, snug and semi-inebriated, Sutton Brothers employees were well settled in armchairs, talking and laughing in small groups. The departure of three colleagues reduced Jack's group to two, Stella Sartori and him. Day two of the program was behind them and this was their last night in Tarrytown. In those two days Jack's opinion of Stella had moved way past simple good looks. She had demonstrated natural leadership, incisive analytical skills and a healthy – and very Australian – scepticism for authority and conventional thinking. He'd felt comfortable with her. Perhaps too comfortable.

'So, you married?' Jack had said, his skin flushing as he realised how much it sounded like a come-on.

Stella had looked at him for a few long seconds. 'Yep,' she said. 'You?'

'Sort of. Pretty much.' Jack's tongue stumbled over the words.

Stella kept looking at him with a curious intensity. Jack remembered the sensation of sweat prickling along his hairline as he held her gaze, saying nothing. At last, she blinked, uncrossed her legs and stood up, lifting a bag onto her shoulder. He saw a brief flash of white teeth as she smiled.

'Good night, Jack,' he heard her say. 'See you bright and early.'

'Jack!'

The computer screen in front of him came back into focus but his cheeks tingled with the memory of his embarrassment.

'Jack,' Matt McCormick was saying, 'Margaret Bland's on the line. They want you upstairs. Again!'

Jack smirked at the insolent tone. A bit of attitude was a plus in this job. He paid a quick visit to the men's room to freshen up. In front of the mirror he straightened his tie and ran fingers through wavy hair, double-checked his mouth and hands for lunch residue. Then, with the prized blue files under one arm, he headed upstairs once more.

Daniel Cross was an impressive-looking man. When he stood for formal introductions he was a good two inches taller than Jack and towered over Frank Spiteri. His head seemed cue-ball smooth until Jack detected a horseshoe of white hair running around the back of his skull, cut so close it was almost invisible. Cross looked all of his sixty-five years but the skin on his strong jaw was tight, his suit tailor-made to emphasise his slim physique. Behind distinctive black-rimmed glasses, his eyes were a sharp blue.

'I've heard of you before today, Jack Rogers,' he said, his voice resonating with authority.

'And I've heard of you, Mr Cross,' Jack replied, unflinching under the client's gaze.

'Call me Daniel. Sit down. Tell me what you know of Stella Sartori.'

Jack chose an armchair directly opposite Cross. 'I hardly know her,' he said. 'We met for the first time at a weekend retreat six months ago. There was another course during the summer. Based on her performance at those two events I'd say she's an impressive operator.'

Cross grunted loudly. 'Oh, she's an operator all right,' he muttered. Then he said, 'You're Australian,' as if it was an accusation.

'Yes, from Sydney. Stella's from Melbourne, I believe. I've been gone twelve years, including four years in London. I didn't know her back home, if that's what you're wondering.'

'It explains your strange accent at least,' Cross said with a smirk, then his expression became serious again. 'Just as long as you remember where your loyalties lie, Jack.'

'Of course,' Jack said, slightly offended.

Cross smiled benignly. 'So, you're prepared to drop everything and come to Peoria tomorrow?' he asked.

Jack nodded. 'If you think it will help.'

'Frankly,' Cross said, in a cynical tone, 'I doubt it will help any but it won't do any harm either. The sooner you get your renegade colleague back into line, the sooner I can think about calling off my lawyers. They tell me I can bring Sutton Brothers to its knees.'

He winked at Frank Spiteri, who winced theatrically. Cross stood up abruptly signalling the end of the meeting. 'All right,' he said. 'Thanks, Jack. I'll see you in Peoria. It'll take you most of the day to get there on commercial flights and I'm going to be in Washington tomorrow anyway. I will see you at the CMS plant first thing Wednesday morning, okay?'

'Uh, right,' Jack said, wrong-footed by the sudden dismissal. He picked up the blue files from the coffee table. Daniel Cross's attention

42

was clearly already elsewhere. Frank muttered a quick thanks to Jack as he directed him from the office.

What an extraordinary meeting, Jack thought, as he descended in the elevator. What an extraordinary man.

The trading floor was, as ever, a flurry of activity. Matt looked grumpy when Jack returned, secretively putting his blue files into his briefcase. A quick glance at the clocks. Still ninety minutes of trading in New York. Only after the bell would he have the space and peace to look at the files and make plans for tomorrow, to imagine himself in the new role. Ninety more minutes.

With an impatient sigh he fitted a wireless headpiece to his ear and prepared to run his last mile as a trader. First stop, voicemail. He punched a button and messages flowed into his ear. Eight new ones since his last check. He made notes and looked at data on-screen, deciding on a final action for each message before moving to the next. He didn't want to leave a pile of loose ends for Matt, who would soon be under enough pressure.

Message four made him smile.

'Give me five hundred grand worth of Sextoys R Us,' a perky female voice said, ''cause the women of America are feeling frisky! Just calling to say hi, loverboy. What time will you be home?'

Jack cancelled voicemail and reached for his cell phone. He punched the 'P' button and pushed call. The same perky voice answered.

'Cancel that order, Jack. I think it was just a coffee rush!'

'What, not frisky any more?'

'I guess I could be persuaded,' she said, seduction in her tone.

'Hey, you're a naughty girl, Peta Fitzsimmons.'

'You better believe it!'

Jack pictured Peta at her enormous easel, curly dyed hair piled up and secured with a shabby-chic clip. A pencil tucked behind one ear, another in her hand, moving in constant artistic fervour, producing sketches and design concepts; at meetings doodling furiously on a pad, sometimes even as she was speaking; at home, on any scrap of paper, magazine cover or napkin. A tight bundle of frenetic, creative energy.

'I should be able to get home early, if you can,' Jack said. 'I've got a lot to tell you. I'll skip the gym.'

'I'll give you a workout, honey, don't you fret none.'

'Stop it, Pete! I'm in a public place.'

'Whoops,' she said with a laugh. 'Wouldn't want the girls in the office staring at the bulge in your pants, would we?'

Jack automatically glanced around the room. 'I'll call when I'm on the way, okay?'

'Leave dinner to me. I have a bit of a craving.'

'Excellent,' he said. 'Can't wait.'

'Me too,' she said, and hung up.

Jack found himself staring at the phone as the line went dead, Peta's voice still playing in his head. The words were fine, but something felt off and he couldn't put his finger on it. She was happy and flirtatious but why did it feel like she was trying too hard? After all these years she shouldn't need to fake it.

The moment passed and Jack's eyes shot to the clocks that ruled the traders' lives. Another sigh, then it was back to voicemail. Messages five, six and seven. Nothing out of the ordinary. Message eight made him sit up, the hairs tingling on the back of his neck.

It was hardly a message at all. Nobody spoke for a long time. He could hear the sound of a television or radio playing in the background. Advertisements, definitely American-sounding. Then, also in the distance, he heard a female voice, faint and difficult to understand. A different woman, close to the phone this time, simply said, 'No one,' and the message ended, with a sudden clunk. Jack played it again, turning the volume up to maximum. The background noise was definitely a television. A commercial, then an announcement: 'Coming up after *Dr. Phil*, the midday news.' He could also make out what the first voice was saying: 'Who ya calling, sis?' And then the blunt answer: 'No one.'

On any other day Jack would have dismissed it as a wrong number, but today he found himself intrigued. He didn't recognise the first voice although it sounded Australian, which was an odd coincidence for starters. The answer was hardly enough for identification, yet Jack's mind made a connection. Was it just because he'd been talking and thinking about her most of the day or could it really be true? It seemed so unlikely that she would pick this day to make her first ever phone contact but Jack couldn't help feeling that the person who'd called him, either deliberately or by accident, was none other than Stella Sartori.

5

Stella's toes wiggled in the sand. She was lying face down on a beach towel, the sun working its magic on her back and legs. The back strap of her bikini top was unfastened to avoid a tanning line. Propped up on her elbows, she was reading a document in the shadow cast by the wide-brimmed hat on her head.

Next to her, Angela was sitting cross-legged on her own towel, dressed in a one-piece swimsuit, writing postcards balanced on her knee. Beside Angela, their mother Freda sat in a low folding chair provided by the hotel, in the shade of a beach umbrella. Behind enormous, round sunglasses, her eyes were magnetically drawn to the passing parade of brown and pink flesh, clad in next to nothing. Being rather diminutive herself, Freda found most of the crowd to be of an intimidating size – in height or mass or both. She was no prude and she delighted in pointing out the skimpier examples of swimwear for her daughters to criticise, admire or simply laugh at.

Without looking up or speaking, Stella reached out one hand, picked up a bottle of sunscreen from the sand and waggled it at her sister. Angie frowned but put down her pen and moved over to apply the cream to Stella's exposed skin. It was a practised act, endlessly repeated during the summers of their youth.

'Are you still reading that bloody file?' Angie said, as she spread sunscreen over a nicely developing tan.

Stella didn't answer. She flicked over another page in the folder and continued reading. Her sister was looking over her shoulder. 'Jesus, Stell,' she said. 'It looks so boring! I've got the latest Grisham in my bag if you want something a bit more exciting.'

'I got some magazines,' Freda offered, her English heavily accented.

'I'm okay, Mama,' Stella said. 'This is exciting enough for the moment. Thanks, Ange,' she added as her sister began wiping her hands on the towel before getting back to her postcards. Angela made a face at her mother, who shrugged and shook her head sadly, the tight curls of her permed hair unmoving.

Stella ignored them but she had lost her concentration. The words on the page in front of her were boring, Angie was right about that. But they were part of the bigger mystery; part of the reason her career was at risk; part of the reason her life had been threatened. They were part of the contract.

Thinking back to the moment when she first heard about the contract, Stella recalled the round, bespectacled face of Harding Collins. It was seven days ago – Monday afternoon. She'd met Harding in his office at the plant on the edge of Peoria. The office of the president of Collins Military Systems, the company started by Harding's great-grandfather.

'I just wanted to welcome you and your team,' he'd said, after the introductions were over. 'Do you have everything you need?'

Harding Collins had a sweet smile and a baby face she found hard to reconcile with the image of a middle-aged manufacturer of military hardware. He'd made her feel comfortable while they chatted about the work, the weather, the trip, the town.

She recollected him saying that he didn't live in Peoria most of the time.

'Chicago's my town,' he'd said. 'I'm partner in a firm of attorneys there. Property law mostly. When Daniel left, the family asked me to take over until a buyer could be found. They promised me it would be quick but it's been nearly six months.'

'You're happy about the Kradel takeover?' Stella had asked.

'Oh, yes!' had been the enthusiastic response. 'I hold a chunk of stock in the company but I have no interest whatsoever in the business, apart from the fact that it's my inheritance. For most of my life, it's been Daniel's baby. Can't wait to give it back to him.'

Stella had felt emboldened to ask some more pointed questions, seeking to soothe the disquiet that had been bubbling inside her since first reading the file on CMS.

'So, tell me,' she said, 'is your research and development division about to announce some big new discovery?'

Harding had looked surprised and said, 'Not as far as I know.'

'R&D shows up on the balance sheet as the company's best source of income. That's unusual, don't you think?'

Harding had looked confused but in no way defensive. 'The accounts aren't my strong suit,' he'd said. 'You should talk to the VP Finance.'

'Without that contribution,' Stella had persisted, 'the company would be in pretty bad shape.'

'That's true,' Harding had said, unconcerned. 'That's why it's important to find a buyer.'

'But, Harding, if you were on the board of Kradel, and you asked me to examine the pros and cons of buying CMS, what would you expect me to say?'

Stella had registered the look of uncertainty on Harding Collins' face, so she rephrased and restated the question. 'What does Kradel get from buying CMS, Harding?'

He had merely laughed a little and said, 'Nothing much, I suppose, apart from the contract.'

'The contract?'

'Yes, the contract. You know about that, don't you?'

Stella recalled her cheeks flushing with anger and embarrassment. This was something Frank Spiteri should have told her. Something central to the deal and she wasn't in the loop. It made her look like a minion, a person not to be trusted.

'I haven't seen it,' she'd said.

'I haven't seen the actual document, either,' Harding had said. 'Never wanted to. But if you don't put a value on the contract you'd probably conclude this deal was pretty ordinary, right?'

'Right,' she'd said, unsure of any other way to respond.

Harding had reached for a folder on his desk. 'It's here in my summary somewhere. I'm sure I saw it last week.' He flicked a few pages. 'Here it is. Now, last year, the contract brought in, let me see . . .' a pudgy finger moved across the page, '254 million dollars.'

He'd looked up at her, a cheeky grin on his face. 'Not bad for doing nothing, is it?'

She'd tried to smile but her heart wasn't in it. 'I know the number; it shows up in the accounts. Surely it's not just given to the company for doing nothing.'

'It is,' Harding had said cheerfully. 'Money for nothing, all these years. Even when I was a kid my father talked about the contract all the time. It was his one big triumph, I guess. He was constantly saying that it not only saved the company, it also made us all very rich. And he kept reminding me of it, right up to the end.'

'The end?'

'He killed himself in 1980,' he'd said, with no emotion.

'Pardon my ignorance,' she'd said, 'but who exactly was your father?'

Harding had glanced away but quickly brought his eyes back to meet hers. 'Ewan,' he'd said. 'Ewan Collins. Third-generation arms dealer. He took over the company in 1968 after my grandfather died. He was president when the company really shone, when it was reaping the great rewards from the contract. But after a dozen years in the job, I guess he couldn't handle it any more.'

'I'm sorry. I had no idea.'

He had waved away her sympathy. 'Don't be silly. Truth be told he wasn't greatly missed. He was no bargain as a father or husband. Or even as a businessman, really. It was all Daniel Cross, before and after. Daniel got us the contract, Daniel was there to take over when my father gave up. That's why Daniel should have the company now. God knows I don't want it.'

'And the contract,' she'd asked, 'do you know what it was about?'

'Detonators,' Harding had said, as if talking about cheese, 'a new form of electronic detonator. They put them in all forms of large ordnance. Shells, bombs, missiles, don't ask me the technical details. My father never seemed to think the detonator itself was anything too special. The thing he seemed most proud of was the accelerator.'

'The accelerator? What was that?'

'He called it that because it accelerated the growth of the company. It was a clause in the contract that required the government to fund our research and development program for decades after the initial deal. As I said, it's still operating today. My father used to go on about the perfect timing. A research subsidy wasn't unusual for defence technology, but ours was based on average sales of the

50

detonators over the first decade of the deal. Of course, in '63, when the contract was signed, nobody realised how much the Vietnam War would blow up or how frantic the arms race would get. What looked like a five-million-dollar deal turned out to be worth nearly ten times that. So the research subsidy was based on nearly fifty million, which has been indexed every year since. You have to remember fifty million was a lot of money in those days.'

'Is this contract a secret?'

'It's not secret exactly,' he'd said, 'but confidential, obviously. And nobody wants to draw too much attention to it either. Not the company and not the Pentagon. It's a bit embarrassing, I suppose, but it doesn't have too long to run. Everybody hopes the Kradel takeover will give the government a better return on its money.'

'I need to see a copy, Harding,' she'd said, 'if I'm going to sign off on this report.'

'That shouldn't be a problem,' he'd said. 'I'll get Maria to dig it out for you. There's bound to be a file somewhere. Finding it will give her something to do.'

He'd been so nice about it all. Not playing on her obvious ignorance of the most valuable asset CMS seemed to possess. Treating her like an adult when her own boss had treated her like a child. And she'd felt better, too, because she could finally do her job properly.

Seven days on from that fateful meeting there was a part of Stella that wished Harding Collins hadn't been so helpful. Because, as it turned out, knowledge of the contract was life-threatening. And by opening the contract file, she had also opened the way to her own downfall.

Stella fumbled with the strap on her bikini as she sat up to ease the strain in her lower back. She closed the file, using a business card as a bookmark. It was one she'd found earlier in the day in the bottom of the pocket in her briefcase where she kept the stolen file.

It was almost identical to her own Sutton Brothers card, but it had raised lettering and a firmer feel. A more expensive version of the same thing.

The day Jack Rogers had given her that card they'd been standing on a grassy slope by the driveway at the Tarrytown mansion where she'd first met him. First exchanged looks with him. Flirted with him a little. There was definitely a buzz between them. She'd seen the way it had thrilled and disturbed Jack, and she admired that he didn't want to cheat on his girlfriend. Then there was the look on his face when she'd introduced her husband, who'd hired a car to collect her from the convention centre. Was it jealousy? Whatever it was, it made her feel good about herself that day.

She'd hardly thought of Jack Rogers since. Life was too busy. His business card had sat, forgotten, until today. At the next retreat he'd kept his distance – unwilling, perhaps, to risk temptation a second time. Whether or not she would have allowed something to happen between them was an open question, but she certainly wouldn't have been the one to initiate it.

She'd called the number on the card when she first rediscovered it that morning. It had felt like fate, finding Jack's card. When she heard his recorded voice, deep and friendly, she froze – unsure of what to say and suddenly unwilling to put his career at risk too. Things aren't that desperate, she'd told herself. I can handle this on my own.

6

The warm air inside Starbucks was heavy with the rich, inviting smell of coffee and baked goods. Each time the door to Broad Street opened, a blast of chilled air swept in but Jack sat at a table around the corner beside the front window, away from the intermittent squall. Once he would have been looking out at the heavy round tables on the sidewalk, occupied, in this weather, by the most die-hard smokers. But in commemoration of 9/11, an enormous flag had been hanging in the front window for a year and Jack's view was of red and white stripes running vertically, backlit by the last of the afternoon light.

On the table in front of him sat the blue files and a large latte. He had escaped the trading floor a little early, leaving Matt at the desk, a telephone in each hand, looking stunned. Before heading home Jack wanted some quiet time with the files, a moment to absorb the reality of his new role and direction. And he needed some space to think about Stella.

Why, of all people, did it have to be her? She had confused him from the moment they met at Tarrytown. For the first time in his

53

life he'd felt clumsy and inane just being in the presence of another human being. It had unnerved him so much that he'd avoided her at the second retreat. Just thinking about her now was befuddling him again. What's my motive? he asked himself. Am I doing this to further my career ambitions by impressing a powerful client and influential partner with my loyalty, discretion and quick mind? Or is my real interest in protecting Stella from unfair treatment and further physical abuse? Are the two objectives mutually exclusive? Will I have to take sides? Could I possibly take sides against her?

He didn't know how to respond to the odd message in voicemail either. He couldn't know for sure that it had been Stella. If it was, it might mean she was reaching out to him, seeking his help. If he could make contact with her it would certainly impress the bosses, but would it also put her at further risk? And would it jeopardise his re-energised career path too?

With a shake of his head, Jack turned his attention back to the files, in particular the file on CMS. The material was dry but he found it absorbing. Starbucks, being located in the base of the building, was a popular spot for the bank's employees, stopping in on a break or getting a last hit of caffeine to arm them for the commute home. Several times people greeted him as they passed by. Jack nodded and smiled each time someone said hello, but did little to invite further conversation. He kept reading.

On one occasion he looked up to respond to a greeting from one of the young women who always seemed to stare at him on the trading floor. As he did, his eyes were drawn to another figure passing behind her. Daniel Cross had entered from the street and was walking purposefully towards the tables along the windows looking out to Beaver Street. Jack watched the square shoulders moving away towards the rear of the cafe and then registered the look of disgust on the face of his young admirer as she realised he wasn't even looking at her.

With a scowl she departed and Jack had a clear view of Cross on the far side of the room, his dome of a head visible until he sat down at a table, the view blocked by the main counter in the middle of the room. The near side of the table was just in his line of sight and Jack saw that Cross was not alone. Sitting at the same table, with his back to Jack, was a wiry man with a shaggy head of thick brown hair, wearing jeans and a worn, tan-coloured suede jacket. From this angle it was impossible to tell the man's age, but he showed no particular deference to the powerful businessman in his pricey suit. He did not stand or even appear to offer his hand.

The interaction between this odd couple was brief. The shaggy man picked up a package from the table in front of him and passed it out of Jack's sight, presumably into the hands of Daniel Cross. Even from a distance, Jack recognised the distinctive colouring of a Fedex envelope. Then he saw a much smaller, plain white envelope appear. The shaggy man took it and glanced inside. He nodded and stood up, tucking the envelope inside his jacket. Jack could not tell if the man was speaking but, this time, he did extend his hand and it was shaken without any apparent hesitation. He turned in Jack's direction and moved deftly around the short line of customers, towards the front door.

A jolt went through Jack and he looked away quickly, casting his eyes down to the files. The man's face triggered a memory. A sunny day, warm with a pleasant breeze. People are waiting for their rides back to the city or waving off those who have their own wheels. Standing with Stella Sartori, close to the driveway. He's just given her his business card – the one with his unlisted direct line – and they're talking about how they should all get together some time. A car pulls up close to where they're standing. It's parked askew, but the driver's satisfied and the door is thrown open. A man gets out, wearing tight blue jeans and a Midnight Oil T-shirt, and he waves at Stella and strides over. His hair is shorter than now, but still thick and unkempt. His face is pale and thin, like his body, but with a strong jaw and friendly eyes. Introductions are made.

'Always a pleasure to meet another Oils fan,' Jack says stiffly. He feels strangely disconcerted. The man is an inch shorter than Stella, even in boots. Half a tattoo is exposed on one arm. Could this really be Stella Sartori's husband?

When Jack looked up he saw Daniel Cross striding towards the door of Starbucks, projecting an aura of authority powerful enough to clear a path through the milling patrons. As Cross opened the door to the street, Jack was stuffing files into his briefcase. He threw on the coat he had draped over an adjacent chair and moved to follow. When he got to the door he could see Cross bending his long body to enter the rear door of a black limousine parked at the kerb. Jack waited for it to pull away before he stepped out onto the sidewalk, where he was suddenly enveloped in cold air and the noise of rush hour.

Water, lying in the street following an afternoon downpour, was adding volume to the harsh song of the city. Taxis, trucks and limos splashed through puddles and potholes as they moved up Broad Street, towards the intersection with Wall Street. People hurried in both directions, heads down against the spray and wind, eyes fixed on the heels and toes of the people in their path. Between cross-streets, pedestrians were penned in on the sidewalk by heavy metal railings, end-to-end in the gutter – the Stock Exchange had to be protected.

Jack peered up and down the street, looking for the tan-coloured jacket of Stella's husband. He was trying to remember the guy's name. Dave, he thought. Dave Something-Other-Than-Sartori. Stella had kept her family name. What the hell was husband Dave doing, meeting furtively with Daniel Cross and making some sort of exchange?

It must be something to do with Stella's disappearance and Cross's determination to get his precious file back. The sudden appearance of Stella's other half had thrown Jack, but it also crystallised his motivation. If the husband was in cahoots with Daniel Cross, then Jack was going to lean towards Stella's side.

A flash of tan – contrasted against the black, grey and beige sea of downtown raincoats – caught Jack's eye just as he was about to give up. He hurried up Broad Street, crossing Exchange Place at a jog. He thought Dave was close to the top of the hill, right opposite the white columns and massive flag adorning the Exchange building. By the time he got to the spot, his quarry was out of sight once more and Jack had to make a choice – street or subway. He picked the stairs leading down to the Wall Street station. If Dave wasn't down there, he decided, he would make his way home.

Racing down two flights, apologising as he went, Jack found himself in a square, tiled space with a rectangular ticket booth in the middle of it. Passages, stairs and turnstiles were visible in several directions, but there was no sign of Dave. Jack slowed, but found himself propelled by the crowd towards the entrance to a tunnel on the far side of the underground room. A sign said it led to the Rector Street station. Jack was about to turn back, when he spotted Dave, caught in the same human tide, further up the passageway. He pushed forward again, hoping to set up a 'chance' encounter with the little guy.

When he emerged from the tunnel, he saw Dave pushing through a turnstile leading to the platform for uptown trains on the 4 and 5 lines. Pulling a MetroCard from his coat pocket, he joined the line of grumpy commuters at the turnstiles and forced his way onto the crowded platform. He'd barely located Dave amid the throng when a line of carriages roared into the station and shuddered to a halt. Doors trundled open noisily and the mass of humanity surged forward.

Jack tried to keep Dave in sight as he struggled towards the closest opening. He wanted to be in the same carriage as Stella's husband but he knew he'd be lucky just to make the same train.

He saw Dave using his small size to duck under outstretched arms and into the next carriage. Using his briefcase as a battering ram, Jack forced his way to the opening and pushed inside, just as the doors closed. When they'd slammed shut behind him, Jack found himself the subject of icy glares from several disapproving fellow passengers, but he adopted his best look of New York disdain and tried to make himself comfortable in the crush, turning around so he had a view through the window.

With a jolt the train started slowly, as if protesting under the weight of its cargo. As it rocked and rumbled through the bowels of the city, picking up speed, the passengers moved in concert with it, rolling from side to side like a closely packed school of multicoloured fish. Mute and impatient, looking around at nothing in particular and avoiding direct eye contact at all costs. The first couple of stops allowed some more aggressive commuters to push their way onto the carriage, but after 14th Street the journey was express to 42nd, much to Jack's relief.

When the doors opened at the stop for Grand Central Station it was as if a giant pressure valve had been released. Humanity spilled onto the platform and Jack went with the crowd. To his relief, he saw a shaggy head of hair and tan-coloured jacket in the throng, barely twenty feet ahead but moving fast. Like a slalom skier, Dave was weaving through the crowd towards the exit, slipping through gaps that Jack could only negotiate by knocking people down. He was quickly getting ahead but he did not follow the throng as it travelled towards the tunnels leading to the main terminus. Dave scurried up the steps to street level and out onto Lexington Avenue. Jack raced after him, desperate not to lose him, and found himself back out in the cold, in the shadow of the Chrysler Building. He saw the jacket on the other side of the avenue, moving north, and hurried after it.

Jack wanted to get ahead of Dave. He could hardly run up behind him, short of breath, and say, 'Fancy meeting you here!' But the little Aussie was quick on his feet, even though his path was marked by puffs of cigarette smoke, and Jack was hustling to keep up.

They stayed on Lexington for a few blocks then turned right into 46th Street. The pedestrian traffic was lighter in the side street, but Dave moved with determination, clearly with a destination in mind. He strode the long block between 3rd and 2nd avenues with Jack about a third of a block behind him. They crossed 2nd Avenue, Jack running as the lights changed, and it seemed as if they would go right on to the East River. Abruptly Dave turned into a doorway and was gone.

As he drew closer, Jack could see that his target had entered a pizza parlour and decided to follow. It was as good a place as any for a chance encounter. As he stepped into the open doorway he froze. Something told him Dave wasn't here to order an early dinner. Behind a long, empty counter, a bored young woman was examining her nails. She obviously had no orders to fill. Round, unadorned tables with matching metal and vinyl chairs were arranged along the wall leading from the door back into the restaurant. At the table closest to Jack, four overweight, middle-aged men of Middle-Eastern or Mediterranean descent sat playing cards. Three younger men were drinking coffee and talking at the next table, two of them looking at folded rectangles of newsprint.

Until Jack appeared. The conversation stopped and the eyes of all the men turned towards the door. One of the younger men stood up. Only the pizza chef seemed unconcerned, concentrating on picking nailpolish from one thumbnail. Jack looked back into the room but Dave was nowhere to be seen. There was a door marked 'private' at the rear of the restaurant. Perhaps Dave was through there.

'We help you?' one of the beefy men playing cards said, eyes narrowing with suspicion.

'I'm rather lost, I'm afraid,' Jack said, making his accent more English. 'Can you point me in the direction of Grand Central Station?'

The men relaxed. The one who had spoken even smiled, as he stuck out a well-muscled arm. 'Just keep walking that way, buddy, 'til you get to Park Avenue. Then make a left, you can't miss it.'

'Thank you,' said Jack as he turned away. Behind him he heard what sounded like a round of disdainful laughter. Outside he took a deep breath and walked back up the street the way he had come. On the corner of 46th and 2nd, he stopped to take stock. Trying to wheedle some useful information from Stella's husband was always going to be a long shot. It was just after 6 p.m. Time to call it quits.

Across the street he noticed a small bar. It wasn't busy, being Monday, but the few patrons Jack could see going in looked like the usual professional crowd. Probably United Nations' staffers, he thought, this close to headquarters. He wouldn't stick out in there. It also had a good view of the pizza parlour and the street. One beer, he told himself. If Dave doesn't appear I'll head home.

Holding a cold bottle of Belgian beer, Jack chose a spot close to the window. The beverage was refreshing and the atmosphere quiet and friendly. Such a different feel to the pizza joint. What goes on over there? Jack wondered as he observed people passing under the streetlights on the sidewalk. Drugs? Gambling? Or was it just an unfriendly restaurant where Dave worked as a kitchen hand? It was an intriguing mystery. What was Stella dragging them all into?

The first beer disappeared quickly and Jack decided to have one more. Even if Peta managed to get home early, it wouldn't be before 7 p.m. He had some time. He made his way over to the bar where another customer was waiting to be served. She was a heavily made-up woman with a fading blonde rinse, a well-worn business suit on her compact body and a pair of sneakers on her feet. The classic Manhattan single office-worker look. While they waited she stared at Jack with obvious hunger and he wished, for once, that he had a wedding ring to flash under the lights. He was relieved when the barman brought his bottle of beer and made sure to avoid eye contact with the predator as he turned away. He was on his way back to the relative safety of his spot by the window when the front door opened. A man was pushing his way in from the dark street. Three paces later, Jack found himself face to face with Stella Sartori's husband.

7

The stolen file was full of sand. Stella took it out to the hotel balcony to gently fan the pages and brush out the crevices. One day it would have to be returned to its rightful owner. And before that it may be needed as evidence in a legal proceeding – either against her or against Daniel Cross. Her only motive in taking the file in the first place had been to preserve it, and when she saw the amount of sand blown between the pages after just two hours on the beach, she resolved to keep it indoors.

Back inside the hotel room the only distraction was the rattle of the air conditioner struggling to keep the room cool. Her mother and sister had left for a half-day organised shopping tour. They'd pleaded with her to join them but Stella could think of nothing worse than a coach ride to shopping malls and factory outlets. Besides, this was going to be her first real opportunity to get some work done since she'd joined them.

Sitting cross-legged sideways on the sofa that converted to her bed each night, she laid out the file in front of her and picked up her pad and pen. The prospect of writing in longhand was oddly daunting, but her laptop was thousands of miles away in New York. And it was vital to get down on record a clear account of the events that had led to this point. Hopefully she'd get the opportunity to explain her actions – to her employer, her client or, if worst came to worst, to the authorities.

Most of all Stella had to justify her actions to herself. Every day since last Tuesday she'd suffered bouts of serious self-doubt. Had she overreacted? Had she put her career and the firm's relationship with an important client in jeopardy just because of some paranoid fantasy? Only by detailing all that had happened – between arriving in Peoria on Monday afternoon to taking off at high speed on Tuesday night – could she explain what she had done. This would have to be a detailed account, not like the sketchy outline in the package she'd dispatched last week. As she began to write down the events, her mind went back two weeks, when Frank Spiteri first told her about Collins Military Systems.

At first she'd been reluctant to take on the assignment. In less than three weeks, her fifteen-day vacation was due to start. But Frank had convinced her the project would take two weeks at most. Her role would be narrower and less taxing than usual. He would handle all the high-level stuff and all he needed was a good project manager to get the job done professionally and quickly.

Hearing that Ben Fisher was available to be her second increased her comfort level. She knew she could rely on Ben to finish the job if it dragged on, because she certainly wasn't going to screw up the holiday plans her sister had made. Ben helped her put together a team of seven analysts to do a fast on-site due diligence exercise and get in and out in record time, which seemed to be what Frank wanted. He'd assured her it was going to be a straightforward job. He told her several times the Kradel board knew exactly what they were buying and needed only a confirming report from Sutton Brothers. Stella's job, as Frank outlined it, was to coordinate team activities, conduct meetings with senior executives as needed and focus her attention on the human resources issues. No need for strategic analysis, he'd assured her, and she'd been satisfied.

On the Friday afternoon of that week, Ben Fisher dropped by her office to say that Jodie Michelson, an associate Stella had worked with several times before, was available to join the team. This was more good news because Jodie's expertise with human resources would reduce Stella's responsibilities even more.

Over the weekend, with her husband moody and riveted to the television, she'd shut herself in the study with all the Kradel and CMS files Frank had given her. Once she'd been through it, she felt as though she knew both companies well, and there was only one question she couldn't find an answer to: Why the hell was Daniel Cross so keen to buy his old company?

It was a strategic question, outside her brief, but she was too much of a big-picture thinker to ignore it. And there didn't seem to be a logical answer. According to all the data, Kradel Electronics was a successful, modern company, formed from the merger of other successful European companies. It had been returning good value to its stockholders consistently and had remained profitable, even through difficult times.

By contrast, the picture she formed of CMS was less rosy. The balance sheet and other data showed a company in decline. Poor asset base, shrinking market for its established products, no excess profit to return to its stockholders. Declining value overall. The research and development department appeared to be the only bright spot on the balance sheet. It wasn't hard to see why CMS was looking for a buyer, but Stella wanted to know why Kradel was lining up to be the sucker.

She'd tried to push the issue aside. She knew Frank Spiteri

wouldn't be pleased, given his specific instructions to leave the strategy to him, but it was galling. This was the sort of thing she was good at and Frank should have trusted her with all the information. It was annoying to think he didn't trust her completely.

The question hadn't been answered until Monday afternoon when Stella had taken advantage of her meeting with Harding Collins and he'd told her about the contract. For the first time, she felt she was beginning to understand the deal. Kradel Electronics was buying not just a foothold in the US, but also an established contract with the Pentagon. Cross and his new company could buy an income stream at a discount at a time when the family had lost interest in the business. Fair enough. But then there was the file.

Maria Petrillo, Harding's assistant, hadn't appeared with the file until the next morning. She'd explained that it was unlisted and because she'd only been at the company for the few months her boss was in charge, it had been difficult for her to locate. She'd finally tracked it to a locked safe, opened only after her boss had intervened personally. Maria obviously hadn't received much warmth from the local employees, and Stella had offered a sympathetic ear as the young woman from Chicago vented her frustration at being stuck in 'hicksville' while her boyfriend was more than three hours' drive away.

The contract file showed its age. The cardboard cover was stiff and yellowing at the edges. The first documents dated from early 1962, beginning with a copy of the initial tender. Stella had flicked through several drafts of the contract itself before reading the final version, dated July 1963, and signed by Gilbert Collins, Harding's grandfather.

A sweet deal indeed, she'd thought, as she took in the terms of the research subsidy. How did Ewan Collins and his cohorts get them to agree to it? She'd read about sweet deals done by the Pentagon before, and the government had been paying up so it was obviously legally valid. A nice asset, no doubt. Pity the company hadn't done more with it.

Flicking through the rest of the file, she noted names but only recognised those of Collins and Cross. Ewan and Daniel must have been a formidable team, she'd concluded, and only in their twenties. The content of the papers were dry, formal and old-fashioned and she was about to push the file aside and move on when she saw a document that didn't fit. The document that would crawl into her psyche and cause her to risk utter professional disgrace. The document that would, before the end of that fateful Wednesday, almost cost her her life. It was headed with the intriguing title of 'The Virgin's Secret'.

8

'Wait!' Dave said. 'I know you. You're that Aussie bloke who works with Stella.'

Jack pretended to think for a second. 'Oh yeah,' he said, 'you're Stella Sartori's husband. We met at Tarrytown a few months back. Dave, isn't it?'

Dave seemed pleased to be remembered. His smile was broad and his eyes twinkled. 'That's right. Dave O'Reilly.'

He stuck out his right hand and Jack shook it firmly. 'Jack Rogers,' he said. 'How've you been?'

'Jack. That's right. I told Stella we should get together for a drink sometime but she's been so busy this year.'

'I'm the same,' Jack said, taking a swig from his beer.

Dave's eyes followed the movement of the bottle. 'I was just gunna get some beers to take home,' he said. 'You want to have one with me?' His eyes flicked to other patrons in the front room, checking if Jack was alone.

'Sure. Join me. I just popped in for a quiet one before heading home.'

Dave hesitated as he looked around the room again. 'I should get home. But we could have one here, I guess.'

He moved towards the bar and Jack followed. When the barman spotted O'Reilly, he was obviously displeased.

'I already told ya, Dave,' he growled, 'I can't serve you no more. You gotta square things with Pauly first.'

'I just come from there, Jimmy,' Dave said with a carefree grin. 'It's all sorted, mate. Ask him if you like.'

The barman looked at him with disbelief.

Dave said, 'Look!' and pulled a brown leather wallet from his jacket pocket. Glancing around, he turned his back on the predatory office worker – who was now sitting at the bar and still trying to secure eye contact with Jack – and leaned forward. Holding the wallet close to his body, he used both hands to open it slightly so that only the barman and Jack could see inside. Dave flicked a thick wad of cash with his thumb, making sure the barman could see the notes were all hundreds.

It elicited a whistle from Jimmy and Jack's eyebrows shot up too. Dave was carrying several thousand dollars in cash. No wonder he was keen to get home.

'You been ripping off your old lady again, Dave?' the barman said, sneering.

Dave shot an embarrassed look at Jack. 'Fuck off, Jimmy. Just get me a beer, okay?'

Shrugging his shoulders, the barman moved away. 'I'm gonna call Pauly,' he said, grudgingly.

Dave smiled sheepishly at Jack. 'Had some trouble with my bookie,' he said. 'He has a lot of influence on this street but it's all sorted now.'

Jack kept his face blank. 'What do you like to bet on?'

'Sports mostly. Trouble is I don't really know the games Yanks like to play. Lost a bundle on the World Series in September. You like a bet?'

'Nah. Wouldn't know where to start. I used to have a few bucks on the Melbourne Cup back home but that's about it.'

'Wise man,' Dave said. 'It's a mug's game.'

Jack nodded towards the wallet, tucked close to Dave's side. 'Still, you obviously win sometimes.'

After a short pause, Dave said, 'Yeah, well, sometimes you get lucky, I s'pose.'

The barman re-emerged from the dark interior of the bar. His face had changed from suspicious scowl to reluctant smile.

'Good for you, Dave,' he said. 'Pauly says your credit's good again. I gotta tell ya, I'm happy for ya, buddy. Wasn't sure you were gonna make it this time.'

Jack saw Dave's eyes darken a fraction. 'Just get me the fucking beer, mate.' Then he turned to Jack, 'The bloke's an arsehole, but they have real Aussie beer here, not the shit they brew locally under licence. I'll put up with a lot of crap for a decent beer.'

The twinkle was back in his eyes. Dave wasn't going to let anyone spoil his day. When a cold bottle of Foster's was placed in front of him, he picked it up and raised it to Jack.

'Cheers, mate!'

'Cheers!' Jack said. 'Congratulations on your win.'

Dave was lighting a cigarette. 'What footy team you support, Jack?'

'The Roosters. Eastern suburbs.'

'Not in Sydney! Aussie Rules, mate.'

Jack racked his brain. 'Carlton, I suppose, if I had to pick. I never followed it too closely. Used to watch the grand final but it's been twelve years since I left Australia.'

'Twelve years! You poor bastard. You been in this cesspit that whole time?'

'Eight years in New York. Four in London.'

'Jeez! No time off for good behaviour?'

Jack smiled. 'I usually get home once a year. I take it you're no big fan of the States.'

Dave shrugged. 'It's all right, I guess. New York'd be okay if you had millions of dollars. But I'm not into all that art and history and shit so it's kinda boring for me. And bloody expensive, too, if you want to do stuff.'

'You work?'

'Nah,' Dave said dismissively. 'When Stella first got this job it was for two years and my visa didn't allow me to work. That was okay with me, 'cos Stella was gonna get paid a shitload and I got a two-year holiday.'

Jack nodded sympathetically. 'And now Stella's doing so well she's not ready to give it up, right?'

'Exactly,' Dave said, draining his beer bottle. 'Now she says I can get some change of status for my visa, but I don't want to work for someone else again and I can't set up my own business if I don't know how long we're going to be here, can I?'

'What do you do?'

Dave puffed out his narrow chest. 'I'm a qualified locksmith. By rights I should have my own business up and running back home. I wouldn't even care if it had to be in Sydney, if that's where Stella needed to be. But Christ knows I can't do it here.'

Dave was bouncing nervously on his toes. He thrust his left hand into the pocket of his jacket again, no doubt tightly gripping his overstuffed wallet.

'Listen,' he said. 'I'd love to keep chatting but I really want to get this home. You'd be doing me a big favour if you walk with me. I'll reward you with another beer back at our place. It's just a couple of blocks away.'

'Sure,' Jack said, 'but it'll have to be a quickie. Will Stella be home? I'd like to say hello. I rarely see her at the office.'

Dave was waving the barman over. 'She's out of town,' he said flatly. 'Don't know where. I lose track all the time.' To the barman, he said, 'Give me a couple of six-packs to go, Jimmy, would ya?'

Dave paid with one of the hundred-dollar bills from his wad and grimaced when he saw the change. 'Bloody outrageous price you gotta pay for a beer worth drinking in this country,' he said, leaving no tip on the bar.

Jack led the way to the street and pulled on his overcoat as he stepped into the bitter wind blowing up from the East River. Dave pulled his own jacket tighter around his slender body and nodded for Jack to follow him, back towards 2nd Avenue. With the hand unencumbered by the bag of beer, he lit a cigarette and sucked on it hungrily, moving fast, apparently uninterested in further conversation. At the corner he turned north, crossing the street against the light. Jack hastened after him and asked what it was like living in midtown Manhattan.

'Boring,' Dave said without hesitating. 'It's pretty dull round here unless you work at the UN. Tourists and diplomats. Where do you live?'

'In the Village.'

'Nice one! That'd be so much cooler than living round all these stiffs. You renting?'

'No, we bought the place five years ago.'

'We?'

'Peta and me. She's American.'

Dave gave Jack a twisted smile. 'So you're stuck, mate. Like a rat in a trap!'

They crossed to the west side of 2nd Avenue at 49th, then ducked across to the northern side of the street. About midway up the block,

O'Reilly turned under a long blue canopy marked 235. It lead to a carpeted flight of stairs flanked by panelled walls and up to glass swing doors where there was a sign that read, 'All visitors must be announced'. The person to do the announcing sat at a desk further inside, a Latino man in a maroon uniform. Dave walked straight past him, showing no trace of the charm Jack knew he was capable of. The doorman's eyes narrowed to almost a scowl as Dave passed by but he nodded politely in response to a smile from Jack.

Walking towards the elevators, Dave glanced back to make sure Jack was still following. 'Where did you meet her?'

'Peta? She was introduced by a mutual friend. I think you'd like her. She's not like the Wall Street types you've probably met. She's a fashion designer.'

A bell announced the arrival of the elevator. As they moved to get in, Dave said, 'Is she successful, too? Business-wise, I mean.'

'Very. She and her partners have eight boutiques in four cities.'

Dave punched the button for the twelfth floor. 'And I bet she'd never give that up to move to Australia, just so you could get your dream job or dream lifestyle, right?'

Jack pondered a moment. 'I don't know. But I like it here anyway, so the issue isn't going to arise.'

'You'll want to go home eventually, Jack. Every Aussie does. I bet you'd be back there now if you hadn't fallen for Peta. You're like me, trapped by the ambition of an independent woman.'

The elevator door opened.

'It doesn't feel that way to me,' said Jack confidently as he stepped out to a long hallway, though deep down he knew there was a kernel of truth in there somewhere. When he'd left on this overseas adventure, there was no way he ever planned to be away twelve years. It would have been unthinkable.

'Hah!' Dave said, walking ahead. 'You try to get Peta to do

something she really doesn't want to do, Jack. Then you'll find out just how much power you have in the relationship.'

'Role reversal,' Jack said quietly.

'What?'

'Role reversal. In our dads' day they had all the economic power. Women traipsed around after their men. Now I guess it's our turn.'

'Well, fuck that!' Dave said. 'I don't want Stella to give up work. I could never make the sort of dough she does. It'd just be nice if she could do it in Oz where I can be happy. Not too much to ask, is it?'

Jack offered a noncommittal smile as Dave unlocked the door to apartment 12C. The entrance opened directly into a living room. 'Take a seat, mate,' Dave said as he walked through the room towards the kitchen.

The apartment was an unusual design, narrow and set out on multiple levels. The living area was decorated in a generic, contemporary style, with white fabric-covered furniture and a glass coffee table. Behind a long sofa, a window revealed city lights in the darkening gloom of the evening. There was little in the way of artwork or personal items or even souvenirs or trophies revealing the personality of its residents. It felt like a typical furnished rental where the tenants hadn't bothered unpacking their own things.

Jack took off his overcoat and put it on the sofa with his briefcase. As he sat down, he saw Dave walking back into the room with two open bottles of Foster's. After passing one across, he took a long, languorous swig from the other. He'd taken off the suede jacket, revealing a tight T-shirt and thin, muscled arms covered with prominent veins. Jack again noticed the tattoo, partially visible towards the top of his left arm. Once more he was intrigued by the bizarre combination of Stella Sartori and her husband. The only sign of affluence on the man was a TAG Heuer watch with a metal bracelet band, hanging loose on his bony right wrist. Jack recognised it because he had one almost identical, with a gold face instead of the blue on Dave's watch. He's a left-hander and has decent taste in watches, Jack thought. Not exactly a treasure trove of relevant information.

'When are you expecting Stella back?'

Dave waved his beer dismissively. 'No idea, mate. She was taking off on holidays at the end of this week. I thought she'd be back before that but she might just keep going.'

'You're not joining her?'

'No way. It's a chick thing. Stella's sister and I don't get along.'

'Where are they going?'

'No idea. They talked about Mexico or the Caribbean or Tahiti. Soon as I found out it wasn't gunna be Australia, I lost interest. What about you guys? Where do you go to get a break?'

'Peta's parents have retired to Florida so we've been there a couple of times. I have a sister with three kids living in Brisbane and my parents and my brother live in Sydney. We went there last year. We've also been to Europe a few times. Love France and Italy.'

'Yeah, we went there. The year after we arrived in New York. Did a whole Euro-tour thing. First time for me. I liked it. Lousy beaches.'

Jack smiled sympathetically. 'You really want to get back home, don't you?'

'Too bloody right, mate,' Dave said, stubbing out his cigarette in an overfull ashtray. He raised his beer. 'Here's to getting home,' he said and stood up. 'I'll get us another one.'

'I should go,' Jack said quickly. 'Peta'll be waiting.'

'You can stay for one more,' Dave insisted and Jack didn't argue. His host was hardly a fount of useful information but the beer was deliciously familiar, as was the instinctive sense of ease felt in the company of a fellow countryman.

They talked sports for a while. Jack had been home for the Sydney Olympics so they talked about that. Whenever Jack tried to steer the conversation towards Stella, Dave would look either sad or angry for a moment, then change the subject before settling back into a contented-drunk look. He chugged beer and smoked cigarettes in a seemingly unending procession and Jack wondered if alcohol and nicotine were going to be his only sustenance that night. On his fourth beer consumed on an empty stomach, Jack, too, was feeling mellow. He even indulged in a cigarette himself, a reminder of his years as a smoker before Peta had insisted he quit.

Inevitably all the liquid followed gravity's course. Jack stood up. 'I need to take a piss,' he said. 'Where's the bathroom?'

'It's called a fucking toilet in this house, mate, and it's upstairs.'

Jack climbed the stairs, found a small bathroom and relieved himself. Afterwards he ducked in to the room next door, which Stella obviously used as her home office. On an oversized, laminated table sat a desktop computer. It was surrounded by piles of documents and the black screen of the monitor was haloed by yellow Post-it notes, like a postmodern sunflower. The only thing he found was an email address scribbled on one of the Post-its: stella.nyc@hotmail. com. Then he noticed the clock on the wall. It was just after 8 p.m.; time to get out of there.

'More beer?' his host slurred, as Jack came down the stairs.

'No, thanks.' Jack picked up his coat and put it on. 'Better get back to Peta. Talking about Stella being away all the time makes me feel guilty.'

'Better to be guilty than bored and broke,' grunted Dave as he laboured to swing his feet from the arm of the chair.

'You're not broke today, Dave,' Jack said flatly.

Dave's beer-induced grin widened substantially as he remembered his thick wad of play money. 'You're right, mate. Today has been a good day.'

Beer spilled from the bottle in his hand as he struggled to stand. 'Don't get up,' Jack said, picking up his briefcase. 'I can see myself out. Thanks for the beers. I enjoyed the chat.'

'Nah, nah, nah, I'll see you out,' Dave said. 'Stella'd never forgive me if I was rude to one of her colleagues.' He laughed much louder than was necessary. 'Thanks for keeping me company, Jack.'

Back out on 49th Street, the cold night air cleared some of the fogginess from Jack's head. He found some breath mints in his coat pocket and tried to suck the taste of cigarette from his mouth. Hailing a cab outside the Smith & Wollensky steakhouse on 3rd Avenue, he gave instructions to head downtown, then called Peta on his cell phone.

'Sorry,' he said, as soon as she picked up. 'I'm on my way now. Get out the champagne; we're celebrating tonight.'

9

Another phone was ringing at that moment, but this one was at twenty thousand feet, in the airspace to the south-east of Manhattan, on a desk inside a sleek corporate jet. Luxuriously appointed, without being gaudy, this top-of-the-line flying office was the single thing Daniel Cross liked most about his new job.

Cross was sitting in a compact but ingeniously designed workspace, lined with mahogany veneers. His chair was upholstered in soft calf's leather, tanned a deep red-black colour. In front of his desk two broad-shouldered men stood awaiting instructions. The larger of the two had red hair, trimmed military style. The shorter man was dark-haired with the physique and face of a second-rate professional boxer.

Cross picked up the telephone from the special holder on the desk, waving his arm to dismiss the men.

'Wait outside,' he ordered, and they exited to the forward cabin, closing the soundproof door behind them.

Replacing the handset, Cross punched a button on the phone and said, 'Go ahead, this is a secure line.'

A male voice crackled from a speaker cleverly disguised in the desktop.

'Did you get the package?'

'I'm fine, Tony, thanks for asking. How're you doing?'

'You're in a good mood. You got the package.'

'Yeah, I got the package.' Cross pulled open the long central drawer of his desk and pulled out a Fedex package, open at one end.

'Return address?'

Cross turned the package over. 'Sure, but it's fake. We checked.'

'How bad is it?'

'Bad. She stumbled on that poem Campbell Reeves wrote to his wife. "The Virgin's Secret", remember? Last night on the boat.'

'Jesus! That crazy thing? That was fucking decades ago.'

'I know. It's probably bullshit. She didn't include a full copy, just snippets. I wish I could remember it but it didn't seem to matter at the time. We had it and Reeves never got off the boat.'

'Does it say anything about . . . you know?'

'Not the bits I have here, but the rest of it might. It mentions my name, and it talks about murder and death and shit like that.'

'Sounds pretty vague. Maybe it's not too damaging. Surely not enough to pin anything on you.'

'On us,' Cross said with determination. 'Problem is, I think the poem is just a pointer. Reeves might have stashed something some-place else.'

'Like what?'

'How the fuck should I know? He was a writer, remember? He used to write everything down and we know Gilbert told him the whole story. There's no way he didn't.'

'So, this is bad.'

'Yes, Tony,' Cross said. 'Potentially very bad.'

There was a pause. 'How the hell did she find it?'

Cross let out an exasperated sigh. 'She found it on the file for the contract.'

'What was it doing there?'

'How the fuck should I know? I haven't looked at that file since 1967. Nobody had access to it without my permission.'

'What's she doing next? Does she say?'

Flicking through the scant few documents in front of him, Cross said, 'She doesn't really say. She's trying to work out what the poem means, I guess. She's convinced it's going to lead her to some prize she can use against me. But remember, Tony, if she finds anything, it's going suck you in too, for sure. This is not just my problem.'

'I understand that, Daniel,' said the voice. 'What do we have to do to shut this down? Does she give any hint where she is?'

'No. But her husband said something interesting today. When I asked if he'd heard from her at all, he mentioned she was going on vacation at the end of this week. Surely we can use that?'

'Of course. Leave that with me. What else?'

Cross was rereading Stella's handwriting. He uttered a brief, ironic laugh. 'She says here her boss was a real shitbag. Listen to this: "Frank Spiteri was rude and unsympathetic and so obviously in awe of Daniel Cross that he will believe anything his client says."'

The disembodied voice of Tony grunted with amusement. 'Well, we know that bit's true.' Then a harsher tone. 'But the violence was a big fucking mistake, Daniel. What the hell were you thinking?'

'I know, I know,' Cross said with a sigh. 'It made her run. My guys overstepped the mark and I gave 'em hell, but it's done. A full description of the whole thing, including my guys, is in this package. And we have another big problem, too.'

'What's that?'

'The attorney.'

'The attorney?'

'She sent a copy to her attorney in New York. He has instructions not to open it unless he doesn't hear from her again. She's sending another package to arrive this Friday, both to her home address and to the attorney. It should have a full copy of the poem as well as all her analysis. If he doesn't get it, he's supposed to take what he has to the authorities.'

'Smart! Who's the attorney?'

'Guy called Alex Trainer at Bloch and Lieberman.'

'Don't know him. Will the husband give up the second package?'

'Sure,' Cross said. 'He might up the price a little now he knows what I'm willing to pay, but he'll do it. He'd love to see her reputation ruined.'

'Man, what a piece of work he must be.'

'A weasel,' Cross said. 'My kinda guy.'

'And he didn't read the stuff in the package?'

'No, just the covering note, in which Sartori told him I might be desperate to get my hands on it. He saw an angle, he called the plant and there I was. Fantastic luck!'

'Yeah, and another potential loose end.'

'Don't worry, I'll keep an eye on him. He can be useful a while longer.'

'Okay. But there are some others too, right?'

Cross's voice was cold. 'Yeah. Harding Collins and the secretary, Maria Petrillo. They both saw the poem and they know about the file. They both know about Stella Sartori taking it.'

'Where are they now?'

'Chicago.'

'What do you propose?'

The response from Daniel was immediate. 'I'll take care of them and you take care of the lawyer.'

'Good.'

Cross stood up, but was forced to sit down as the jet was buffeted by an updraft. 'I'm a bit sorry about that guy coming out to Peoria. Jack Rogers. I know more than I did this afternoon. If he finds out about the damn poem . . .'

'It's only a problem if he gets his hands on a copy. And he might find out what the rest of the Sutton Brothers people know. I'm betting one of them knows where she is and I doubt he can make things any worse for us. Relax, we've done this sort of thing before, Daniel, it's easy. One loose end at a time, right?'

Cross gave the speaker a grateful smile. 'We're a good team, Tony. We'll get through this.'

'Of course we will, Daniel, of course we will.'

10

The material possession Jack valued most did not fly. It was his home on 4th Street in the West Village. From the outside, it was an unremarkable square brick box painted a creamy lemon colour, but Jack loved this house, partly because it was so very different from everything around it. Only two storeys high, it was surrounded by brownstones and red brick apartments at least twice as tall. On the flat roof, the ragged foliage of an unkempt collection of plants could be seen from the street. The French windows of Jack's den, underlined by a long flower box, dominated the facade on the upper level. At street level, there was a rectangular window, a few shrubs behind a simple iron fence, and two doors. The one on the right was the entrance to the home; the other led down the left side of the building, where there were more plants. It could almost be called a garden – a distinctly improbable feature for a Manhattan address.

But beyond the architecture the true joy in this house for Jack was what it represented. Like most middle-class Australians of his generation, his upbringing had indoctrinated him in the virtues of owning property. Why pay somebody else's mortgage if you can afford to pay off your own? To have achieved that Aussie dream in one of the most glamorous and expensive cities in the world was a source of great pride and satisfaction. Even Peta thought he was crazy when he first suggested it, a little over five years earlier. But together they had done it. It had provided fuel for their ambitions in business, an outlet for their creativity and a focus for their partnership in life. It was the embodiment of Jack's success and the land alone was worth a small fortune.

When the cab pulled up the wind had dropped and it felt warmer than earlier in the day. Jack looked up and saw lights on in the windows. For the briefest moment, as he often did, he stood on the sidewalk, gazing proudly at his little slice of New York City.

As he opened the door, he was met by warm, aromatic air riding on waves of heavy metal music. Metallica, backed by the full San Francisco Symphony, was flooding from the speakers concealed in walls and ceilings throughout the house. The food smells made his stomach grumble as he walked down the long hallway past the second bedroom – which doubled as Peta's weekend studio – and a small bathroom. The hall opened up to the kitchen and living area at the back of the house, and the staircase leading to the upper floor. He put his briefcase and coat on a chair then followed his nose towards the cooking.

'Hi, babe, it's just me,' he called out over the music.

'Hi there, handsome,' Peta called back. 'Where've you been?'

She was dumping a dirty saucepan in the sink, and she had food stains and flour down the front of her T-shirt and jeans. The domestic look made Jack smile, as it was rare for Peta. With her other hand she reached for the remote and turned the music down.

'Sorry,' she said with a smile, 'I couldn't work out how to get it to just play out here. You really need to give me lessons in this stuff.'

Jack laughed. 'You've been saying that for five years.'

'How are you doing?' he asked, as he bent down to kiss her cheek. 'Mmm, something smells great.'

'You mean me or the food?'

He gave her another kiss, close to her right ear, and said, 'You smell good too.'

His hands were moving towards her hips when Peta turned and gave him a sour look. 'Speaking of smells,' she said, 'your breath stinks of beer and cigarettes. I thought you were coming straight home. Isn't that what you said? And since when did you start smoking again? You know I can't stand it.'

Jack moved away, embarrassed by his breath. 'I got sidetracked as I left the office, sorry. But it was important. It's all to do with this new assignment I've been given by Frank Spiteri. It's part of a whole new career opportunity for me and I —'

'Tell me while we eat,' Peta said tersely. 'The pie is about to burn. If you want to get out of your suit, go do it now.'

'You made pie?'

'Yeah, from scratch. I told you I had a craving.'

'I just thought you were going to get one of your favourite take-outs. I had no idea you even made pie!'

'Oh, don't be stupid, I've made pie for you before.' She gave him an expectant look. 'Are you getting changed or not? I'm about to serve up.'

The odd feeling of disquiet had returned to Jack's stomach. Their enormous bedroom was at the back of the house, right above the living space. Like the rest of the place – originally a commercial building converted to a residence before Jack and Peta bought it – the bedroom had high ceilings and was decorated with modern furniture and dark but striking colours chosen by Peta and her designer friends. The renovation had been trying at times but truly satisfying when it was all over. Now the home was worthy of *Vogue Living* and the only annoying thing was how neat and tidy that look required Jack to be. Even his trackpants and sweatshirt had a place to be stored each day, out of sight.

After changing, he hustled into the adjacent bathroom to clean his teeth. Even after two minutes with the electric toothbrush, his mouth still felt furry so he hunted around for some mouthwash. There was none in the cupboard reserved for his toiletries but he found a bottle among Peta's jumble of products in the cabinet behind the mirror over the sink. After a good gargle, he replaced the bottle and was closing the door when something caught his eye. On the top shelf, a long blue and white box lay on its side, the writing upside down but still easy enough to read: home pregnancy tester. And the box had been opened.

He vaguely registered Peta's exasperated voice, calling him down to eat, but he was transfixed by the blue and white box. Now he understood the sense of impending doom he'd been experiencing since his phone conversation with Peta that afternoon. Now he knew why she had made pie. She was about to announce that she was pregnant!

Oddly, his first concern was that he wouldn't be able to keep the horror from his face when she told him. Could he summon the resources to pretend to be happy or would she see right through him and feel shattered? Either way, he was already experiencing his most unwelcome of emotions – guilt.

He reached for the box, feeling the need to confront Peta, but then he reconsidered. What if I'm wrong? he thought. Do I really want to raise this subject? No, he decided. Why make it easy for her? Let her stew.

'Are you coming or what?' Peta's voice held a hint of pique.

'Coming,' Jack answered, and he shook his head to clear away the nervous prickle creeping across his scalp.

Downstairs, at the table separating the kitchen from the living area, Peta had put out two helpings of pie and vegetables on large white plates. A bottle of red wine was open on the table, half empty like Peta's glass.

Jack's eyes fixed on the wine. Would she drink if she was pregnant? Maybe life could go on unchanged for a while longer.

'No champagne in the fridge, I'm afraid,' she said as she watched Jack reach for the bottle, pour a generous slug into his own glass and take a gulp. 'What is it we're supposed to be celebrating anyway? What happened to you today?'

With some relief, Jack turned his mind back to the extraordinary day he'd just had. 'Well, it's been pretty amazing,' he said. 'Not only do I have a fascinating new assignment, but I've also been offered an opportunity to move to M&A.'

'What? You're kidding!'

Peta usually listened with patient indifference on those rare occasions when Jack shared a work story. But this time, as she heard about his meeting with Spiteri and the mysterious disappearance of Stella Sartori, she leaned in closer, apparently enthralled, and asked occasional, concerned questions between mouthfuls of food. When he told her about the meeting he'd witnessed at Starbucks she dropped her fork, her mouth hanging open while he described his clumsy attempt to casually run into Dave O'Reilly and their subsequent drinking session.

Telling the tale rekindled the buzz Jack had been feeling before he'd opened the bathroom cabinet, and by the end, he was too excited to stay seated. He paced around the table, red wine in hand, adding gestures to his description of the apartment on 49th Street and its odd inhabitants.

When he'd finished, he looked at Peta expectantly but the look on her face told him at once he wasn't going to like what she had to say.

'Are you sure you want to get into this, Jack? It sounds pretty screwed up to me. It has the potential to put you in the middle of some major disputes. Between your boss and his star employee, between the firm and its powerful client. And, even worse,' she added, 'it's going to put you between a husband and wife. How can this be good for you?'

Jack's enthusiasm wasn't going to be easily deflated. 'It gets me off the damned trading floor for starters,' he said.

'There are plenty of other ways to do that. You could get a job paying just as much, more even, anywhere in the world.'

Jack sighed dramatically and sat down again. 'Just doing the same old thing, Peta. You know I've wanted to work in mergers for a long time. And I like working at Sutton Brothers. Here's my chance. You want me to just ignore it? Just say no thanks, Frank? Come on! Does that sound like me?'

Peta sighed too. 'No, baby, I can't imagine you knocking back an opportunity just 'cause it's risky. But I'm telling you this could blow up in your face. You can't play both sides of the fence for long. You'd be risking it all, and for what? Some chick you hardly know?'

An image of Stella jumped into Jack's head. Green, intelligent eyes looking directly into his. He looked at Peta, whose blue-grey irises conveyed both concern and resignation. 'What have I really got to lose?' he said. 'If it all goes sour I can leave the bank. Like you said, the world is full of opportunities. But if it goes well and we end up with a happy client and a reconciled employee, I'll be off to a great start on a new career path. I'd be learning stuff again, Pete.'

Peta opened her mouth to argue the point but closed it again. He wanted her approval but he wouldn't change his mind to get it. She'd seen how boredom was beginning to wear him down and it had been a long time since he'd come home from the office so excited. Her eyes flicked to the far end of the table, where her drawings sat, unnoticed. This was meant to be her night for big news but the moment wasn't right any more. Jack had trumped her.

Jack had noticed the movement of her eyes. He was so used to her sketches collecting around the house and, although her ability to draw still impressed him mightily, he rarely gave them a second glance. These drawings, however, were obviously very different. They were architectural, for a start. Not cocktail dresses or fabric designs, but shopfronts and interior layouts. He pulled them closer and flicked through the stack of oversized notepaper.

This was not how Peta had imagined this night. She tried to distract him.

'I guess you're right, Jack,' she said. 'Sorry to be such a negative nelly. It's great to see you so excited again. Just be careful, okay?'

Jack gave her a grateful smile but was aware of the change in her demeanour. That strange nervousness was in her voice again. Oh God, he thought. Here it comes. As if reaching for a lifeline, Jack spread the large documents across the table and bent over to examine them.

'What are these?' he asked. 'Did you do them? They look great. Are these ideas for new stores?'

Peta thought for a moment as she felt her jangling nerves return. She had a whole speech planned and the drawings were meant to come in the middle, not at the beginning. But maybe this would work too. She swigged the last of the wine and said, 'The top bundle is a concept for a new store in Paris. Underneath there are some plans for a refit of the London store.'

'Fantastic!' Jack said. 'How is it going in London?'

'Our clothes are a big hit with the critics and the press but the store isn't making money. There are staffing problems, landlord problems. The location's not ideal and the design and layout clearly aren't working.'

'Some more investment is required to get it going?'

'Yeah. And if we're going to be in Europe, we have to be in Paris too.'

'An even bigger investment. What do the boys think about that?'

The 'boys' were Anton and Bill, Peta's business partners. Anton was ostentatiously gay, creatively brilliant and Peta's closest collaborator. Bill was older, a serious man with a well-trimmed grey beard, the accountant, business manager and investor. The three of them made a bizarre but effective team.

'Well, they're worried, of course. The bank's willing to give us the money, but for a couple of years there could be a serious dent in the bottom line.'

Opening a store in London had been Peta's pet project, and Jack knew it meant a great deal to her. 'Have they seen these drawings? They'd have to be impressed.'

'Yeah, they like the drawings. They're happy with all my plans. They've agreed to let me go ahead with the whole thing, on one condition.'

Jack jumped up and came around the table to plant a loud kiss on her cheek. 'Congratulations, my girl. Your talent wins out again.' The grin on his face was genuine – fed by pride but also by a sense of relief. If she was going to be crossing the Atlantic every second week, how could they possibly start a family? 'What's the condition?'

Her answer was soft. 'I have to move to London.'

Jack froze. 'What did you say?'

'I have to move to London,' she said, louder, her gaze fixed on his face.

Jack was lost for words. This, he hadn't expected. He returned to his seat, relief turning to dismay. 'They want you to move to London?' was all he could think to say.

A voice in his head said, 'London? I've already done London!' He thought of Dave O'Reilly, restless and unhappy after following his wife to a place he didn't want to be.

'When?' he said, sounding grumpier than he intended.

'Soon,' she said, with equal determination.

They sat in silence, contemplating the implications.

'Bummer,' he said.

'I guess.'

Another long pause.

'I really want to go,' Peta said, 'but I don't really expect you to follow me. Especially with all that exciting new stuff happening at your work. I was kinda hoping you'd still be bored. Maybe this is kismet.'

'Kismet?' he said angrily. 'It's appalling!'

'Oh, come on,' she said, 'let's not kid ourselves that we weren't facing a crunch with the whole baby thing.'

Jack's face screwed up in disbelief. 'So you're saying we should walk away now, just like that? So you can go off to London and what? Have babies with someone else?'

'I suppose so. I don't know. Oh, Jack, I don't know what I'm saying.'

Her voice cracked. She came to him and sat in his lap. Her arms went around his shoulders and she pulled him into a long, tight embrace. He was tense at first but loosened up as her fingers ran over his back. Her face was pressed to his chest and Jack's heart softened when he realised she was crying into his shirt.

'Oh Pete, Pete, Pete,' he said gently, patting her back. He felt terrible but had no idea how to make either of them feel any better.

After a minute, he stood, easily coping with Peta's light frame, and carried her to a sofa in the main sitting room. She clung to him like a lost child and they sat, locked together, for nearly an hour, saying nothing while they both pondered the end. The Metallica CD had finished and the only noise was the faint, omnipresent hum of the city and Peta's breathing. Then, saying nothing, she disentangled herself and shuffled across the room and up the stairs. As she disappeared, he heard a small, exhausted voice say, 'I'm going to bed. We can talk again tomorrow.'

I'm going to Peoria tomorrow, he thought, but said nothing. For a long while he sat there on the sofa, feeling empty. He didn't like seeing Peta upset, but the guilt it generated only made him resentful. There was a part of him that yearned for the freedom of not being responsible for someone else's happiness. But there was also a big part of him that drew strength from this relationship. It seemed unthinkable that it might suddenly disappear.

It had turned out to be quite a day. And tomorrow Jack faced a whole new set of challenges, solving the riddle of Stella Sartori, the angry client and the untrustworthy husband. Maybe fate would play a further hand. If it turned out to be a disastrous career move, returning to London might be a good option for him.

A shiver ran down Jack's spine and he got up from the sofa and began cleaning up the dinner mess. After the dishwasher was packed and the counters wiped down, he took a soda from the fridge, turned out all the lights downstairs and went up the stairs, collecting his briefcase on the way. The door to the main bedroom was open and light streamed into the room from the hallway – it didn't bother Peta when she needed to sleep. Jack could see her, looking tiny in their king-size bed. She was either asleep or giving a very good impression of it. He padded softly into the room in thick woollen socks and leaned down to kiss her right temple. She didn't move.

He left the bedroom and headed towards the den, a generous space with hardwood floors, as wide as the whole house. In the silvery wash from the streetlight outside he could just make out his antique desk and leather chair, his treadmill and free weights in the corner, and his plasma screen dominating the far wall. Through the French windows – which looked like they should lead to a balcony, but didn't – occasional passing cars and pedestrians could be seen between the thinning branches of the trees lining 4th Street. He collapsed into his much-loved armchair next to the tall glass doors, the Sutton Brothers files in his lap, his Diet Coke on a small table next to the chair.

With his foot he prodded a switch, turning on the standard lamp behind the chair, throwing light on the files but keeping his face in shadow. He spent ten minutes thinking about Peta and London and marriage and babies but only came up with complicated questions, no simple answers. With a sigh he opened the top file and worked his way through the dry, detailed documentation, making a few notes on yellow legal notepaper as he went.

It was well after midnight by the time he was done. Before heading to bed, Jack moved over to the computer on his desk. On a scrap of paper he wrote down the email address he'd memorised at Stella's apartment. Frank had told him she didn't have her work laptop with her, but Jack knew she could access hotmail anywhere. He didn't hold out much hope – he had no way of knowing if the address was still active or if Stella would be checking her mail, wherever she was. On the other hand, there was little to lose. All he wanted was to open a channel of communication.

After struggling to find the right words, Jack finally settled on a message titled 'Jack Rogers' followed by his cell phone number.

Hi Stella,

This is Jack Rogers from Sutton Brothers. Remember me from the Top Gun course? Earlier today I was briefed by Frank Spiteri on recent events at the CMS plant in

Peoria. Daniel Cross asked Frank to find someone outside M&A to look into what went on, and he picked me. Tomorrow I'm flying out there to talk to your team.

Both Cross and Spiteri seem convinced that you've gone feral, Stella. They are both frantic about the file you've apparently taken. Cross seems ready to sue the firm for its last dime and Frank, of course, is going to put his reputation, and the firm's, ahead of anything else. I'm sure you know how close he is to Cross; they've known each other for decades. So in short, whatever the truth is, it seems pretty clear to me that you are setting yourself up to be the scapegoat.

Now, maybe I don't know you all that well, but I find it hard to believe you would do all this without good reason. I'd really like to understand what that reason is. And if there is a way I can help resolve the issue or act as a go-between so that you and Frank can start talking again, just say the word. I want you to know that I have your interests in mind too, not only the bank's or the client's.

Of course, if you have turned crim, it would be nice if you could let me know before I make a fool of myself!

Seriously, Stella, send a reply to this address, which is private, or call me on the cell number I set out up top. You don't have to tell me where you are. Just tell me what's going on and how I can help. The sooner we start talking, the sooner we can defuse the situation.

By the way, did you try to call me at the office yesterday? Also, do you know anything about a meeting between Daniel Cross and your husband?

Anyway, I'll be in Peoria the next two days, so call me, please!

Jack

He clicked on the send icon with a hopeful sense of anticipation. If the message wasn't bounced by the system it might still be valid. Even if that were true, he couldn't force Stella to reply. If she didn't want to communicate with him there was nothing he could do about it.

11

Six hours later, weak morning light filtered in through the bedroom window as Peta watched Jack drying his naked body next to the bed. She remained under the blankets and wasn't planning to rise for another hour. When he noticed she was awake, Jack wrapped the towel around his waist, bent down over her pillow and kissed her quickly on the lips.

'Morning.'

'Morning. How did you sleep?'

'Not so well,' he said. 'Had a lot on my mind.'

'Yeah. I had the weirdest dreams.'

'Dreams would have been nice.'

He moved to the dressing room to pick out a shirt and tie, and pack a small suitcase for his trip west. When he emerged, fully dressed except for his trousers, Peta's head and bare shoulders were still the only parts of her visible. The clock radio next to her read 7.36. He saw a sadness in her eyes as they followed his movements around the room. With trousers on and belt buckled, he sat down on the edge of the bed and gave her backside an affectionate pat.

'Pete, I have to go Peoria today but I should be back tomorrow, okay? I know we need to talk and the timing sucks but this trip can't wait. I promise I'll get back as soon as I can.'

'Mmm,' she said, snuggling down in the bed. 'You keep patting my butt like that and you'll send me right back to sleep.' Then she said, 'Our discussion can wait a couple days, Jack, but after that I have to make some decisions, 'cause things are going to start moving pretty fast.'

She reached out one hand to give his ribs an affectionate tickle. 'But hey, high-flyer, I wouldn't want you to miss out on a trip to Peoria, Illinois. That's gotta be the highlight of your career so far!'

Jack smiled, though he couldn't help thinking that her sarcasm was motivated by more than just good humour.

A gentle rain was coming down when he stepped out on to 4th Street, towing his suitcase. The roadway glistened like a black-backed mirror and when a cab stopped in front of him to discharge an elderly passenger, Jack moved to grab it. The city seemed as busy as ever, despite the weather, and it took a good twenty minutes to crawl the two miles to Broad Street. With nearly an hour to spare before his scheduled meeting with Frank Spiteri, he went down to his desk on the trading floor, where he exchanged some good-natured banter with Matt, who seemed content with his new responsibilities, despite the barbs he threw at Jack about avoiding the real work.

As always, the voicemail light was flashing on the phone and Jack forwarded messages from clients to Matt or Kevin Fields. There were also two messages from Margaret Bland, one to say flights to Peoria had been booked and the other informing him that an office had been found for him on level twenty-seven, the home of the mergers and acquisitions division. Jack was delighted. A new work life was starting today, and it came with an office – every trader's dream come true, privacy at last!

When Jack met with Spiteri at nine, he received terse instructions about being nice to Daniel Cross and moving things along as quickly as possible.

'By the time you get out to Peoria,' Spiteri reminded him, 'Daniel won't be available. You'll meet with him first thing tomorrow. You should be able to get the ball rolling with people like Ben Fisher. I'm convinced that Ben, and maybe one or two of the others, know how to contact Stella. They may even know where she is. Your job is to try to get that information or at least get into the communications loop somehow. If you can talk directly to Stella, then do so, but try to get her to call me, would you? I'm sure we can sort this whole thing out if she and I can get some quality time.

'I promise to behave myself next time she calls,' he added, with a wry smile. 'If you can't get any information from the staff, see if you can track Stella's activities at the company. Try to understand what she was looking at when she decided to do this silly thing. Maybe we can get some idea about what motivated her.'

Jack nodded, wondering if he should tell his new boss about the meeting he'd witnessed at Starbucks the previous evening. He hadn't learned anything directly useful from Dave O'Reilly – and he didn't want to give Spiteri any reason to doubt his impartiality or loyalty – so he decided to keep it to himself, at least until he understood the implications of this piece of information.

After the briefing on level twenty-eight, Spiteri took Jack down to his new office. Space wasn't a problem – the mergers division had been downsized, and there'd been several offices to choose from. Spiteri had picked out the best of the bunch for Jack, with a view and plenty of natural light. This floor wasn't usually visited by clients and was decidedly downmarket compared to the opulence of the senior partners' floor. The light grey carpet showed signs of wear and the decor was functional, completely lacking in personality. Behind a glass wall separating Jack's small office from the hallway, modular wooden furniture formed a desk, a shelving unit and bookcase.

Jack surveyed the room with satisfaction. It wasn't glamorous but it was the sort of space he'd imagined himself working in. Spiteri explained that the phones were being rejigged so Jack's number would follow him, and he suggested a well-constructed voicemail greeting, directing trading-related calls downstairs. Jack told him it would be okay; his direct line was known only to a select few and most business calls went to one of the other phones on his trading desk.

'Right,' Spiteri said, uninterested in telephones. 'I think you've got an hour or so before you leave. You can finalise things downstairs if you like, and check in with Margaret for your travel arrangements. Keep in touch with me regularly.' Spiteri handed Jack one of his personal business cards. 'This has my cell number on it. During daylight hours you can usually find me or Margaret here.'

'No problem, Frank. Track Stella, be nice to Daniel Cross and keep in touch – I think I've got it.'

Spiteri moved towards the door. 'Margaret's arranged for you to take over the room Stella had at the Holiday Inn in Peoria. I found out yesterday we've been paying for it since last week because Stella never checked out. The hotel says she left some of her stuff behind. Who knows, you might get lucky and find the file there, but I doubt it. Be sure to have a good look around. And if you find it, give it back to Dan Cross immediately. Don't wait for further instructions from me on that score.'

'Yep,' Jack said, confident he wouldn't be put in that position.

'Any questions?'

'If I come up with any I know where you are.'

'Good, good.' Spiteri extended a manicured hand to shake Jack's. 'Good luck then, Jack. When we get this sorted out I look forward to sitting down and giving you a proper introduction to the division. This is hardly typical work for us, thank Christ, but I'm sure your interviews with Ben and the others will give you a taste of the process.'

When Spiteri was gone, Jack sat down in the swivel chair behind his new desk, and took in his view of downtown Manhattan. For a moment he wondered if he would've been able to see the World Trade Center towers from this west-facing window, but it was already hard to remember exactly which part of the sky they'd occupied. He'd spent the critical moments of 9/11 on the viewless trading floor, watching open-mouthed as events unfolded on multiple television screens. It seemed to be happening in another place, another world even, but the swirling dust and chaos that enveloped him when Sutton Brothers was evacuated to the streets brought it all home with shocking clarity.

Jack shook off the sense of dread that always accompanied these memories and turned back to his new office. It was so quiet. There were other people on the floor, as he could hear them in the distance, but this space was so calm he could actually hear the air-conditioning. It was a little disconcerting.

He rang Margaret Bland and heard that he was booked on a noon flight to Chicago. A limo would take him to La Guardia. He had just enough time for an expedition to the trading floor to clear out his desk and bring up the few personal items he kept there. He found an empty box in a photocopy room and it proved more than adequate – the atmosphere of the trading floor didn't exactly encourage personal touches. There was one photograph in a frame, capturing Peta and Jack at some fashion industry party with happy grins on their faces, and a few academic books from the MBA course, which looked inadequate on the large bookshelves in the new office. Other favourite items of stationery and sundry personal items disappeared easily into the drawers of the desk so that when he was finished Jack still thought the office looked unoccupied. There was no computer monitor; that was the biggest difference. He made a note to ask about a new PC, then moved the photograph to a more prominent position, facing the doorway to the office. It was his way of marking the territory.

With a little time to spare, Jack took a walk around the floor to find Stella Sartori's workspace. Most offices he passed were a jumble of reports, files and loose papers, but there were remarkably few people. Mergers and acquisition specialists apparently spent most of their time away from head office. In the centre of the floor he found a nest of cubicles where young analysts banged away on their computers or talked in low voices. A few glanced at Jack as he passed but otherwise showed little interest.

On the opposite side of the floor from his new base Jack found a glass wall with Stella Sartori's name on it. The lights were off inside the office. The room was identical to his in size and shape and it, too, had a window to the outside world, signalling Stella's seniority. He stood in the hallway, uncertain. Entering felt like a violation of privacy and Jack found himself glancing both ways to see if anyone was watching. There was nobody around but still he moved to the doorway without going all the way in. Something seemed odd. Unlike all the other occupied spaces he'd seen, Stella's office was almost as sterile as his own. There were no papers and files to be seen. The bookshelves were filled with neatly arranged books and reports, but virtually every other surface was vacant. Jack couldn't see one personal item and he was immediately reminded of the apartment on 49th Street. Was this just Stella's fastidiousness or had the office been cleaned out? Frank said her laptop wasn't with her, but it didn't seem to be here either. The desk was a bare rectangle of polished wood.

Jack left Stella's office. Even if he'd been invited, he wouldn't have felt comfortable in the cold space. It told him nothing about

Stella and it was disquieting that seemingly little more than a simple name change on the glass would be enough to erase her from the corporate memory altogether. He had the odd feeling that he was setting out to search for a ghost. He hurried back to his own office to collect his bags.

The limo waiting downstairs was an immaculate Mercedes. On the way to La Guardia, Jack used his cell phone to call Peta and tell her he was on his way out of town. She ribbed him some more about going to Peoria but there was no hint of anger or discontent in her voice. Jack found it simple enough to push aside the memory of the previous night and all the implications of her news about London. Avoiding the difficult questions had worked for seven years; maybe it would work a little while longer.

Getting out of New York on time had Jack in Chicago shortly after 12.30 local time. He waited two hours in the Admiral's Club lounge, offered by American Airlines to its first-class passengers, before boarding a small jet with no more than thirty other passengers for the last leg to Peoria, Illinois. As he flew south-west from O'Hare, he sat glued to the window. Apart from a few trips directly into Los Angeles and San Francisco, he'd never touched down anywhere further west than Chicago before. This was going to be Jack's first visit to small-town America.

From the air, the great patchwork plain that stretched west from Chicago seemed as flat as a gently heaving ocean. As the aircraft descended, Jack was surprised, and a little disappointed, to see that Peoria wasn't such a small town after all. It looked more like a little city.

Separating east and west Peoria, a bright blue river snaked its way across the landscape and, before they came in to land, Jack could see an impressive iron bridge connecting the two sides. Then it was gone, dropping behind a decidedly commercial skyline of brick, concrete, steel and glass boxes. Although on a tiny scale compared to Manhattan, the buildings stood as a solid testament to Peoria's success. A brochure he found in the seat pocket of the aircraft claimed that more than 300 000 people lived in the 'urban agglomeration' around this 'small' town.

The rain clouds that had been mobbing New York for the last few days didn't extend this far west and the sky was clear as Jack walked out of the airport terminal. It was cold, in the low forties, and a sharp wind cut right through his business suit. There was no sleek limousine waiting to collect him at this end but before he jumped in a cab, he noticed a courtesy van from the Holiday Inn pull up close by.

With inch-perfect precision, the shuttle driver – who was, Jack decided during the wild ride, a frustrated Indy car racer – drew up to the kerb at the hotel entrance just before 5 p.m. The manager on duty escorted Jack to his room – or perhaps it was still technically Stella Sartori's room, as her belongings remained inside. The manager's name was Dalton, but he told Jack he wasn't on duty the night Stella was attacked. He was aware of the event, though, as indicated by his assurance that security had been tightened. He also told Jack the hotel wouldn't be charging Sutton Brothers for the nights when the room was unoccupied, nor for Stella's last night as their guest. A complimentary fruit basket and a voucher for two free drinks at the bar downstairs were presented as tokens of the management's goodwill. Jack accepted the apologies and obsequious gestures with practised politeness.

The hotel was reasonably modern and much larger than Jack expected. Eight or nine floors of unimaginative concrete and glass on the outside but pleasantly furnished inside. The deluxe room Stella had occupied was comfortable, dominated by a king-size bed with a small sitting area, desk and all the usual conveniences. Except a minibar, Jack noted, after a search of the closets.

A small roller suitcase, very similar to his own, sat in the corner where, the manager assured him, it had remained untouched since Stella's departure. As soon as he was alone, Jack took a careful look through it. He found only a hair dryer, a large hairbrush and a few of the bulkier items from Stella's toiletry kit, plus some clothing, underwear and a pair of shoes.

The clothes were about the same size as Peta's, Jack guessed, but the style was about as far from Peta's taste as you could get. Peta would've carried a bag full of bright colours, interesting textures and many choices of fancy lingerie. Stella's business wardrobe was expensive, but monochrome. A black suit by Donna Karan, albeit with a short skirt, and black shoes that were obviously pricey – Peta would have classified them as 'boring'. The underwear was more of a surprise – a lacy bra and two black thongs that seemed a little out of place next to the power suit.

Jack found no hidden documents, computer disks or other convenient clues, either in the bag or anywhere else in the room. Stella had left nothing behind relating to her work. Nor were there any scraps of paper under the bed or behind the desk or in the trash can that might hint at her destination after leaving Peoria. She could have gone anywhere.

When the search was over, Jack called Ben Fisher on the number provided by Frank Spiteri. Fisher didn't seem surprised to receive the call and agreed to come by Jack's room once he'd returned to the hotel. He said he'd be leaving the CMS plant shortly and should be knocking on Jack's door round six. Good enough, Jack decided, and he settled back on the bed to watch CNN until his colleague arrived.

12

A satisfying calm had descended on the Sartori family suite. Freda and Angie had risen early to take a coach tour that held no attraction for Stella. Determined not to obsess over the file, Stella had promised herself a morning by the pool, but when room service arrived with her breakfast and she could find nothing of interest in the newspaper, her mind filled at once with lines from the poem. It was haunting her, and she knew she would have to look at it one more time before she could do anything else. With a sigh of resignation, she pulled the file from under her bed and opened it to the critical page.

The Virgin's Secret

The Virgin's purse a secret hides
riveted by her metal sides.
Her drawers reveal a hidden box
four by two the key unlocks

A past of death and murder vile,
Oh Danny Boy, all style and guile.
The Virgin, innocent and serene
bore witness to the awful scene.

Thus in her heart you'll find the truth,
don't forget to check the roof.
A lesson learned, amid the gloss,
death stalks the man who crosses Cross.

If I fail to make it home,
don't hesitate, pick up the phone.
Choose your allies carefully,
solve the puzzle, use the key.

The Virgin's path will lead you there,
down curving hall and sloping stair.
Truth and justice will be your gain
or else my death will be in vain.

I love you truly, Beth, you know,
so for my sake take care, go slow,
tho' your loving arms I can't replace,
The Virgin may have my last embrace.

8 December 1967

Her eyes slowly followed the words on the page, although she barely needed to read it because the poem was etched in her brain. She kept coming back to the original document, wondering if she'd missed something in the verse or overlooked some other clue on the paper.

An uncomfortable feeling of dread stirred in her stomach, as it often did when she revisited the poem. Was this really the reason she had put her whole career in jeopardy?

The date troubled her. Thirty-five years had passed since Campbell Reeves had penned this page. She assumed he was the author. The paper was fine linen writing paper, embossed at the top with the name 'Campbell Reeves'. The penmanship was elegant: old-fashioned strokes of a fountain pen in black ink. The matching envelope, addressed in the same hand to Elizabeth Reeves at an address in Peoria, was in the file next to the poem. There was no stamp or other postmark on the envelope. It appeared to be a letter never sent. Yet here it was, surviving many years later, in a file about a Pentagon contract with a relatively minor defence contractor in the Midwest.

It was part love poem, part puzzle. Yet from the moment Stella first encountered it, these six verses seemed to speak directly to her. They were obviously written to be obscure but they clearly hinted at Daniel Cross. They told of a murderous past. Her personal experience of the man was limited to one unhappy telephone conversation. Why was she so ready to believe her client was a man with a despicable secret?

Her mind went back to that Tuesday morning in Peoria when she'd first read the verses. She reminded herself that her initial reaction had been far from suspicious. If anything, it had struck her as an amusing curiosity, perhaps a flowery piece of slander penned by an embittered employee or business rival.

She took her questions to Harding Collins, who seemed to welcome the distraction. 'Campbell Reeves,' Harding had told her, 'was VP Finance for, like, a million years. He and my grandfather were best buddies, just like my father and Dan Cross were in the next generation, though I'm sure Cam had more respect for his boss than Dan ever did.'

'So this Campbell Reeves wasn't some sort of crank?'

'Heck, no! He was a prince among men, according to the old timers. I was pretty young when he died, but I remember him as a kind man who was closer to my grandfather than anyone.'

'When did he die? Do you recall?'

Harding's face had turned serious. 'Yes, I do,' he'd said. '"Black December", we called it. In that month in 1967 we lost both Campbell and my grandfather within three weeks of each other. It was the end of an era. Grandfather's funeral was held on Christmas Eve.'

Stella's curiosity was in overdrive. Campbell Reeves, long-term loyal lieutenant of the company, had written 'The Virgin's Secret' just before his death. Perhaps, as the poem hinted, he hadn't made it home. It was only then that she'd opened the contract file to show Harding Collins the mysterious verses. She'd watched his face carefully as he read it, and saw his eyebrows knit together, a deep fold appearing above the bridge of his nose behind the frames of his spectacles.

'Bizarre!' he'd said.

'You don't know why it would be in this file?'

'No idea. Never heard of it before.'

'So, you never heard rumours about Daniel Cross? No skeletons in the closet or accusations of any kind?'

'No, nothing like that. He's one of the most ambitious and business-focused people I've ever met, and sure he's ruffled a few feathers in his time, but no, I never heard anything like that. Do you really think that's what Campbell was trying to say? This poem is pretty vague.'

Stella had shrugged her shoulders. 'I can't even be sure he wrote it. Anyone could have used his stationery, but it was addressed to his wife.'

'Oh, it's his writing all right. I recognise the penmanship from my birthday cards. My mother was always at me to write like Uncle Cam.'

There had been a long pause in the conversation as they each tried to understand the implications of the poem. Harding had pushed the file back across the polished mahogany of his desk and said, 'We'll just have to ask Dan about it, won't we? He's in London but I have a telephone conference with him scheduled for one o'clock. I'll ask him if you like. I'm sure it's nothing but I know you want be thorough.'

Stella had been confident it would turn out to be nothing, or certainly nothing relevant to her work, so she'd spent the next few hours working with her team on more mundane matters. It was only when Maria Petrillo brought word of Daniel Cross's reaction to her discovery that Stella felt sure she'd stumbled onto something significant.

'The conference call with Mr Cross is not going well,' she'd said in a rush. 'Look!'

She'd thrust a piece of paper towards Stella. 'Get Stella Sartori up here!' was written on it in an untidy scrawl.

'I was listening,' Maria had said, her Latina complexion unusually pale. 'Harding likes me to take notes. When he asked Mr Cross about this virgin thing, Mr Cross goes nuts! "Why the hell did you let her see that file?" he screams. "I can't trust you to do one simple thing," he shouts. Oh my God, you should have heard the language!'

Stella had felt a little sick and kicked herself mentally. Why had she raised this trivial thing with Harding? What would Frank say when he heard she'd started a brawl between the heads of the two companies she was supposed to be helping to merge? It was his fault too, she'd reassured herself. He should have told her about the contract.

She'd followed Maria back up to the third floor, down the long hallway and into Harding's enormous office. He was seated in the far corner of the room, at the round meeting table, a speakerphone in front of him. He was leaning back in his chair, pale, his glasses pushed up to his forehead and his hands flat on the table at the end of outstretched arms. He looked tired and was breathing deeply, but he'd waved them in when he saw them, indicating the phone connection was dead.

'He's coming,' he'd said, as if he didn't quite believe it.

'Who?' Stella had asked naively, unable to believe that she was causing the head of the giant Kradel group of companies to scurry across the Atlantic Ocean to deal with a problem of her making.

'Daniel,' Harding had bleated. 'He's coming tonight! I tried to dissuade him but he's mad as hell!'

'But he doesn't even work here any more, does he?'

For the first time, Harding had given Stella a look of disdain. 'He's unstoppable, Stella. And he has more sway with the stockholders than I do, even if they're mostly members of my own family. He can pretty much do what he likes.'

Without waiting for an invitation, Stella had sat down heavily in a leather office chair across from Collins. 'I'm sorry, Harding,' she said earnestly, 'I had no idea . . .'

'I'm sorry too,' he'd said, looking at her seriously. 'He wants me to hold you in custody until he arrives. He told me to call security if you resist. He wants me to get the file back, along with any other documents you have in your possession.' Then the bleak look on his face had intensified. 'And he also wants me to destroy the Campbell Reeves poem. Shred it. Immediately.'

Stella's mouth had dropped open. And now, almost a full week later, the memory of that moment still triggered an uncomfortable, empty feeling in her gut. It had felt as though a powerful force was suddenly enveloping her, seeking to pin and cage her. And her instinctive thoughts had been of escape.

Clearly Harding Collins had also been shaken by the instructions he'd received. She'd felt a wave of sympathy for him but knew she couldn't make it that easy for him. 'Cross can't ask you to destroy the poem,' she'd said. 'I'm not sure you should even let him have access to the file. Technically, legally, he really has no business coming here without your invitation.'

He'd made a helpless gesture. 'What do you expect me to do? Everybody who works here is still loyal to him. They can't wait to get him back. He's a natural leader, Stella. I'm not!'

'Harding, we can't let him destroy the documentation. It could be important evidence.'

'You could photocopy it,' Maria had suggested. She was still in the room, fidgeting nervously.

'No!' Stella had said quickly. 'If the original gets destroyed, an uncertified copy isn't going to be any good. It should be kept in the file. I'm sure it's there for a reason. It has to have something to do with the contract. I think somebody has to protect the file until we can work out what "The Virgin's Secret" is all about.'

'I can't let you do that,' Harding had said softly, 'officially.'

She had been hoping he would offer a way out, but part of her knew all along, it had to be her. 'I had a call this morning,' she'd said tentatively. 'My mother has taken ill quite suddenly. She's in the hospital. They're saying I might need to fly home at short notice. It was pretty upsetting, you know?'

She'd watched Harding to see if he would play along. 'I imagine,' he'd said, 'hearing news like that you might like to be alone for a while. You know, make a few calls, look into flights, that sort of thing.'

Stella had glanced at a gold carriage clock on a bookcase behind Harding Collins. The hands indicated quarter to two. 'You're right, I do feel the need to get to a more private place. I might take the afternoon off, go back to my room at the hotel and try to make some arrangements. Of course I'll take some work with me to keep the project on track. Ben Fisher can keep an eye on the team here until I return in the morning to meet with Daniel Cross and sort this whole thing out.'

'An excellent plan,' Harding had said. 'What time do you think you'll be leaving the plant? I can get Maria to arrange a cab, if you like.'

'That would be very helpful. I think I'll leave at noon.'

Maria Petrillo had been following the strange conversation with a quizzical look on her face until she caught on. 'Oh, right,' she'd said, a small smile breaking the tense line of her mouth. 'When I came to get you just now —'

'She was already gone,' Harding volunteered. 'What a pity!'

Before leaving Harding's office, he'd taken Stella by the elbow and whispered a final piece of advice. 'Be careful where you, uh, work, Stella. Daniel still has plenty of influence in this town. Even the local sheriff might agree to search for stolen property if it's for Daniel. If he calls me again I will have to tell him where you've gone, understand?'

She'd understood very well, which is why those two wannabe rapists hadn't found the file in her hotel room. But why did Cross have to send thugs? Cops would have been much easier to deal with and she wouldn't have felt the need to flee. In sending his goons, Cross had forced her to the conclusion that she could not face him until she had solved the puzzle of 'The Virgin's Secret'.

Staring out the window, only vaguely aware of the cloudless blue sky and the sounds of fun in the sun being had many floors below, Stella came to another conclusion. I need more information, she told herself. Her trip down to the pool would have to be via a payphone. She needed Ben Fisher to do her one more favour.

13

Ben Fisher didn't have the look of a player in the high-powered world of mergers and acquisitions. He looked more like a techno-geek. Tall, pale and skinny, he had the build of a college high-jump champion. Jack was prepared to bet the clothes Ben wore when he was seventeen still fit, although his face said he had to be in his thirties. He had large, rectangular black-rimmed spectacles, which gave him a permanently surprised look. His grey suit pants were rumpled and his bright white shirt was open at the neck.

Jack felt overdressed as he shook Fisher's hand and invited him in, discarding his jacket and loosening his tie to create a more casual atmosphere. Even so, it was obvious that Fisher was nervous and uncomfortable. His eyes darted about as if he expected a surprise attack.

'Something wrong?' Jack asked.

'Do you know what happened in this room?' Fisher said, his voice tight with tension.

'Frank said Stella was assaulted,' Jack said. 'Did that happen here? What do you know about it, Ben?'

Jack sat down on the bed and gestured to a nearby chair, but Ben remained standing, as if he wanted nothing to do with the furniture. 'She wasn't just assaulted, Jack. She was told she was going to be raped and killed. That's what she told me. If I hadn't come back when I did . . .'

Jack's expression was one of genuine surprise. Raped and killed? Frank hadn't mentioned that. And if it was true, it was little wonder Stella had decided to run. He stood up.

'Maybe we'd be more comfortable in the bar, Ben. I have these vouchers for some free cocktails. Want to go downstairs and talk?'

Fisher didn't need a second invitation and headed straight for the door. Once outside in the hallway he relaxed and as they walked to the elevator, Jack said, 'Tell me what you know about the assault, Ben.'

'All I know is two guys forced their way into her room. One had a knife, the other a gun. They said they were going to kill her but before they did that, they had plans to . . .'

'Were they serious? Not just trying to scare her?'

Fisher shook his head. 'It would take a lot to scare Stella, and I've never seen her so shaken. She was convinced it had been a very close call. And if you saw those guys . . .'

The elevator arrived and they stepped inside.

'You saw them? What happened exactly?' Jack asked. 'What did they look like?'

Fisher took a deep breath. 'Stella called me during the afternoon,' he said. 'This would have been last Wednesday. Jesus! Nearly a week ago. She'd left the plant early, taken some work back here. Not sure why, but she was working on something she said I didn't need to know about. That's not unusual. She calls me and says I should come by after I'm finished at CMS for the day. So we did – Jodie Michelson was with me. You'll meet her tomorrow. We came to her room about

6 p.m. I was sure I heard voices inside but when I knocked on the door, it went quiet.'

The elevator doors opened on the first floor and Fisher led the way to the bar of the hotel's gaudy Irish-American restaurant.

'Something told me I should keep knocking. I called out to Stella and said I wasn't leaving 'til I saw her. There was no reply so I kept knocking and sent Jodie off to find the hotel manager or security or something. Suddenly the door opens and these two guys walk out. Both of them were big. The shorter one was about your height, maybe a little smaller, but broad and muscular. He had dark hair and a face only a mother could love, you know? Broken nose, pock-marked skin. The other guy was a redhead with a buzz cut. Pale, freckly skin. He was taller than me and huge! Weighed at least 250 maybe even 300, I'd guess. Little piggy eyes.'

'Did you see weapons?'

'Nah, they had their hands in their pockets but Stella said they had a knife and a pistol. They just walked right by me like I didn't exist. I went into the room, your room now, and found Stella on the bed crying. It freaked me out. She said they threatened to rape and kill her. They had searched the room, emptied everything out of drawers and her suitcase. She said she thought it had something to do with our work at CMS but then she wouldn't say any more. When the hotel manager turned up with Jodie, Stella said she didn't want him to call the police or anything. I think she just wanted out of here.'

'Did you tell Frank all this?'

'Of course, but I don't think he believed me. Thought I was exaggerating. Those guys looked like professional thugs to me. They were wearing shirts with the logo of some security company but apparently they're well-known troublemakers round here. The hotel manager knew them from Stella's description. Said their names were Hollis and Hoyle. Don't know which is which.'

Jack shook his head in bewilderment as they settled at a table and waited for someone to take their order. Fisher was still edgy and Jack needed him to relax. He kept the conversation general, talking about the work to be done for the merger, while they had the two free cocktails and then a couple more.

With about thirty minutes of inconsequential talk behind them, Fisher could wait no longer. 'So,' he said, 'Frank's sent his star trader out to Peoria to sort out our little M&A team. That makes a whole lotta sense.'

'Did Frank tell you I was a trader?'

'Hell no! Frank tried to tell me you're a new member of the M&A team, but you're famous, pal, I know who you are.'

'You do?'

'Sure!' Fisher seemed annoyed by Jack's pretence at anonymity. 'Every year they publish the names of the firm's top performers in the staff newsletter. For the last few years you've always been on the list for the big bonuses. I notice things like that. Jealousy, I guess. No way you'd give up all that cash to join our shrinking little gang.'

'I never read the newsletter,' Jack admitted.

'Why would you? You already know you're getting the big money. You don't need to read about it!'

'Well, you should know that my transfer to M&A is actually one part of the story that is completely true. I've wanted to make this move for some time but I never expected it to happen this way.'

'You gotta be kidding!' Fisher exclaimed and started to laugh. 'They screwed that up, didn't they? They paid you so much down there you don't need to go after it any more.'

In a way, Jack thought, he's absolutely right.

'So you're really here to find Stella, right?' Fisher said cautiously.

'That's right, Ben. Frank wants her back on the team.'

'But why would they send you?'

'Pretty much because I was willing and in the right place at the right time.'

Fisher's eyes narrowed with suspicion. 'A dangerous pick on their part, wouldn't you say?'

'What do you mean?'

'I mean you're obviously already rich so you won't be easy to control. You've got options. If I was Frank I'd send some sucker who needs me more than I need him.'

'I think you're exaggerating the money bit for a start.' Jack was embarrassed by the fixation on his income. 'But it's interesting that you use the word "control". Is there some reason why you think someone would be trying to control me?'

'Look,' Fisher said, getting serious, 'you and me both know something weird is going on here. You may be new to the M&A business, Jack, but you don't have to be Einstein to work out this is no normal due diligence exercise. Stella gets attacked and takes off with a bunch of papers, Frank descends on Peoria and turns out to be best buddies with Daniel Cross, and then I get told to keep half the team here, even though we finished our work last week, just so you can come question us. Our own Sutton Brothers' goddamned Sherlock Holmes! If you expect me to believe you're here for any reason other than to advance Frank's interests, or Daniel Cross's, you must think I'm pretty fucking dumb!'

Jack shook his head to suggest he thought no such thing. 'I take it you're no fan of Frank's, then?'

'Oh, I used to be.' Fisher played with his empty glass. 'And maybe I will be again soon enough. But lately his behaviour hasn't really impressed me, you know?'

He waved a waitress over to the table and ordered another round.

'I've been drinking more than usual this past week,' Fisher mumbled, more to himself than to Jack.

'What did Frank do that you didn't like?' Jack asked.

Fisher looked at him sharply before responding. 'I shouldn't have said that. Please don't go repeating it. I'm just worried about Stella, and Frank's total focus is on the client. That's all. It's his job, I guess.'

'Look, Ben,' Jack said quietly, realising he'd have to take a little risk if he expected Ben to do the same, 'I have my own reasons to be a bit suspicious of Cross's motives in all this. And I'm worried about Stella too. I think your concern that Frank isn't looking after her best interests may well be justified.'

Fisher was watching Jack's face intently. Their eyes were only a foot apart as they leaned together like conspirators sharing a secret.

'Like what reasons?' he said, challenging Jack to up the ante.

Jack didn't want to tell the story of the mysterious package slipped to Cross by Stella's husband. 'Well, for example,' he said, 'I know how close Frank is to Daniel Cross, and he completely glossed over the assault on Stella. His only interest seems to be in keeping Cross happy. He hasn't shown any interest in whatever Stella found in that file, he just wants it returned to the client. It's pretty clear his only priority is to get the client relationship back on track. My priority is to safeguard Stella's interests.'

'Right,' Fisher said slowly, sitting back a little. He didn't seem convinced.

'And Daniel Cross's aggression about the file is suspicious too, wouldn't you say? Why did he rush back here in such a hurry? My guess is Stella stumbled on to some information that throws the whole takeover strategy into question, and Cross isn't happy about it. Maybe Frank's professional judgement is being clouded by his long relationship with Cross, I don't know. I've read the files, Ben. This whole deal is a bit wonky, isn't it?'

'You seem to know more about it than I do,' Fisher said defensively. 'What brings you to that conclusion?'

'The numbers just don't seem to add up, do they? Why is this big multinational conglomerate trying to buy a tin-pot defence contractor in Peoria? Just because Cross used to run it? On the face of it, it's not a particularly good deal and Frank appears to be blind to that fact.'

Fisher nodded, almost imperceptibly. 'I just assumed it was all confidential. It often is in this industry. And that's what Frank kept telling me.'

'If we assume Stella was doing what she thought was the right thing, professionally speaking, she must have taken the file because she thought it was in the best interests of Kradel, right?'

'Cross says Stella's put national security at risk. He says she's breached her confidentiality obligations to her clients, the firm and even the nation, for Christ's sake. He'll tell you all this tomorrow, for sure.'

'He's told me already,' Jack said. 'I met him in New York yesterday. But what the hell's he doing out here, Ben? Have you ever heard of that happening before, when one company is considering buying another? He's the CEO of Kradel. What right does he have to interfere with his old company? What about the current boss of CMS?'

'They only had a temporary guy in the job since Cross left six months ago,' Fisher said. 'And he got the elbow last week. But you've met Cross, Jack. He's a man used to getting his own way.'

'What do you mean the boss got the elbow?'

'Poor old Harding Collins,' Ben said with a regretful smile. 'He seemed like an okay guy but he was no match for Daniel Cross. And it's his family company too, poor sap. He and his secretary got packed off back to Chicago on Friday afternoon on Danny's orders. He came through the place like a tornado.' Ben circled an index finger in the air to emphasise his point. 'And do I think it's unusual for Cross to be here instead of in London? Damn right I do, but what can I do about it?'

'Have you raised it with Frank?'

'Yeah, kind of,' Ben said uncertainly. 'We had a brief conversation about it when he was here last week. He claims CMS can't risk undermining customer and stockholder confidence and Cross is the only person who can provide leadership until the sale goes through. He claims it's the best thing for both companies, and apparently both boards agree.'

'That doesn't make sense. If you want to buy a company, you don't normally take steps to prop it up. That would result in you paying more than you need to, wouldn't it?'

'I guess so. But maybe things are so finely balanced that the company could collapse completely, or maybe CMS has some big contracts out there that would be at risk if their customers thought there was a problem with leadership at the company. Frank's the strategy adviser – he should know all this stuff.'

'If he does, he didn't tell me.'

'Like I said, it may be confidential.'

'Mmm, maybe.' Jack wasn't persuaded. 'Did you see any evidence of big contracts like that during the last week?'

'No, not really. But there are lots of secrets with defence contractors. We were told right from the start we mightn't be able to see all the stuff we'd normally get to see.'

'Who told you that?'

'Frank,' Fisher said. Then the implications of the conversation seemed to strike him for the first time. 'Are you saying Frank is dirty?'

'No, I don't think so. I don't know,' was Jack's inadequate response. 'How could he be? He's been at Sutton Brothers forever. But then again I'm not sure I'd trust him one hundred per cent. Not with this client.'

'Yeah, maybe you're right.'

They sat back to ponder this latest information. Jack took the opportunity to order another round of drinks. He wasn't sure he really needed another one but it would do no harm for Fisher to get even looser. The bar was filling with after-work drinkers and the restaurant looked pretty busy already. They were early eaters in the Midwest, Jack noted.

He looked across at Ben Fisher and decided to say nothing. He left a big space there for Fisher to fill, inviting him to share his thoughts rather than answer questions. It took a few minutes but Jack was comfortable holding the silence. It was a good negotiating tactic. The drinks arrived with a bowl of pretzels, which they both began to munch automatically.

Ben shifted around in his seat. He looked away but his eyes were focused, as if he was conducting a debate in his head. Eventually, having reached some conclusion, he leaned forward again and spoke, softly and carefully. 'Between you and me, Jack, I don't think Stella's risking national security. I think she's risking exposing Daniel Cross.'

'How do you mean?'

'I don't know much about it.' Fisher licked his lips nervously. 'But I do know Stella's sure Cross did something bad in his past and wants it kept under wraps.' He leaned in closer. 'According to her it's not some government secret he's trying to keep quiet. It's murder!' The last word was almost whispered.

'Whose murder?' Jack hissed back, his nerves jangling.

There were people at all the tables around them now.

'I don't know,' Fisher murmured. Then he straightened in his seat, looking at Jack strangely through his big lenses. 'And I don't really know you, either. Maybe I've said too much already.'

'Look, Ben,' Jack said, as earnestly as he could. 'I know we've only just met, but believe me, I'm only looking for a fair and reasonable outcome to this mess. And I guarantee to protect Stella unless and until she demonstrates that she doesn't deserve my support. To do that effectively I need more information. Daniel Cross will give me a convincing story tomorrow, you know that. Who's going to put Stella's case? She's not talking. You can help her.'

'I can't put Stella's case,' Ben exclaimed. 'I have no idea what her goddamn case is!'

'So how do you know about the accusation of murder? How do you know Stella hasn't breached national security?'

'Because she told me,' Ben said with finality, 'and that's good enough for me. If you knew Stella it'd be good enough for you too.'

'When did she tell you?' Jack kept pushing. 'Before or after she left Peoria?'

'After,' Ben admitted. 'I've spoken to her a couple times on the phone, okay? But I don't know where she is so don't bother asking.'

His attempt to look belligerent came out looking surprised. Jack ignored it. 'On her cell phone?'

'No, she turned her phone off. The phone company can tell where she is if it's switched on. She called me from a payphone.'

'Did you tell Frank?'

'No way!'

'Do you know what her plans are?'

'No, she didn't share much. She said it wasn't in my best interests to know.'

'When did she call?'

'On Friday and over the weekend. And earlier today. She's still okay, which is good news. She wanted me to . . .' He hesitated.

'She wanted you to what?' Jack insisted.

'Nothing,' Fisher said, looking away again. 'She wanted me to finish up the job and not make any more waves, that's all. We're out of here tomorrow night, unless you say otherwise. I gotta tell you, I can't wait to wrap this up and get home.'

Fisher was holding something back but Jack didn't push. He suggested dinner instead, and the two men moved to a table in the restaurant, where they ordered steaks with baked potatoes and a bottle of red wine. Despite his thin build Ben seemed to hold his booze better than Jack, who was grateful for the meat and potatoes to soak some of it up.

Over coffee he decided to prod at Fisher's defences again. 'So what have you been doing out there at the plant these past two days, Ben? Twiddling your thumbs?'

'Pretty much. We've started outlining the structure of the report for the board of Kradel. Frank's still determined to get it done by the end of the week but it's difficult doing it out here in the sticks. We need to get back to the city.' He gave Jack a dark look.

'Hey, it wasn't my idea to keep you out here,' Jack said. 'But I'm glad you'll be there tomorrow. You can show me around, then I can tell Frank I did what he asked and we can all go home.'

'Yeah, well,' Fisher said begrudgingly, 'it turned out to be a good thing we're still here.'

Jack's ears pricked up. 'Why's that?'

'Because Stella had a few jobs for us to do.'

Jack looked up and saw Fisher was teasing him. He had a mischievous look on his face. Sometime during the course of the meal he'd decided to trust his colleague, but was having some fun with it.

'So give it up,' Jack said, smiling. 'What did she get you to do?'

'It was no big deal. She wanted some old information about CMS; names of company executives in the 1960s, that sort of thing. Most of it's publicly available information.'

'What did she want that wasn't already in the public domain?'

Ben hesitated a moment before going on. 'Current addresses to go with the names. Also the names and addresses of surviving spouses if the employee's no longer around. My guess is she wants to contact some former senior employees to get a better handle on the documents she found.'

'But you said the issue was murder,' Jack said, confused. 'Was the victim associated with the company?'

'Look, Jack, I don't know what the story is, okay? But I figure it has to have something to do with the company, or the file wouldn't be relevant, right? I'm sorry I mentioned the murder thing but it was what Stella said when I pushed her on the whole national security angle. See, when she called me on Friday, Daniel Cross had already given me his spiel. He'd pretty much convinced me that Stella had screwed up badly.

'But Stella's convincing too. I've known her ever since she started with the bank. In those days, she was junior to me and now I work for her, but I gotta tell you, I never had a better team leader. She's impressive, Jack, and she's raised the standard of our work a hell of a lot in the time she's been with us. Of course, she's gorgeous too.

'When she called me,' Ben went on, blushing, ' I tackled her on the national security stuff, but she insisted she could see nothing in the documentation she'd taken that risked any government or military secret. That's when she said she thought it had something to do with murder. She said she'd found some strange document hinting at some past crime, possibly murder, but she needed time to work on it. Maybe it's coded or something. She needed the names of past office-holders to help sort it out. She also said she'd given Daniel

Cross the opportunity to explain the documents, but he couldn't do it – not in a way she believed, anyway.'

Ben rocked back in his chair and drained the last of his wine. 'Now I've told you everything I know. And it feels good, I gotta say. I don't like keeping dirty secrets.'

Jack wasn't quite finished. 'How did you get the names and addresses Stella wanted, Ben?'

'Mainly from old annual reports and organisation charts. The spouses' names and the addresses were a little harder to find but the pension plan had all the details.'

Fisher looked a little sheepish. As well he should, Jack thought. 'How the hell did you get at the pension plan records?'

'It was a good deal easier than it should be. The plan is managed by an outside firm but an updated copy of all the records is dumped down to the CMS system every month. With a bit of hunting around we were able to fill in most of the gaps.'

'We?' Jack said, alarmed. 'Who else knows Stella's been in touch with you?'

'Well, I couldn't get into the system without help so Stella told me it was okay to get some discreet assistance from Maria Petrillo, Harding's PA. Stella made some sort of connection with her, apparently. She even gave us her password – which still works, by the way, even though she left on Friday.'

'Shit, Ben, are you crazy? You don't want to be found using that network access, especially after Maria's gone.'

'Don't panic,' Fisher said. 'We finished with it this afternoon and we covered our tracks pretty well.'

'Ben,' Jack said with some exasperation, 'you're still saying "we". Do you mean you and Jodie?'

'Yeah, but don't worry about Jodie. She can be trusted to keep quiet and she worships Stella.'

Jack was impressed by the loyalty of Stella's teammates. Frank Spiteri had certainly been right on that score. 'How'd you get the information to Stella?' he asked.

'Email. Don't worry, we didn't use the Sutton Brothers' system.'

'Will you give me the address?' Jack was eager to know if it was the same hotmail address he'd used.

Ben paused for a second then shook his head. 'No,' he said, 'but tell you what. Stella's due to call me tomorrow. I'll ask her if she's okay with me giving you the address. I'll tell her you seem like a decent guy, all right? You sure are a good dinner companion, I'll say that much, but now it's time for me to sleep all this booze off. And you'd better stay sharp too, Jack. You gotta face Danny Cross in the morning.'

'You think maybe I could talk to Stella tomorrow too?'

'I'll ask her, okay? That's all I can do. I'll give her your cell number if you like.'

Fisher unfolded his lanky frame and Jack followed as he weaved his way tentatively towards the elevators. On the way up Ben told Jack he'd collect him at 8.30 for the 9 a.m. meeting with Cross – it was only twenty minutes to the CMS plant by cab. Fisher's room was on the eighth floor, like Jack's, but they tottered off in different directions after getting out of the elevator.

'You be careful in that room, now, ya hear?' Fisher called out as a parting remark. 'Be sure to use the security chain, and don't open the door to strangers, okay?' He staggered down the hallway with a tipsy giggle.

Jack giggled too, realising that he was in little better shape than Fisher. Already he was dreading the hangover waiting in the wings of his skull. He moved unsteadily to Room 808 and scanned the door thoroughly for signs of forced entry. Nothing was apparent. When he finally managed to get the electronic lock to click open, he cursed his failure to leave the room lights on. The interior was dark and unfamiliar and he squinted into the gloom to be sure there were no large, dangerous shapes lurking inside. It would have looked very odd to anyone passing in the hallway.

Eventually he reached inside to flick the light switches. All suspicious dark shapes dissolved into the familiar forms of furniture, luggage and other standard hotel fixtures, but he was still cautious as he entered the room and he checked all the obvious hiding places before satisfying himself that he was completely alone. He sat on the bed heavily, exhausted. All that alcohol on top of a few hours' sleep the night before caught up with him in a rush. The booze also fed his paranoia. Not only did he carefully attach the security chain and roll the big knob over to deadlock the door, he also dragged a big armchair down the narrow corridor beside the bathroom and pushed it firmly into the entrance space against the door.

Nobody's getting in or out of here in a hurry, he thought, as he stripped off clumsily and prepared for bed. From beneath warm blankets in the gloom broken only by the faint light of the city coming through the window, he contemplated with satisfaction the big obstacle in the hallway. As sleep crept over him, the final image in Jack's head was of Stella, running.

14

Stella was, in fact, strolling. The light, cool breeze coming off the ocean felt good on the skin of her bare arms, still glowing from a long afternoon sun-worshipping session. The streets around the hotel remained busy as the sun began to leave the sky. Souvenir and food vendors were still plying their trade and Stella moved patiently around family groups blocking the sidewalks, peering at menus and arguing about where and what they would eat.

It took her less than ten minutes to reach the copy shop and Fedex agent she had found earlier. The place was also an internet cafe and booking agent for all the local tours. Paying for a half hour of computer time, Stella sat down at a monitor in a booth plastered with advertising material and hints for the budget traveller, but she was only interested in her email.

As her hotmail inbox loaded she found herself frowning. She had received a message from Jack Rogers. How could that be? How could he get this address, and why would he be writing to her in the first place? Her mouse hand hovered impatiently as the rest of the page loaded and, as soon as she could, she opened up Jack's email.

As she read it, the feeling of disquiet in her gut only intensified. Jack Rogers had been selected by the bank as the best man to hunt her down. She had almost reached out to him a day earlier, probably at the very moment he was up in Frank's office discussing her and the mess she'd caused and deciding how best to neutralise the problem. She had decided against involving him because she didn't want to compromise his career too, but now he was adding himself into the equation and she wasn't sure she liked it.

At the very least it was embarrassing. Frank and Jack had obviously concluded that she might be having some sort of breakdown. It was galling to think of her smugly successful fellow Australian viewing her as some sort of loose cannon and discussing her shortcomings with her boss. When they met on the Top Gun program, they were both on a fast track to partnership. Now he was patronisingly offering his assistance as if to some damsel in distress, still the golden-haired boy of Sutton Brothers, while her prospects for advancement were being flushed down the toilet. And that line about David meeting with Daniel Cross had to be wrong. There was no way those two could have connected.

By the time she'd read the message through a second time, indignant, defensive anger replaced the knot of concern in her stomach. If she decided to communicate with Jack, it would be at a time of her own choosing. A time when she had better evidence than an obscure and, so far, indecipherable poem written decades earlier. And if she wanted to talk to Frank she knew where to find him, she didn't need Jack Rogers to hold her hand. But she wasn't ready to talk to Frank. And she wasn't ready to explain herself to Jack either. She sent his message to print but closed it without sending a reply.

The message from Ben Fisher was more welcome and Stella managed a smile as she read his colourful and lengthy account of the latest events at the CMS plant. His descriptions of Daniel Cross were both amusing and a little frightening, but the news of Harding Collins' dismissal wasn't funny, and Stella felt a pang of guilt, knowing she had precipitated his confrontation with a man who clearly terrified him.

Attached to the message was a document containing the information Stella had asked Ben to collect. After opening it and reading through the few pages on the screen, she printed out three copies. One she kept to review later. The other copies she added to each of the two large envelopes she had been carrying in her shoulder bag. They also contained her detailed retelling of the events leading up to her departure from Peoria, a complete copy of the contract and 'The Virgin's Secret' and her interpretation of its meaning so far.

With the new information from Ben the packages were now complete. The envelopes were already addressed; one to Alex Trainer, the attorney in New York, and one to her home address. Before going to the counter to arrange their dispatch, she felt their weight in her hands and the meaning of their existence. They were her insurance, her only ace in the hole. If something happened to her, or the accursed file, it would be up to her attorney to make sure it hadn't all been in vain.

I must call him, she told herself. This wasn't his area of expertise but he was the only lawyer she'd used for personal matters in the US and who the hell knew what sort of expertise was relevant to her situation, anyway? He would need more explanation but it was too late to call him now. It would have to wait for the morning.

Using a made-up name and return address, she paid for the courier service at the counter and was assured the packages would arrive in New York by lunchtime on Friday. Then she purchased a pre-paid phonecard to be ready for what could be a lengthy call to Alex Trainer. Only then did it occur to her that it wasn't too late to call her husband. Jack had to be wrong, but it would do no harm to put it to the test.

She waited until she was back in the lobby of her hotel where there were payphones with some measure of privacy. It seemed to take a while to connect, then even longer for the phone to be picked up at the other end.

'Hello?'

'David, hi! It's me.'

'Yeah, I thought it had to be you, ringing this late. Where you calling from?'

Just the sound of his voice was enough to make Stella feel irritated and defensive. She detected alcohol in his speech, which wasn't uncommon, but there was something else too – a forced pleasantness that worked its way under her skin. Maybe he really was hiding something.

'Didn't interrupt anything, did I?'

'No, no, not at all. Just on my way to bed.'

Then Stella heard the clinking sound of glass against glass and, more faintly, what could easily be interpreted as a short, girlish giggle.

'Is there someone there with you, David?'

'No, love, it's just the TV. I'll turn it down, okay?'

He never called her 'love'. She felt her hackles rise.

'Look, I was just calling to see if you got the package I sent home last week.'

'Yeah, yeah, I've got it here somewhere. Put it in the study, I think. Your note said you'd be sending another one.'

'I've just sent it. It will arrive on Friday. Just keep it safe with the first one, okay?'

'No worries.' There was a disturbing note of satisfaction to his voice. 'How's the holiday going? Where are you again?'

'I can still hear the TV, David, or whatever that is.'

'Oh, right. Sorry.'

She heard his breathing change as he moved about and she pictured him scurrying to another room. When he spoke again there was an echo on the line that convinced her he was in the bathroom adjacent to their bedroom.

'There,' he said, 'I've turned it off.'

Stella's anger peaked and then suddenly melted away as it had countless times before. It would rise up and up in her, but only to the point where she realised that she didn't have the energy to maintain it. She just didn't care enough to stay mad.

'David, do you know who Daniel Cross is?' she said, her voice flat.

'Isn't he the guy you mentioned in your note? What about him?'

'Have you had any contact with him?'

'Me? No! Why would I?'

It would have been useful to be able to see his face, but Stella wasn't sure it would help her know the truth. He was obviously lying about something, but was it about Daniel Cross or about the whore he had stashed in their matrimonial bed? Disgust ran through her. The phone in her hand felt unclean and she wanted the conversation to be over.

'I have to go, David.'

'Oh, right, if you say so. Don't want to update me on the holiday? It's freezing back here, you know, and raining. What's it like where you are? What time is it there?'

'Just keep the package safe, please!' she said and put down the phone.

She began to run, through the broad open-sided hotel lobby and out to the street, as quickly as she could manage in her sandals. She was panting for breath by the time she reached the Fedex agent where she pushed past a slow-moving backpacker to get to the head of the line. The shift must have changed because she didn't recognise any of the people serving behind the counter.

'I need to get back a package I sent just a little while ago,' she gasped to a smiling brown face topped with a baseball cap emblazoned with the company logo.

'Where was it going?' the man asked pleasantly.

'New York.'

'If you sent it before the turn of the hour then it's on its way to the airport.'

'Can you stop it?'

'Maybe.' His eyes turned to a computer screen. 'What was your name, Miss?'

Stella hesitated, trying to remember which false name she'd used on the package, but then she heard the words that made her ragged breathing stop.

'And I'll need to see some ID, please.'

15

Flames danced in front of Jack's eyes. Blue, red, yellow, orange, scorching flames rising up from the floor. Stella Sartori was in the armchair in front of the door to his hotel room, burning like Joan of Arc, her arms outstretched like a martyr. He dived from the bed into deep, cold water. Astonished, he went under for a moment then struggled back to the surface, gasping for breath, kicking to stay afloat, only to find the air above the water burning vigorously. The flames were at the level of his face, toasting his cheeks. His eyelids were melting, his nose burned and smoked. His cheeks began to blister.

Suddenly he was awake. His heart was pounding. Beads of sweat ran down his brow and soaked the sheets. And he was blinded. The rays of the morning sun were pouring through the window directly on to the bed, washing over his upturned face. He turned away from the bright light and his eyes adjusted painfully to a more moderate glare. The nightmare images still hurtled around his brain and in his confused and dehydrated state, he imagined he could still hear screaming in the distance, like the eternal cries of the damned. He shook his head a couple of times, instantly regretting the movement.

The face that greeted him in the bathroom mirror was another shock. Grey skin pulled tight across his cheekbones, in need of a shave, making him look gaunt and unhealthy. Grey eyes, bloodshot and sitting deeper in his sockets than usual, as if trying to avoid the outside world. There appeared to wisps of grey hair peppering the hairline at his temples. His head was pounding, his throat was screaming for water. Jack made a pact with himself to avoid alcohol for the rest of the week.

The tap water had a metallic flavour, but he swallowed four glasses of it in quick succession. Then he eased himself into a hot shower and let the water drum away on his head and shoulders until they tingled on the outside, distracting him from how he felt from the inside. Slowly he came to life, like a drought-starved animal receiving the first rains of the wet season. When he emerged from the steamy bathroom he was feeling almost human again, but he popped a couple of Advils to speed his recovery and ordered fruit and coffee from room service.

The trip out to the CMS plant with Ben Fisher was informative, if not picturesque. Jack saw a little more of Peoria and even crossed the big iron bridge he'd seen from the air. It was pretty obvious that Caterpillar, the huge multinational, was the biggest employer in town. Just a couple of blocks from the hotel, the cab driver pointed out the worldwide headquarters of the company as they drove past on largely empty streets. A huge, gloomy concrete box that looked indestructible. Across the river, in East Peoria, Caterpillar's manufacturing plants were massive in scale.

Jack read billboards by the side of the road advertising something called the Par-A-Dice Riverboat Casino. Others, paid for by the Auto Workers' Union, denounced Caterpillar's labour practices and called for a better contract. Beyond Caterpillar's facilities, other smaller businesses occupied the industrial spaces around the edge of the city, taking advantage of the infrastructure that had accumulated around the bigger corporation.

Among them Collins Military Systems sat on a large piece of land of which, Jack guessed, less than twenty per cent was taken up by man-made structures. High fences, low white cinderblock buildings no more than three storeys high and a large asphalt parking lot, only half full. The whole facility looked like its glory days were long gone. From the architecture he guessed most of the buildings dated from the 1950s and 1960s, but there were a few modern structures visible towards the rear of the complex. The gardens lining the visitors' entrance to the main building were, by contrast, immaculately maintained, sporting colourful blooms despite the season.

The third-floor office Daniel Cross had taken over wasn't grand by Manhattan CEO standards but it was impressive enough. It was lined with rich wood and furnished with expensive contemporary pieces as if it had been redecorated using a single photograph from an interior design magazine.

Jack was wearing one of his most impressive suit-and-tie combinations and Cross was no sartorial slouch; they looked like a couple of powerbrokers sitting down to lunch in a gentlemen's club. The fact that they were three hours' drive south-west of Chicago in the middle of an overgrown cornfield seemed incongruous to Jack, but Cross looked very much at home.

'You like being back here?'

'You know it's strange,' Cross said, waving Jack towards a chair, 'but I really do. London's big and impressive and all, but this place is very . . .'

'Friendly?' Jack suggested.

'Familiar,' Cross answered.

'Well, if Kradel buys CMS you'll have plenty of legitimate reasons to be here, right?'

Cross's blue eyes narrowed at the implication that his presence in advance of the sale was somehow illegitimate.

'You look ill, Jack. Are you feeling okay?'

'I'm fine. Just a little hungover. I spent the evening drinking with Ben Fisher.'

'Did you, now? Learn anything useful?'

'He seems like a decent bloke but we didn't talk much about Stella Sartori. I wanted him to get comfortable with me, you know, gain his trust. I'll be talking work stuff with him in more detail after we finish up here. But I do know that Stella has been in touch with him.'

'Really?' Cross looked at Jack with renewed interest. 'And?'

'And nothing really. She rang to say she was okay and to tell him to get on with the work for the Kradel board. He doesn't get the impression she's trying to sabotage the deal. Far from it.'

Cross shook his head, his mouth hardening. 'She's doing something I'm not going to like, Jack, otherwise she'd be here and the file would be back in the safe where it belongs.'

Jack had no answer for that. Cross contemplated a spot on his desk for a moment and then said, 'Still, you've already done better than Frank. He got diddly-squat out of 'em.'

'I think Stella contacted Ben after Frank's trip out here.'

'But Ben didn't pick up the phone and let Frank know she'd been in touch, did he?'

'No,' Jack said, 'that's true. He and the others are caught in a bind, aren't they? They admire Stella and are naturally loyal to her, but they're professionals too. I'm pretty sure that if Ben thought Stella was doing something unethical, he'd be the first to let Frank know.'

'Unethical!' Cross's tone was incredulous. 'She stole a confidential file from a client company, Jack, and she's disappeared with it. If that's not fucking unethical —'

'I'm sorry,' Jack said, holding his hands up in a gesture of surrender.

'You're right, of course, but she hasn't caused any real harm yet, has she? I'm sure that whatever she is planning, she'll be discreet.'

Cross grunted his scepticism and Jack tried to change the subject. 'What will you do next if I don't come up with any more leads about the file or her location?'

'First thing is to get the sale completed,' Cross said firmly. 'Despite what Stella Sartori might think, there are a great many strategic advantages for both CMS and Kradel in this deal, and I refuse to let her jeopardise it. Frank's guaranteed me a report by the end of this week so we can keep this thing moving.

'And as for Sartori,' the sharp edge returned to his voice, 'she's bound to make a mistake soon enough. I *will* find her and get my file back, no matter what it takes.'

Jack felt the chill of unmitigated malice in Cross's voice and swallowed hard. 'Have you heard from her again?'

'I have yet to receive her demands, if that's what you mean.'

'I'm sure it won't come to that.'

'Is that so?' Cross said. 'And I was under the impression you were to be impartial in this matter, Jack.'

'I'm not rushing to any conclusions, Daniel. I would only ask that you do the same.'

'There is no other conclusion to be drawn,' Cross said, his tone chilly. 'The woman stole company property. I want my property back. I want to know what she's been doing with it and I want every copy she has made of the material in that file. And I want it sorted out fast and quietly. Maybe then I won't insist on her dismissal from Sutton Brothers.'

But then Cross gave Jack a smile, though it was hardly warm. 'I'm sorry, Jack. You're quite right. You must make your inquiries and I must be a little more patient. Go and talk to your colleagues. Make them understand how important it is that we locate Stella as soon as possible. Find out what you can and report back to me this afternoon. We'll get Frank on the phone and you can brief us both, okay?'

Jack found this sudden change in mood disconcerting. He stood up, again feeling dismissed by Cross, but he still had some questions.

'Can you tell me any more about the file Stella took, Daniel? Maybe it would help me understand her motivation.'

Cross's eyes flashed but his manner remained friendly. 'Frank knows all the details, Jack. It's highly confidential, relating to one of our older contracts with the US Government. Very sensitive. Not something we'd like to see plastered all over the papers. Nobody at the company has looked at the file for years so it's hard to say exactly what's in there. I imagine there will be information regarding the negotiations and the terms agreed and so on.'

'So what on earth could Stella hope to gain with that sort of information?' Jack said. 'If she reveals any of it, she'd be breaking the law, wouldn't she?'

'I can only assume she's planning to sell it to one of our competitors,' Cross said. 'Or threaten to. As I said before, I can come to no other conclusion. If you expect me to change my mind on that, Jack, you will have to bring me something new.'

Cross pressed a button on his telephone and summoned a severe-looking, middle-aged Englishwoman, who escorted Jack down to a meeting room on the first floor where the Sutton Brothers team had their temporary home. Only four members of the team remained in Peoria. Apart from Ben Fisher, Jack saw three twenty-somethings in the room – two men and a woman.

The woman was obviously Jodie Michelson. Ben had talked about her. She was short, about five three, and at least twenty pounds heavier than when she married, judging by the bulging flesh around her wedding ring. Mousy blonde hair in a pageboy cut framed a pleasant but serious-looking face. No smiles from Jodie. She greeted Jack with formality and little warmth.

The two men looked like fraternal twins. They were younger than Jodie, maybe twenty-four or -five. Their near identical uniforms of white shirts, dark ties, blue suit pants and close-cropped brown hair blurred the facial differences between them. They also shared the smiling, enthusiastic expression that often marked out Wall Street newcomers. They were introduced as Aaron and Andrew, and Jack immediately forgot which one was which. They both pumped his hand vigorously then turned their attention back to their notebook computers.

Ben explained that Aaron and Andrew were working on the production of graphs and tables for the final report. 'We've only got 'til Friday to have a polished draft ready to go to the client,' he added in an exasperated tone. 'Jodie and I have been working on the words.'

He pointed to the whiteboard in one corner of the room where they'd set down the major points to cover. 'Lucky they only want a short report,' Ben said as he sat down.

They were in a meeting room designed for eight people, separated by one central table too large for the room. It was a windowless, claustrophobic space, hardly conducive to creative thinking.

Jack didn't sit down. 'Is there some place we can get some fresh air and have a chat?' he asked.

Jodie rolled her eyes and looked up at the whiteboard, as if to say, 'We don't have time for this,' but Ben nodded his head and said, 'Good idea, let's go into the garden.'

16

Well before dawn, Stella was punching phonecard numbers into the keypad of a payphone in the comparatively peaceful lobby of the hotel. Sleep had been out of the question. Since the conversation with David, her mind had been racing with paranoid thoughts. Her level of distraction had sparked a shouting match with her sister, who considered Stella's inability to switch off the work and have some fun as a personal affront. Some unfair things had been said by both sisters and it had only been the sad and shocked look on their mother's face that had stopped them from going further.

Exhausted, angry and a little fearful, Stella dialled the number she had memorised last night and waited for someone in New York to pick up. Nothing happened. The ringing tone droned on and on before becoming an annoying beeping sound. She tried again with the same result and felt her heart begin to pound. She should have connected with voicemail at the very least.

Digging out a battered filofax from her bag, she flipped the pages until she found a different number. This one should connect her to the central switch. Nervously she waited while the tone played its monotonous tune in her ear.

'Bloch and Lieberman, Annie speaking. How may I direct your call?'

'My name is Stella Sartori, Annie. I was just trying to call Alex Trainer on his direct line. He does still work there, doesn't he?'

'Yes, of course,' Annie said quickly, but then she seemed unsure how to proceed. 'Mr Trainer is, uh . . .'

An awful image leapt into Stella's mind, of a man bleeding and hurt, but it was a generic image as she could barely even remember Alex Trainer's face.

'My God!' she said. 'Is he all right?'

'Why yes, I'm sure he is,' the operator said, taken aback that her caller would jump to such a grim conclusion. 'I believe he's just fine. But he's had some, uh, there was some trouble. No, no, I think he'd better tell you himself. If you'll hold the line I'll try to locate him or perhaps you'd like him to call you back? What was the name again?'

'Sartori. Stella Sartori. I would prefer to talk to him immediately if that is at all possible. The matter is very urgent. I am also calling long distance from a payphone, if you could be quick.'

'Hold on,' Annie said and Stella's earpiece filled with a well-worn classical music track.

Willing the phonecard to last the distance, Stella fidgeted with her filofax and turned around to watch two drunken Englishmen support each other in a stagger across the lobby towards the elevators, singing a football anthem, while a hotel employee hustled along behind begging them to keep it down.

'This is Alex Trainer, Ms Sartori. How can I help you?'

Stella felt a rush of relief at the sound of his voice, which she now remembered clearly, but she was concerned at his apparent ignorance. 'You don't know why I'm calling?'

'I do apologise.' The attorney's embarrassment was obvious. 'I don't have access to my records right now. I remember your name from a few years back, but to be honest . . .'

'Yes, that was me,' she said. 'You helped me out back in 1999. I work for Sutton Brothers, remember?'

'Yes, of course,' Trainer said, his tone more confident. 'You're Australian, aren't you? How's your time in the States been so far? Did the job work out or —'

'Alex,' Stella interrupted. 'Did you get my package?'

'Package? No, I don't think so. Hold on.'

Stella could hear him talking to someone and a female voice responding, but she couldn't make out what was being said. Then he was back on the line. 'I just spoke to my assistant,' he said. 'She has no recollection of a package arriving from you either. Perhaps it hasn't arrived yet.'

'It should have got there last Friday,' Stella said, 'Monday at the latest. It was a Fedex courier package but the return address was fake. I didn't use my real name, either.'

'Is that so?' Trainer said. 'Why would you —'

'Just ask your assistant about a Fedex package, please?'

There was pause. 'Hold the line.'

After another frustrating thirty seconds, Stella's lawyer was back on the line.

'Yes,' he said, 'Jenny remembers it now. She didn't recognise the name so she thought it might be personal. She put it in my in-tray unopened. But, Stella, I wasn't in the office Monday and then —'

Stella's pulse began to settle. 'You do have the package? It's still safe with you?'

'Well, no,' Alex Trainer said.

Stella's heart rate accelerated again. 'What do you mean, Alex? What's going on?'

She heard a deep sigh. 'We had a break-in Monday night,' he said. 'Vandals, drug addicts, anti-Semites, we don't really know. They did quite a lot of damage. Set fire to my office and some adjacent workstations. Unfortunately they destroyed a great deal of original documentation in the process. If your package was among the papers on my desk I'm afraid it's been destroyed. I hope the contents can be easily replaced. Your passport wasn't in there was it, Stella?'

'No,' she said quietly, 'not my passport, but —'

'Good, good. I think we lost a few passports. They can be reissued, of course, but the hassle . . .' He sighed again. 'So, Stella, what were you writing to me about? A change of status, perhaps?'

'No, no. Actually nothing in your normal line of work.'

She felt as if a great weight was pressing down on her. Could she even be bothered trying to explain? What difference would it make now?

Then she heard a tone on the line warning her that the phone-card was running out of juice. 'Alex, listen, I have to go but this is important. I've sent you another package. I just need you to keep it safe. I had more detailed instructions in the first package but there's no time to explain it all again. It will arrive Friday morning, I think. Another Fedex envelope, again with a fake name and address. Don't let anyone get their hands on this one, please. Do you have a safe in your office?'

'Yes, we have a safe, but what on earth —?'

'Somebody might try to get it, Alex. It seems they got the first one.'

'Are you saying it was your package these guys were after on Monday?'

'I don't know. It's possible. When the envelope arrives, put it straight in the safe. You can look at it, of course. It's only some documents, and they won't mean much to you, but I need you to keep them secure until I call you again. If you don't hear from me by Friday afternoon, take them to the authorities.'

'Authorities? What authorities?' Trainer's voice was heavy with curiosity and suspicion.

'Cops, FBI, I don't really know. Will you do this for me, Alex? You may not be the right attorney for this but you're the only one I know.'

'Look, Stella, if you know something about our break-in you should be talking to the police. Where are you? Can you give me any more information? What's this all about?'

The warning tone on the phone line picked up speed.

'Will you take care of the package for me, Alex? Can I trust you as my attorney?'

'Of course you can, but I —'

'I'll call you again soon,' Stella said, as the line went dead.

17

Ben Fisher and Jodie Michelson led Jack to a group of chairs out in the sun. They were between the main administration building and the manufacturing plant, which were connected by a covered concrete walkway and separated by a wide swathe of manicured lawn, scattered with almost-leafless trees and well-tended flowerbeds. Garden seats and tables were grouped in various locations on the lawn and some CMS employees were making the most of them, enjoying a mid-morning smoke and coffee break.

'I've spent a bit of time out here this past week,' Fisher said as they settled themselves. 'This is where I make all my phone calls.' He patted the compact Motorola hooked on his belt.

The sky was wide and blue and calm but the air was frigid, making the warmth of the sun welcome on Jack's back, though he hadn't quite forgiven it for his rude awakening that morning. He told his colleagues about his conversation with Daniel Cross and Fisher said he'd heard it all before. Jodie didn't say anything and continued to look glum. Jack asked whether they thought he should talk to the other two young associates toiling away inside.

'Not if you want to talk about Stella,' Fisher said. 'They don't know anything about that.'

'They must be suspicious, surely,' Jack said. 'The whole team must have been thrown when Stella took off. How did she do that, anyway? And what did you say to the team after she'd gone? It must have seemed very sudden.'

'Oh, you don't know the half of it,' Fisher responded excitedly.

Jodie gave him a glare that said 'Shut up', but he waved it off. 'I've already told him the important stuff,' he said to her, 'so I may as well tell him the rest of it. If you don't want to say anything that's your choice.'

He turned back to Jack, eyes shining. 'Stella's getaway was like something out of a spy movie. After she was attacked in her room, Jodie and I cooked up a plan to get her away from Peoria in this rental car she had. I have no idea when or where she got the wheels, but that's Stella for you. Anyway, the whole bunch of us got together to go eat downstairs, you know, where we ate last night?'

Jack nodded but Fisher wasn't waiting.

'Stella's car was parked in the hotel garage but she was worried the hotel exits might be watched and she didn't want anyone to know she'd gone. If they went after her she'd be alone, you see? We got a table by the window in the restaurant with a view of the street and right away we could see one of the men who attacked Stella. The dark-haired guy with the broken nose was on the street across from the hotel. And get this – he was talking to a cop, laughing even. Sharing a joke!'

Fisher's face flushed at the memory. 'Okay, so we ordered some food and drinks, there were eight of us, right, Jodie? And then in the middle of the meal the two thugs, Hollis and Hoyle, walked into the restaurant. They made no attempt to hide either, and took a table across the room and ordered some beers. It was real creepy, and Stella must've hated seeing them but she was too tough to show it – I was sitting right next to her, which made her feel better, she said.'

Jodie rolled her eyes. 'She was making you feel better, you mean, dweeb!'

Fisher ignored the jibe. 'We didn't expect them to come in, and I suggested going to the manager and asking him to get 'em tossed out of the place, but Stella said she was happy knowing where they both were. And these guys didn't mind Stella knowing they were keeping an eye on her. The big guy, the redhead, even toasted her with his beer. I could have shoved it down his throat.'

'Yeah, right,' said Jodie.

Fisher ignored her. 'After the meal we put our plan into action. Most of the group had no idea something unusual was going on, only Stella and Jodie and me. Nobody else was looking out for guys tailing us or anything like that. We just looked normal – a happy bunch of colleagues having a meal after work. I think most of the team were pretty surprised when Stella and I kept buying more drinks. We wanted to keep them there as long as possible. The two thugs kept drinking too. Stella was drinking club soda but it looked like something stronger.'

Jack gave a 'let's move this along' signal and Fisher started talking even faster. 'Our group was getting kinda merry, and the two thugs looked pretty relaxed too because they were getting louder and flirt-ing with the waitresses. Stella went to the ladies' restroom a couple times and they watched her like a hawk but by the third time, they hardly bothered. The fourth time it was, like, nearly midnight, and she went with Jodie.'

'I was carrying a shoulder bag she'd packed earlier,' Jodie said quietly, not wanting to be forgotten.

'Right,' Fisher said. 'So Jodie gave Stella the bag in the restroom and they waited a long time. Meanwhile I had my cell phone open under the table. When I saw the two thugs getting antsy I called Stella's number. That was the signal for Jodie to come back. So she sauntered back into the restaurant, and of course they were watching her. Then, pretending to be smashed I called out "Hey, where's Stella?" and Jodie said —'

'I said she'd gone up to her room,' Jodie interjected. 'And I don't think you had to pretend to be smashed.'

'Whatever,' Fisher said, dismissing the barb. 'Anyway the thugs both jumped up and raced out into the lobby. I walked after them like I was off to take a pee and I saw them going into one of the elevators. Then I called Stella's number again and she came out of the ladies' restroom and blew me a kiss as she raced by on her way to the parking garage. Just after, we saw her screeching past the front of the hotel in her rented wheels. Eventually the thugs returned to the bar and finished their drinks. They didn't look happy but they had to conclude she was in her room and she wasn't going to let them in again, that was for sure. I called Stella's cell one more time and she knew she'd got off scot-free.'

'That's quite a story,' Jack said, and the smile on Ben's face broadened. Jodie continued looking glum. 'You both did great,' he added, but it sounded patronising, even to Jack's ears. He returned quickly to his original question.

'Ben, what did you end up telling the rest of the team? They must have been surprised when Stella didn't turn up for work the next day.'

'I told them Stella had a call to say her mom was dying of cancer,' Fisher said, as if it was a ruse he used every day. 'Cancer's always good, nobody likes talking about it so you don't get too many questions. I also said that's why she left work early, just in case anyone had noticed. Everybody knows Stella's real private so it was no surprise to them she hadn't shared. Pretty neat, huh?'

'Yeah, pretty neat, if a little macabre,' Jack replied. 'Have you seen the two guys since?'

'Shit, no,' Ben said, with an involuntary glance over his shoulder. 'I wouldn't forget them. I've never seen two uglier-looking specimens. Big as buses. And for some reason they didn't seem too intimidated by me!'

He flexed a thin arm and Jack joined in his laughter. Jodie Michelson didn't smile; she only rolled her eyes again. Jack decided it was time to turn his attention to her. 'If there's no point talking to Andrew and Aaron, and the rest of the team has gone home, and Harding Collins and Maria Petrillo are in Chicago, that would seem to leave you, Jodie.'

She stiffened but said nothing.

'Would you like me to leave you two alone?' said Ben cheerfully.

'That might be a good idea.'

Jodie didn't comment so Ben loped away, saying, 'I've got a few things to sort out, anyway,' accompanied by a conspiratorial wink. Jack knew he had Ben on side but he had a feeling Jodie would be a tougher nut to crack.

He started with familiar tactics, saying nothing. He just sat back and enjoyed the sun and fresh air, but Jodie wasn't going to fall for that. She looked perfectly comfortable, despite her sour face, and he knew he'd be waiting a long time before she volunteered anything. At last he said, 'You don't seem very happy.'

'Don't patronise me.'

Her response was so immediate that Jack knew she'd been practising the words in her head. They sat in silence for another minute, Jodie's face still stony.

'You know,' Jack said, 'if you ever need extra cash, you'd be great at pretending to be a statue in Times Square.'

The hint of a smile crossed her lips, then it was gone.

'Look,' she said, 'if you've got some questions for me, ask them. I'll answer if I can. If you don't, let me get back to my work. I'm not like Ben. Don't expect me to open up and pour my heart out.'

'I can assure you, Jodie, Ben didn't share anything with me until he was convinced my main interest was protecting Stella. She's not just some stranger to me, Jodie, like she is to Daniel Cross. I have a lot of respect for her.'

'You don't even know her,' Jodie spat out accusingly. 'You're just another Member.'

'I'm sorry,' he said, 'what did you say? I'm a member? A member of what?'

'The WSBC,' she said.

Jack went to work on the initials in his head but nothing stuck.

'The Wall Street Boys' Club,' Jodie explained darkly. 'A Member is what we call the slick guys on the street who are all good looks and charm face-to-face but the first to knife you when your back is turned. Smooth as silk on the outside but greedy and dangerous inside. Manhattan's swarming with Members.'

Jack had to smile at the description and the double entendre. 'Did you come up with that?'

'No, it's one of Stella's.' She tensed and squeezed her eyes shut as if fighting the urge to cry.

'I can't claim to know Stella as well as you,' Jack said quietly, 'but I do know her. She was in the same Top Gun group as me. You know Top Gun?'

Jodie nodded reluctantly.

'We spent the weekend up at Tarrytown not long ago and we had to reveal a whole lot about ourselves to each other. I had to learn to trust Stella during that course, but it wasn't hard. I was impressed with her the moment we first met.'

'I didn't know that,' Jodie said. 'I thought they picked you for this job precisely because you didn't know us.'

Us and them, Jack mused, it always comes back to that. 'Frank knows about the Top Gun program,' he said, 'although he probably doesn't know just how intense it is. He wouldn't realise how well you get to know your peers on a program like that. They didn't have those courses in his day.'

He was right to talk to Jodie about Stella. Her defences were beginning to crumble. He softened his voice and said, 'You're really worried about her, aren't you?'

'Of course I am,' she said. Her tone was friendlier but still bitter. 'It's her against the world, isn't it? She's out there alone somewhere, trying to save her job and her reputation, and we all just sit around acting like nothing's happened. Let's get the damn client report written, that's the most important thing, right?'

'How do we help her, Jodie?' he asked, trying to get some eye contact.

'We can't,' she replied with desperation. 'Stella won't accept help – from me or anyone else. She says it's too dangerous.'

'Well, it seems I have no choice *but* to try and help,' Jack said. 'For whatever reason, I've ended up as the referee in some high-powered game. And I don't even know the rules. Now my ass is on the line too.' He needed Jodie to feel a bit sorry for him.

'Can you really be independent? You get your bread buttered by Sutton Brothers and its clients like the rest of us, don't you? Are you prepared to risk your career like Stella is?'

'Those are reasonable questions, Jodie, but you need to remember Sutton Brothers is more than just Frank Spiteri. He's a powerful guy but there are more powerful players in the firm. In the end it'll be up to them what happens to Stella's career, or mine. Anyway, I'm arrogant enough to think I could find some other opportunity out there if I happen to burn all my bridges at the bank. I've been with the company eight years, maybe it's time to move on.'

'Ben told me you've moved to M&A.'

'That's right.'

'You could set a record for the shortest ever time on the team,'

At last she was smiling, just a little, improving her appearance enormously. Jack smiled too, always one to appreciate a laugh in the face of adversity.

'So, Jodie,' he said with mock seriousness, 'in my role as independent arbiter of this puzzling conundrum, I only have one question for you. Is there anything you can do to help me help Stella?'

Jodie chewed her bottom lip for a few seconds while she thought about it. 'I suppose I could give you her papers,' she said.

'Papers?'

'Her working papers: notebook and photocopies of documents and bits and pieces like that.'

'You've got her notes?' he said incredulously. 'Didn't Frank ask you for them?'

'No, he asked for the files so that's exactly what I gave him.'

Now Jodie had a smug look on her face and Jack was again struck by the delight Stella's subordinates seemed to take in their little acts of defiant loyalty.

'Not that it's any big deal,' Jodie went on. 'I would've given the papers to him if he'd asked. I don't think you'll find anything useful. She had another notebook that she took with her.'

'That's okay,' Jack said, 'it will be something I can give to Daniel Cross.'

'You wouldn't! Why the hell would you do that? Let the bastards do their own dirty work.'

'I have to give them something, Jodie. If I go back to them with nothing, they'll conclude that either I can't be trusted or I'm useless to them. I've been told to report back this afternoon and it's already pretty obvious I'm going to have to bullshit my way through the meeting. Anything I can produce that Frank didn't discover when he came down here will help, even if it's not directly related to the missing files. I need to stay in their good books, don't you agree?'

'I suppose so,' she said uncertainly. 'But where will you say you found them? You can't say I was keeping them back. You wouldn't, would you?'

'Don't worry,' he said. 'You and Ben will come out looking like champions, I promise. I'm a Member, remember? I have the skills.'

Jodie had no choice but to smile again. 'All right,' she said. 'I'm going to trust you for the moment but if you screw things up for me or for Stella or Ben, you'll have made yourself a dangerous enemy.'

The look she gave Jack was about as intimidating as could be expected from a short, round woman with a cherubic face, and he felt sure she meant every word.

Jodie left to get Stella's working papers while Jack leaned back and stretched his arms out along the top of the bench to do some quiet thinking. After a few minutes, Ben Fisher came around the far corner of the large courtyard, talking into his phone. When he saw Jack was alone, he moved closer and snapped the phone shut.

'That wasn't Stella by any chance, was it?'

'Nah, that was my broker,' Fisher said, sitting down. 'The market's having another shitty day. The Dow's down nearly two per cent, Nasdaq is down nearly three. Looks like it'll have to be coach seats for the kids next vacation.'

Such are the terrible sacrifices made by the children of the upwardly mobile these days, Jack thought. Sitting in the back of the plane to Cancun or Aspen or Disney World. Fisher had a happy smirk on his face so he obviously wasn't too distraught about it.

'When do you expect to hear from Stella?' Jack asked. 'I really need to start talking to her, Ben.'

'I know, I know. I've done all I can. I sent her an email this morning and I have to wait for her to call back. Sometimes it only takes a few hours but if she's moving around she said I might not hear from her for up to a day.'

'And if you don't hear from her at all?'

'Then she told me to get in touch with some lawyer in New York.'

'Really? Do you remember his name?'

'Trainer. Alex Trainer, I think. I've got it written down somewhere.'

'Jesus, Ben. Don't leave information like that lying around. Don't make notes unless you really have to, and if you do, keep them with you and destroy them at the first sign of things going sour, okay? You know how serious this could get, right? And remember Hollis and Hoyle.'

Ben sat up straight. 'I'm not frightened of them,' he said, and Jack could see he really wanted to believe it. 'But you're right, we should be more careful.'

'What else have you got in writing?' Jack asked. 'You didn't keep a copy of the names Stella asked for, did you?'

'She told us not to.'

'But . . .'

'I thought it was crazy not to have backup copies,' Fisher admitted. 'We wouldn't be able to get into the system again if they got lost. But I carry them with me all the time, like you said.'

'You've got them here?'

'Well, no, they're in my bag.' He pointed to the admin building.

'Get them,' Jack ordered tersely. 'And anything else like them.'

'There's nothing else,' Fisher said, but he didn't argue. 'I'll make sure Jodie does a complete cleanout too.' He stood up and flashed a sly grin. 'By the way, where are your notes, Mr Smarty Investigator? I seem to recall your bag's inside too.'

Jack shook his head. 'Sorry, Ben. You'll find nothing in that bag except the two blue company files produced by the firm that you and at least eight other people have a copy of. I've got Stella's.' He tapped a finger to his right temple. 'Everything else is in here.'

18

While Jack sat in the sunshine, Daniel Cross paced the length of the president's windowless office on the third floor of CMS, his hands clasped firmly behind his back. The main phone on the desk rang often but the highly efficient secretary who came with his new position at Kradel was doing an excellent job of thwarting all attempts to bother him. Today he didn't care if Kradel thought he was failing the duties of his office. He had far too much history on his mind to be able to concentrate on the present.

It had been more than forty years. Forty long years since he'd found his path from poverty to prosperity. Forty years of blocking out the memories of his beginnings and thinking only of the future. But Stella Sartori's accursed curiosity had, with one astonishingly simple act, brought all that murky history back into sickening focus.

He'd still been a young man when he stumbled across his ticket out of an ignominious existence in the slums of Chicago's southside. Out of a brutal neighbourhood of street gangs and casual violence; a neighbourhood dominated by corrupt police and Mafia standover men, where being Polish and poor meant a constant struggle for survival.

Danilo Kruszelnicki did more than just survive, driven as he was by an overwhelming desire to escape – and to raise his parents out of squalor and up into the full bright light of the American Dream. And it was his smarts that made all the difference. He was book smart and he was also street smart. By the time he was a teenager, he could defend himself against Italian street punks with knives, and he could defend his father's meagre business from corrupt government officials and usurious landlords. As a kid he had rejected the lifestyles of the marginalised and dispossessed who surrounded him. Strict moral and religious values had been in abundant supply at home and Daniel had always known that the family was looking to him to deliver a brighter future. For him that brighter future required only one thing – money.

He won scholarships to attend decent schools, culminating in his acceptance to the University of Chicago's business school at the age of twenty-three, and it was there he found his ticket to a better life. A ticket that came in the form of the spoiled scion of a great Midwestern family, whose privileged future was predestined from conception to the grave. A ticket by the name of Ewan Collins.

Ewan was a year older than Danilo, who by this time had changed his distinctively downmarket name to the more waspish Daniel Cross. In stark contrast to the life of a poor immigrant outsider, Ewan Collins had never had any responsibility in life other than matching the expectations of his forebears and living relatives. Yet he found that single responsibility to be an onerous burden.

The whole heir-to-a-fortune thing he was okay with. He even loved the company. It paid the bills, it carried his name and it gave him a much-needed feeling of self-importance, but he felt oppressed by it too. The entire company, from the lowliest employee to the largest stockholder, throbbed with admiration for his father and grandfather. They were constantly hailed as the great founder and the great builder, the source of all wisdom and knowledge about business and, more particularly, about matters military.

They'd both served their country – grandfather during the Boxer Rebellion in China and father in World War I. Ewan had been encouraged to spend time in the army too – see a little action in Korea – but the idea had appalled him and he used every means at his disposal to ensure it didn't eventuate. He knew he didn't have what it took to impress his family on the battlefield, so he decided to focus all effort on proving his mettle in the world of business.

That was why he found himself so quickly drawn to the tall Polish kid he met during his first year at graduate school. Not only was the guy smart, he seemed genuinely interested in Ewan and his family business. And he was quick to offer his assistance in class – assistance that Ewan sorely needed to allay his growing sense of panic. He'd barely made it to business school. His grades were hardly better than average. Each failure to top the class or make a single dean's list during his college years had fuelled his growing sense of insecurity. He thought it would all come so naturally, but his genes had failed him. He blamed his mother, whose polite encouragement of his meagre efforts galled him each time he returned home to Peoria with his grades. Obviously the second-rate traits from her side of the family had overwhelmed the winning instincts from his father's line. With a few drinks in his belly, he would sometimes theorise to his new Polish friend that maybe Gilbert Collins wasn't even his real father. His mother was clearly a slut!

Daniel took an instant dislike to Ewan Collins and his opinion of the man never changed – from the moment they met to the day Ewan met his ignominious end, twenty years later. In general, he despised soft, insecure types, especially those who came from the privileged classes. But one thing they had in common was enlightened self-interest. Ewan knew he needed a strong lieutenant to boost his own performance. Even Gilbert had always relied on the trusted counsel of Campbell Reeves – an old friend who was smart and loyal. He thought Dan Cross was ideal for the role as his own right-hand man: clever and motivated, yet sufficiently in awe of Ewan's family history to remain notionally subservient. And Daniel instinctively knew that Ewan, this weak-minded excuse for a business leader, was a quick path to riches and power.

The partnership had been formed back in 1960. Daniel applied his intellect and savvy, first to helping Ewan look good at business school and later as official adviser to the heir apparent of CMS. As Ewan rose rapidly through various middle-management positions at the company, Daniel was there by his side, keeping a low profile, making sure his sponsor was credited with the big wins. Perform-ance improved, costs were cut, new capabilities were added to the business, making more sales possible. CMS prospered.

Daniel smiled ruefully as he remembered how pleased Gilbert Collins had been in those early days. The old man knew his son's achievements were due in large part to Daniel's brilliance but he gave Ewan credit for bringing such talent to the firm. He would often ramble on about the importance of his own working relationship with his best friend Campbell, and happily forecast great success for the pair of youngsters when it came time for his son to run the whole show.

But therein lay the problem for Daniel. He didn't want to wait for the old man to die, and he showed no signs of retiring. Although almost forty years older than his son, Gilbert remained robust and energetic. And more importantly, he had the full confidence of the board and the stockholders. They'd all watched Ewan growing up and shared long-held fears for the succession. The arrival of the boy's dynamic new lieutenant was a source of great comfort, but niggling doubts remained and Ewan's youth meant there was no hurry. Daniel knew that something momentous in the history of CMS would be required to convince the people who mattered that the younger generation was ready to take over. He and Ewan needed a really big win.

An exotic burbling came from the cell phone sitting on Cross's desk, interrupting his thoughts and bringing him back from the distant past. 'No cell phones in the sixties,' he muttered nostalgically as he walked to the desk and picked up the phone. The caller's name was displayed as 'The Professor' and Cross was quick to accept the call.

'Tony,' he said. 'I've just been thinking about the old days, right around the time we first met.'

'Yeah, me too,' said the deep voice on the other end of the line. 'Just thinking about the contract brings it all back. I dreamt about the ship last night.'

'That so? I had a weird dream too. When I think about it, I'm pretty sure it took place at the Willard Hotel. You remember that day at the Willard, Tony?'

'Of course I remember, Danny. Who'd forget a day like that?'

Cross chuckled. 'We had a few days like that back then, didn't we?'

'A few, yes, but none quite like that one,' Tony said, his voice serious. 'And if it wasn't for those days we wouldn't be where we are now, would we? Everything we are, Danny, all comes back to the contract.'

'True. And we don't even know where the damn thing is any more.'

'I've been thinking about it,' Tony said. 'There can't be anything in that file to cause us real trouble, can there? It was all just business stuff, wasn't it? But I have to say this virgin's secret thing has me worried. Don't you remember anything else about it?'

'I only read it once,' Cross said. 'It didn't make any sense to me at all; just the poetic ravings of an old crank. And it was only one page. How could it be anything important?'

'You remember the look on his face that night, Daniel? When you pulled his letter out and showed it to him? He thought it was going to hurt us. He was horrified that we'd intercepted it; that nobody would get to see it. And now, forty years on, someone is seeing it, aren't they? It obviously rang some bell for her.'

'That bitch! I just wish I knew how it ended up in that file. It should have been destroyed that night on the boat.'

'Too late to worry about that now,' Tony said, 'but we still have to find the girl. Any news on that score?'

'That Jack Rogers guy has arrived out here. He's already found out that she's been in touch with at least one of her colleagues. Who knows, he might get a bit more out of them before the day is out.'

'What do you make of him?'

'Rogers? Seems smart, a Sutton Brothers' man through and through. I'd say he's more interested in protecting the bank's ass than anything else.'

'Gotta respect him for that,' Tony said. 'But if he kicks over a few rocks, who knows what might come scurrying out?'

'What about the attorney? Did you get the package she sent to him?'

This time Tony chuckled. 'Oh, that guy. He had a fire in his office, poor sap. Got some paperwork to catch up on.'

Cross smiled. 'You still got it, Professor.'

'Damn right! Gotta go. Talk to you later.'

'Later,' Cross said, and snapped his cell phone shut. The Professor, he thought to himself, where would I be without that man? His thoughts returned to the 1960s.

It was 1962 when Cross was first introduced to Antonio

Castelluzzo, a remarkable, handsome young Sicilian. The kid's story had fascinated Daniel. Only twenty-two years old, born and raised in a land being torn apart by war, Tony Castle, as he preferred to be known, had already graduated from a small but prestigious college located on the outer edges of Chicago. His ability and eagerness to learn as a child had inspired his grandmother to nickname him *U Prufessuri*, the Professor, and it became the title by which he was generally known in the family.

And what a family it was. Tony's uncle, Don Francesco, was the most powerful man in his region, not far from Palermo. Like other Mafia families, they had suffered greatly under two decades of Mussolini's brutal regime. When the Americans invaded in 1943, Tony was only two years old and he didn't comprehend the tremendous joy his relatives felt as the Italian army fell back in disarray. The family was soon back in business and, before long, not only were they prospering once more, but men loyal to the Castelluzzos also held many influential positions on the island – including two of Tony's uncles, appointed provincial town mayors by an occupying force who were interested only in finding good anti-Fascists to work with. Local patronage and protection were once again more important than membership of the Fascist party. The destruction caused by the invasion was a small price to pay and it was just one more chapter in Sicily's long history as the meat in some foreign power's sandwich.

Better still, the American army turned out to be the perfect ally for the Mafia dons. There was much the local powerbrokers could do to assist the Americans in controlling the island. And in return, many soldiers chose to turn a blind eye as their bloated supply lines were slimmed down by profiteers and lucrative contracts were corruptly distributed.

Young Antonio had found himself an English tutor, a bored quartermaster serving out his time before returning to his former life as an economics professor at a small New England college. Glad of the distraction, the officer was happy to invest his energy in Tony, whose overwhelming enthusiasm – and maturity beyond his years – added some simple joy to an otherwise humdrum routine.

Not only did Tony master English, he also learned about capitalism and the American way. The left-wing professor didn't hesitate to point out the injustices and exploitation he saw at the core of the American economic system. He would have been astonished to learn that the Sicilian youth he was mentoring recognised every small fault in the system as an opportunity ripe for the picking.

Tony yearned to be a part of that system. Sicily was destroyed. It would be decades before his homeland could offer opportunities close to even the worst of those that lay across the Atlantic. He kept learning. When the quartermaster was shipped home, Tony found another tutor and continued to study America; he believed that knowing all about the country would bring him closer to it. The GIs stopped laughing at his English. By the time he was fourteen, his accent was slight and his only limitation was vocabulary. His intelligence and aptitude shone, together with a ravenous hunger for knowledge. On the street, in the classroom, in the guardhouse and barracks, Tony was always adding to his brain store. He dreamed of going to college in America, and his nickname, which had once embarrassed him, became a source of pride.

The bookworm did not neglect the family business either. He was a quick student in the school of the streets. From the age of five, in the lean years immediately after the war, Tony learned how to steal, lie and charm to great effect. At the age of fifteen he killed for the first time, slicing the throat of an older rival for a case of stolen American medical supplies. He also pilfered books and college mementos he found while systematically searching the officers' quarters. He learned to present two faces to the world, one charming and helpful – for the benefit of the foreigners – the other coolly cunning, dangerous and resourceful. He fantasised about combining the training and education available in the US with the skills learned on the mean streets of his homeland.

In 1958, when Tony's father was killed in a dispute over a reconstruction contract, Don Francesco decided to sponsor his nephew's dream. He thought it wise for Tony to disappear for a while, but he also liked the idea of the family gaining some legitimate business credentials. The experience with Mussolini confirmed the danger of complacency about the future. Governments had a habit of turning nasty every few decades. Next time they'd be prepared with a string of legitimate enterprises supported quietly by the tactics and resources of the family. Tony would lead the way.

And so he came to America. Admittance was arranged to a college in Chicago, a city where the Castelluzzo family connections were strong. The local bosses Trafficante and Giancarna were amused by this kid from the old country who was desperate to get an elite American education. Although the entrance procedure wasn't entirely above board – supported as it was by fake records of an entirely fictitious high school career and some well-placed bribes – Tony soon allayed any doubts by demonstrating that he was definitely university material. With characteristic dedication and single-mindedness, he blitzed his undergraduate program in two years, earning himself a place in graduate school.

His drive to succeed grew stronger. The respect and praise of upper-crust Americans was a powerful incentive to keep achieving. If they'd only known his true heritage, they'd have been amazed. There was even talk of a doctorate on the subject of the role of American capital in the rebuilding of Europe.

Then things fell apart.

At twenty-one, Tony was about to become the youngest graduate in the school's history. In truth, he was only twenty, having relied upon a falsified birth certificate for his immigration papers. His dark good looks and maturity deflected any doubts about his age. But looks can be deceiving – in reality, Tony wasn't yet sufficiently grown up.

When he was told he'd just missed out on a prestigious award, his response was automatic. Two days later, the prizewinner was found floating face down in a storm drain. The award went to Tony but he was dismayed and annoyed by the fuss made over the death of the other student. All the grief and angst completely overshadowed his moment of glory. Clearly life was valued quite differently in middle America, compared with the middle of Sicily. It was a useful lesson, and he was about to learn another.

Although no clear link was ever established between Tony and the death of the star college student, the incident focused unwanted attention on his background. Rumours flew around the campus and the business community, hinting at a mob connection. He was no longer warmly welcomed in the upper echelons of the academic world and there was no more talk of a PhD. Despite his stellar academic record, Tony found the prestigious Chicago firms unwilling to offer him a position worthy of his talents. By 1961, when Bobby Kennedy was just beginning his crackdown on organised crime, it was no longer fashionable in serious business circles to have mob connections. The family could open some doors for Tony but not to the big investment banks, stockbroking houses or consulting firms he coveted.

While he waited for the dust to settle, Tony repaid his American friends for their support by streamlining the finances of the Chicago families and designing new money-laundering schemes, but this put the nail in the coffin of his legitimate reputation in the city. He needed to go some place he wasn't known. Some place where he could begin again. He dreamed of conquering the Big Apple but relations with the New York families weren't good at the beginning of 1962 and he had no useful contacts in the legitimate business world. Until he met Daniel Cross.

It took many years for Cross to learn the full story of Tony's early life but when he recalled the memory of their first meeting, he imagined it was all there, in the face — and particularly the eyes — of the diminutive Sicilian. He already knew Tony Castle was well connected because it had been his search for a man with the right connections that had brought them together. The kid's bizarre passion for big business and his qualifications were an unexpected bonus.

Tony's cousin Tomasino was responsible for the introduction. Cross and Tommy were sparring partners from the old days on the gritty sidewalks of the southside. They'd met one oppressive summer afternoon when the Italian tried to beat up fourteen-year-old Danny Kruszelnicki as part of an 'anti-Polak day' gang outing. The torrid stalemate that ensued fashioned a grudging respect between the two boys. Nearly twelve years on, Daniel Cross had returned to the neighbourhood in his newest and most stylish business suit, seeking a favour. And for Tommy — who now had his own crew to feed — someone in need of a favour was always welcome. Danny wanted assistance with a business problem. He thought his old acquaintance with powerful connections might be able to help out. Tommy was delighted. 'Do we have the man for you!' he'd said.

Daniel's connection with Tony had been immediate. Neither he nor Tony had any interest in judging each other or trying to appear superior. And Tony's interest in Daniel's business opportunities was matched by Daniel's fascination with the ambiguous morals of the underworld. Mutual respect and mutual self-interest formed a powerful bond. Forty years ago when Tony had asked how he could help, Cross hadn't hesitated. He'd simply said, 'We're having some trouble with a contract.'

19

Jack's jaw ground away at the chewy crust of a tasteless sandwich bought at the company cafeteria. He gave the food little thought as he concentrated on the small pile of documents accumulated by Ben and Jodie after a thorough search inside. Out of the breeze, the sun was warm. And the colourful gardens – tended by flitting butterflies and insects – exuded such an air of peace and tranquillity that it was somehow inconceivable that they formed part of a military industrial complex.

'This disk has a copy of the stuff we sent Stella,' Ben Fisher mumbled through the food in his mouth.

Jack took the CD and nodded. Swallowing hard, he said, 'Everything else is shredded or deleted?'

Fisher nodded, and Jack waited for Jodie to do the same.

'Okay,' he said, 'I have about thirty minutes before I'm due upstairs. Better leave me with this stuff so I can go through it.'

They rose from their chairs, Jodie looking worried as she eyed the papers she'd handed over to Jack. 'If you find anything in her notes . . .'

'If I find the address of where Stella was heading I won't hand it over to Daniel Cross, all right? I can't see how anything else is going to make much difference now.'

There was a flash of defiance in Jodie's eyes but Jack had his head down and was oblivious to it. Jodie pursed her lips and reluctantly started walking after Ben Fisher, who was already halfway back to the building entrance.

The loose papers in Jack's lap were mostly photocopied from innocuous company publications recording the long history of CMS. Organisational charts, lists of board members and senior executives at various dates, even some black and white photographs of men in suits, which copied so poorly they were of little use. Jack could see nothing sensational in any of it and concluded that most of the material would be available to Joe Public, if Joe could be bothered seeking it out.

The one item Stella clearly should not have had in her possession was a list of current beneficiaries from the company's pension plan. It suggested she was seeking out some retired executive and needed his contact details, but her methodology was highly unethical. It was also the only item that conceivably pointed to her next steps – and possibly her proposed destination – but the list was long and the beneficiaries' addresses were spread not only across the country, but also around the world. As a pointer it was pretty useless but it might mean more to Daniel Cross.

Stella's notebook had a metal spiral binding and a yellow cover. Inside the pages were faintly lined and her handwriting was neat and femininely rounded. Most pages were blank and it seemed likely to Jack that her habit was to start a fresh book for each new client company or transaction. Her time on this deal, officially at least, had been short.

There were a few pages of notes relating to CMS's human

resources policy and practices. These were the random phrases and comments Stella would later turn into professional language for her report. Mostly she seemed satisfied with the company's practices, as the expression 'within normal range' – or its abbreviated equivalent, WNR – was repeated several times.

It got more interesting when Jack opened a double page headed, 'What is K.'s strategy??' One page appeared to be a list of reasons why Kradel should buy CMS. The other, a much longer list, cited many reasons why Kradel should leave the deal alone. There was a good deal of jargon, abbreviations and shorthand on these two pages, plus many alterations and a few circles and arrows. But it was not hard for Jack to work out Stella's conclusions on the proposed purchase. She didn't like it.

On the next page, Jack saw the words 'Maria Petrillo, Harding Collins third floor 2 p.m.'. Stella had lined up a meeting with the boss, as Collins was at the time. According to Ben Fisher, Harding Collins was dismissed from the role before the end of the week, a dismissal that probably had its genesis in this very meeting. Maria Petrillo was the secretary who'd helped Ben and Jodie to access the company's system; this must have been where the whole mess began.

Jack flicked ahead two pages and found Stella's notes from her meeting with the acting president of the company. Harding's name and the date – Monday of last week – were written neatly at the top, but her other thoughts were obviously jotted down rapidly as the letters were less well formed than her other notes.

Future of CMS? No future! Takeover only chance. HC no love for business. Only interim pres until DC returns. HC major shareholder (inherited). Real job is partner at Leggat's. HC main concern is stock price.

R&D division? No big discovery.

So why would Kradel buy? CMS no value except for <u>the contract!</u>

HC says without contract, deal would be 'dodgy'. HC no expert but always knew contract v. important to CMS.

What is contract??

Deal with govt in sixties. Vietnam War. Pentagon guarantee CMS R&D funding for 60 yrs!! Contract has decade or so left. Initial grant indexed. Has grown to big $$. HC says this year worth $250m+!

Lucky timing? Accelerator clause??

Contract secret? No, but 'embarrassing'. Kradel takeover should bring better value to govt side of deal.

Then there was a gap, and towards the bottom of the page, Stella had written, *Maria to get file to me tomorrow. What about Frank? Why no brief on this??*

Jack re-read the notes twice. The contract under discussion was presumably the one to which the stolen file referred. Daniel Cross had said it was about a confidential government deal. This one sounded like a contract both CMS and the Pentagon would prefer to fade away quietly over the next decade. Jack could also understand Stella's thinking – she obviously thought the contract was central to Kradel's decision to buy CMS so she wanted to see it. That much was perfectly reasonable. But why did she steal the bloody file?

Hoping to find the answer, he flicked ahead in the notebook but he only found one other handwritten page and the notes were bizarre.

DC negotiated with P!

Executed Jan '64. Will last til 2014.

Boring

Boring

What is THE VIRGIN'S SECRET??

Murder?!

Dec '67. Campbell Reeves.

Ask HC?

What the hell is this? Jack thought. It must have something to do with the Pentagon deal. 'DC' was presumably Daniel Cross and 1964 to 2014 was a span of sixty years, the agreed duration of the mysterious contract, but the rest of it made no sense. Could the virgin's secret, whatever that was, be the cause of Stella's strange behaviour? Who was Campbell Reeves and was he supposed to be the victim or the perpetrator of some murder? And most perplexingly, what on earth could Stella have found in this old file to prompt her to write the word 'murder' in the first place? Apparently she was planning to ask Harding Collins about it. Was that what got him into trouble with Cross?

He was still struggling with these questions when the stern Englishwoman appeared to tell Jack that Cross required him upstairs in five minutes. He hurried inside to collect his briefcase, into which he stuffed the documents and the disk, while he exchanged banter with the Sutton Brothers team. He made his way to the third floor.

He found Daniel Cross sitting at a round table in one corner of the large office. On the table was a conference phone that looked like a *Star Wars* cast-off, right down to the three blinking green lights that warned Jack the line was active. He was joining a conversation already in progress.

'I have Frank on the line,' Cross said as Jack took a seat at the table.

Spiteri's deep voice boomed from the speaker. 'Hey there, Jack. How's it been going?'

'Pretty good thanks, Frank,' Jack said. 'How are things back east?'

'Good, good. What have you found out?'

Straight to business. Jack could sense Cross's attention on him. 'I haven't found out where Stella's gone, I'm afraid. I don't think any of the team know. I'd say the only one she might confide in is Ben

Fisher and he reckons she won't tell him because she says it will put him in harm's way.'

'What utter crap!' Cross said. 'What sort of harm does she think he's going to come to? She's living out some fantasy, that woman.'

Jack shrugged. 'She was pretty shaken by the invasion of her hotel room, Daniel. Ben was too. I'm pretty sure that's the only reason she left Peoria in such a hurry and why she's staying out of contact. Those guys were truly frightening by all accounts. They threatened her with rape and continued to stalk her after the attack. Did you know that?'

Cross was stony-faced but Spiteri's voice registered surprise. 'They did what? What do you mean?'

'On the evening after Stella was attacked, the team gathered in the hotel restaurant for a meal. Apparently the two guys who'd assaulted her – with a gun and a knife – were hanging around the hotel. One was seen talking to a police officer out front. They even came into the restaurant and openly watched her, drinking beers and leering and so on. I can understand why she was feeling threatened. It's little wonder she took off. She just didn't feel safe here any more.'

Cross was shaking his head and his eyes were downcast. 'I didn't know that,' he said.

'There's a chance Stella doesn't have the file at all,' Jack went on, watching Cross closely. 'The thugs searched her room. They may have taken it.'

'No,' Cross said, 'they didn't.'

Jack tried to keep his voice even. 'They were working for you, were they, Daniel?'

Cross shifted defensively in his chair. 'When I heard the woman had removed confidential and important information from the plant, I thought it prudent to keep an eye on her. I asked a local security firm to send over some guys to watch her. They got carried away, I guess.'

'She is a very beautiful woman,' Spiteri's disembodied voice said, and Jack looked at the speakerphone with disbelief.

'The rape stuff is a bit far-fetched,' Cross said. 'They weren't authorised to approach her at all. These two guys were off duty when they were called in. Apparently they'd been drinking. It was all very unfortunate but it was over quickly. They tried to scare her to get my property back. Fortunately she wasn't harmed, but the real point is she didn't have the file with her. Either she had an accomplice or she'd gone to great lengths to keep the file from being returned to its rightful owner. What possible reason could she have for that?'

'It has something to do with the contract,' Jack said.

A pregnant pause followed. Cross's eyes narrowed. 'What contract?' he said.

'*The* contract,' Jack repeated. 'Isn't that what's in the file Stella took?'

'Yes,' Cross said slowly, 'but who told you about it?'

'Stella did. In her notes.'

Cross sat up straight in his chair. 'You have her notes?'

'What notes?' Spiteri asked. 'Where did you get them, Jack?'

Jack reached into his briefcase, which was leaning against the leg of the chair. 'From Jodie Michelson. She only came across them yesterday as she was packing up to go home. She didn't think it important because there isn't much in here.'

He placed the spiral-bound notebook on the table and saw Cross reach for it instinctively, then withdraw his hand. Opening the book to the double page list of pros and cons, Jack pushed it across the polished mahogany towards Cross, who eagerly pulled it closer and started reading.

'What did she write, Jack?' The frustration was clear in Spiteri's voice.

'She had some issues with the strategy behind Kradel's acquisition

172

of CMS,' Jack said. 'She discussed these concerns with Harding Collins who, I understand, was company president here at the time.'

Cross glanced up from Stella's notebook. 'Technically Harding remains president until the sale goes through,' he said, smiling insipidly. 'Obviously it wouldn't be appropriate for me to formally fill the role while I'm heading up Kradel.'

'No,' Jack said, with a hint of sarcasm. 'That might be interpreted as a conflict of interest.'

'Jack!' Spiteri cut in. 'We've been over this.'

Not to my satisfaction, Jack thought.

'To be quite frank,' Cross went on, watching Jack coldly, 'Harding was never interested in this job. He's a property attorney; he likes to buy and sell office buildings. He doesn't want to do this.'

'Yes, well, anyway,' Jack continued, 'it was Harding who pointed Stella in the direction of the contract.' He reached across the table and turned the pages of Stella's notebook to the record of her meeting with the titular president. Cross started reading again. 'Stella found out the contract is central to the strategy. It has to be one of the most valuable single assets CMS possesses.'

'Of course it is,' Cross said, in a patronising tone, 'and of course it's central to our decision to merge. The point is we didn't want every Tom, Dick or Shirley sticking their noses into it. Sartori should never have been talking to Harding about the strategy in the first place. And Harding shouldn't have been talking to her. Frank was supposed to give her clear instructions on that point.' He scowled at the phone on the table.

'I did!' Spiteri boomed.

'Yeah, well, she ignored you, Frank,' Cross said bluntly. Then he looked at Jack. 'If she'd raised her concerns about the strategy with her boss, she would have discovered that I briefed Frank on the contract right at the very beginning of this exercise. We agreed the information was highly confidential and would only be discussed at the partner level within Sutton Brothers. Isn't that right, Frank?'

'Absolutely!' was the loyal reply. 'I told the team all along to keep to the brief they'd been given. Defence mergers can be very tricky. The wider business and security issues are extremely sensitive. We didn't even know if we had the government's permission to share information about the contract with anyone, did we, Daniel?'

'That's right,' said Cross, and then he went silent.

'Well,' Jack said, 'whether Stella should have known about the contract is neither here nor there now. The fact is Harding Collins told her about it. According to my reading of her notes, he even said it wasn't a secret but he did describe it as "embarrassing".'

'Did he just?' Cross muttered.

'He must have told you this himself.'

'I knew about the meeting,' Cross said after a slight pause, 'although it's interesting to read Sartori's version of what was said.'

'The impression I get from the notes,' Jack continued, 'is that Harding Collins arranged for Stella to see the files relating to the contract.'

'There is only one file relating to the contract,' Cross said.

'Right,' Jack said, 'but my point is he instructed someone called Maria Petrillo to get the file to Stella. She didn't steal it.'

'She's stolen it now!'

There was a murmur of assent from Frank.

'Perhaps,' Jack said. 'But again, my point is there's nothing in the notes to suggest she was setting out deliberately to uncover sensitive material that could be embarrassing to the company or the government. I found no evidence of a plan to blackmail you, Daniel. There was no premeditation. She was just reacting to new information.'

'Look, Jack,' Cross said amiably, 'you've done a great job digging this out.' He waved the notebook about. 'But these notes only go up to the date of the meeting with Harding. She hadn't even seen the contract file then. Whatever plans she made to damage the company or me obviously formed in her twisted little mind after she got her hands on the file.'

Jack took a moment to ponder his options, then he said, 'Ever heard of the virgin's secret?'

Again, Cross's face showed little reaction. Just a twitch at the corner of one eye. There was a lengthy period of silence and Jack was surprised when Spiteri did not jump in to fill it.

Eventually Cross said, 'Actually, it rings a bell. And she mentioned it when I spoke to her on the phone.'

'Stella talked about the virgin's secret?' Jack reached for the notebook and found the page with Stella's strange notes. As he pushed the notebook back towards Cross, he wondered what reaction they would receive. 'Then it must be at the heart of her concerns, wouldn't you say?'

As he watched, Jack saw Cross's eyes flick to the open page but they did not linger as before. The faintest hint of colour flushed the pale skin of his cheeks as he quickly closed the notebook and pushed it away dismissively.

'It's nothing,' he said, 'and it's old. Why she expected me to know about some obscure letter she'd found, sent by some crank four decades ago, is beyond me. Defence contractors get crank letters from peaceniks all the time – it goes with the territory. Whatever it is, Jack, this thing that has Stella so excited – it is most definitely none of her business.'

Jack began to argue the point but Spiteri interjected. 'I agree,' he said. 'All the material in CMS files belongs to the company. However good her intentions, there can be no excuse for Stella's behaviour. She must return the file, complete and unaltered.'

Cross seemed pleased by Spiteri's support. 'Thank you, Frank,' he said. 'I think that's the first time you've been completely clear on that point.'

'On the contrary, Daniel, I have always agreed that the file must be returned. It is Stella's motivation that we disagree on. I don't believe Stella would ever set out to deliberately harm a client and I think Jack would agree there's no evidence that she has done so now, is there, Jack?'

'No,' Jack said emphatically. 'None.'

Cross leaned back in his chair and gave first the phone, and then Jack, an incredulous look. 'What the fuck do you two geniuses think she's doing out there with my file? A little bedtime reading?'

'Maybe she just got scared when those thugs attacked her,' Spiteri said defensively. 'Maybe she just took off and forgot she even had the file with her.'

'Bullshit!' Cross said. 'She asked me about the damn file, remember? She demanded information about that crank letter, even though I haven't seen the fucking file in ages. She's doing something with it, Frank, and the sooner you accept that, the sooner we'll get somewhere with this.'

'Actually,' Jack offered, 'I have to agree with Daniel on that point. She has been looking into something, and I assume it relates to the file. She asked Ben Fisher to dig up some more information for her. After she left.'

'Are you serious?' Spiteri said, his tone stern, 'And he did this for her without telling me anything about it?'

Cross smacked the table with the flat of his palm. 'What else has the bitch got her hands on now?'

'It's nothing sensational,' Jack said calmly, reaching into his briefcase again. Carefully he took out the photocopies, keeping the pension plan records concealed, and placed them on the table. 'I have copies here.'

Cross did not wait to be asked and reached out and grabbed the small wad of documents.

For Spiteri's benefit, Jack summarised. 'It's all the stuff you should be able to find in libraries, Frank, or in institutions like Sutton Brothers. If she'd written the company a letter and asked for it I'm pretty sure they would have been forthcoming – if the circumstances were different, of course. Extracts from annual reports, lists of company executives, some organisational charts, even a couple of photos. It doesn't tell me much about what Stella might be looking into but, like the contract, it obviously relates to the past, rather than the present.'

'How can it relate to our work?' Spiteri asked, exasperated. 'What the hell is she doing?'

'How did Fisher get this to her?' Cross said. 'Are you sure he doesn't know where she is?'

Jack shook his head. 'He scanned the pages and sent them to an email address, hotmail, I think. She could have picked them up anywhere.'

Spiteri's voice was becoming more menacing. 'I'll be having a little chat with Ben Fisher as soon as he gets back to New York.'

'There's no point taking it out on Ben,' Jack said. 'He's just very loyal to Stella and to the bank. And she assured him it was all in the best interests of the client.'

'Hey, hello!' Cross said, raising his right hand. 'I am the fucking client. And this doesn't feel like it's in my best interests.'

'I assume,' Spiteri said in a conciliatory tone, 'she meant the board of Kradel Electronics rather than you personally, Daniel. And technically she's correct. The board is our client.'

'Semantics,' Cross spat, 'that's all that is. You both need to know that if I'm pissed, so is the board.'

Jack nodded to show that he understood, and then decided to change the focus slightly. 'I think I should interview Harding Collins and Maria Petrillo,' he said. 'It seems likely Stella talked to them some more about the contract and the secret virgin thing. Maybe they can shed some light on her thinking.'

'That won't be necessary,' said Cross. 'I've already interviewed them at length and I'll talk to them again if I need to. They're not your colleagues, Jack. There's no advantage in you talking to them.'

Jack looked to the phone for support, but none came. Instead, Spiteri said, 'Is that all you have, Jack?'

'He got a hell of a lot more than you did, Frank.'

'I didn't mean it that way, Daniel. Jack's done a great job. I just wondered if his briefing was over.'

Jack thought about the pension records in his case. If he showed them to Cross he might be able to detect some spark of recognition, some clue as to their significance. But then again, Cross was still poker-faced and this evidence of an ethical breach would implicate not only Stella, but Ben and Jodie also. 'That's it from me,' he said. 'What would you like me to do next?'

'Nothing much more you can do out there,' Spiteri offered, 'unless there's something else you'd like Jack to do, Daniel?'

'No, not here,' Cross answered, his eyes fixed on Jack, 'but let's keep him on the team.'

Jack examined the client's face. Does he value my input or does he just want to keep an eye on me? he wondered.

'Okay, Jack,' Spiteri said, 'you get back to New York and we'll decide what you do next.'

'Fine,' Jack said.

Daniel Cross disconnected the call abruptly and stood up. 'Are you flying out tonight?' he asked Jack.

'Yes. I'm booked on United to Chicago at 7.25.'

'Cancel it.'

A small jolt of alarm sparked in Jack's brain. 'Why?'

'You can come with me,' Cross said mildly, looking at his Rolex. 'I have an aircraft standing by to take me to Chicago. You need to pick up luggage?'

'No, I have everything with me,' Jack said, thinking of the papers in his briefcase he hadn't shared with Cross. Should he risk transporting them on Cross's own plane?

'Good,' Cross said. 'Then meet me out front in ten minutes.' He picked up Stella's notebook and the photocopied pages. 'I'll hang on to these,' he said, the silk in his suit glistening as he turned his back and walked towards the desk, completely uninterested in Jack's reaction.

Downstairs Jack ran into Jodie Michelson as she was leaving.

'I'm going to visit my family in Ohio on the way back to New York,' she said, as if daring Jack to stop her. 'My flight leaves in an hour. Ben's looking for you outside.'

'Have a good trip, Jodie,' Jack said. 'Thanks for your help. See you back in the city.'

In the garden he found Ben Fisher, looking very excited. 'I just spoke to Stella,' he said.

'And?'

'I asked her about giving you the email address and she said she's already received an email from you. Is that right?'

'I did try to send her a message,' Jack admitted, 'but I didn't know if the address would work.'

'Stella wants to know how you got it.'

'You mean the hotmail address?'

'Yep. I'm afraid it's made her mighty suspicious. That address was only known to a few of us. How'd you get it?'

'Ben,' Jack said with sincerity, 'it's a long story, and one I only want to tell Stella. I can explain it all to her, but I can't tell you, do you understand?'

Ben contemplated Jack's face for a second or two. 'I don't have much choice, do I? Anyway, it's out of my hands now. I think I managed to convince Stella to get in touch with you. I told her you're one of the good guys so don't let me down.'

'I won't,' Jack assured him, 'and thanks for putting my case.'

'No problem. Besides, I think Stella can use the help.'

'How is she?'

'Pretty frazzled, I'd say.'

'Will she accept my assistance?'

'I don't know.'

Cross's assistant burst out of the building. 'Mr Rogers,' she demanded, clearly upset by his bad manners, 'Mr Cross is waiting in the limousine.'

'What?' Ben said, his eyebrows shooting up over the rims of his big glasses. 'You're going with Cross? Now?'

'He very kindly invited me to fly to Chicago with him,' Jack said, as evenly as he could. 'I have to go.'

'But —'

'Sorry, Ben, I'll try to call you later.'

'But —'

It was obvious Ben wanted to say something else but it would have to wait. The officious Englishwoman wasn't going to let Jack dally. She led him inside at a trot to collect his bag. He had planned to take Stella's small suitcase with him but had asked Ben at the last minute to see it safely back to the office. Ben was leaving Peoria in a couple of hours – and clearly couldn't wait.

A long white limousine was sitting next to the perfect little gardens framing the entrance to CMS. The windows were tinted almost black and a broad-chested Latino man with a chauffeur's cap was holding the door open for Jack. In the back, there was a bench seat facing forwards, covered in soft, grey leather. Daniel Cross sat on the far side of the long seat, reading a newspaper. He indicated Jack should sit next to him.

As they swept away from the plant and back over the Illinois River towards the airport, Cross acted as if he was alone. He studied his newspaper while Jack took in the views and the opulence of the car's interior. He tried to relax and enjoy the smooth ride but as they were picking up speed on the freeway, with the centre of the city passing away on the left, his cell phone rang loudly. He gave his client an apologetic look as he opened the phone but Cross didn't appear to give it a second thought.

'Hello?' Jack said.

'Hello, Jack? Is that Jack Rogers?'

A woman's voice. Jack's temples started to pound.

'Yes, hello,' he said.

'Jack, hi! This is Stella Sartori.'

20

Jack took a deep breath.

'Peta!' he said, quickly correcting an involuntary sideways peek at Daniel Cross. 'Hi, how are you?'

'Is that Jack Rogers?'

'Yes, fine thanks, on my way back. But I won't be home 'til late.'

'You can't talk?'

'No, babe, not right now. I'll call you from Chicago to let you know what time I'm getting in.'

'You're going to Chicago?'

'Yeah, but it's cold. Winter's on the way. Is it still raining in New York?'

'I'll call again later, say, after eleven Chicago time.'

'That's good. I'll talk to you then.'

'Want me to say I love you?'

Jack smiled and relaxed a little. Cross was still buried in the *Wall Street Journal*. 'Love you too.'

He terminated the call but a buzz was still running through him. Stella had decided to trust him. A connection had been made, right

under the gaze of Cross. Discreetly he switched the phone off, just
in case the real Peta called, and tucked it into his suit.

Cross put down his newspaper. 'Your wife?' he asked, though his
tone implied no interest in the answer.

'Girlfriend. Actually, she'd prefer I said partner.'

'She Australian too?'

'No, she's a New Yorker, through and through,' Jack said. 'Although
it looks like work's going to take her to London.'

'Really? For a long time, like me?'

'I guess so.'

'You don't sound very happy about it, Jack. Don't you like the
UK?'

'Been there, done that,' Jack said glumly. 'It would feel like a
backward step.'

'I know what you mean. For me the move from Peoria to London was clearly a step up. But from what you've achieved on Wall
Street . . .'

'Exactly,' Jack said, oddly satisfied that Cross saw the point.

'Pity about Concorde being phased out soon. On that baby, London's closer to New York than Los Angeles. Without it countless
trans-Atlantic relationships are doomed.'

Jack looked at Cross and saw the hint of a smile. 'So, Daniel, what
about you and your family? How have you settled in London?'

And so the conversation proceeded – detached, friendly and
uncontroversial – all the way to the Greater Peoria Regional Airport.
Jack followed Cross up the stairs of a small, jet-powered five-star
hotel which, once airborne, needed barely thirty minutes to fly them
to Chicago. Just enough time for the steward to serve strong cocktails
in cut-crystal glasses.

As the plane began its descent, Jack pressed his face to the window to watch the gathering gloom of the evening envelop the earth

below. He registered just how close they were flying to the city's spectacular parade of skyscrapers. He turned to his client, who was examining documents under the glare of a halogen reading lamp, oblivious to the sights.

'We're not landing at O'Hare?'

'No, Midway Aiport,' Cross said. 'Much closer to the business district and easier for small craft like this. Don't worry, I've arranged a car to take you over to O'Hare.'

Jack nodded but didn't enjoy the feeling of being conducted every step of the way. As the executive jet taxied to a dark spot away from the main terminal buildings, Jack saw two black limousines parked a little way apart from each other. The aircraft stopped close by and Cross was on his feet, hurrying down the stairs as soon as they were extended. Jack was delayed by a friendly contest with the steward, who insisted on carrying his suitcase down the stairs, even though he had to be twenty years Jack's senior.

When he got to the tarmac he saw Cross standing by the closest of the limos, its back door open. He was reaching into his suit jacket. As Jack approached, wheeling his bag, Cross produced a lizard-skin wallet, from which he took out an embossed business card. 'These are my personal numbers,' he shouted over the roar of engines. 'I want you to call me direct if you get any new information. Don't wait for Frank to catch up – we have to move fast on this thing, understand?'

Jack nodded vaguely and shivered. Frigid air was whipping across Lake Michigan right into his bones. Cross waited until the card was tucked away safely and then shook Jack's hand with a powerful grip. 'You seem like a smart guy, Jack. I like you. I get the impression you don't take crap from anyone, am I right?'

Jack had no automatic response but Cross wasn't waiting for one. 'I'm not going to tell you what to do. You'll do what you think is best,

I'm sure. You know by now how determined I am to see my interests are protected. I won't let Stella Sartori or even dear old Sutton Brothers get in the way of this deal. But I also want you to know how appreciative I will be if you can help resolve this mess quickly and quietly.'

Here it comes, Jack thought, the carrot after the stick.

'I can be a tough client, Jack – Frank'll tell you that. But I can also be a generous client. When I'm sure my file is secure and my interests are unharmed, there'll be big bonuses for everybody who helped make it happen.'

Jack tried to look interested but all he really felt was cold, and Cross's approach wasn't exactly warming him up.

'Oh, I know you're not short of money, Jack,' Cross went on. 'Frank told me you're used to big bucks. No bonus you've ever received could compare to my potential generosity. You're in a different league now, my friend.'

'Thank you, Daniel, I'll keep that in mind,' Jack said, still shaking Cross's hand slowly. 'But you should know I'm not starting out from an assumption that a good outcome for you has to mean a bad outcome for Stella.'

'Of course.'

Cross was still smiling but he let go of Jack's hand.

'And if it turns out she's been acting in my best interests this whole time, I'll be happy to reward her too. But,' he added, putting his hands in his pockets and dropping the smile, 'she'll find out just how tough life can get if she tries to screw things up for me.'

Cross's glare was steely, and Jack marvelled at his ability to go from snake-charmer to snake and back again with such consummate ease. With a final nod, Cross strode away across the tarmac towards the other limousine. Jack stood stoically in the freezing wind and watched the tall, elegant figure move into the fading light, the wind flapping the tails of a fine cashmere overcoat around his legs. His shiny head was tucked down into the upturned collar as he skirted around shallow puddles on the concrete apron. Observing the man at that moment – with his private jet, his limousine, his servants, all the symbols of his power – the only possession Jack found himself coveting was the cashmere coat.

As Cross approached his limousine, the passenger door on the far side opened and Jack saw dark shapes emerge. The outline of two men with broad shoulders was silhouetted against the bright flood-lights on a hangar in the distance. For a moment the men stood next to the vehicle, then one of them rushed around to open the door as Cross arrived. On the way the man passed through the beams from the headlights on Jack's limo, providing Jack with a brief glimpse of a dark-haired man with pale skin and a nose that, even from this distance, looked decidedly bent.

Jack froze and the chauffeur standing beside him holding the door gave him a quizzical look. 'Sir, we need to go if you're going to make your flight,' he said, in a thick Eastern European accent.

Jack didn't move. His eyes were fixed on the man standing on the other side of Cross's limo. It was a big man, no doubt, but his features were all in shadow. The dark-haired guy with the twisted nose followed Daniel Cross into the back of the car, then the big guy reopened the passenger door on his side and bent down to join them. As his head dipped, the light from behind glowed orange around his head and Jack did a double-take. Was that red hair? Were the guys Ben Fisher described – the thugs who had attacked Stella – really here, in the car with Daniel Cross? Or was he just imagining it?

Feeling self-conscious, gazing after Cross like an abandoned puppy, Jack finally acknowledged the driver standing in the cold next to him and climbed into his own limousine. As both vehicles swished smoothly across the rain-soaked tarmac, his mind was rac-ing. If his instincts were right, and Cross was still making use of the thugs from Peoria, then what task were they performing? Were they reporting back on their own search for Stella or were they just acting as bodyguards? Jack was sure Stella wasn't in Chicago because she'd suggested calling back at eleven, 'Chicago time'. She had to be in some other time zone. What was going on?

The sense of restless excitement returned to Jack with a rush. He shook free the complacency induced by an hour or so of Daniel Cross's hospitality, charm and threats. Stella would be calling again in a few hours. Eleven p.m. Chicago time would be midnight in New York. Jack should be on the ground in plenty of time and he could hardly wait. He needed to hear her side of the story.

The limousine was soon sweeping along the freeway away from the city towards O'Hare International Airport. Jack stared vacantly through tinted glass at the passing traffic, feeling uneasy. His eyes and ears took in multiple grey ribbons of concrete humming the song of countless rubber tyres, backed by rhythmic da-dumps as the wheels hit each join in the roadway. His mind paid no attention to the freeway. It was occupied by a predicament: what to do next?

It was pretty clear from the meeting earlier that afternoon that Frank Spiteri had no particular plans for him now that he'd completed the snooping job in Peoria. When he got back to New York, would he be shuffled over to some other M&A project? Or would he be asked to help Ben and Jodie finalise the report for Kradel Electronics? Cross said he still wanted Jack on the team, but to do what? Spy on Frank and the others? Is that what he meant by 'call me first, don't wait for Frank'? How would any of that help Stella or protect her against another attack from the likes of Hollis and Hoyle?

As the muddle of questions and possible answers whirled around in his brain, Jack's thoughts kept returning to Stella's notebook. 'The virgin's secret', she had written. Mysterious, provocative words that obviously had some impact on Daniel Cross. 'Murder', she had also written. Perhaps it was not so hard to imagine Cross ruthless enough to order a killing, but proving a charge like that would be a monumental task, especially if it related to events forty years in the past. When she called in a few hours, would Stella tell him what it was all about, or would she be as cagey with Jack as she had been with her close friend and colleague, Ben Fisher?

The limousine was powering up the exit ramp to O'Hare when Jack reached a conclusion. He had to stay in Chicago. Harding Collins and Maria Petrillo were the only other people Stella had spoken to about what she found in the file, and they were in Chicago. And Sutton Brothers had its headquarters in town, too. The afternoon teleconference with Frank Spiteri had convinced Jack that his new boss rated his relationship with Daniel Cross more highly than Stella's welfare, or Jack's for that matter. And the only partners who could rein in Spiteri and protect Stella's career were located in Chicago. Jack needed to be in Chicago for the moment.

First he had to go through the pretence of leaving. Cross's driver was obviously under instructions to escort him all the way and he wheeled Jack's bags to the first-class check-in line for the American Airlines flight to New York. However, he didn't stay. He wasn't going to risk the limo being towed while Jack went through the rigours of twenty-first-century airport security. With a polite smile and nodded thanks for Jack's over-generous tip, he raced back to the car.

When he'd disappeared through the terminal doors, Jack stepped out of the line and waited a few minutes. He went to the American Airlines' ticket counter and changed his reservation to the same flight twenty-four hours later.

The cab ride back into the centre of Chicago wasn't as physically appealing as the trip out. Noisier, smellier, less comfortable – but in that cab, Jack felt more relaxed than he had all afternoon. He was free of minders, clients and bosses for a few hours. Everybody who cared, except maybe Stella, thought he was on his way back east.

Including Peta, he realised with a pang of guilt. Another day would go by before they discussed their future. He turned on his phone and called her number. She sounded disappointed when she heard he was staying and suggested it was just another avoidance tactic, but didn't push it further when he reassured her. Jack told her a little about Peoria but he could tell she was distracted, so he didn't bother with detail.

The cab dropped him at the InterContinental Hotel, at the river end of Chicago's famous shopping strip, the Magnificent Mile. On the strength of Jack's status as a frequent guest of the chain, he was upgraded to a spacious corner suite on the twentieth floor in the older of the hotel's two towers. The sun was long gone, but from the window Jack had a grand view of the ornate, illuminated Wrigley Building across the street.

Jack was a fan of Chicago's diverse and imposing architecture but on this cold and windy night, he had no desire to linger over the view. He closed the drapes, took a long shower, ordered a club sandwich from room service and settled down to watch local TV news while he waited for Stella to call. He saw the usual depressing stuff. Homeless numbers up, followed by live pictures at the scene of a gruesome suicide downtown, then belligerent words being exchanged by world leaders about chemical weapons in Iraq, a vicious storm front cutting its way across Canada towards Chicago and a sad tale of medical negligence at a city hospital. The New York Giants, the football team Jack adopted when he came to America, were predicted to lose on the weekend.

On the plus side, the club sandwich was excellent, the room was warm and comfortable, the Diet Coke in the minibar was cold and refreshing and the 'Do Not Disturb' sign was on the door. Jack was keyed up by the prospect of Stella's call and anticipating a good night's sleep under soft sheets, once she had set his mind to rest. A couple of *Star Trek* re-runs came on the television and he half watched them while he paced around the room, resisting the urge to look at his watch.

He tried to picture Stella, to imagine where she might be. She could have made it to any part of the globe by now. Maybe she was even back in Australia in the secure fold of her family. If that were true, it would drive her homesick husband nuts, Jack thought.

His eyelids were starting to droop as 11 p.m. came and went. The minutes were starting to drag. At 11.30 the news came on and Jack was complaining out loud about how much he hated waiting for the phone to ring. He hated waiting for anything. But a second later he was startled to full alertness by what appeared on the television screen and then by the harsh screech of his cell phone, which he'd turned up especially loud.

With his left hand, Jack reached for the phone on the bedside table. With his right, he grabbed the remote control from the bed to turn up the volume.

'Hello?' he said into the phone.

'Jack?'

'Stella! Hold on a sec.'

'What?'

'Just hold on a minute. There's something on the news.'

'What?'

'Just shut up for a second, will you?'

It wasn't the friendly exchange he'd planned but then the news item was over.

'Sorry Stella, I'm back,' he said, breathless as if he'd run upstairs, 'I had to watch that story on the TV, and I'm afraid it wasn't good news for us. Harding Collins is dead.'

21

There was a long pause.

'What did you say?'

'Harding Collins is dead,' Jack repeated. 'It was just on the news. There was a story I saw earlier about a jumper from one of the city buildings, but on the late news they named him. Harding Collins, partner in the distinguished legal firm of Leggat and Leggat, president and major stockholder of Collins Military Systems. Fell from an office window on the thirty-second floor of the building where his firm's located. Destroyed a minivan when he hit bottom.'

'You're joking!'

'I wish I was. They showed a black-and-white photo of a thirty-five-ish man with a round face and round glasses.'

'Shit!'

'Shit is right.'

'Was it really suicide?'

'According to the news the police are investigating, but there are no suspicious circumstances.'

'They wouldn't say that unless they were sure it was suicide, right?'

'I don't know, Stella, but even if the police think it was suicide, it might only look that way.'

'Why do you say that?'

'When you called earlier – when I couldn't talk – I was in a limousine on the way to the airport in Peoria with Daniel Cross.'

Stella gasped. 'Really? That must have been uncomfortable. Was he as charming as everybody seems to think?'

'He has his charming side, yes, but that's not the point,' Jack said. 'I flew to Chicago with him this evening in his private jet and I think Hollis and Hoyle were in the limo that picked him up at the airport.'

There was another sharp intake of breath in Jack's ear. 'And you think they killed Harding Collins?'

'I'm just speculating but it seems like a bit of a coincidence, doesn't it? And Cross seemed very keen to make sure I was out of Chicago tonight.'

'Hang on,' Stella said, 'let's go back a step. How do you know about Hollis and Hoyle?'

'Ben Fisher told me about your run-in with them in Peoria. He described one as dark-haired with a broken nose and the other guy, much bigger, was a redhead. I'm pretty sure the same guys were at the airport. Cross wouldn't have another team that fit that description, would he? But why would he use that security firm again, after they screwed things up with you?'

'He owns the company,' Stella said, grimly. 'That part was easy enough to find out. Turns out he owns a number of companies that provide services to CMS.'

'Not too good with the ethical boundaries, is he?'

Stella grunted in agreement. 'Is that what he told you? That Hollis and Hoyle screwed up? Because I reckon that's bullshit. They might have been stupid but those guys were definitely following orders. I think Cross planned for me to disappear that night.'

'Know what Frank said when we discussed the attack? He said you're a very beautiful woman. As if it explained why they couldn't contain themselves.'

'He didn't! That arsehole! Jesus, I know Cross has been his client since Adam was a boy but you can take client loyalty too far, don't you think?'

'That's the main reason I stayed in Chicago tonight. I'm going to try to see Bob Schubert tomorrow.'

'Really? You think Frank needs leaning on?'

'You tell me. From where I sit, he ain't exactly looking out for your best interests, is he? I just didn't think you deserved to have your career destroyed over this.'

There was a lengthy pause, until Jack felt compelled to say, 'Stella? You still there?'

When Stella responded, there was an edge to her voice. 'I didn't ask for your help with my career, Jack. And I don't like the idea of blokes I hardly know getting together to discuss my strengths and weaknesses before deciding whether or not I deserve the bank's support. And why should I trust you more than a man I've worked with more than three years and admired for longer? Frank may be a sexist pig sometimes, but at least I know what makes him tick. What's in it for you, Jack, going in to bat for my career and reputation? Ben told me you've always wanted to join M&A. Now you're in, why would you jeopardise it all by pissing Frank off just to protect my job?'

Jack was taken aback. 'I'm sorry,' he said automatically, before feeling a surge of defensive anger. 'But hey, excuse me for being the only person outside your team who assumes that whatever the hell it is you're doing, it's gotta be above board. And don't think for one moment that I'm happy putting my new career at risk in my very first week. But Stella, this thing that you've started, it's getting serious. People are turning up dead.'

There was no response from Stella, so Jack added, 'I just thought you might need my help, that's all.'

'I do need your help,' Stella said, her voice softer, 'but not with my career. If I've fucked that up then so be it. But the last thing I want is for you to get caught up in a mess of my making and screw up your career too.'

'I can take care of myself.'

'So can I!'

'Yes, of course you can. But you're operating at a distinct disadvantage. Cross has you marked down as the enemy. At least I can play the role of impartial broker trying to resolve a dispute with an unhappy client. I'm betting you're a long way from the action right now, but I'm here on the ground. I can do stuff to help. I was planning to try talking with Harding Collins tomorrow.'

Jack heard a soft, choking sound from the telephone.

'Oh my God,' Stella said. 'That poor man may be dead because of me. What have I done?'

'A good question,' Jack said. 'What have you done, exactly?'

Stella took a deep breath. 'You know I took one of the company files.'

'Yes, something about a contract with the government. Is that what you're worried about?'

'No, not exactly. I'm pretty sure the contract is kosher. But there was another document in the file.'

'The virgin's secret,' Jack said, and he heard Stella gasp again.

'You're good,' she said. 'How did you —'

'It was written in your notes. I guessed it had to come from the file.'

'Oh, right. I didn't think Cross would have told you about it. He freaked out when I raised it with him.'

'He didn't like me raising it either, but he dismissed it out of hand. Is it really forty years old?'

'Nearly,' Stella said. 'Still think you've picked the right side?'

Jack chuckled. 'Hey, it's not too late for me to jump ship but convince me, if you can.'

'Well,' Stella said, 'it's a poem that was written in December 1967 by a man named Campbell —'

There was silence.

'Stella?'

'Yes.'

'You've stopped talking.'

'Yes. That's all for now.'

'What?'

'That's all for now. I'm sorry, Jack, but you said it yourself – lives may be at stake. I can't just trust you because you say I should. I've already been let down.'

'You mean David.'

'Yes. After I saw your email I called him. He denied contacting Cross but he was lying, I'm sure. I sent home some information about the file for safekeeping.'

'I saw him give a Fedex package to Cross at Starbucks,' Jack said, 'and he had a wad of cash later. Had to be ten grand or so. Less after he paid off his bookie.'

'So you —'

'Yeah, I followed him. Managed to run into him in a pub. I was trying to find out if he knew where you might be and what he was doing with Cross. He was in a great mood, even invited me back to your place for a beer. I visited your upstairs bathroom, next to the study. That's where I got your email address.'

'Wow, you're quite the spy, aren't you, Jack? What else did David say?'

'Nothing much. Complained about being stuck in New York, being bored all the time. You've probably heard it all before. He has no idea where you are, by the way. He assumes you'll be vacationing with your family next week, but he doesn't know where.'

'Thank Christ he never pays any attention,' Stella said bitterly. 'I know how unhappy he's been but I can't believe he betrayed me like that. The only instruction I gave him was not to give the package to Cross, and what does he go and do?'

'I think he'd be happy to see things screwed up for you here,' Jack suggested. 'He really just wants to go back to Australia.'

'As if I'd have anything to do with the bastard now,' Stella said angrily. 'But it had to be more than that. He must be in real trouble with the bookmakers.'

'Not this week. For the moment at least he's cashed up.'

'It won't last. It never does. And he'll be doing it all again on Friday.'

'What's that?'

'I sent another package to him, Jack. It has much more information in it, including a full copy of "The Virgin's Secret". It will arrive in New York on Friday. That's why I need your help. I need you to get back to New York and stop David from selling it to Cross. Like you said, Cross remembers something about "The Virgin's Secret" but I doubt he recalls the detail. I don't think anyone other than me has looked at this file for many, many years. The poem's full of cryptic clues, which will probably mean much more to Cross than they do to me. I need time to work through it, but if Cross gets his hands on the full text . . .'

'What?' Jack said, with frustration. 'What will he do, exactly?'

'I don't know, but probably destroy evidence, for a start.'

'Evidence of what?'

'Murder, I think.'

'Murder, you think! Jesus! Whose murder, Stella? An old murder you hope to pin on Daniel Cross by virtue of some forty-year-old evidence that you might find – if it still exists – but only if you can work out the clues in time, is that it?'

'That's a fair summary, I suppose,' she said defiantly.

'And how does all this relate to our work for the bank, Stella? Are you able to show that you've acted responsibly and ethically?'

Stella made a blowing sound. 'God, I don't know. I've probably crossed a few lines. But yes, I believe I'm pursuing the best course professionally. I'm trying to be discreet, after all. I haven't run off to the cops or anything. I'm investigating quietly, knowing there's a good chance it will all go nowhere. If that happens I will apologise and face the consequences with the bank. But if it turns out to be important and it relates to the contract, as I think it does, then I don't think I have any other choice. I have to investigate. I can't risk the destruction of the documents and I can't trust the client or my boss. My only option was to get away, especially after the attack.'

'This is the stuff I want to get across to Bob Schubert,' Jack said. 'He needs to know all this so he can watch your back. The contract is at the heart of the deal between our client and CMS. "The Virgin's Secret" is clearly linked to the contract. The attack on you and Cross's reaction to the file being safely held in your custody are signs that something is fishy – Cross himself may even be a murderer – and you have a responsibility to the board of Kradel to look into it. And Frank's closeness to the client is preventing you from sharing all you know with him. You don't think I should take this to Bob?'

'No, I don't,' Stella said. 'Apart from anything else, we all know that while Chicago is notionally the head office, New York is where the power lies. On paper Frank reports to Bob Schubert, but in reality nobody tells Frank what to do. If he decides my career is over, then it's over.'

'But we should at least get your side on the record —'

'I tried to do that,' Stella interrupted, 'and the copy I sent to my husband was sold to Daniel Cross. The copy I sent to my attorney was stolen or destroyed in a suspicious fire on Monday night. I mentioned the attorney's copy in the letter I wrote to David – so Cross would have known about it. I've sent a second package to my attorney too, but that one should be safe this time. Unless you help me, a copy of my records will be in Cross's hands on Friday. Stop worrying about my career, Jack, and start worrying about how you're going to get my package back.'

'Your lawyer, too? Jeez, Stella, maybe you should go to the cops. Can't you stop the packages being delivered?'

'I tried, but I used a fake name and I can't stop them. And I can't go to the cops – I have no real evidence.'

'But the poem, the link to the contract, the mention of Cross as a murderer. Can't you —'

'I'm just guessing about the link to the contract right now, okay? I know there's a connection, more than just being in the same file but I haven't found it yet.'

'What? I thought you said —'

'The truth is that while the poem implies Cross was responsible for some dire acts in the past, including murder, it doesn't actually say that he murdered someone in particular. Maybe he just murdered good taste or the environment or something. I don't know for sure.'

Jack groaned. 'Maybe I would understand this a bit better if you read me the whole poem.'

'There's a complete copy in the package arriving on Friday,' Stella said. 'Get your hands on that and you'll have almost as much information as I do.'

'What do you expect me to do? Steal the package from David?'
'Yes.'

Jack sighed, flopped back on the bed and stared at the ceiling. 'How am I supposed to do that? Any tips on hijacking a Fedex truck?'

'Hey, you've got an MBA. Work it out for yourself!'

A reluctant laugh escaped Jack's throat and Stella said, 'Don't worry. I'll think about it. I'm sure we can come up with something before Friday morning.'

'So,' Jack said, 'I'm guessing you're not close to New York. Care to tell me where you are?'

'No need for you to know that.'

Jack smiled wryly. He hadn't really expected anything more. 'I suppose I could make another house call. Dave said I was always welcome. He called me mate.'

'David calls everybody mate. It means he doesn't have to remember names.'

'I'm shattered,' Jack said. 'I thought we were close.'

Stella laughed. 'You take a six-pack round there and you'll be best mates again. Or, if you prefer, you can do it behind his back.'

'How?'

'There's a spare set of keys to the apartment in my desk back in New York. I keep them there in case I lose my keys while I'm travelling.'

'You're an independent soul, aren't you? Do you rely on David for anything?'

'Absolutely not,' she said, with humour. 'But you don't know me well enough to ask a question like that.'

'I'll just have to get to know you better, won't I?'

Jack was suddenly embarrassed to find himself flirting. The confusion he'd felt after their first meeting six months ago was flooding back, and he wasn't sure whether he found it exhilarating or terrifying.

'Where are the keys?' he asked quickly, wanting to steer the conversation back to business.

'There's a plastic piggybank in the bottom drawer of my desk,' Stella said, seemingly oblivious to Jack's discomfort. 'Pull out the stopper in its belly – the keys are inside.'

'Your office looks like it's been cleaned out. It doesn't look anything like the other offices on twenty-seven.'

'No, that's just the way I keep it. I don't like clutter.'

'Okay, so I could sneak in when Dave goes out, and hope he leaves the package behind. When is he likely to be out of the apartment?'

'There's bound to be something on Friday afternoon that he'll be betting on. And sometimes he likes to go bar-hopping Friday nights, so you may have a chance then.' Her voice took on a sarcastic edge. 'Of course, now he has money of his own, his routine may change. Maybe you'll find him at the opera or the ballet!'

She was mocking her husband but Jack decided it was fair for her to feel hurt. 'Okay,' he said. 'Leave that with me.'

'Great, thanks,' she said, sounding relieved. 'Please be careful. If we're right about poor old Harding, Cross is obviously prepared to play hardball.'

'Don't worry,' Jack said. 'I'm not going to take any chances with —'

'God!' Stella suddenly exclaimed. 'What about Maria Petrillo? Harding's secretary. Do you think she's okay?'

'I don't know. Why, do you think —?'

'She was there at the discussion I had with Harding about "The Virgin's Secret". She knows about the file and about my concerns. She's knows about as much as Harding did. If they're prepared to kill him . . .'

'Do you know how to contact her?'

'I know she lives in Oak Park with her parents. Her father's a doctor, I think. They're quite a well-to-do family. He should be in the phonebook.'

There was a set of phonebooks in the cupboard and Jack hauled out the relevant volume while Stella was talking.

'She is such a nice kid,' she said. 'I hope she's okay.'

'Here it is,' Jack said. There was only one Doctor Petrillo listed in Oak Park. 'You want me to call?'

'No, let me call her,' Stella said, 'I know her at least. Give me the number.' She took it down as Jack read it out and then said, 'I'd better do it right away.'

Jack's phone went dead but in a few minutes it rang again.

'He was a bit cranky,' Stella said. 'I forgot it was so late there. Anyway, Maria's apparently out with her boyfriend. They don't expect her back tonight. Her father gave me the boyfriend's cell number. I left a message. Maybe they're in a noisy club or something.'

'Give me the number,' Jack said. 'I'll try again in the morning.'

After reading out the number, Stella said, 'She'll be so upset about her boss. She really liked him, it seemed.'

'If I talk to her I'll be sensitive, but I'm sure somebody will have given her the news by then.'

'Listen, Jack, I have to go. My phonecard's running out and I'll have to get a recharge. I'll call you tomorrow, around noon your time.'

'Okay, but make it closer to 11 if you can, 'cos I'm going to try to make the noon flight to La Guardia.'

'Okay. Good night. And, Jack, thanks.'

Before he could respond, the connection went dead and as the sound of Stella's voice faded away, Jack found himself missing it already.

22

In New York, Tony Castle was watching the sparkling lights of Manhattan from a window high above the Upper East Side. Behind him, his study was decorated in an opulent masculine style, with rich veneers on the walls and burgundy leather softening the heavy timber furniture. The room was dark, a Tiffany lamp on the antique desk the only source of illumination. His wife was in bed – accustomed to her husband's late nights and frequent absences – and the vast apartment was silent. Until one of the telephones on the desk began to ring. Although he was expecting the call, Castle was momentarily startled. He turned away from the window and picked up the handset.

'Hello,' he said.

'It's been a good night, Tony, my old friend,' said the cheerful voice of Daniel Cross. 'Loose ends tidied up nicely.'

'You've been drinking.'

'Yep. Been to a fundraiser here in Chicago. Was seen by hundreds of people. Important people, people of note. They were the perfect alibi.'

'For what, Dan? What have you done? I thought we agreed to play the waiting game, let Stella Sartori make the first move.'

'Yeah, yeah, but we had to take care of things here sooner rather than later. And I decided sooner was better.'

'You should have cleared it with me first,' Castle said, the muscles in his jaw tightening. 'Loose ends don't have to mean dead bodies. If any heavy work needs to be done it should be done by professionals. Your amateur thugs will screw things up for all of us.'

'I've got professionals,' Cross said in a petulant tone, 'which is more than you have these days. You've been legit too long, Tony. You just don't have the muscle you used to.'

Castle spun back toward the window and glared at his own faint reflection in the glass. 'I'm going to ignore that, Daniel,' he said slowly, 'on account of the fact that you're drunk. Why don't you call me back when you've sobered up?'

'No, no, sorry, Tony. I didn't mean to offend, sorry. I'm just happy we've struck a blow, that's all. Feel a bit more in control. It was all done neat and tidy, don't fuss.'

Castle released a deep sigh of frustration. 'You've never done it yourself, have you, Daniel? You've never felt another man's hot blood wash over your hands while you twist the knife in his belly. I bet you've never even pulled the trigger that ended a life. It's easy to give the orders and go to the parties but you have no respect for the process.'

'Just like you back in the old days,' Cross countered. 'When we got the contract you didn't do any of the wet work yourself – you just gave the orders.'

'I'd earned that right,' Castle snarled, 'with hands-on action. And I was good at it, too. Had quite a tally by the time I was seventeen. But twice I was caught, Daniel, and other people had to clean up the mess. That's when I understood killing is an art best left to true professionals – men who live and breathe the skills and pass them on from one generation to the next.'

'Like that family you used in the sixties,' Cross said, his petulance fading.

'The Nicolisi boys, yes. They've been supplying specialists to my family for more than five generations. They still do. I used them at the attorney's office. It's in their genes, Dan, and they're almost never caught. Like the contract negotiations, remember? The air force colonel in the Pentagon car park? Cops said it was a mugging gone wrong. The admiral's aide they found in the alley behind that gay bar? Queer bashing, they said, though we know the kid was straight. Or that scientific adviser who disappeared? He's in a sealed drum at the bottom of Chesapeake Bay. That's what I call neat and tidy, Daniel.'

'And Cam Reeves and old man Collins too, right? On the ship? That was the father and son, wasn't it? He had that little suitcase full of drugs, I remember. Are they still around after all this time?'

'The son's still in the business. Works with his nephews. Nicolisi senior died years ago peacefully in his own bed, you should know. They're still based in Sicily but can usually get people here within twelve hours. They're excellent at getting in and out of the country because they have clean records and impeccable documentation. So from now on, please keep your amateurs on the leash and let me decide who best to use for the tricky stuff, okay?'

Cross cleared his throat. 'Um, I'll be bringing my boys to New York on Friday, Tony, to get the next package from the husband.'

'I think my people should handle that,' Castle said. 'The last thing I need is your hopped-up hooligans knocking around the city.'

'No!' Cross said, his voice pitching higher. 'The husband will only deal with me and I need my boys around in case he gets difficult. Don't worry, I'll be there to supervise. We'll be in and out before you know it.'

Castle stood motionless at the window, saying nothing, the cogs of his brain turning over. Eventually he heard Cross trying to change the subject.

'Have you had any luck tracking her down, Tony?'

'I should have some useful information tomorrow. There's a guy who works for her credit card company. Took me a while to get the details, but for the right gratuity he's going to provide details of her recent purchases. If she was planning to join her family on vacation at the end of this week she'd have bought the ticket before she went out to Peoria. There might even be some hotel reservations in the system. Even if we don't find her, locating her family will give us some leverage.'

'That's great,' Cross said. 'You know, I asked the husband about credit card statements and the like. He said all the bills go to her office.'

'We've already been through her office. Found nothing like that. She pays her bills quickly and discards the paperwork.'

'Jesus! What is it with this woman? Is she some kind of efficiency nut or what?'

'She obviously likes to keep on top of things,' Castle said. 'Like you, Dan, she doesn't like loose ends.'

Cross gave an incredulous snort. 'You like the bitch, don't you? You do realise she's trying to destroy me? And if she brings me down, you can kiss goodbye to all the luxuries and the power and that fine view you love so much. You do understand that, don't you, Tony?'

Castle traced the outline of skyscrapers against the grey-black night with his eyes. 'I admire her, that's all,' he said, before his tone turned sarcastic. 'But your loyalty and friendship are heartwarming, Daniel. You'd go a long way with that attitude in a Sicilian family.'

'Oh, don't be stupid, Tony. I'd never snitch on you. I'm just saying if she finds something that incriminates me there's a good chance it'll hook you too.'

'But what could she possibly find after all this time?'

'Who knows? But we can't take the chance, can we? It's just too big. Reeves knew something. We know old man Collins had all the details, 'cause he was obviously lying when he said he was sound asleep in that hotel room. And we know Collins always told Reeves everything. What if Reeves wrote it down? He was always writing shit down. What if that damned poem was meant to lead to something more substantial? I wish I'd looked at it more closely back then. It didn't seem to matter because we had the poem itself. But now she's got it.'

'We searched his cabin thoroughly that night,' Castle said. 'Didn't find anything hidden that he could've referred to. And nothing has surfaced in nearly forty years.'

But Cross clearly wasn't convinced and Castle detected a dangerous note of fear in his voice. 'You found nothing in his cabin, no. Nor in Gil Collins'. But the ship, Tony, remember the ship. It was fucking enormous!'

'Yes,' Castle said, nodding at his own reflection, 'it certainly was.'

When the conversation was over, Tony sat down heavily in the high-backed, black leather chair behind his desk. He swivelled round to face the window once more. Laying his head back on the soft padding, he closed his eyes and allowed his mind to wander away from the present and take him back in time. He saw an image of the ship in the great harbour of Rio de Janeiro as they were brought out to join the cruise. Spectacular from a distance, but tired-looking and worn out up close. And the passengers all lined up on the deck, dressed to the nines despite the heat of November and the almost-useless air-conditioning on board. Vague recollections of vast, over-decorated rooms filled with nosy, pretentious people all competing with one another. But then a clear vision of the faces of the two men, Reeves and Collins, whose deaths he was there to arrange. They were strong faces, as he remembered them now – wrinkled, friendly and wise. About the same age as me, he thought, and he brought the reflection of his own face back into focus. Back then I thought they were old and decrepit. The memory felt strangely distasteful and Castle pushed it aside.

He recalled instead his early days with Daniel and that snivelling toady, Ewan Collins. Fresh out of college but so full of Sicilian bravado, Tony's ambition had been boundless. Denied access to the stockbrokers and banks where he wanted to work, the opportunity to 'consult' on a Pentagon contract and get close to a well-respected company was too good to pass up. He didn't care what they were selling or how the Pentagon normally went about evaluating a tender or negotiating a contract. The only thing he needed to know was: who needs their mind made up for them?

It wasn't only the killing, he remembered with a smile. The gentler tactics were actually more satisfying. The bribes and blackmail, including the army guy who wanted a fancy motorcycle and the naval officer they photographed fucking his secretary. And the gambling sting on that other navy guy, that was the best.

Except for the other thing, Castle thought, and he felt a familiar surge of pleasure course through his veins. It was that other thing, that single stroke of genius that really set him apart – only a man with his unique history and courage could have made a leap of logic like that.

In his mind's eye, he was in a suite at the Willard Hotel, Washington – adjacent to the White House itself – on a sunny day in May 1963. Daniel had just received the call. The panel's recommendation had been made. The contract was theirs! A year of hard work and brutal manipulation had finally paid off. The champagne in the ice bucket was frothing over as the unlikely trio toasted each other.

When the initial euphoria had mellowed to a self-satisfied sense of hubris, he made his move. It was as fresh in his memory as if it had happened last week.

'You know, Daniel,' he'd said, 'if you really want to maximise the value of your new contract, we need to do more.'

'What do you mean?'

'I've been looking at the terms of the deal. You have this research subsidy clause in there. It's your long-term security, right? Five decades of subsidy based on average sales in the first decade.'

'My idea,' Ewan had claimed. 'The averaging thing and the indexing. We did a case study in college —'

'What's your point?' Daniel had said, demonstrating his typical level of respect for the man who was notionally his boss.

'Fundamentally it means that the more product you sell and the quicker you sell it, the richer you're going to get.'

Daniel had nodded but didn't look impressed, yet. 'I know the clause. I helped write it.'

'What's going to drive your sales numbers up?'

'Our detonator will be used in all sorts of things: bombs, shells, missiles. The more they use, the more they'll need.'

'Exactly! It's the perfect product because when you use it, it destroys itself.'

Daniel had given him a look of bemusement. 'What are you suggesting now, Tony? You want to start a war?'

'We have the beginnings of one in Indochina,' he had said, 'but we can't wait around for it to heat up. The missile crisis was good for raising the tension but we need more than stockpiling; we need your detonators going bang in large quantities and soon.'

'So you want a change of policy on North Vietnam?'

'I'd like to see a more aggressive policy, yes. That would be good for you, and for me, of course, when I get my cut.'

Daniel was shaking his head. 'How do you plan to achieve such a rapid change of policy?'

Tony Castle, sitting high above Manhattan, felt the same tingle of anticipation he'd experienced forty years earlier, when he'd turned to Daniel Cross and said, 'I believe I have the perfect solution.'

23

After a frustrating night of fitful sleep dominated by strange dreams, Jack rose early and reached for his cell phone. First he called the number at Maria Petrillo's family home but reached an answering machine. Then he tried the boyfriend's cell, again with no luck. Finally he called Frank Spiteri in New York.

'I missed my flight last night,' he said, not enjoying the act of lying to his new boss. 'I'll be back at the office later in the day.'

'You stayed in Chicago last night?' Spiteri asked.

'Yeah. Why, is there a problem?'

'No, not at all. Still no word from Stella. You have any news?'

'Only Harding Collins. You hear about that?'

'No, what's he done?'

'Killed himself apparently. It was on the news here last night.'

There was a shocked silence before Spiteri said, 'You're kidding!'

'Wish I was. They say he jumped from his office building. You think that's likely, Frank?'

'God, I don't know. I only met him briefly, years ago, but there were rumours.'

'Rumours? What sort of rumours?'

'Oh, just personal stuff. I'm told he was gay and had a lot of grief from his family, that's all.'

'Who told you that?'

'What are you suggesting, Jack?'

The tone of Spiteri's voice made Jack hesitate. Clearly the boss wouldn't appreciate hearing unsubstantiated allegations about Cross from a subordinate.

'Nothing, Frank,' he said. 'It just feels wrong, you know, Collins deciding to do himself in just after all this stuff with Stella.'

'What could Stella's behaviour have to do with Harding's suicide?'

'Maybe nothing,' Jack said, wanting desperately to share his suspicions and his possible sighting of Cross's thugs at the airport but knowing it was not the time. 'It's just a bit off, that's all.'

'I imagine suicide always feels a bit off,' Spiteri said sagely, 'but whatever Stella has done, I can't imagine it leading to Harding Collins' decision to take his own life.'

Again, Jack felt a wave of disloyalty, keeping back his conversation with Stella and their pact to work together. But he could not risk sharing with the man who'd been advising Cross for so many years. They were just too close.

'I'll have a look at the Chicago papers,' Jack said. 'Maybe there's more information this morning.'

'Okay, you do that and I'll see you when you get back to New York.'

'Fine.'

And the call was terminated. Jack tried the Petrillo numbers once more but was again only offered the option to leave a message, which he declined to do.

After ordering breakfast and a local newspaper from room service, he took a shower and shaved. Then he collected *USA Today* from outside his door but found no reference to the local tragedy. The morning news on television was repeating the story running the previous night but when the *Chicago Tribune* arrived with his muesli and fruit, there was a small front-page article about the Collins death, with the promise of a fuller obituary in the next edition. The story mentioned a suicide note found at the scene and speculated that a failed property deal may have been the impetus for the attorney's decision to jump, although it acknowledged that the fallout from that deal had long passed.

After checking out of the hotel, Jack was guided by the doorman into a taxi on Michigan Avenue, where he gave instructions to head first towards an address in Oak Park before going on to the airport. As soon as the cab turned into the elegant, tree-lined street where Doctor Petrillo and his family lived, Jack could pick out their large brick mansion, even from a distance. What gave it away was the gaggle of police cruisers parked out front. With dread Jack realised something unpleasant had happened. Sure enough, as the cab drew closer, the number on the letterbox confirmed it was Maria's address.

Feeling a little cowardly, Jack told the cabbie to drive on and take him straight to the airport. He just couldn't think of a reasonable explanation for turning up at the home of a possible victim of a violent crime whom he'd never met, asking if she was all right. How could he explain his interest in Maria's welfare without revealing all the background, which could lead nowhere good? The last thing he wanted was to get stuck in Chicago. He had to get to New York.

The cab drove on and, until he saw the TV news in the airport lounge ninety minutes later, Jack had no way of knowing for sure whether the cops had been there because of Maria. For a while he entertained the hope that the police were just asking questions about the suicide of her boss. But his worst fears were confirmed by a news anchor informing her viewers that a young female resident of Oak Park, as yet unnamed, had been the victim of a hit-and-run accident the night before. She'd been struck down and killed when crossing the street outside a nightclub where she'd been celebrating with friends, just before 1 a.m. Her boyfriend was also injured. The police were appealing for anybody who may have seen a dark-coloured SUV speeding away from the scene to come forward.

There was no doubt in Jack's mind that it was Maria. She'd apparently paid the ultimate price for trying to be helpful to Stella. And as he stood watching the news, he knew with absolute certainty that Daniel Cross must have ordered this. SUV or not, he could imagine who was at the wheel. If not Hollis or Hoyle, then some close facsimile – some mindless individual prepared to take an innocent life because some arsehole in a suit paid for it.

Jack felt weak at the knees and light in the head. He had to sit down to absorb the impact of the truth. One coincidental death was bad enough, but two just confirmed that neither could be coincidence. Which meant Daniel Cross wasn't only dangerous – he was lethal.

He also knew for certain that Stella was doing the right thing. No way would Cross be resorting to such extreme measures if Stella didn't have something important and potentially damaging in her hands. And if she was right, and 'The Virgin's Secret' was actually a signpost to incriminating evidence, then she had to take a shot at finding it. And he had to help her.

He glanced at his watch and saw that it was almost the time when she'd said she would call back. Although he wanted badly to talk to her again, the thought of having to pass on this terrible news made him feel sick to the stomach. As if on cue, his cell phone burbled to life. As he moved it towards his ear, Jack noted the usual 'unknown caller' on the screen that he always saw when Stella called. His heart beat faster in his chest and his mouth went dry. He swallowed hard and touched the button on his phone.

'Jack Rogers,' he croaked.

'You okay, Jack? You sound like you're getting a cold.'

'I'm all right, Stella, but I'm afraid I can't say the same for Maria Petrillo.'

'Oh God, no!' Stella said, and was quiet for a few long seconds. 'What happened?' she said, her voice barely audible.

'Hit and run, early this morning. The boyfriend's still in hospital. No names have been given yet but they say she was young and lived in Oak Park.'

'Jesus! And she's definitely . . . ?'

'Dead? Yes.'

'Fuck, fuck, fuck.' Stella's voice had a new edge of panic. 'You know what this means, don't you?'

'Yeah. Whatever you've stumbled on, it's pure dynamite. And Daniel Cross is much more dangerous than we thought. We have to pursue this, Stella. We have no other choice.'

'Do we go to the police?'

'With what? We have no proof. The only way to convince them would be to bring you out of hiding, and then you'd be an easy target and Cross would soon know I'm working with you. I think we have to see it through, Stella, see where "The Virgin's Secret" leads us. We'll just have to hope it leads us to something the authorities can use against Cross.'

Jack heard Stella give a deep sigh. 'We stick to the plan then. You get the package back tomorrow and I'll try to solve the puzzle. What about Frank?'

'I spoke to him this morning. He was shocked to hear about

Harding Collins but wasn't open to any suggestion of foul play. And I can't tell him about Maria without it sounding suspicious, can I?'

'Please, don't do that,' Stella said. 'Not yet.'

'No way,' Jack said. 'I'm not going to risk it getting back to Cross. Both our lives would be on the line if he found out.'

'It's not just our careers any more, is it?'

'Hell, no. He's playing for keeps.'

'Okay,' Stella said, and Jack pictured her shaking free the shock to regain the focus required, 'I've had an idea about how you can get the package back.'

'Really? That's great, because nothing was coming to me.'

'Packages usually get delivered to the doorman on duty at our building, right? Normally he calls upstairs to say something has arrived.'

'You know the doorman well?'

'I know the main guy pretty well. Manny's usually on duty during the day. He's a very honest type of guy so he may take a bit of convincing. But then again, he doesn't like David much.'

Jack recalled the Latino man Dave O'Reilly ignored as they'd entered the building on 49th Street three nights ago. 'I think I saw him. He kinda sneered as Dave walked past.'

'It might have been him,' Stella said. 'Most of them seem to have some issue with David. Probably they don't approve of his lifestyle.'

'And I bet you pay the tips.'

Stella managed a chuckle. 'Well, yeah, there is that.'

'You think you can get the doorman to give me the package?'

'I'm going to call and try. I should be able to get him to hold it for a short while. You know, not make the call upstairs immediately? He may not be prepared to hand it to you himself but if he left it on his counter for a few minutes, maybe you could sidle in and —'

'Sounds a lot better than trying to knock over a Fedex truck.'

'I'll give Manny your phone number,' Stella said. 'If he sends you a text message once the package's arrived you can do the rest. You'll need to be close by though, because David will be expecting the delivery, and Manny won't be able to hang on to it for long. If David turns up to claim it, Manny'll have to give it to him. After all, it is addressed to him. Then we're back to plan B, C or D.'

'What if I get arrested and thrown in jail for stealing?' Jack asked, only half joking.

'Oh, shit, don't!' Stella said. 'Don't take any unnecessary risks. If the stuff falls into Cross's hands it'd be a disaster, but it's not the end of the world. Certainly not worth getting arrested for, or worse.'

After two deaths in twenty-four hours, the risks seemed much more real to Jack. 'Would it really be such a disaster if Cross got the package?' he asked.

'Well, if the poem really is pointing the way to better evidence, there's a good chance he could get to it first and have it destroyed. If that happens, we're done.'

'Like a dinner,' Jack said, in automatic agreement.

'I'm sorry, Jack. I hate the idea of dropping you in it like this. I'd do it myself but I'm too far away.'

'Where was that again?'

Stella released half a laugh. 'No need for you to know. But I am looking forward to buying you a drink when the time is right. It feels so good not to be all alone in this.'

'You still don't trust me?'

'Of course I do. I just think —'

'It's okay, Stella. I agree with you. It's better that I don't have to lie about knowing your whereabouts.'

'Thanks for understanding.'

'No worries. I'm going to have to play it pretty coy with Frank as it is, but if I miss my chance with the package —'

'Then the particular vat of shit I've landed myself in will have just gotten a couple of inches deeper.'

'We're in it together,' he assured her.

'Take a deep breath,' Stella said grimly, 'because we may be about to go under.'

24

As Stella replaced the handset of the payphone, she felt a surge of anger and revulsion. Looking around the hotel lobby, she could see the smiling faces of tourists and beach bums, passing through on their way to start another day filled with sun, sand and sea. It felt surreal, as if the bright light and blue sky of this paradise, indifferent to the ugliness of the world, was as fake as the plastic plants in their plastic pots. And yet these were real people around her – pink or tanned or new-arrival white, in gaudy clothes and broad hats, their eyes hidden behind expensive dark glasses. She could not deny that she was a part of this disturbingly trite existence. Her bikini was covered with a sheer wrap. Her feet – in tiny, strappy sandals – were as brown as the glowing olive skin of her torso and, next to them on the floor, her beach bag held little more than an escapist thriller and a bottle of suntan lotion. Many miles away in the real world, two people she knew just well enough to like were lying in the cold drawers of some dark morgue in Chicago.

Disgusted, she picked up the phone again and dialled the New York number of her immigration lawyer. She was told that Alex

Trainer was in a meeting but she insisted on talking to him right away, and when he came on the line, he sounded pleased she had called.

'Stella,' he said, 'it's good to hear from you again. When we last spoke, you said you might know something about the fire at our office this week. I would really love you to talk to the police about that.'

'It's just not possible right now, Alex,' she said, 'but I would like to stop another tragedy happening, if I can. My package will be arriving tomorrow. I want you to secure it immediately and take every precaution you can.'

'I know, I know,' he said, sounding slightly irritated, 'put it in the safe as soon as possible. You've already given me that instruction. What's it all about, Stella? Can't you tell me what's in these packages and who is trying to get at them?'

'I'm not in a position to make specific accusations just yet. But if my husband David O'Reilly or a man named Daniel Cross make contact with you, say nothing, deny everything. It's best if you don't mention the package to anyone at all.'

'This is all very mysterious and sensational, Stella, but I am a professional. You can talk to me about anything, anything at all. Everything you tell me is privileged information. Please confide in me a little.'

Stella thought for a moment but decided it could do no good to explain. 'Don't your clients ever keep secrets, Alex?'

'Not normally. Not in my line of work.'

'Well, like I told you before, this has nothing to do with your area of expertise. I just need a safe place to secure some sensitive material and if anything happens to me, I want you to give the material to a man named Jack Rogers.'

'I thought you wanted me to go to the authorities if that happened.'

'You can trust Jack Rogers. If he doesn't make contact with you for some reason, then go to the authorities with the material.'

'If he doesn't —,' the attorney repeated. 'What on earth have you got yourself involved in?'

'Can you just follow my instructions, Alex, please? Take care of the material and take care of yourself.'

'Myself? Why would I —?'

'Two people are dead already, Alex, but I can't prove they were murdered and I can't prove who might have done it. Please believe me, this is very serious. Please!'

Trainer sighed deeply with frustration, but said, 'Okay, if that's how you want to play it. But two people dead? Stella, you should be going to the police with this.'

'I know, I know. And I will, but not yet. Just as soon as I can, all right? Until then, do nothing until you hear from me again or from Jack.'

'Jack Rogers,' he recited, with resignation. 'Got it.'

'Thanks, Alex. You're a good man.'

Again, Stella found herself standing next to the bank of phones in the lobby, feeling helpless and guilty. Guilty for starting a chain of events that had resulted in unfair and unjustifiable deaths. Guilty for spoiling the vacation of her mother and sister with her absences and detachment. Guilty for putting Jack's life and career in harm's way. And guilty for sunning herself on the beach while people were dying.

Not knowing what else to do, she picked up her bag and made her way slowly through the hotel towards the beach, just a short walk away. Completely oblivious to the people and hustle around her, she slipped off her sandals and trudged toward the spot where she knew her family would be waiting. In her catatonic state she almost walked right by them until she heard her sister shouting, 'Hey, Stella, wake up! We're over here.'

Mustering up a facade of holiday joy was beyond her and, as Stella sat on the towel spread out for her, Freda Sartori was immediately aware that her daughter was even more disturbed than usual.

'Darling,' she said, 'what's wrong? You look so sad.'

'Yeah,' her sister Ange added, 'you look like crap. Where have you been? We missed you at breakfast. Did you have a bad night? Couldn't sleep?'

Trying to summon the hint of a smile, Stella just shook her head. 'I'm sorry, you guys. You've come such a long way for us to be together and I'm not being much fun, I know.'

By the look on Ange's face it was clear she felt the apology was more than justified but Freda was more understanding. 'Don't you be silly, darling,' she said. 'We don't need you to entertain us. It's so good to spend time with you. We're just sorry that you can't get away from your responsibilities for a while.'

Stella gave her mother a look of loving gratitude and ignored her sister's pout.

'It's wonderful to spend time with you too, Mama. It has been too long.' Lying back on the towel, she felt the morning sun's rays beginning to warm her exterior. On the inside she felt cold and empty.

25

With the time difference and travel time, Jack wasn't back in Manhattan until 4.30 in the afternoon, and the sky was already beginning to darken. To his surprise, and considerable relief, he discovered that Frank Spiteri was unavailable and wouldn't be back that day. And he found a string of voicemail messages on the phone in his new office, most of them relating to his old trading role. As he worked his way through them, pushing most to Matt McCormick, he came across the strange message he'd heard and saved on Monday afternoon, which seemed like a lifetime ago.

'No one' was the only word spoken by the caller, but after several conversations with Stella this week, Jack was even more convinced that it had to be her. She'd definitely reached out to him, even before he got involved in her dangerous dealings, and it made him feel good.

Listening to the message twice more, he also heard the voice of the woman asking 'Who ya calling, sis?' and the noise of the television in the background and it struck him that it sounded very different from Stella's later calls. The background noises during their recent conversations were more consistent with a payphone in a public place. This message sounded like it was coming from a hotel room or some other enclosed space, with a TV and a sister close by.

Turning to the computer that had miraculously turned up on his desk while he was away, he logged in and found the Sutton Brothers' directory. He found the number he wanted and punched an extension into the phone, hoping the tech department were not early finishers. Seven rings, then on the eighth, 'Help desk,' said a bored male voice.

'This is Jack Rogers, from the —'

'Yeah, Jack, I know who you are. I see your number on my screen. What's the problem?'

'I had a call last Monday from a client who's not at his usual number this week. I need to get back to him. He left a message on this number around 2.15, Monday afternoon. Are you able to tell me where that call came from?'

'Maybe. Depends.'

'Could you check it for me, please? As quickly as you can.'

'Probably won't get to it today. Tomorrow okay?'

'Sure. You'll call me back?'

'If we have the data, it will be emailed to you. That's how the system works.'

'Right, thanks, I appreciate your help.'

'Sure,' the voice said, clearly uninspired, and the line went dead.

A slight feeling of self-satisfaction brought a smile to the edges of Jack's mouth. Perhaps he'd surprise Stella yet. Then, with nothing else to do, he pushed back from his desk, took a long look at the view from his very own window and then said aloud, 'Right. I guess I get an early mark. Maybe I'll surprise Peta, too.'

His heart skipped a beat. The idea of a quiet evening at home –

and his own bed, with Peta in it – had always been extremely comforting at the end of a working day, but lately it also seemed to elicit a vague sense of dread. There were so many unresolved issues swirling around his personal life, yet Jack doubted he could summon the energy to resolve even one of them. Which won't please Peta, he thought, and he found himself guiltily hoping that she might have a party or opening to attend. An empty house, for a couple of hours, would be perfect.

When a cab delivered him to the West Village, he discovered that Peta was reading from a different script. There was a party going on. As soon as he came through the front door, he could hear voices raised in laughter and good cheer from further inside. Feeling instantly grumpy, he dropped his bags unceremoniously and moved down the hall towards the living space, trying to form a smile.

At the big kitchen table, he found his partner in her natural habitat, enthralling her guests with wicked stories and outrageous gossip. It was a small group, but they had the volume of a larger crowd, thanks to the champagne that had once occupied the empty bottles on the table. Anton and Bill, Peta's business partners, were there, as well as Kate and Susie, two of the company's store managers. It looked to Jack like they'd been celebrating something – perhaps someone was getting married or promoted or they'd scored a big sale.

Whatever it was, they all looked sheepish and uncomfortable as soon as he walked in, as if the school principal had turned up to spoil the fun. It wasn't the first time Peta's friends had behaved that way. They mostly assumed they wouldn't relate to a Wall Street type so they didn't even try. It didn't bother Jack in the slightest.

The group sensed his mood because excuses were made shortly after he'd said his hellos and kissed Peta's cheek. He fixed himself a strong gin and tonic while Peta saw her giggling friends to the door.

When she returned, she busied herself moving glasses and plates to the bench above the dishwasher but seemed to be avoiding him.

Jack took a large gulp of his drink. 'What were you celebrating?' he asked.

Peta stopped clearing up and plonked herself down in a kitchen chair at the table. She picked up a half-empty glass of champagne, drained it, then took a deep breath.

'I'm moving to London,' she said.

Jack felt the muscles in his face tense. 'That's what you were celebrating?'

'Yep.'

'You're moving to London.'

'That's right.'

'When?'

'Next week.'

'Next week! Next week for a visit or next week for good?'

'Next week for good but I'll be back to sort things out.'

'Next week for good.'

'Yep.'

Jack was numb. A great nothingness filled him from the belly out. She was going to London. She'd made the decision. She didn't wait for his input. Whatever he thought or did or said, she was still going to London. Their once-perfect life together was over. Just like that.

Then, slowly but surely, the emptiness in Jack's guts transmuted to anger. 'You didn't want to wait to discuss this with me?'

'You're never here,' she said sternly, 'and besides, you're the greatest avoider on the planet. You didn't want to talk about me going to London any more than you've wanted to talk about starting a family for the last two years.'

'That's not fair. You only raised the London thing with me three days ago.'

'I told you it was urgent.'

'But surely you could have —'

'What the fuck difference would it make, Jack?' she interrupted hotly. 'You tell me. If we had another month to decide, what would you do differently? Would it make the slightest difference to the outcome? I don't think so.'

The cold anger in Jack's eyes made her look away. He was sensing the loss of one of the best things in his life, and in his mind she was to blame. Through tight lips, he said, 'What is it you expect me to do exactly, Peta?'

'I don't expect you to do anything you don't want to do, Jack,' she said matter-of-factly. 'What I would like most is for you to come to London with me. I know you'd prefer not to but that's what I want. Come to London with me. It'll be fun.'

Jack stared down at the ice cubes in his glass as he absorbed her words. Peta reckoned it would be fun, and life with her could certainly be that, but he didn't want to go back. All his dreams for the future were in New York. Somehow going back to England would feel like defeat, taking a step backwards because he couldn't stick it out.

And he didn't want to go now, when Stella needed him and the prospect of going to work was more exciting than it had been in a long while. America was offering a new start. England only promised more of the same old grind. Besides, there'd still be an unresolved issue with Peta, the big one.

'What about your family plans?'

'You know what I need,' she said bluntly. 'Soon I'll be too old, but I'd really like to do it with you. I love you. And you'd make a great father.'

The flattery had no impact on Jack.

'And you were prepared to make me one, weren't you?' he asked, accusingly. 'Whether I wanted it or not. Why else would you need a pregnancy test?'

'Oh, you saw that?'

'Yes, I saw that. Is there anything you think I should know? Perhaps something I have a right to know?'

'I'm not pregnant, if that's what you're worried about.'

Jack shook his head and flexed his fingers, trying to dissipate some of the fury that seemed to keep boiling up.

'Peta, did you stop taking the pill without telling me?'

The look of real fear that crossed her face surprised him, and he consciously softened towards her. Then he realised she was projecting her dread of being caught out.

'How long?' he asked, through gritted teeth.

Peta shrugged her shoulders. 'About four months.'

Four months! Jack felt a new surge of indignation but could think of nothing rational to say. Peta stood up, genuinely concerned by the pained expression on his face. She moved towards him, opening her arms for what she hoped would be an embrace of mutual forgiveness, but Jack moved away as if repelled.

The rejection cracked Peta's defences. Tears filled her eyes and rolled down her cheeks. All the consequences of the change she was bringing washed over her and she needed a hug of reassurance. But Jack's body language and expression made it clear that she could no longer look for comfort there.

'I'm sorry, Jack,' she said with a sniff. Then she rushed up the stairs with one hand to her face.

After a slow circuit of the house, switching off the downstairs lights, Jack followed her but at the top of the stairs, he turned right rather than left, seeking the sanctuary of his favourite armchair. For a long time he could hear Peta sobbing quietly in the darkened bedroom across the hall, but he felt no urge to move from his chair by the window.

26

At ten the next morning, Jack was hovering around on the sidewalk opposite Stella Sartori's apartment building. Forty-ninth Street was still pulsing with rush-hour traffic but the pedestrian cover was fast dissipating as the stream of commuters from nearby subway stops thinned. Glancing up, he wondered if O'Reilly was watching the street. His recollection of the apartment suggested views were limited to the rear of the building but it was possible there was another vantage point. Still, Jack thought, there's no good reason for him to be watching.

Jack was in his workout gear, right down to the sweat accumulated by running most of the way from his home. His aim was to look like a local jogger returning from a run along the East River, but he hadn't counted on how silly he'd feel running up and down the same block, always keeping an eye out for the distinctive colour and shape of a Fedex van.

As he moved at a steady pace up the slope from 2nd Avenue to 3rd for the fifth time, he knew he couldn't keep it up for the whole morning. Some attentive doorman along the street was bound to call the cops. And, apart from anything else, he wasn't in any condition to run a marathon. He was physically exhausted from a week of too much activity and too little sleep; he was mentally punch-drunk from the night before, unable to focus on more than one thought at a time. For the moment, he was concentrating on Stella's problems, pushing his own issues to one side.

When he got to 3rd Avenue he turned north, past Smith & Wollensky, and began to stroll calmly up the block. He decided to stay away from 49th Street until the cell phone in his runner's backpack beeped. He'd have to risk being a little further away. The wait turned out to be another fifty minutes, and Jack was glad of the decision to walk rather than run. He was two blocks south-east when his phone beeped, and he saw a message on the screen saying simply, 'OK'. He started running again.

He was aware of his heart pounding in his chest, mostly in response to the nervous tension he was feeling rather than the exertion. Apart from one undiscovered shoplifting caper as a teenager, he'd never done anything so deliberately illegal in his life before. As he rounded the corner into 49th, Jack could see the white Fedex van pulling away. His eyes focused on the dark, arched doorway of Stella's building and his heartbeat quickened as each stride brought him closer to it.

The dimly lit hallway was empty when Jack turned in under the blue awning. His eyes had to adjust to the gloom before he could see the stairway leading up to the lobby. He leapt up the stairs two at a time and then slowed to a less conspicuous pace as he passed through the glass doors. The doorman's position was on his right and was unattended. A single package sat atop the counter and Jack rushed over to pick it up. With a silent hoot of joy and a pump of the fist, he read David O'Reilly's name on the address label. Triumph and relief flooded through him, and the urge to run was overwhelming but he stayed calm, tucking the promisingly thick, document-sized envelope under his right arm and turning to leave the building.

Just as the tension began to leave his body, he heard a shout from behind and he looked back to see one of the elevators standing open. A man was moving towards him shouting with one arm raised and, much to his dismay, he saw that it was Dave O'Reilly. O'Reilly's eyes moved from Jack's face to the Fedex package and back again. He didn't look happy.

O'Reilly started to run but he had to get through a set of doors, which gave Jack a short headstart. Adrenalin flooded into Jack's tired heart and legs as he realised the pretence of impartiality was well and truly over. Even if O'Reilly didn't catch him it wouldn't be long before Daniel Cross knew Jack was working against him.

Suddenly O'Reilly was right on him, and Jack focused all his attention on speed. Despite his drinking and smoking, the little guy was surprisingly quick. His wiry frame weaved through the maze of pedestrians, trash containers and sundry other objects on the side-walk as he pursued Jack along 49th Street, shouting abuse with all the colour available to the Australian vernacular.

In Jack's favour, he was wearing the right gear for running – his only burdens were the small pack on his back and the package under his arm. O'Reilly wore tight jeans and his suede jacket – ready for another meeting with his new corporate sponsors. Jack hurtled up the street towards 3rd Avenue. The one-way traffic on 49th coursed by to his left, moving in the same direction. As it slowed for a change at the lights, he ducked between two cabs to the downtown side, just before the corner, then bolted south down the avenue. Jack's instinct told him to get to Grand Central Station. If he could make it there it should be easy enough to lose O'Reilly in the crowd – but the back entrance to the station was still four blocks south and two long blocks west. And right behind him, he could hear O'Reilly pounding the pavement, closing in on him fast.

Third Avenue was suddenly terrifyingly wide. All the vehicles on it, mostly buses and cabs, were moving towards him as he ran close to the edge of the sidewalk – avoiding people and hot-dog vendors and looking for a way to cross six lanes of traffic, four of them moving pretty fast. The sound of laboured breathing close to Jack's left ear and a hand clutching at his shoulder forced him to take a risk. He moved right, out into the stream of motor vehicles, crossing each lane as a gap appeared. At a full run, he dodged around cars and vans, eliciting a few angry honks from bored drivers. A long, angry horn blast at his back and more swearing suggested his pursuer had had a near miss as he tried to follow, and O'Reilly's footfall seemed further behind as Jack hit the other side of the avenue at the corner of 48th Street. He put in a short burst of extra speed as he kept running east, trying to widen the gap.

With typical detachment, most of the New Yorkers observing the chase ignored it. To some, Jack must have looked like the bad guy, but nobody chose to interfere. A few people hurled some abuse of their own but most moved out of the way, self-preservation being their primary instinct. Jack prayed that some well-meaning cop wouldn't take a pot shot at him.

Lexington Avenue finally loomed in front of him. Narrower than 3rd, this avenue – where tourists hovered in a group around the T-shirt vendor on the corner – hardly slowed Jack at all as he bounded over its kerbs and between slow-moving cars. O'Reilly was shouting again and it was only at the last minute Jack saw the trap. Still on 48th Street, he was approaching the carpeted sidewalk in front of the InterContinental Hotel. Two hotel porters in dark uniforms stood there, looking Jack's way as he ran towards them. He realised that O'Reilly was shouting to them, maybe even knew them. Sure enough, Jack could see the men forming a line of scrimmage next to the small crowd of guests at the main entrance. To Jack's left, the street was full of traffic, flowing against him now. The station, where he wanted to be, was still three blocks south – he had to get to Park Avenue, at the other end of this long block.

He had only a split second to decide what to do, so he let instinct take over. The two doormen were poised like wrestlers, making themselves as wide as possible on the sidewalk, legs and arms outstretched to stop him. The guy on the left looked big enough to be a sumo. The one on the right was smaller and thinner, the younger of the two. He became the target. Jack tucked his precious package under his left arm, put his head and shoulders down like a footballer and stuck out his right arm to fend off the tackle.

He hit the poor kid like a train. The young porter was bounced to the side with a loud grunt, collapsing over a neat row of suitcases. Jack heard the screams of indignant guests and staff, but by then he was past the hotel and running across the street, which had conveniently emptied of cars. A glance behind saw O'Reilly still in pursuit, but further back and looking the worse for it. Sweat poured down his ruby-red face and he was heaving for air. Fewer smokes would be my advice, Jack thought, but at that moment he was glad of O'Reilly's habit.

Park Avenue is the widest of all the avenues but Jack didn't need to cross it. Looking up as he ran south along the broad and sparsely populated sidewalk, he could see the massive hulk of the MetLife Building – still known to most locals as Pan Am – straddling the avenue. An entrance to Grand Central Station was there, through the square tunnels of the Helmsley Building and down the escalators. He'd been this way before.

Three city blocks will normally take three minutes to walk briskly, if the lights are favourable. Jack made it in less than half that time, virtually ignoring the traffic as he sprinted over the cross-streets. By the time he hit the escalators down to the main concourse of the terminus, O'Reilly was a good forty yards behind him, still struggling through the brass revolving doors.

Jack sailed down the escalators, three steps at a time, looking for the most crowded part of the station. O'Reilly's lack of height would work to Jack's advantage here. On the main concourse, the Aussie wouldn't be able to see over the heads of the milling crowd. So Jack kept low, moving towards one of the big arches down to his right, following a few would-be passengers also scurrying in that direction. He hoped they were racing to catch a train about to depart. He skidded down the steps at a dangerous clip and found himself approaching open carriages on track 25. Jack didn't care where it was headed, he was going to ride that train. He dived into the first carriage and collapsed on a padded vinyl seat with a good view of the platform.

Time seemed to go on strike. Each second waiting for the train to move felt like a minute. Jack's chest was aching as he fought for air. His trackpants and top were heavy with sweat, turning cold. His face burned. Still the train didn't move, but there was no sign of O'Reilly. The car was nearly half full but nobody paid any attention to Jack. He felt that special invisibility that goes with looking dangerous or unhealthy in the big city.

At last the doors closed with a solid clunk and, with no fanfare or announcement, the train rattled out of Grand Central and under the expensive real estate of Park Avenue. O'Reilly hadn't appeared on the platform and finally Jack's heart began to slow down. He felt a great rush of relief and exhaustion. He still gripped his stolen prize, but didn't yet have the energy to open it. For five minutes he sat there, trying to empty his mind.

He was interrupted only once, to buy a ticket from a conductor who didn't seem phased in the slightest by his appearance. He just took five bucks and gave Jack a torn piece of paper in return. All very normal. To Jack's dismay, the conductor informed him their first stop would be White Plains, thirty minutes away. He'd landed on an express train heading upstate. There was little he could do about it so he went back to his meditation. The gentle, regular bang and rattle of the train helped soothe his jangled nerves.

His recovery from the run was satisfyingly rapid, but he still felt physically fragile and, after a while, he realised that it stemmed from a sick feeling in his stomach – a reaction to anticipated consequences flowing from the morning's events. As soon as O'Reilly made a phone call to his new mate, Daniel Cross, Jack would join the list of Cross's enemies, which was not an ideal list to be on. Even worse, Sutton Brothers could be pressured to do something about him. He'd conveniently given them plenty of grounds, having acted way outside his brief and in a way that reflected very poorly on the firm. Possibly even worse, he'd been observed in the act of stealing mail, which he knew was a big deal in the US. It'd be difficult for him to deny the theft and Stella could hardly be expected to come forward to explain that she'd asked him to do it. He'd thought he was being so clever playing both sides but now he was in deep trouble. For the first time he wondered if he should have stayed a trader.

And all because of this, he mused, contemplating the package in his lap. The fake return address was in a town he'd never heard of, apparently somewhere in Florida. In every other respect the package was innocuous, identical to millions floating around the world every day. Nervously he eased open the flap on the outer packaging. Inside there was another envelope with Stella's distinctively neat handwriting, with a note for her husband to keep the envelope safe until her return. His sense of anticipation rose and the end of the second envelope was quickly torn away. Inside there was a small stack of documents held together by a bulldog clip. Removing the clip, he noted a copy of a formal legal document, presumably the vaunted contract at the heart of the CMS deal, which he put to one side. Then there were several pages setting out the management structure of the company in 1966. These, Jack had seen before, because they were the pages Ben Fisher had coughed up in Peoria. Four pages of Stella's handwritten notes followed, which Jack quickly scanned, but they didn't seem to reveal anything he didn't already know. And finally, on a single page, the real prize – the mystery poem that had caused Stella to run and had caused Daniel Cross to react with such deadly force. This had better be good, Jack thought, as his eyes struggled to make sense of the elegant handwriting, which had not photocopied well.

The Virgin's Secret

The Virgin's purse a secret hides
riveted by her metal sides.
Her drawers reveal a hidden box
four by two the key unlocks

A past of death and murder vile,
Oh Danny Boy, all style and guile.
The Virgin, innocent and serene
bore witness to the awful scene.

Thus in her heart you'll find the truth,
don't forget to check the roof.
A lesson learned, amid the gloss,
death stalks the man who crosses Cross.

If I fail to make it home,
don't hesitate, pick up the phone.
Choose your allies carefully,
solve the puzzle, use the key.

The Virgin's path will lead you there,
down curving hall and sloping stair.
Truth and justice will be your gain
or else my death will be in vain.

I love you truly, Beth, you know,
so for my sake take care, go slow,
tho' your loving arms I can't replace,
The Virgin may have my last embrace.

8 December 1967

Jack read the poem through several times, hoping to see more than first appeared. Christ, he thought, is this really what the fuss is all about? No question the words were intriguing, conjuring up images of a young virgin with metal sides – a wheelchair perhaps? – with a secret hidden in her handbag. But could this really be the impetus behind the deaths in Chicago? And was it really worth the destruction of two great careers? What the hell had he done?

At the bottom of the photocopied page, there was an address, and Jack could see that Stella had also copied the envelope that matched the personalised stationery. Both the handwritten page, and the envelope it was found in, fit on one sheet of copy paper. The notepaper was imprinted with the name Campbell Reeves in the top right-hand corner. The envelope, unstamped, was addressed to Elizabeth Reeves at an address in Peoria. The Beth in the poem was presumably the wife of Campbell, the poem's author. And Campbell's name was highlighted on the organisational charts in the other papers. In 1966, at least, he had been Senior Vice President Finance at CMS, reporting directly to the then President of the company, Gilbert Collins.

The author of the poem was a company insider, not the crank peacenik Daniel Cross had suggested on Wednesday. Jack took some consolation from that fact but he felt a sudden anger with Stella for the way she'd handled her accidental discovery. Why hadn't she just quietly taken a copy of the poem and returned the file? Then she'd have had time to work on it in the comfort and safety of her office in New York and Jack's future wouldn't be in jeopardy. And Harding Collins and Maria Petrillo might still be alive. And even if she could decipher the message in the cryptic verse, how could she know the promised prize would be worth the lives and livelihood of innocent bystanders?

Although she couldn't have anticipated the violent response from Cross and his thugs, she could certainly have been more discreet. And now it seemed the only way to stop Cross was to find the elusive evidence alluded to in a love poem penned almost thirty-five years ago, when Jack was still a baby. What were the odds it was still in the virgin's purse, whatever and wherever the hell that was? As gamblers go, Dave O'Reilly was emerging as the more reasonable risk-taker in the family. And like an inexperienced rube at the roulette table, who'd put all his chips down with the ball already bouncing around the wheel, Jack's fate was also sealed. He'd placed his bet and would have to live with the consequences. His skull started to pound.

He rolled his head sleepily to one side, letting his forehead rest on the window, and watched Harlem, then the Bronx, then the northern suburbs of the great city roll past. More and more vegetation entered the picture as the train rumbled north. His unfocused observations picked up the occasional point of interest, like an abandoned car or some bright graffiti, but mostly it was a blur of tenement roofs, gloomy streets and tired billboards.

By the time the train stopped in White Plains he felt the weight of the world leaning on him. He'd spent the previous night on the sofa, something he'd never done before. He'd never had a clash like that with Peta, not something serious enough to necessitate separate sleeping arrangements, but after an hour or two in his armchair, contemplating the mess his life had suddenly become, Jack couldn't face her, asleep or awake, so he'd decided to try the couch.

He'd been very tired, but not tired enough to overcome his discomfort or the machinations of his mind. He'd managed barely an hour or two of snooze before light streaming in through the big front window had rendered any further attempt useless. He'd snuck into the bedroom and gathered up his exercise gear, not bothering with a shower or shave, before taking off early for his stakeout. The two hours before his run over to 49th Street had been spent in the familiar territory around his home. He'd perused bookshops, called in sick to the office and sucked down several coffees to inject some life back into his system.

Now it was just past noon, and he was in White Plains, New York, shivering in clammy sports gear, with a headache the size of a small moon and all the energy of a sea slug. Rather than turn around and head back to the city, Jack sought out the nearest drugstore, where he purchased shaving gear, deodorant and painkillers. Then he checked into the nearest motel. He paid cash at the drugstore and used a credit card at the motel, and both clerks serving him reacted with a mix of trepidation and revulsion. When he got into the motel room and in front of a mirror, Jack could see why. His unshaven face was grey and his eyes sunken. Dark rings around his eyes made him look like a junkie and his unkempt hair was plastered with sweat and grease. His trackpants and top were crumpled and stained and starting to stink, while his left hamstring was aching from the run, giving him a strange limp. He was a mess.

He took out his cell phone from the backpack. He knew he should call Frank Spiteri but couldn't face the conversation. He realised it wouldn't be long before Daniel Cross was on the line to Spiteri, screaming accusations about yet another fugitive felon from Sutton Brothers. Spiteri would be livid but Jack didn't have anything to say that would make it better. He couldn't even share 'The Virgin's Secret' with him; Stella had laboured that point. It was hard to see how it would help. He turned off his cell phone, rationalising that he needed to save battery life but feeling a strong twinge of disloyalty. He recalled Jodie Michelson's prophetic words in Peoria – the record for the shortest M&A career in the history of corporate takeovers was his for the taking. From star employee to outcast thief in less than one working week.

He was depressed and hungry. For the promise of a generous tip, he persuaded someone at the motel front desk to get him some food. He was hoping for something hot and nutritious but the guy came back with lukewarm McDonalds. Lukewarm or not, the burger and fries were gone in a flash. A long shower and a shave followed and, to his great relief, the water pressure and temperature were good. He put his damp clothes in front of the heater to dry and then crawled naked into the double bed and was asleep in seconds.

Four hours later he woke feeling better. His leg still ached and his clothes were even smellier but a little deodorant sprayed here and there made the odour less offensive, if no less powerful. His mind was much clearer after some decent sleep, but he was still reaching the same conclusion he had come to on the train. The die was cast. Whether Stella had been right in the choices she'd made no longer mattered. By his actions, he had hitched his fate to hers.

He had planned, after his mail theft, to go straight home to wait for her call but now he thought it unwise. It wouldn't be difficult for Spiteri or Cross to find him there. Turning on his cell phone with some dread, he discovered there were four messages. The first was from Spiteri, but to Jack's relief it was just a well-wishing call, hoping he was feeling better. One message from Matt McCormick with a query about a client's portfolio, and one was from the bored voice at the IT help desk, saying that the information Jack had requested was being forwarded via email. The final message was a few concerned words from Stella, wondering how things had gone that morning and suggesting he make contact with Alex Trainer, the attorney. He felt guilty about that one but part of him felt she deserved to share some of his ill feeling after what she had started. Hopefully she'd call again soon and he would give her the news. He gave himself a mental kick in the pants for not thinking of the attorney sooner. With Dave's package in Jack's hands, Cross would almost certainly go after the only other source.

To save battery power he used the motel's phone to call the offices of Bloch and Lieberman, his heart in his throat, and was relieved to find Alex Trainer safe and sound with Stella's parcel securely in his possession.

'In the partners' safe already,' Trainer said, sounding pleased with himself, 'as per instructions. Stella said you might get in touch. Are you able to tell me what this is all about, Mr Rogers?'

'I can try,' Jack said, 'but it's a little complicated. I just wanted to be sure you were okay.'

'Of course I am. I'm on the twenty-fifth floor of a busy office building. We have very good security here.'

'Not good enough to stop a break-in, I hear,' Jack said.

'Well, no, but we've asked for things to be tightened up. I can assure you, Mr Rogers, the documents are safely locked away.'

'Call me Jack, okay? It's 4.40 now, and it will take me a little while to get in to the city. Can you wait for me to get there? I'll fill you in as much as I can, and we can decide what to do next.'

'Of course I'll wait,' the attorney said. 'I'm eager to learn more about this mystery. If you arrive after office hours, just check in at the security desk in the lobby of the building. I'll let them know I'm expecting a client.'

'Please stay in your office, Alex, until I get there. There may be some guys in town who will try anything to get to Stella's package.'

'I'm not going anywhere,' Trainer said. 'I look forward to seeing you soon.'

When Jack dropped off the room key, the clerk at reception gave him a knowing smirk, as if he knew exactly why Jack had paid for a night but was leaving after only a few hours. Leaving the man to his imagination, Jack returned to the station. The next available train into New York was a local so it was a slower journey back to the city. At Grand Central Jack made his way outside as quickly as he could, keeping one eye out for O'Reilly or anyone else suspicious. It was a short walk to the Bank of America Building on Madison Avenue, and he presented himself to the security guard in the foyer just after 6.20 p.m. Outside, it was already dark, but the reddish hues of the marble interior were warm and well lit. When he told the guard he was here for a meeting with Alex Trainer, the man looked confused.

'He didn't call down to tell you he was expecting someone?' Jack asked.

'Yessir, he did, but his clients went up there already 'bout thirty minutes ago.' The security guard pointed vaguely up the big central atrium forming the core of the building. 'You going to the same meeting? 'Cause they haven't come down yet.'

'I'm not sure,' Jack said slowly, warning bells ringing in his head. 'What did they look like, the other clients?'

'There were two guys. Big guys, too. Dressed a bit like you.'

Jack had forgotten his own shabby appearance. A sweat-stained tracksuit just didn't command as much authority as a Valentino single-breasted.

'One guy had red hair. Looked like a pro footballer,' the guard continued. 'You guys doin' a deal for some local team? Is it the Jets?'

Hollis, Jack thought immediately. Or was it Hoyle? He couldn't remember and didn't care. His mind raced. Could it be somebody else? Two big Polish guys looking for a visa? Maybe, but what if it wasn't? How the hell do you deal with two mindless thugs who are probably armed and certainly very dangerous when all you have in your possession are some documents you don't want them to find and some useless toiletries?

Jack looked over at the security guard who was smiling and still yabbering on about football or something, probably glad of the company. He was a middle-aged, greying-at-the-temples African-American whose name, according to his badge, was Stan. Stan was about six inches shorter than Jack and at least twenty-five years older. He was thick around the middle, flabby and wrinkled in the face. He looked about six months away from retirement. But as far as Jack was concerned, Stan had one important thing going for him. He had a gun.

27

'You any good with that thing, Stan?' Jack asked, indicating the pistol on the guard's belt.

'Sure, I'm okay with it.' Stan gave the holster a friendly tap, amiably unaware of any danger. 'I was top marksman in my squad in 'Nam, but I was shootin' an M16 back then.'

And it was also a hell of a long time ago, Jack thought.

'We only put these on after 9/11. Some of us didn't even have an up-to-date licence, but I go out to the range every year a couple times. I ain't bad for an old fat guy.' A happy chortle burbled up from deep in his barrel chest. 'Now, you want I should ring Mr Trainer, tell him you're here?' His hand reached for a phone behind the high desk.

'Yes, please,' Jack said, 'but before you do I want to tell you a little story.'

Stan withdrew his hand and gave Jack an untroubled smile. 'Sure thing. I like a good story.' He relaxed, leaning on the countertop, arms folded, waiting. He thought Jack was going to tell him a joke.

'First, I have a couple of questions,' Jack said, 'like names. Did the two guys give you their names?'

Stan looked confused at first, disappointed this wasn't to be a gag, but then he caught on. 'Sure, everybody got to give a name.' He consulted his register. 'Whaddayaknow,' he said, eyebrows raised. 'They both signed A. Smith. They sure didn't look like no brothers to me.'

'And the big one was pale, freckles, short red hair, like a marine?'

'And a tattoo —'

'— on his left forearm,' Jack finished.

'So you know the Smith boys, then?' Stan looked pleased.

'And the smaller one?'

'About your size,' he said, 'maybe a bit bigger.'

'Dark hair, down his neck.'

'And his nose is all over the place. Like he tried hitting on Mike Tyson's girlfriend or sommit.' Stan was grinning.

'These are bad men,' Jack said, trying not to sound too melodramatic. 'These are killers, Stan. Alex Trainer could be in a lot of trouble up there.'

Stan's smile turned into a puzzled frown. 'What you say?'

'Their names are Hollis and Hoyle.' Jack knew he had to be quick. 'They come from Peoria, Illinois, and they're here to steal some important documents from Alex Trainer. It's why I'm here. Alex and I were going to work out a plan to protect the documents from these guys.'

Stan didn't look convinced. 'Look,' Jack said, 'I know it sounds weird but it's a long story and we need to act fast. If I'm right, they're already up there, holding Alex until the place empties out. They'll hurt him. They could even kill him if he doesn't give them what they want. They might do it anyway. They've done it before.'

'That office would be empty already,' Stan said carefully, trying to size Jack up as either a real problem or a lunatic distraction. 'They go home early on Fridays, 'specially with the days gettin' shorter. They mostly Jews in that firm, they gotta get home before sundown, y'know.'

'All the more reason to act fast.'

'How do I know you ain't pullin' my leg?' The security guard was suspicious. 'I don't want no part of no silly-assed stunt. I don't even know you.'

'Look,' Jack said, his frustration beginning to show. 'My name is Jack Rogers. I'm a banker on Wall Street and Alex is helping me with a very sensitive matter. There are some bad people trying to stop us —'

'You're a Wall Street banker? Sure y'are!' Stan was looking Jack up and down and recoiling from the strong odour of cheap deodorant mixed with dried sweat. Jack was losing him. He fumbled around in his bag to find his wallet, and slapped a business card down on the counter. Stan still didn't look convinced. He rubbed the embossed business card, probably thinking how easily it could be faked or stolen.

Jack groaned with annoyance. 'At least try to call him,' he said, reaching into his bag for some photo ID. 'Alex Trainer, I mean. Please!'

'No problem,' Stan assumed a more professional and distant manner. 'I recall offerin' to do that right at the start.'

Jack watched as the call was placed but, as he feared, there was no answer. Stan left a message telling Trainer he had another client waiting downstairs and asking him to call the security desk. 'Maybe he's on the phone,' he said as he hung up.

'Maybe he's been hogtied and beaten up.'

Stan gave Jack a stern, paternal look. 'Sounds to me like you need the cops.' He said it as if he wasn't sure whether the police were needed to assist Jack or take him away.

'Maybe I do,' Jack said, bouncing up and down on the spot in frustration, like a kid with an overfull bladder. 'But it would take too long to explain to them and we need to do something right now. At least to slow them down, make sure Alex is still okay. We need to go take a look, Stan.'

Jack didn't really relish the idea of confronting Hollis and Hoyle. But he hoped, with Stan backing him up, he could scare them off by making his presence known, just as Ben had done in Peoria. If skinny Ben could get them to back down, then surely Jack and Stan could do the same.

The ageing security guard finally agreed to go take a look, but only after Jack told him there was a direct link to the fire in the office tower earlier that week. That got the man's attention, but Jack knew they'd already wasted valuable minutes. Stan picked up his white phone and called a colleague called Rita. A sturdy-looking Hispanic woman in her late thirties soon appeared, wearing the same blue cop-like uniform Stan was squeezed into. It was tight, like Stan's, but in very different places. She was carrying a paper bag holding a steaming drink or soup.

Stan explained that he had to escort Jack upstairs to Bloch and Lieberman. Rita asked no questions and settled her broad beam comfortably on the stool behind the counter. Jack took the pack from his back, took out his cell phone – the only tool he could see a possible use for – and passed the rest to Rita. He wasn't going to risk losing the package he'd worked so hard for. 'If we're not back in thirty minutes, call the cops, and give them that,' he said to her, and she responded with a look of surprise before turning to Stan for confirmation.

Stan just shrugged his big shoulders – in the affirmative, Jack hoped – and led the way up two flights of escalators from the main lobby to a mezzanine where banks of elevators offered a ride to different levels of the building. Jack was led through an opening marked

246

'21–30' and Stan waved an electronic key and pushed the button for the twenty-fourth floor. Nervous tension gripped Jack's body again. By contrast, Stan looked positively bored.

'They could be armed, you know,' Jack said, hoping to stoke the embers of a fire in Stan's belly. The guard gave him an annoyed look but unclipped the leather strap holding his pistol in its holster.

When the doors opened, there was a short corridor running left, alongside the clear glass of the central atrium, to a wide reception area. In contrast to the modern feel of the building, the furniture was decidedly Victorian. Some fuddy-duddy in the firm had resisted the wave of modernism by using woods, colours and fabrics that belonged in a nineteenth-century setting. Looking out across and beyond the wide, square atrium, Jack could see into many of the offices and work areas of the firm, both on this level and the one above. The space was still brightly lit, awaiting the cleaners. Pure modern decor out there, Jack noted; only the public areas suffered from an identity crisis.

As Stan had predicted, the place was devoid of people. Jack could see unoccupied rooms and passageways piled with papers and spotted here and there with office technology and potted plants. To the right of the reception desk a large, thick glass door led directly to the open-plan work areas, which were separated by rows of modest offices. It was pretty similar to Jack's new floor at Sutton Brothers. On the other side of the reception desk there was a long hallway stretching in both directions, leading to rows of wood-panelled meeting rooms – also projecting the time of Teddy Roosevelt, just like the reception area. All the rooms were empty, their doors standing open, ready for another deal on Monday morning. One was closed due to fire damage. Stan pointed out some other damage in the reception area and Jack marvelled at how much they'd managed to conceal in a few days with some replacement furniture, fresh paint and carpet.

'Do you know where Alex Trainer's new office is, Stan?'

'Nope, no idea. Don't normally go in there.' He pointed to the glass door leading to the working heart of the firm.

'Did you take a tour of the fire damage this week?'

'Yep, came through Tuesday.'

'One of the offices hit was Trainer's.'

'Izzat so? Well, then most likely it's upstairs. Most of the damage was done on twenty-five.'

'How do we get there?'

'Take the elevator or use the stairs. They have a staircase between the floors. Over in that direction.' Stan pointed towards the south-west corner of the building.

'Do you have a pass to go through here?' Jack asked, standing close to the glass door leading to the interior.

The security guard came closer. 'I think I do,' he said, but when he pushed against the door, he found it was already swinging freely. 'Huh. That's not right. Somebody musta jammed the lock open. There's usually a button under the reception counter but it shoulda been turned off.'

He made a move towards the counter but Jack stopped him. 'I don't really care how they got in, Stan, but we need to scare them off. We need to make some noise.'

'Ha!' Stan said dismissively. 'This door being open don't mean nothin'. Happens all the time. Some kid forgets his pass so he sticks some tape over the button or sommit.'

'Stan, have you been listening to me? There are some dangerous men in here and we have to make some threatening noises, get them to run. We can't confront them – they're too dangerous for that, you understand? But we must try to flush them out, force them to back away from Trainer.'

Jack was peering through the glass into those offices he could see, looking for some sign of Hollis and Hoyle. The floors were large. Between the central atrium and the outer windows on each level, the building was deep enough for two large open-plan work areas, surrounded by rows of offices. Each side of the building was long enough for three of these work areas, all identical. It was a maze of pale grey partition and glass walls, with few landmarks for reference.

Stan still wasn't moving. 'I dunno,' he said. 'Everything looks okay from here.'

He shuffled about on the spot and Jack was beginning to think he'd have to do this on his own. 'Look at it this way, Stan,' he suggested. 'If I'm right and Trainer's being threatened or hurt by these guys, it's going to look real bad if we just walk away, isn't it? You could be a hero, Stan, if we save him.'

'Don't wanna be no hero,' Stan mumbled.

'If I'm wrong,' Jack persisted, 'what harm have we done? So we find Alex in a friendly meeting, sipping coffee. I'm a little embarrassed and you've brought Alex his next client, safe and sound. There's no downside, you see?'

'You said they was dangerous.'

'We just scare them off, from a distance. Make noise, call out to Alex, that sort of thing. If they come at us, we duck and run.' Jack wasn't too convinced about this part.

'We could use the PA system,' Stan offered.

'Can you work it?'

'Sure!' He gave Jack a frown. 'I have to know this stuff.'

Stan moved behind the reception desk, looking for the right switches and knobs. Normally the system was used to call employees to the phone or to reception, but it seemed a perfect tool to send Hollis and Hoyle a back-off message. Stan picked up the microphone that stood on the counter. He cranked up the volume and, when he pressed the button to speak, a loud click and buzz could be heard from the speakers located in the ceiling panels around the firm.

'This is building security.'

He has a real radio voice, Jack thought, deep like James Earl Jones, and perfect for the part.

'Mr Alex Trainer, please contact building security on extension triple one or contact one of the officers coming through the floor. That's Mr Alex Trainer of Bloch and Lieberman. Mr Trainer, you are needed urgently.'

There was another loud click as Stan disconnected. He looked over to Jack with raised eyebrows.

'Perfect,' Jack said, 'let's hope that does the trick. How will we know if we've succeeded?'

Stan unhooked a walkie-talkie from his belt and connected with Rita down in the front lobby. He asked her to buzz back as soon as two guys matching the description of the men from Peoria left the building or if she received a call from Alex Trainer. Then he looked at Jack. 'What next?'

'Let's stay out of sight, away from the reception area or the elevators.'

'Okay.'

They went though the open glass door into the first work area and found a small meeting room on the far side of the atrium with a good view back to the elevator lobby. On the way, Stan saw a shadow moving past the windows on the floor above so they kept low and moved quietly into position. Then they sat there, like two ornithologists in a hide waiting for the first glimpse of some rare species.

And then nothing happened. They waited ten minutes, though it felt much longer, but there was no sign of escaping felons and no call from Rita. Apparently the plan hadn't worked. The look on Stan's face said Jack's credibility was in doubt again. Before he could say anything, Jack raised a hand to deter him. 'I know what you're going to say but I swear I'm on the level. Are you sure there's no other way out of here?'

'Everything's locked down. If they broke out it would show up on Rita's screen.'

'So they're still here,' Jack said. 'Or maybe they made it into one of the fire escapes or something. Either way, we're going to have to go out there. Alex may need help or medical attention.'

Stan looked glum but he nodded in agreement. Jack pointed at the holstered gun again and said, 'I really think you should take that out.'

'Man, if I had me a dime for every time I heard that!' Stan chuckled to himself.

'I meant the gun.'

'I know, son, I know, but it won't do you no good losin' your sense o' humour, now will it?'

Jack was bubbling with frustration but forced himself to calm down. 'You're right, I'm sorry.'

'S'okay, s'all right. I can see you're real upset. That makes me believe you. You wouldn't be this uptight if these two guys were a coupla pranksters, now would you?'

'Absolutely not!' Jack sounded a little defensive.

'All right then, you get behind me.'

Stan moved into a low, hunched walk, like he was back in the jungles of Vietnam. His belly was almost resting on his knees. He pulled the pistol from its holster with his right hand, flicked the safety catch, and held the gun loose, hanging straight down as he loped forward between the rows of workstations and offices. Jack padded behind him on the soft carpet, keeping his head at the same height as the guard's – a more pronounced crouch for him. Stan made straight for the internal staircase up to level twenty-five and Jack was very glad of his presence. He seemed to know what to do, even if he wasn't quite the physical specimen he'd once been.

'If anything happens,' Stan whispered as they rounded the landing at the top of the stairs, 'you drop to the floor, flat as you can, you understan'?'

'Got it. You think we should make some more noise?'

'No, you shut the heck up, okay, Jack? That plan didn't work already.'

'Fair enough.'

Stan flashed a quick, reassuring smile. They made their way along yet another panelled wall and around another corner identical to the last. Crouched down, Jack lost his bearings entirely. He just had to hope Stan's knowledge of the building would give them the edge.

They meandered on, crab-like, between walls, around blind corners and large potted plants. In Jack's hypersensitive state, the hum of office equipment seemed loud and intrusive. Then, from the corner of his eye, he saw a shadow scurry across the ceiling, as if someone had just walked past a low desk lamp. It was off to the right, only about thirty feet away.

Jack's pulse leapt up a gear or three. He reached out to warn Stan but then noticed the security guard was already rigid and staring straight ahead. Jack followed the gaze along the short passageway ahead of them to a small meeting room, with the door shut and slim venetian blinds closed over the windows.

In the near silence of the empty office space, Jack thought he heard a man groaning and then, very distinctly, a slap. Skin against skin. The hair on the back of his neck stood to attention and he instinctively straightened up as he realised they'd found Alex Trainer, and he wasn't alone.

Then all hell broke loose.

'Well, what the fuck we got here?'

It came from behind them. A rough, menacing voice, echoing loudly around the vacant workplace.

Jack acted immediately, just as Stan had instructed, and threw himself to the floor. As he went down, he twisted his head and caught a glimpse of the dark-haired thug only fifteen feet away. To Jack's horror, the man's extended right arm was moving down, following his progress to the carpet. In his fist, a big black gun was pointed directly at Jack's head. In that split second, Jack watched the killer's eyes, focusing first on him and then on Stan, who became a large, easy target as soon as Jack dropped flat.

The security guard was turning around, attempting to point his pistol the right way, and as soon as his weapon came into view Jack ceased to be the main focus of attention. The muzzle of the big black gun swung up and away and then exploded with a deafening roar.

Stan was hit on the left side, spinning him around. Hot blood spattered Jack's hair and the back of his neck. As Stan fell down on top of Jack, the guard's momentum lifted his pistol arm up and, with his last moment of consciousness, the old veteran pulled the trigger. Jack was stunned by the loud blast so close to his ear, and was completely winded as his partner's considerable bulk landed on his back.

But all the time, with his face pressed to the carpet, Jack was watching their attacker as he rebalanced himself from the recoil of his own shot. At that instant, the bulbous broken nose that so identified the man seemed to collapse inward and a fine red spray burst from the back of his skull. His body fell in a heap on the carpet. One moment this was a living, breathing, threatening human being and the next he was just so much dead meat piled up on the floor. The suddenness of it gripped Jack with horror and amazement.

He was still alert enough to realise that Stan's incredible shot had solved only half the problem. The other one – Hollis or Hoyle – was either in the meeting room at the end of the hall or already on his way to investigate the shots. Jack was still deafened by the exchange of gunfire and he couldn't see back over Stan's body, half-draped over him. The valiant security guard was still alive – his ragged breathing was evidence of that – but Jack had no time to tend to him.

Stan's pistol had fallen to the carpet, right in front of Jack's face. Almost before it stopped bouncing, he reached out his left hand and grabbed it. The gun was hot and heavy and greasy with oil. It was the first time he'd ever held a gun – and he only had a couple of seconds to get familiar with it before he'd have to convince an experienced criminal he knew just how to use it.

With a grunt and a heave, and a mumbled apology to the unconscious man, Jack pulled himself out from under Stan's bleeding body. As he rose up, he turned to face the door to the room where Trainer was being held, swapping the gun to his right hand, where it felt a little less heavy, but just as unfamiliar.

His breath caught in his throat. The door was open, the doorway filled with the huge mass of the redhead. If he'd been carrying a gun, Jack would be dead already, but his weapon of choice was a knife – long, lethal-looking and stained red.

The redhead was obviously at a loss without his partner. His eyes darted repeatedly between Jack and his dead friend, whose misshapen head on its twisted neck was fast developing a deep red halo on the pale carpet. He seemed as shocked by the sudden turn of events as Jack was. Raising the pistol up in his right hand, Jack gripped it with the other hand, mimicking the stance he'd seen on TV cop shows. He pointed it at the broad chest of the redhead – where he felt he had the best chance of actually hitting the guy.

Jack was determined to shoot if he had to, and he hoped the determination showed, because he didn't really want to kill anyone, not even a thug like this. For a second, the big man looked as if he was going to charge, as his face turned from shock to horror, and then anger lit up his beady eyes. The man was built like a tank and a flash of uncertainty zinged across Jack's mind as he pictured his bullets bouncing aside harmlessly.

Fortunately the redhead wasn't so confident. More frightened of the gun than the man holding it, he backed away into the room where Jack could make out the figure of a slender man slumped in a chair. Moving faster, the redhead turned and darted through the room and out a door on the other side. Now it was clear to Jack that this meeting room was accessible from two sides and, from the work area on the other side, he soon heard the thump, thump, thump of heavy footsteps as the man ran away.

Only then did Jack fully register the pool of gore he was standing in and the sickly sweet smell of blood. He stepped aside, swallowing his revulsion, and stood still, dazed for a moment, trying to gather his faculties. The whole battle, from discovery by the dark-haired guy to the flight of the redhead, had taken only a few seconds. Two bodies lay on the carpet; another was strapped to a chair with duct tape. Jack stood with a smoking gun – literally smoking – in his hands. He let the pistol drop to the floor. He was looking around for a telephone when he heard the walkie-talkie on Stan's hip squawk to life with Rita's excited voice reporting the departure of the redhead. Jack grabbed the blood-soaked device and screamed at her to call for the cops and an ambulance.

Stan was still unconscious and breathing loudly with a nasty-sounding rattle. Jack hastened to check on Alex Trainer in the meeting room that had become a makeshift interrogation and torture chamber. He found the lawyer alive but in bad shape. He was attached to a simple office chair with loops of tape around his torso, his arms taped to the arms of the chair. Duct tape had also been used to secure his legs by his ankles to the table in front of him, so they were spread in an uncomfortable and completely exposed fashion. His trousers and underwear had been cut away in slices by a sharp instrument and Jack could see several gashes on Trainer's legs where his torturers had been clumsy. His underpants had been stuffed in his mouth, and Jack quickly pulled the tattered, bloodstained material away to allow the unconscious man more air. Fortunately, they'd had no time to do more than threaten the mutilation of the attorney's genitals before they were interrupted. His face was in far worse shape, with one eye swollen shut, his mouth torn and bleeding.

There was more evidence of the brutal beating around the room. Splatters of blood formed a ring around the base of the chair. And there, on the floor, Jack saw something that made him wish he'd shot the redhead when he had the chance. It was a finger. Trainer's index finger from his right hand. When Jack examined the damage to the lawyer's hand, he could see a second finger was cut almost through to the bone.

That did it for Jack. His lunch of burger and fries was soon hurled into the nearest wastepaper basket and he sat on the floor in a cold sweat, concentrating hard to stop the retching and willing the paramedics to arrive soon. Even the faces of the first police officers to arrive on the scene turned decidedly green as they worked to free Alex Trainer from his sticky cocoon.

Stan hadn't moved, but Jack could still hear his breathing, and Rita had come up to sit with her colleague, holding his hand and talking quietly to him. Jack prayed to whoever would listen for the safe recovery of these two men. More innocent bystanders, just trying to do their jobs, whose lives had been horribly impacted by the violent power of one man. The virgin's fucking secret better turn out to be spectacular, he thought.

He spent more than two hours with the police, who treated him with politeness and respect despite his sorry appearance and strange story. Given that he was the only conscious person at the scene and looked like an abattoir worker out for a jog, he thought he was dealt with fairly. The questions were blunt, frequently repeated and numerous, but he received no abuse, no sneers or rolled eyes at his answers. They made notes, two of them, neither in uniform. They didn't even bat an eyelid when he told them his Daniel Cross theory and filled them in on all the drama of an eventful week.

He answered their questions completely and honestly. It seemed the only logical approach. Now there was some clear evidence of criminal activity, hopefully the cops could link it back to Cross. Maybe that would stop Cross, without the need to solve 'The Virgin's Secret'. He even encouraged the two detectives to contact their colleagues in Chicago and look deeper into the deaths of Harding Collins and Maria Petrillo.

When they were done with their questions, they told him to wait, and a concerned paramedic took the opportunity to look him over and clean most of the gore and vomit from his skin. Stan and Alex Trainer were long gone to the hospital; Trainer's finger had left with them. It had been an extraordinary day and Jack felt an overwhelming longing to tell Stella all about it – the burden seemed too much to carry alone.

Eventually the cops came back and said his version of the story was, so far, borne out by the physical evidence and their conversation with Rita. However, both the nature of the crime and the conspiracy theory Jack had offered up meant they'd need a more thorough statement. To Jack's great relief, the older cop – Robertson – said it could wait. An officer would come by to collect Jack at ten the following morning. A cop would also drive him home if he was ready. Man, Jack thought, am I ready.

Out on Madison Avenue, cars were inching past the group of flashing police cruisers double-parked in front of the building. A young uniformed cop named Thompson escorted Jack to a blue and white vehicle and invited him to sit in front. Jack was in no mood to chat, and Officer Thompson didn't push it as they pulled away from the kerb and out into the sparse night traffic. It was after ten. Peta would be wondering where he was. She'd think he hadn't called because of the blow-up last night.

He looked in the pockets of his trackpants for his cell phone, but it wasn't there. He searched the backpack he'd retrieved from Rita, but he knew already he wasn't going to find it. He'd taken it upstairs in his pocket. It must still be there somewhere. He couldn't believe it. Apart from anything else, it was the only way Stella knew how to reach him!

He sat in sullen, frustrated silence in the darkness of the police car, kicking himself and watching the homeless get settled for the night as the car moved west along one of the streets in the upper forties, before turning onto 7th Avenue. They passed through the sparkling lights of Times Square where hordes of tourists still milled about, waiting for something to happen. Pushing through an undisciplined swarm of yellow taxi cabs, Officer Thompson edged the cruiser south towards Greenwich Village. The cross-streets grew darker and narrower as they travelled downtown and away from the theatre district.

As they crossed Greenwich Avenue, just a few blocks from his home, Jack felt his usual warm anticipation of coming home being insidiously supplanted by a stomach-churning feeling of dread. Something felt terribly wrong. Even before they reached the turn into 4th Street, his radar was screaming danger. As Officer Thompson completed the turn, blue and red flashing lights reflected back from dark windows further down the street. Noises and sights and smells unlike any Jack had experienced overwhelmed his senses. The street was blocked with emergency vehicles of all kinds. Water and steam were forming a dense tropical storm front over his street. And his home, his treasured safe haven in this crazy city, was burning.

28

The sheer horror of the scene seemed to suck Jack towards it, as if gravity was operating horizontally. His forehead was pressed against the windshield of the police car, his knuckles forming a line of white ridges as he gripped the dashboard tight to stop himself from falling into the pit. His mouth hung open and slack. His eyes, filling with tears of helplessness, were wide and unblinking.

Thompson said something but Jack wasn't listening. All he could hear was a strange whooshing sound filling his ears. It might have been the whirlwinds of water, smoke and fire or it might just have been in his head, he couldn't tell. It felt as if someone had reached into his skull and removed his brain, replacing it with cotton wool. Not a single cohesive thought was being generated in his cerebellum, which had already been close to overload.

Through the fog of sound, a voice emerged, slowly getting stronger and clearer, rising in volume until it became a scream. Repeating, repeating, repeating a single word – 'Peta!' It was Jack's voice.

'Who's Peter?' Officer Thompson was shaking him.

Jack's mind slipped back into first gear. The cruiser was stopped

259

short of the crowd of onlookers and the line of emergency vehicles and was still half a block from his home.

'Why the fuck have we stopped?' he screamed. 'My house is on fire. My partner's inside.'

'Shit!'

Thompson turned on the siren and lights atop his car. Like magic, the knot of rubberneckers in front of them parted and the car shot forward, pulling in behind a massive red and chrome fire truck that filled the narrow street. Jack was out of the vehicle before it had stopped, ignoring Thompson's shouting, drawn in disbelief by the sight of everything that defined him going up in flames.

A bright white fireball, almost too bright to look at, was eating his house from the inside out, starting upstairs in his den. Even from down on the street, the intense heat was searing and Jack thought he could see the steel frame of the French window twisting and melting away. A man in firefighter's black and yellow rubber pulled him back from the building by his shoulders. Even so, his eyebrows were singed. Officer Thompson appeared and led him to a safer position, next to another fire truck. Only then did Jack register the frantic activity going on around him. Men and equipment were being hurled into action. One man seemed to be in charge and Thompson was briefing him.

'You think your partner's inside?' the firefighter shouted over the din of calamity.

Jack nodded, not prepared to speak.

'It's too intense to send my men in,' he said. 'As soon as we get it under control, I'll send a team in. I'm sorry,' he added, almost as an afterthought.

'What about the neighbours?' Jack asked.

'What? Louder!'

Thompson shouted, 'He said, what about the neighbours?'

'We think they're all out,' the fireman said, pointing to a small group of observers on the sidewalk about fifty yards away. 'Anyway, it's a good solid structure – it's well contained.'

Jack could see he was right. The neighbouring brownstones didn't seem at all threatened by the flames. Even the roof garden seemed okay, flooded as it was by water from high-powered hoses. The fire was eating into the fabric of his home, not trying to escape it. Part of the floor in the den collapsed and flames spread downstairs, but they seemed almost timid, compared to the intensity of heat and destruction upstairs. The shrubs in the window box were smoking twigs, and a roar like a jet engine accompanied the firestorm on the upper level.

Anyone observing Jack – standing in the street dressed in blood-stained and filthy clothes, drenched by the fine mist of spray from fire hoses and totally bewildered by the events of the past few days – saw a man stripped of all his armour, physical and mental. He'd been so very wrong. About everything. Fine suits and platinum credit cards couldn't protect him from life's cruellest blows. A beautiful, vibrant lover and a stylish home and cash in the bank were not security. They just bred dangerous self-confidence and illusions of invulnerability. And it turned out that the skills Jack prized so much as a successful player in the business world were totally meaningless and completely useless against the fury of violent destruction and death. He was not equipped. He wasn't trained for this.

All he could do, for the forty-five minutes it took for the fire to completely destroy his home, was pray that Peta was safe. He couldn't know for sure she was inside. She had a busy life and could be any-where. Occasionally, he'd scan the crowd, hoping to see a shock of dyed hair pushing through, Peta's face emerging to relieve him of this terrible burden of loss and guilt.

But she didn't come. Part of him knew she wouldn't. They'd

parted unhappily and there was only one place he could imagine she'd be. At home, up there, waiting to mend the fabric of their relationship with the honesty and individuality that made her so special. He looked up at the blazing wreck and focused all his will on her survival, wherever she was. People tried to speak to him, first Thompson and later Detective Robertson, who'd interviewed him at the last crime scene and had arrived in response to a call from Officer Thompson.

Jack had no idea what they said. He couldn't hear them, and they stopped bothering him, standing back behind him like bodyguards while he waited for the judgement of this fiery god. Would it be life or death?

It was death.

The hungry fireball at the centre of the blaze seemed, for a long time, totally impervious to the thick columns of water pouring into the den. Liquid turned to gas with a roar and steamed in billowing clouds into the cool night sky. The inferno seemed unstoppable. And then, quite suddenly, almost as if a switch had been flicked, the water seemed to win. The fireball turned from intense white and blue to softer yellow and orange and then fizzled out to black, dense, swirling clouds of smoke. The wooden beams and floorboards continued to burn, but small, localised areas of flame were quickly extinguished by the torrent of water flooding the place.

Even before the flames died down, Jack saw a group of firefighters race in through both doors, dressed like astronauts, with breathing apparatus and masks. Eventually they emerged close to the gaping hole in the upper floor and directed the efforts of their colleagues down on the street.

Jack's ears registered the sounds of two-way radio traffic. Maybe they were talking about Peta. He shook his head to restore some function to his brain. The fire chief was back, his ear pressed against his walkie-talkie. His face looked grim. 'They've found a body,' he said.

Thompson was at Jack's side, gripping his left elbow. Detective Robertson shook his head sadly and the fire chief's face said he'd seen it all before. 'It's not possible to make an identification at this time,' he said. 'The body was too badly damaged by the bomb.'

'Bomb? Did you say bomb?'

It was Robertson who spoke. Jack's mind wasn't moving quickly enough to react.

'Sorry, that was premature.' The fire chief held up one hand to calm everybody down. 'I can't say for sure it's a bomb but it sure wasn't no electrical or gas fire. And did you see that fireball? It behaved like an incendiary device. When the fuel ran out, it virtually extinguished itself. Like there was no oxygen left up there.'

He frowned at Jack. 'Either you're into some weird shit, buddy, or you got yourself some serious enemies.'

Detective Robertson was looking at Jack with intense interest. The fire chief turned to him. 'We'll get a complete report together in the next day or so, okay?' And then, turning back to Jack, 'Sorry for your loss, sir.'

Jack watched the firefighter walk away. Obviously experience, like the 9/11 catastrophe, had hardened this man, taught him there was little point in holding out false hopes. And at that moment Jack felt his own hopes begin to fade, to be replaced by a horrible truth: he was responsible for the death of an amazing woman, full of promise and life. The receding back of this anonymous firefighter had extinguished the last dregs of Jack's optimism.

Reality settled on him like a dead weight. His body shut down. He couldn't feel cold or hunger. He couldn't hear the shouts and sirens and he couldn't smell the awful stench of the fire. He couldn't even feel the rage he knew was boiling up within him. Tears rolled down his cheeks but no sound came out of his mouth. Well-meaning officials tried to ease him away from the scene gently, but he was glued to the spot, watching the medical examiner's van arrive. When a body bag was carried out into the street, he stared in mute agony. Only when the van drove silently down the street did he turn away, unable to watch any longer.

Detective Robertson led him to the back seat of an unmarked police car and got in the other side. Jack sat silently while the policeman talked quietly, expressing sympathy and his determination to see whoever was responsible punished. He asked Jack if there was anyone he could call, to come spend some time with him.

The realisation that there was nobody within twenty hours' flying time overwhelmed Jack. Although he was in the middle of Manhattan, he felt like a man alone in the wilderness; like a child deserted by its mother. This wasn't the comfortable isolation borne of self-confident independence, but the terrifying loneliness of abandonment. He tried hard to resist the waves of self-pity washing over him but failed. He began to sob, loudly at first, but then the sobs settled into a sporadic series of wracking, breathless heaves that made his ribs ache.

Robertson didn't seem embarrassed. He put an arm around Jack's shoulders and tried to soothe the pain with a little human warmth. When Jack managed to say he'd like to be alone, the detective nodded grimly and climbed out of the car, leaving Jack in the back seat, crying as he'd never cried before.

He lost track of the time. Robertson pulled open the door and stuck his head in the car. 'I called your boss – I hope you don't mind. You need a familiar face.'

'How did you —?'

'You gave me his details earlier, over at the law firm, remember?'

It seemed such a long time ago.

'Besides,' Robertson went on, 'you said he's wrapped up in your whole conspiracy theory thing, right? If this fire's connected, I think he oughta see it, don't you?'

Spiteri's handsome features appeared over Robertson's shoulder and the detective was right – it was an enormous relief to see a familiar face. It also grounded Jack's emotions a little. In front of Frank he wasn't going to show his vulnerability, so he took a couple of deep breaths, wiped his face and eyes vigorously with his hands and climbed out of the car. Frank's shock at his appearance showed for an instant before he composed his features. He took Jack's hand and held on to it, putting the other hand on his shoulder. 'My God, Jack, were you inside? Are you injured?'

'No, Frank, don't worry. It's not my blood.'

'Detective Robertson says that Peta . . .'

'Yes, they found a body. They haven't identified it yet.'

Jack's eyes searched Spiteri's for some reassurance that a miracle was still possible, but Frank just frowned with concern. 'The detective said it might be a bomb, Jack. You don't think this could have anything to do with —'

'It's Cross, Frank, it has to be.'

'Good God, can you be sure?'

Jack was feeling anger now. 'Yes, I'm sure Frank. Absolutely sure. You have no idea what that bastard is capable of.'

Spiteri glanced nervously at Robertson, who was closely monitoring the conversation. 'Jack, please be reasonable. What evidence do you have? You need something solid to back up an allegation like that before speaking out about it. Remember, I've known Daniel a long time. I can't accept that he's responsible for this.'

'Frank,' Jack said, through gritted teeth, 'all I have is a trail of dead and injured people, all of them caught up in the hunt for Stella and the missing file. All of them completely fucking innocent, I might add. Well, except for one of Cross's henchmen, who was shot dead in a building over on Madison Avenue this evening. I know – I was there. And I personally witnessed another one of Cross's thugs fleeing the scene. A scene of torture, Frank! They cut off a finger. And the man being tortured was Stella's attorney. The guys were the same ones who attacked Stella in Peoria. They work for Cross. How much more of a connection do you need? Wake up, Frank! Your old friend is a fucking killer!'

Spiteri shook his head in disbelief, but Jack could see he was taking in what he said. Frank looked up at the smouldering ruin of Jack's luxury condo. 'And you think he's responsible for this too? Why would he do a thing like that?'

Jack heaved a big sigh. 'Because I stole Stella's second package from Dave O'Reilly.'

Spiteri's eyes were wide. 'That was you? Daniel rang me this afternoon about some guy who'd stolen a package from O'Reilly. He said O'Reilly was sure it was someone from Sutton Brothers. But even if it was, I never thought it would be you, Jack. I thought it had to be one of Stella's team. I never thought you would do something like that without talking to me first.'

'Stella didn't want the package to fall into Cross's hands. And when she found out her husband was working for Cross —'

'How the hell did Stella know that?'

'I told her.'

'You told her? You've been talking to her?'

'Yes.'

'And how did you know?'

'It's a long story, Frank, but it wasn't too hard to work out. I knew Cross bought the first package from her husband.'

'What package? And that doesn't explain —'

'It's complicated, Frank and, quite frankly, you'll forgive me for not giving a flying fuck about any of that right now!'

He threw up his hands to terminate the discussion. He knew Spiteri was dying to learn how he contacted Stella and what had been said, but just thinking about Stella's mess right then was infuriating, and Jack wished with all his heart he'd never heard of her. Curse Stella, he said to himself. Curse strong independent women generally. He slumped back against the hood of the police vehicle, imagining Peta's last few moments.

'That's enough,' Robertson said, intervening. 'We'll pick up the discussion about Daniel Cross and this Stella dame tomorrow. Right now we need to get Jack somewhere warm and friendly.'

'Of course,' Spiteri said, moving forward and putting his arm around Jack. 'What was I thinking? Detective, you leave Jack's welfare to me.'

'I just need to know where he's going to be,' Robertson said, 'And you too, Mr Spiteri. We'll need to talk to both of you tomorrow.' He coughed nervously into a closed fist and looked at Jack. 'And we may need you to identify . . .'

'I understand,' Jack said.

'What about your partner's next of kin?' Robertson asked.

'Peta's parents retired to Florida. I'm not sure I could bear talking to them tonight.'

'Then I suggest we wait until the ID's confirmed. No use upsetting the folks tonight and a few more hours won't make any difference one way or the other.'

Jack nodded gratefully, and Robertson asked where he'd be staying the night. 'He'll be staying with me, Detective,' Spiteri offered. 'You have my address and telephone number.'

'Frank,' Jack said, 'no offence, but I'd rather stay in a hotel if you don't mind. I'm very used to hotels and not very good in other people's homes.'

Spiteri didn't push it. 'Whatever makes you most comfortable,

Jack, of course. I'll stay with you as long as you need me. And the firm will pay for the hotel.'

'I think your insurance company will contribute to that, too,' Robertson said helpfully.

This wasn't the kind of assistance Jack was looking for. The day's events were fast catching up with his body. 'I don't give a shit who pays for it, but I know I need to get cleaned up and sleep as soon as possible, so can we get on with it please?'

'Let me make a coupla calls,' Spiteri said, ever the organiser.

Within the hour, Jack was safely ensconced in a suite at the Millennium Broadway Hotel, just around the corner from the flashing neon of Times Square. A new outfit of casual clothes by Ralph Lauren, in almost the correct size, was delivered to his room as he and Frank arrived and they were whisked upstairs without the bother of a formal check-in procedure. Spiteri poured him a drink from the minibar and had one himself, but after that – and much to Spiteri's frustration – Jack shooed his boss out the door so he could shower. He didn't know if he could sleep but he knew he had to try.

As it turned out, a deep, dreamless, exhausted sleep overtook Jack almost as soon as his head touched the soft cotton of the pillow. His body had decided for him – the only way to deal with all the new horrors in his life was to shut down completely.

29

The clock in Tony Castle's hallway was chiming midnight when Daniel Cross arrived at the front door of the condominium. It was only with a strong will that Tony controlled his temper as he ushered his old friend inside, down the long hall lined with original artwork and into the grand space of his study. He was telling himself to stay calm – to remember what he owed this man – but still he felt an overwhelming urge to slap the self-satisfied smirk from Daniel's face.

When he had closed the soundproof door of the study, Tony turned to face the taller, older man. 'What the fuck are you playing at, Daniel?' he said. 'I told you I should've handled the package. Now we have dead bodies piling up and Stella Sartori hasn't even made a move. You risk bringing us down without any push from her.'

Cross looked shocked at the outburst. 'You sure it's safe to talk in here, Tony?'

'Of course I'm sure! You think I'm stupid? I get the place checked regularly and why would anyone be bugging me these days, anyway? I've been pretty much legit for thirty years. Thirty great years, Daniel, since I had to get my hands dirty. And now you and your team of perfect assholes are fucking things up right under my nose, on my own patch. What the hell am I supposed to do with you?'

'I thought I was out but they keep pulling me back in,' Cross said, in a bad impression of Al Pacino's ageing Godfather. Then he laughed at his own joke and stopped when he saw the rage dancing in Tony's eyes. 'Jesus,' he said, 'relax, will you? It's all taken care of. There's no way any of this is coming back to us.'

'Are you out of your fucking mind? One of your guys is already dead, they have witnesses in the hospital and they have a suspicious fire to investigate. It's all over the late-night news. Why the hell did you send your guys after the attorney? If you'd just thought it through, you would have realised that it doesn't matter what the woman sent to her lawyer, it all goes back too far in time. But you're giving them every reason to dig deep now. You have to know they're coming after you next.'

'With what?' Cross said, looking smug again. 'They've got nothing, especially without the Sartori bitch. Even with her. Just wild accusations and conspiracy theories. There are no loose ends, I've taken care of them, like I said I would. And we had to go after the package, Tony, you have to see that. I have to know what she knows. I have to know if she has a chance of resurrecting the truth. The stakes are too high to sit back and take our chances that she won't.'

'I never suggested we do that,' Tony said, 'but there are better ways to handle it. I just hope you have your other thug on a short leash.'

'You don't have to worry about him,' Cross said grimly. 'He's not going to be talking to anyone. I took him down to show him the river, just before I came here. Took your advice and did it myself.'

Tony was momentarily stunned. 'Another one? Jesus, what have you become, Daniel?'

'You,' Cross said, with a note of satisfaction, 'but you thirty years ago. You got squeamish, my friend, over the years.'

'I got smart, is what I got, while you got stupid.'

'Hey, back off would ya? Remember who's been punching your ticket all this time. Where the hell would you be without me? Probably dead, or behind bars, is where.'

Tony sighed deeply. 'You might still put me there, Danny, if you don't get yourself under control.'

Shaking his head, Tony moved to a door in the wood panelling of his office and opened it to reveal a backlit bar, sparkling with crystal and glass. He poured two whiskies over ice and handed one tumbler to Daniel, who took it as a sign that he was forgiven. Then they both sat in leather armchairs and observed each other in silence for a few moments.

'Now, if you promise to be good and get out of the country for a while, I'll tell you where Stella Sartori is.'

Cross sat up straight, his eyes shining like a kid who's been told he's getting a new toy. 'You've found her?'

Tony nodded.

30

When Detective Robertson knocked on the door at ten the next morning, Jack wasn't long out of the bath, where he'd soaked his aching body for an hour after waking. He felt better, physically, and he'd woken with a renewed determination to see that Daniel Cross was stopped.

As always, the things outside his control were pushed from his mind. Like his burned-out home and his dead lover and the mutilated lawyer. There was nothing he could do about any of that. Let the police and the insurance companies and the funeral parlours deal with those things. He just wanted to get at Cross, to stop him before he could do any more harm. To hurt him before Jack or the people Jack cared about were hurt again.

As Jack opened the door, he was tightening his new belt around the waist of a pair of trousers one size too large for him. The legs were rolled up like he was at the beach. The shoes Frank had organised were way too small, so he was wearing his old grubby sneakers, which he had wiped clean of obvious bloodstains. A navy polo shirt and windbreaker completed the ensemble. He looked in the mirror and decided it would do until he could get to the stores.

His only other possessions were the few things he'd carried in the small backpack when he left 4th Street a day earlier. Keys to a home that no longer existed, his office security pass and his wallet containing credit cards, driver's licence, some cash and a few crumpled business cards. There were the toiletries he'd purchased in White Plains, which he had used to shave his pale, drawn face. And he still had Stella's precious package, the small bundle of innocuous and infuriating documents that had spawned a night of death and destruction. Sitting on the desk in his suite, it seemed to mock him every time it caught his eye, so he stuffed the papers back into his backpack.

Detective Robertson led him from the room and dismissed a uniformed officer as they went by. Jack noticed a chair placed just outside his door. 'Was he here all night?' he asked as they entered the elevator.

'Someone was there all night. We discussed this before I left, remember?'

'I have absolutely no recollection of that.' Jack shook his head. He was trying valiantly to pick out the lost details of the night before, but his memory was pretty vague. 'You know, normally I have a pretty sharp mind but somehow . . .'

'Don't worry about it, Jack, you had a rough night. We just wanted to keep an eye on you. After all, someone bombed your place last night. They could've been after you.'

'I don't think so. I think they were just after a package of documents. A copy of the same stuff they were after at Bloch and Lieberman. If they couldn't find the package, Cross would've wanted it destroyed. That's the only reason they could've had to burn my place.'

'Better to be safe.'

Jack looked at Robertson, trying to gauge his true feelings. Had he placed a guard outside the door at city expense to protect him or to stop him from leaving? Maybe a bit of both. The detective was watching him with sleepy but intelligent eyes. He was about Jack's age, with very thin hair and a thick moustache to compensate. 'Do you think the package was destroyed?'

'No, what they were after wasn't there, although they must have destroyed the only other material I have, including my notes and other papers that were in my study or my briefcase.'

'So where's the package?'

'Well, I've got —'

Jack stopped, unsure if he should relinquish Stella's package. With Peta now added to the list of Daniel Cross's victims, this business had become extremely personal. If he gave up the package would he be forgoing some avenue of attack against the enemy? His only way to reconnect with Stella was via email and that would take time. Maybe another look through the papers would reveal some clue he hadn't noticed before, something that would unravel Cross's web of violence and deceit.

'I already know you've got it, Jack,' Robertson said. The tone reflected his disapproval of Jack's reticence to share. 'I heard you tell Frank Spiteri last night that you took it from —' he consulted a notebook pulled from inside his jacket, '— a guy called David O'Reilly.'

Jack looked at him with a blank expression, but it was as if Robertson could read his mind. 'You've got to leave this to the proper authorities, Jack. Don't be holding back any evidence. If you want the people responsible to be brought to justice, you're going to have to work with me.'

Silently, Jack pulled open the backpack he had slung over one shoulder, extracted the package that had cost him so dearly, and handed it to Robertson. The detective took it gingerly, and carried it out in front like a dead rat, as Jack followed him out through the revolving door of the Millennium on to 44th Street. They entered a white unmarked police car parked right in front of the hotel, much to the disgust of the doorman, who shooed them away with an indignant wave. Behind the wheel, Robertson's partner, whom Jack had met the previous evening, looked bushed and grumpy. Jack sat in the back, while Robertson placed the package into an evidence bag and then explained that they were heading over to 35th Street, Midtown Precinct South. 'The first homicide, at Bloch's, was in my patch, Midtown South,' he said. 'Your home is in the Sixth Precinct, so there'll be a detective present from 10th Street.'

Jack nodded, but Robertson hadn't finished. 'The fire department's also sending over a guy, some kinda arson expert or something. And there'll be a guy from the FBI.'

'Seriously?'

'Very seriously. This is very serious stuff. We've been up all night with this.'

That explained the fatigue written all over their faces. 'Wow, that's great. So you believe me then?'

'I don't believe nothing 'til I get some hard evidence, but we don't like it when attorneys get their fingers hacked off and investment bankers get their homes firebombed. It's not the image the mayor wants for the city. And so far your story checks out. You have good alibis for last night and a story to tell, so we're gonna start by listening to that story. Then we'll decide what to believe.'

'Fair enough,' Jack said, satisfied. 'What about Alex Trainer and the security guard, Stan? How are they?'

'They're going to be okay. Stan was lucky. The bullet missed all the vital bits, but he's retired now, that's for sure. I spoke to him this morning. He said you tried to warn him about those guys.'

'He saved my life.'

'Yeah, he was pretty pumped up about that shot. Hasn't stopped talking about it ever since he regained consciousness and was told about it.'

Jack smiled with genuine relief. 'And Trainer?'

Robertson looked at his watch. 'He'll still be in surgery. They're trying to sew his finger back on.'

An unpleasant knot tightened in Jack's stomach at the thought of the operation. Looking out the window at the grey sidewalk passing by, he could see New York was taking its time to stir this lazy Saturday morning. The sun was shining weakly but the streets were still empty and it took only a few minutes to drive to the stationhouse on 35th Street. Robertson's partner – whose name was Eastern European and unpronounceable – pulled the nose of the car in right outside the entrance. Above a few steps leading to glass doors, a large white portico announced Midtown Precinct South, but apart from that, it looked like any other office building in the area.

Jack was escorted through the overcrowded workspace to a meeting room with a worn, rectangular table in the centre and vinyl-covered chairs scattered around it. There were three people in the room already, two of them sitting, and looking like they could use a good night's sleep. The third, a young woman with straight blonde hair, dressed as if she worked at Sutton Brothers, was standing as they entered. She looked fresh and sharp in a pale grey tailored suit. She introduced herself as Shannon Winters of the FBI.

The other two were introduced as Ted Fiske, from the 6th Precinct, and James Tong, an accelerants expert with the New York Fire Department. They both carried the lines of experience on their faces. Jack was offered coffee but declined as they all sat down around the table. Automatically, as he did at most business meetings, Jack handed around the last few business cards from his wallet. Only Agent Winters reciprocated.

When they were settled, Detective Robertson flicked a switch to start recording the interview and in a clear voice noted the date and time and the names of those present. He turned to Jack. 'For the record,' he said, 'the matters under discussion today remain the jurisdiction of the New York Police Department and the New York Fire Department. Agent Winters of the FBI is present as an observer only.'

Winters frowned but made no comment.

'Also for the record, at this time the interviewee, Mr John Rogers, is not considered a suspect in any crime. However, we reserve the right to treat Mr Rogers as a suspect if the emerging evidence supports that conclusion. For that reason I will now read Mr Rogers his rights.'

And he did. It made Jack a little nervous, wondering about the need for legal counsel, but only a little. In the scheme of things, he didn't think the theft of a package would be considered such a big deal. Apart from that, he couldn't see how he'd done anything wrong.

Robertson started by asking personal questions. Age, place of birth, when he had come to the US and why, and so on. Mundane stuff – too mundane for Jack.

'Look,' he said, 'I'm happy to get to all that. I'm happy to cooperate fully, guaranteed. But can we just talk about Peta first? Please?'

'Your partner?' It was Ted Fiske who spoke – the official most interested in the death that had occurred in his precinct.

'Yes,' Jack said, turning to him. 'Do you know if the body has been . . .' He couldn't find the right words.

'No formal identification has been made yet. We'll probably need dental records. The corpse was badly damaged.'

Jack winced.

'Sorry,' Fiske said, and he fumbled with his notebook. 'All we have is an approximate height. Five six or five seven. Quite short.'

The height matched. The feeling of overwhelming dread returned. 'Short?' Jack said.

'For a man.'

'A man?'

Fiske furrowed his brow. 'Yeah, a man. Your partner was a man, right?'

'No!' Jack thumped the table. 'Peta was a woman. Peta, P-E-T-A. Her middle name was Samantha, for Christ's sake. She was a woman. Not everyone who lives in the Village is gay, you know!'

Fiske's face had become a little red. He looked at Robertson for support.

'The point is, Jack,' Robertson said, 'the medical examiner says the victim was a man. That's all we have, five foot six or seven and a man. You said your partner's name was Peter – it was a reasonable assumption to make, right?'

'Then it's not her!'

Jack pushed his chair back from the table and stood up, filled with new energy. 'If the body was a man's then it wasn't Peta. It couldn't be Peta, right? Are you sure it was a man?'

'Ted, ring the ME's office. Get a confirmation,' Robertson ordered.

Jack waited and watched, unable to move on until he knew. A faint trickle of hope had been rekindled. Maybe he wouldn't have to make that awful call to Peta's parents after all. And maybe the terrible guilt that was weighing him down might begin to abate. He followed every movement of Fiske's eyes and mouth as the detective talked into the telephone. Fiske was obviously asked to wait and looked like he was about to hang up until he caught the expression on Jack's face. So he stayed on the line, patiently waiting as the minutes ticked by. The others talked among themselves but had the good grace to leave Jack to his wishful thinking.

At last, Fiske snapped his cell phone shut. 'No doubt about it,' he said, 'it's a man.'

Jack's usual reserve was cast aside as he gave a whoop of joy and bounced around the room, shaking everyone by the hand, Robertson twice. The grin on his face was stretching his mouth to the limits.

'Peta's alive, Peta's alive,' he kept repeating, until logic brought him back down to earth. 'So where the hell is she? I've got to find her.'

He paced aimlessly, his mind whirling with hypothetical thoughts. Was her body still in the ruin? Had she been abducted by Cross? What should he do next?

He marched over to Detective Robertson and held out his hand. 'Give me your phone,' he demanded. 'I have to call her.'

The detective could see there was no point in arguing. He passed his cell phone to Jack and watched him punch in the number.

'Nothing,' Jack muttered angrily as he disconnected and dialled again. For a moment his spirits lifted when he heard a female voice, but then he registered her words: 'The telephone you are calling is switched off or outside the network area. Please try again later.'

More uncertainty. Jack snapped the phone shut and dropped it on the table. Then he grabbed it up again, as if it represented his only hope of ever seeing Peta alive.

'Jack!' Robertson used a stern tone to get his attention. 'Sit down, relax. We'll find her. But we need you to tell us what you know about all this, please.'

'But what if they've got her?'

Visions of Peta in the clutches of that big redheaded psychopath swam in front of his eyes. His skin prickled with fear and trepidation. It was far from over.

Agent Shannon Winters spoke with a calm that seemed incongruous for her age. 'Even if they've got her, Jack, you can't do this on your own. We can help you.'

Jack glared at her. 'What are you doing here, anyway?' he demanded. 'What has the FBI got to do with this?'

Winters held his gaze calmly. 'Kidnapping is a federal crime.'

'It's a good question, though, isn't it?' Detective Robertson said. 'There was no mention of kidnapping when I put this on the wire. Just why are you here, Agent Winters?'

The young FBI agent turned to face the detective. She seemed to be considering her answer. 'I'm here because my boss told me to be here. It wasn't my idea to schlep into the city on my day off, believe me.'

Robertson responded with a quizzical look and a shake of his head, which elicited a flash of petulance from the agent. 'Look,' she said, 'I'm just here to listen to what Jack has to say.'

'If you say so,' Robertson said, after a moment's consideration. He made a welcoming gesture with his arms, inviting Jack back to the table. 'Come on, Jack, let's hear the full story, soup to nuts.'

Jack sat down reluctantly and tried to concentrate. 'Let's do this quickly,' he said, and they all nodded in agreement.

He gave them a complete account of his week. Notes were taken, eyebrows raised and questions asked. He answered them all without hesitation, no matter how embarrassing, incriminating or libellous. It was like a purge and he felt so much better when it was over. He didn't care whether Stella would approve or not – it wasn't her million-dollars-plus worth of real estate and personal belongings that had gone up in flames. This was just as much Jack's fight as hers. And he didn't care about Frank Spiteri either. He could stick his job as long as Peta was all right.

Jack's listeners were each interested in different parts of the story. The detectives wanted to solve the particular crimes in their jurisdiction and they asked lots of questions about the events the day before. The FBI agent was interested in the conspiracy angle, with the events in Peoria and Chicago and the issues of government contracts and national security at the top of her list.

The man from the fire department was there because his initial examination of the remains of Jack's home had revealed some disturbing evidence. 'It was some kind of sophisticated incendiary device,' he reported to his colleagues, his right hand resting on a pile of large photographs of the ruin on 4th Street. 'This was no homemade weapon – this was an expensive piece of hardware, almost certainly military in origin. There was no blast as such, just a tremendous heat, enough to bring the entire space to the point of combustion. That's why the body was still in one piece, just severely burned. We've never seen anything like it before in a civilian setting.'

'Mmm,' Jack mused, his wit resurfacing. 'Can anyone think of somebody who has good military connections?'

'Somebody better have a chat with Daniel Cross,' Agent Winters said.

Jack thought, Hooray! Now the spotlight was going to be turned on the right people. 'And find the redhead,' he suggested. 'He's a dangerous bastard.'

'Yeah, William Hoyle,' Robertson said. 'Quite well known in his hometown, according to the local sheriff's office. He shouldn't be too hard to track down.'

'If the body in my townhouse isn't Peta, who is it?' Jack wondered out loud.

James Tong had also been pondering this conundrum. 'When we thought the victim was a resident, our theory was that he, or she' – he gave Jack an apologetic glance – 'was killed when he triggered the device, like with a letter bomb. The body was found close to the primary source of combustion.

'But if the victim wasn't someone who normally had access to the residence then it's more likely to be the perpetrator himself.

Maybe the device was triggered prematurely. If he was a terrorist, he may not have been properly trained in the use of a sophisticated weapon like this. Usually terrorists deal with much simpler devices. Maybe he just screwed up somehow. Either that or it was some other male person who had access to the home and may have touched the device. You don't have a male housekeeper or anything like that do you?'

'No,' Jack said. 'We have a cleaner, usually on Mondays. But she's a woman, and shorter than five six.'

Detective Fiske cleared his throat. 'Um, I brought along a few items that were found with the body.'

He reached down beneath his seat to pick up a small cardboard box with no lid. 'I thought you might recognise something belonging to your partner, I mean, girlfriend. I guess it wouldn't hurt for you to take a look anyway.'

He pushed the box over to Jack. Inside there were several clear, zip-lock plastic bags, all numbered and dated, containing blackened objects that were almost unrecognisable. There was a shrivelled wallet, probably made of leather but now just one lump of charcoal. There was a set of melted keys and some fused coins.

And there was a watch. Jack picked up the bag. Even though the watch was black with soot, it had a familiar feel in his hand. And it was obviously strong, still whole despite the great heat. The weight of it, the feel of the metal band, even through the plastic bag, was just like Jack's own watch. The raised dial around the face confirmed it. It was a TAG Heuer. He rubbed the face of the dial through the bag and was surprised to see the glass was still intact. He used a thumbnail to try to scrape a gash in the soot, much to Ted Fiske's horror.

'What the hell are you doing? That's evidence. It hasn't even been to the lab yet, for Christ's sake.'

'Sorry, but I think I know who this watch belongs to.'

The law enforcement officials watched in silent anticipation as Jack held the watch up to the light. The face was definitely blue. 'I know who died at my place last night,' he said. 'It was David O'Reilly.'

31

'The Australian?' Detective Fiske said. 'The runaway's husband?' He consulted his scribbled notes, trying to get the story straight in his head.

'Yeah, Stella Sartori's husband,' Jack said. 'He has a watch just like this. He was working with Daniel Cross and he knew I had the documents Cross was after because he saw me take them. Maybe Cross sent him to get them back or, at the very least, destroy the evidence. O'Reilly was a locksmith, and a little guy, no more than five seven, I'd say.'

'Is that so?' Fiske was writing everything down. 'And where does this O'Reilly live?'

Jack gave the address on 49th Street and told them what little he knew about O'Reilly and his habits. 'I'll check it out,' Fiske said, hopeful of a quick solve.

Agent Winters snapped shut the black leather portfolio she'd been writing in. 'I need to discuss this with my boss,' she said. 'I doubt the FBI will play an active part in this investigation, but if you come up with some hard evidence of a federal crime . . .'

Detective Fiske – whose bandwidth for tolerance didn't extend to young female FBI agents – rolled his eyes, but Winters ignored him. Robertson, who was sympathetic to Fiske's view but too smart to show it, said, 'We have this,' and held up the evidence pouch containing Stella's second package.

'What's in it?' Winters said, pushing her hair back behind one ear.

'There's a copy of "The Virgin's Secret" poem,' Jack volunteered, 'some old organisation charts for the company in Peoria and a few other lists of personnel. Oh, and there's a copy of the defence contract I was talking about. You probably need to be pretty discreet with that as Stella really shouldn't have copied it.'

'I'm glad she did,' Robertson said. 'I doubt we'd get another copy easily, certainly not from the Pentagon.'

'I might want a look at that, Detective,' Agent Winters said.

'Sure. But only after I get the whole package processed by the lab first, just to be thorough.'

'You'll just find Stella Sartori's fingerprints, and mine,' Jack said.

'Not these days, Jack,' Winters said, in a slightly condescending voice. 'We might also find fibres that tell us where the package was prepared. We can analyse the paper and the ink and we may even get DNA from whoever licked the envelope.'

Jack gave a frustrated sigh, wanting things to move faster, and Detective Robertson said, 'Now you mention it, we'll need to get some prints from you, Jack. Maybe a DNA sample too.'

Agent Winters stood up, as if it was her place to end the discussion. She looked at Robertson and said, 'You will keep me informed of developments, won't you?'

'Why of course, Agent Winters,' Robertson said, straining to hide his irritation. 'I'll be sure to check in with you before I make any move.'

Her response to the sarcasm was a long, cold look. 'That won't be necessary, Detective. Just a little professional courtesy, that's all I ask.'

She put a business card down on the table and then, seemingly oblivious to the impact she was having on her colleagues, Shannon Winters swept towards the door, stopping only to shake Jack's hand. 'I hope you find your partner safe and sound.'

'Thank you,' Jack said automatically.

Just before she opened the door to leave she flicked her hair once more, turning her face towards Robertson, and said, 'If it turns out to be a kidnapping, let me know.'

When the door banged shut, Robertson's partner muttered something under his breath and the other cops joined him in a low chuckle. Only James Tong and Jack remained oblivious to the joke. Then the explosives expert also said his farewells and departed.

The detectives discussed next steps among themselves and Jack pretty much ignored them. He was preoccupied with disturbing thoughts of Peta. Was she being held for ransom, in the form of Stella's package? Would that make sense? If Cross got hold of the package, it might help him stop Stella but he'd just end up as an obvious suspect in the kidnapping. Had he lost his marbles altogether? But if Cross didn't take Peta, then where the hell was she? And if he did take her, why hadn't Jack received any demands?

Because I have no phone, Jack realised with a start. His home phone was just melted plastic and his cell phone was missing. Nobody could contact him. Not Cross. Not Stella. Not even Peta!

'We need to go to Sutton Brothers,' he said loudly, interrupting the police talk.

'What?'

'We need to go to my office. If they're holding Peta they'll be trying to contact me. I lost my cell phone last night. The only number that works for me is my office number. I need to get downtown.'

'Right,' Robertson said. 'We'll take you. Ted, I'll talk to you later.'

Fiske nodded and stood up, jealously reaching for his precious box of evidence. Jack was already out in the hall, trying to remember how to get back to the entrance. Robertson was quickly at his shoulder pointing the way, but as it turned out it was the way to a processing area. Jack's frustration boiled while a woman in uniform took his prints and swabbed the inside of his cheek. He was still rubbing ink from his hands with a paper towel when Robertson's partner Vlad – as everybody called him – held open the car door for him.

Vlad took the wheel and followed Jack's directions to Sutton Brothers. Robertson was in the passenger seat. 'I'm gonna need to talk to Frank Spiteri again,' he said as they moved quickly through the traffic. 'You think he'll back up your story?'

'I don't know,' Jack said from the back seat. 'I hope so. But Frank has his own agenda. He'll be keen to keep Sutton Brothers out of it as much as possible.'

'A little late for that now, wouldn't you say?'

Jack found his own instinct to protect the bank was still strong. 'Maybe. But the bank's involvement is incidental, don't you agree? Nobody at Sutton Brothers has done anything wrong.'

'So you say. Yet I'm aware of at least two admitted cases of robbery by bank employees. What am I supposed to do about that? And I still haven't heard Daniel Cross's side of the story.'

Robertson shifted his eyes front, leaving Jack feeling vulnerable. Vlad twisted and turned the car downtown and Jack swayed against the seatbelt, imagining Cross telling his side of the story. He knew Cross would do it very well – he'd be thoroughly convincing. The story would be smooth as silk and watertight in every detail. Unless he was pretty stupid or one of his minions squealed, it would be tough to mount any serious case against him based on the evidence to hand. At the very worst, Cross might be forced to sacrifice an employee or two, but getting anything to stick to him personally would be close to impossible.

So, Jack figured, as far as the NYPD were concerned, it might be much easier to book him for stealing the mail than to get involved in the complex power games Daniel Cross was playing. The self-defence shooting at the law firm was pretty open and shut. They could go after Hoyle for attempted murder or mutilation or something but even if they could find him, would the trail lead back to Cross? And it looked like the man responsible for setting fire to Jack's home was himself a victim of it so there was little more for the cops to investigate there.

It was fast dawning on Jack that he was still way out on a limb. There were so many ways in which the story could be twisted to make him look bad. He had little or no hard evidence, apart from a pretty outrageous tale that seemed to fit all the facts. He really needed Stella.

'Do you think you can find Stella Sartori?' he asked Robertson.

'We'll try. I put a rush order on the forensic examination of her package. And we can try to track credit card usage, check with immigration, that sort of thing. But if someone really wants to stay hidden, it's a lot harder to find 'em than you might think from watching TV. Legally, anyway.'

'What about the documents held by Bloch and Lieberman? Alex Trainer said they were in the firm's safe.'

'They won't cough 'em up without a court order or clear instructions from their client, which brings us back to square one.'

Jack raised his eyes to the roof of the car. 'So I have nothing and nobody to support my claims about all this.'

'That's why I wanted to know if you thought Frank Spiteri would back you up,' Robertson said, turning around to look Jack in the face, his left arm draped around the front seat. 'I'm wondering if he's gonna give me a different version of events.'

'I could go back to my house and see if anything survived the fire,' Jack suggested.

'Like what?'

'Like the notes in my briefcase or the material Ben Fisher gave me. At least that would prove I wasn't making all this up.'

'Were they upstairs?'

'Yes, in the den. On the desk and in the drawers.'

'Then they didn't survive, believe me. I was there this morning. Nothing in that entire room survived the fire. There's no desk left. No furniture I recognised, except the remains of a big flat-screen TV on one wall. Even most of the floorboards are gone. I think you had a treadmill upstairs, right?'

Jack nodded sadly, and Robertson said, 'Well, now it's downstairs. I've never seen damage like it. That guy James Tong said he thinks it was one of those devices the military puts into its own installations. Designed to destroy everything in the room if security is compromised. You know, like a self-destruct thing.'

'Really? That shouldn't be too hard to trace.'

'You'd think so, wouldn't you? Apparently it's not as hard to get hold of these things as it should be.'

'Oh, great!'

'It's still a good angle,' Robertson said. 'We'll try to trace it. It'll be interesting to see where the trail leads.'

Robertson was looking at Jack strangely, making him feel increasingly uncomfortable. From the start, the detective had seemed like a decent guy, but Jack warned himself not to place too much trust in him. Hollywood had spent millions of dollars over the years teaching him American cops were more interested in clearing cases off their books than getting the right guy for the crime. He didn't want to believe it, but he had absolutely no personal experience to go on, so how else could he judge the New York police?

'I'm telling the truth.' He looked directly into Robertson's eyes, projecting sincerity.

'Good,' Robertson said impassively and turned back to look out the front window. 'Just keep doing that and you'll be okay.'

32

The familiar surroundings of the office building on Broad Street were strangely comforting to Jack. This place was his only remaining anchor in New York City. The guard manning the security counter noted their details as the two detectives flashed their badges and Jack showed the security pass fished from his tiny backpack – the one containing his entire catalogue of possessions. Then he led the way to the elevators. Without thinking, he pushed the down button first, heading by instinct for the trading floor downstairs. Then he realised that even here, his workplace of eight years, home turf was no longer all that familiar. A great deal had changed in the space of one week.

With another pass of his electronic key, Jack reprogrammed the elevator to go to level twenty-seven. Being a Saturday, the floor was eerily silent and gloomy – weak natural light from distant windows the only source of illumination. And it remained that way because Jack had no idea where the light switches for the floor were located. When they came to Jack's small office, it looked forlorn and useless. Vacant bookshelves and no papers or even a pen – such a contrast to the crowded surfaces of the police station. Robertson and Vlad exchanged a look. 'I just moved in,' Jack explained defensively. 'In fact, I haven't really moved in yet, as you can see.'

Robertson just nodded. He was looking at the framed photograph. 'Is that Peta?'

'Yes.'

'Very pretty.'

Jack nodded and moved to the phone, which was blinking its message light. He knew it would be blinking – the damn thing was always blinking – but would there be some message there telling him what had happened to Peta? He picked up the handset.

'Can we do it on speaker?' Robertson said as he sat down in the visitor's chair.

Vlad leaned against the door, saying nothing. Jack was unsure about playing all his messages out loud, but could hardly say no, so he put the handset back and pushed the phone to the middle of the desk. Then he touched the voicemail button. The speaker was activated and he punched in the code to retrieve new messages. Robertson pulled out his notebook but soon got bored. There were eleven messages.

Five related to Jack's old job downstairs. There was a message from his sister in Sydney, thanking him for her birthday present and giggling about her love life. One gruff message from Frank Spiteri asking where he was – from Thursday morning, before Jack had called from Chicago to say he'd missed his flight. Then another from Frank, left on Friday afternoon, wondering why he was getting no response from either Jack's home or cell numbers. Late in the afternoon of the same day, there was a message from Steve, his buddy from the gym, suggesting either a workout or a drink after work.

Then, to Jack's overwhelming relief, the last two messages were from Peta. Not about Peta but from Peta. They'd both been received today, Saturday, the second one less than one hour before he'd arrived at the office. She was obviously furious. Jack was ecstatic.

'Jack, this is Peta. Where the hell are you? Why haven't you called me? Are you trying to punish me? Don't be so childish! I asked you to call me, whatever time of day it was here. Didn't you read my note? Please call me. I hope you're okay. Um, look . . .' There was a long pause. 'Just call me.' She recited a telephone number.

'She's in London,' Jack said excitedly, grabbing Robertson's pen out of his hand and scribbling on a scrap of paper from the top drawer of the desk. 'That's a London number.'

The second message was even terser than the first. 'John! This is getting ridiculous. I tried calling you at home and I tried your cell phone. I've left messages all over the damn place. Look you might be pissed with me, I get that. But please at least call and tell me you're okay. It's cruel to leave me hanging like this. Just call me. I'll feel like shit until I hear from you, okay? Don't be a bastard!'

'She called me John,' Jack said happily. 'She must be really mad at me.'

'I think you'd better call her,' Robertson said, smiling.

'Here, take this,' Jack said, holding out his electronic passkey. He wanted some privacy and was prepared to breach security to get it. 'Go up one level – you might find Frank Spiteri up there.'

He was already punching buttons on the phone as the two cops walked out into the hallway. They were immediately dismissed from his mind as he listened with nervous intensity. Someone picked up.

'Peta?'

'Jack! Thank God! You prick! Where were you last night?'

The wave of relief that washed over Jack was almost euphoric. Stella's machinations had resulted in tremendous death and destruction, but at least Peta was safe. As he told her about his incredible Friday and the destruction of their Manhattan townhouse, he was almost cheerful.

Peta was shocked and appalled. 'Oh, no! All our beautiful things . . .'

'They were just things, Pete. And they were insured. For a while there I thought I'd lost you.' His voice cracked as he felt a sudden yearning for her, a need for the comfort and familiarity that only she could provide.

'Oh baby, you poor thing. You must have had a shitty night. And here I am thinking you're punishing me for leaving. I'm so sorry. I should've been there.'

'I'm bloody glad you weren't!' Jack said. 'But, I sure wish I knew where you'd gone. It would've saved me a lot of heartache.'

'I'm sorry,' she repeated, 'but I did try to call. And I left a note at home. You seemed so angry Thursday night. And then on Friday you left so early without speaking to me. I thought you must hate me.'

'Oh, Peta, how could I possibly —?'

'We were both hurting, Jack, and I wasn't going to change my mind about coming to London. So I decided not to drag out the agony any longer. I packed a bag first thing Friday morning and came over here to do what I have to do. But you know I still love you. I still need to know you're okay.'

'I'm okay,' he said, sounding a little unsure.

'Tell me the rest of it.'

They were on the phone for over forty minutes and could have talked much longer, but Jack was put off when he saw Vlad hovering around outside, looking impatient. Peta was full of good advice. She would get her partner, Bill, to organise the company's attorneys to take care of the insurance claim for 4th Street. 'They deal with property stuff all the time,' she said.

'There might still be some of our things that can be salvaged,' Jack said. 'It was mainly the den that was damaged, I think. I don't even know if we're allowed to go in there.' He wasn't sure he could face it anyway.

'Leave that to the attorneys, Jack. If necessary, I'll get Jan and Mrs Adriano to go through it all. I'd better call Mrs Adriano anyway.' Mrs Adriano was their cleaner. Peta's sister Janet was a student living in New Jersey. 'Where are you going to stay?'

'Frank organised a room at the Millennium Broadway. If I get bored I can go to the theatre.' He laughed weakly.

'Why don't you come here?' She said it almost nervously, as if asking him on a first date. Jack was unprepared for the question and had no ready answer. 'After all,' she persisted, 'you deserve a break and you've got friends here. Get away from Daniel Cross and that whole mess for a while. The police will take care of it now. Why not come to London and get some TLC? Then you can decide what you want to do next.'

It sounded tempting, but Jack was torn. Could he really walk away after all that had happened to him? Could he really leave Stella out there on her own?

On the other hand, what more could he do to help her? He still didn't know where she was. Even if the cops tracked her down, why would they tell him how to contact her? And virtually all the evidence was either lost or destroyed or hard to get hold of, and it would be the police who'd get to it first anyway. He had nothing more to go on than what was in his head. And with no cell phone, there was no longer any way for Stella to contact him. He'd have to go through the whole email thing again.

'Maybe I will come over for a few days,' he said. 'But I need to sort a few things out at this end first.'

'Of course.' Peta was clearly pleased by the prospect. 'Just call me as soon as you know what your plans are. I'll give you my new numbers.'

He wrote down several long phone numbers. Vlad's head appeared around the corner. 'I'd better go,' Jack said. 'I've still got the police here.'

They ended the call on a happy note, but Jack was a little sad as he put the phone down, noting that they'd finished a conversation without saying 'I love you' to each other.

'We're upstairs,' Vlad said as soon as Jack was off the phone. 'We found that Spiteri guy up there. Robertson's talking to him. You wanna come up?'

Jack shrugged his shoulders, no longer quite as interested, but he followed Vlad to the elevators. When they got to Spiteri's office, Jack wasn't surprised to see the boss looking dapper and relaxed. He was dressed as if he was scheduled to play eighteen holes at Augusta National. Detective Robertson looked positively shabby next to him.

The conversation stopped as Jack neared the office and Spiteri rushed out into the hallway to meet him, like a father greeting his son home from the army. He gave Jack a big hug and seemed to be fighting the urge to kiss his cheeks. 'I'm so happy to hear Peta is okay. You must be so relieved, my boy. Is she well? How did she take the news about your beautiful home?'

'She's fine, Frank, thank you. She had to go to London for business at short notice, but she's just fine.'

Jack was trying to extricate himself from the hug and get a bit more Anglo-Saxon space between them. 'And yeah, you're right, it is a huge relief.'

'For me too, Jack. For me, too.'

Spiteri put one arm around Jack's shoulder, guiding him back into his office, where Robertson sat in one of the big armchairs. 'How long will she be gone?'

'It could be quite a while, I think.'

'Then you must go to her!' Spiteri exclaimed.

'You think?'

'Of course you must. After all you've been through this week you need the bosom of a good woman. How else do we warriors recover our strength after battle?'

Jack would have laughed but Spiteri looked very serious, and the macho logic had a certain appeal. A few days of good old-fashioned loving would do him the power of good, and whatever else might be wrong with their relationship, the physical chemistry he shared with Peta hadn't suffered. He looked over at Robertson.

'I doubt if the good detective would approve if I took off for London.'

Robertson was thinking about the question already. 'I don't know. I was gonna suggest you get out of town for a few days anyway. So long as I can contact you I see no good reason for you to make yourself an easy target for Daniel Cross or his associates. In the circumstances, I guess there's no reason why you shouldn't go to London. It's a big town. Just stay with your girlfriend or your family, though. Don't go wandering about.'

'What about the FBI?' Jack asked. 'You think they'll mind if I disappear for a few days?'

'You heard Agent Winters,' Robertson said derisively. 'The FBI ain't even decided they want in on this case. And you saw how green she was – this is obviously no big priority for them. Their focus is all the war on terror these days.'

'Then it's decided,' Spiteri said resolutely. 'You get out of the crossfire, Jack, and we'll let the authorities deal with Daniel.'

'Are you serious, Frank?' Jack said. 'I thought you didn't believe Cross was capable of all this.'

Spiteri shook his head. 'I still find it hard to believe, Jack, but after last night, it's difficult to reach any other conclusion. Detective Robertson told me about the shooting at Bloch and Lieberman, and what they did to that poor attorney. And he told me about the type of device they used to attack your home. It all seems to point to Daniel, though why he would turn to such desperate measures is completely beyond me. Stella must have stumbled on something extraordinary.'

Jack smiled. It was good to know Spiteri was finally on side. It had felt extremely disloyal operating behind the boss's back, but now it looked like his actions, and Stella's, would be vindicated. He suddenly felt more relaxed than he'd done in days. And now that Stella had some powerful new allies, she wouldn't need his help as much. He said, 'Maybe I will go to London for a few days.'

'Take a week, you've earned it. And there will be no deduction from your vacation entitlement.' Spiteri's generosity with the firm's money showed no signs of abating. Automatically he looked over to where Margaret Bland normally sat during the working week, ready to instruct her to make the bookings.

'It's okay, Frank. I can take care of the travel arrangements,' Jack said. 'Besides, I need to do a few things here in New York first. My home just burned down, remember?'

'Of course, son, of course. You can take care of things, I know. But you let me know if there's anything we can do for you, all right?' He took Jack's hand firmly with both of his, exuding genuine affection. Jack was almost embarrassed.

'I'm very proud of you, Jack,' Spiteri said. 'You've acted with great moral fortitude and courage. I should have been supporting you all the way.'

Now Jack was blushing. 'Thanks, Frank. Just remember Stella needs the same kind of support.'

'Absolutely! Don't worry – when I see her, the hug she gets will be twice as big as yours!'

Jack chuckled at the thought. He looked over at Detective Robertson. 'Do you need me any more?'

'I guess not. I wanna stay and talk to Frank a while longer now our paths have crossed. It'll save me a lot of time.' He pulled his tired body out of the armchair and shook Jack's hand. 'Thanks for your cooperation. Just give me your contact details and forgive me in advance if I have to haul your ass back across the Atlantic at short notice for some reason.'

'Consider yourself forgiven,' Jack said, and he read out the numbers Peta had dictated to him. Spiteri copied them down too.

Jack said his goodbyes and declined the offer of a ride back to the hotel. He was planning to shop for a new set of clothes.

As he was leaving, Vlad called out to him. 'Hey, Jack!'

He turned back. 'Yeah?'

'I think I know where your cell phone is.'

'Is that so?

'Yeah, a phone was found at the scene last night. At the attorney's office. Maybe you dropped it during the gunfight.'

'Maybe. Can I get it back?'

'Nah, it's evidence now, sorry. Anyway, it got blood all over it.'

The policeman shrugged his shoulders and a wry grin played around his mouth. Was he trying to be nice or just funny? As Jack walked away, he decided he really didn't care.

Waiting for the elevator to arrive, Jack found his mind flipping from thoughts of a reborn Peta to questions about the elusive Stella, to images of her husband's charred corpse and back again. Then the doors opened and he stepped inside.

When he saw Frank Spiteri hurrying towards him across the thick carpet, Jack stuck out his arm to prevent the elevator doors closing. Slightly out of breath, the boss was gesturing with one arm. 'Sorry, Jack,' he panted. 'Thanks for waiting. I just wanted to ask you —'

'What?'

'About Ben Fisher,' Spiteri said. 'You saw him in Peoria on Wednesday, didn't you? Do you know where he is? He was due to return on Thursday but he never showed up for work.'

33

Back in his office, Jack stared, unseeing, out the window. He was trying to calculate the cost of Stella's well-meaning actions and could only imagine how she would react when she learned the truth. Four people dead. Two others grievously injured. One more missing. The grief of their families multiplying the effect exponentially. It was an overwhelming tally.

Focus, Jack told himself, shaking his head to try and clear his mind. He added a few items to the sparse collection in his backpack, including pens, a notepad and his passport – which, thankfully, he always kept at the office. Then he stuck his head out into the hallway and looked both ways. Satisfied that he was alone, he went back to the desk and turned on the computer monitor on his desk.

His email inbox was overflowing with new messages, but he was only interested in one. It was from the IT help desk and set out a list of numbers and times – all calls received at his number on Monday afternoon. The one he wanted was obvious, a short call received just after 2 p.m. local time, apparently from a hotel – the Outrigger, Waikiki Beach.

Hawaii, he said to himself triumphantly, Stella's in Hawaii. Immediately, he picked up his phone and called the number. The operator who answered was polite, but unhelpful. She had no record of a guest by the name of Stella Sartori, either currently or during the past week. Confused, he turned to look out the window. Was she using a false name, he wondered, or was the room booked in the name of one of her relatives, like her sister, perhaps? Or maybe the call wasn't from her at all.

It was a frustrating dilemma. Stella needed to be told what had happened. She needed to know about David and the attack on Alex Trainer and the fire. And poor Ben. And she should hear it from me, Jack thought, not some cop interrogating her.

Banging down the phone, he marched over to Stella's office on the other side of the floor. In the drawers and cupboards, he found plenty of evidence of professional activity. Well-ordered files, reports and folders filled the cupboards. He closed the doors, no longer interested in her mergers and acquisitions work.

The top two drawers of her desk contained the usual office equipment – envelopes, pens, scissors and the like. The third and bottom drawer was obviously reserved for Stella's personal items, which looked almost as organised as her work-related material. Jack had nothing against a well-ordered workplace but it all felt a little anal.

The most prominent item in the drawer was the pink plastic piggybank she had described. When he pulled the rubber stopper from its belly, a few coins of various foreign currencies fell out, as well as a small bunch of keys. Now he had access to the 49th Street apartment, but as soon as the keys hit his hand, it felt creepy. Imagine, he thought, sneaking into the apartment of a guy who just died in the process of destroying your home. He shuddered involuntarily. Then he looked through the other items in the bottom drawer and found a bunch of photos, some postcards, two birthday cards, a packet of painkillers and a hair clip.

Many of the photographs featured Stella but there were plenty of faces Jack didn't recognise. A few showed work colleagues, including Frank Spiteri and Ben Fisher. Almost all the shots were taken at social events over an extended period, as evidenced by changing hairstyles and fashions. Smiling faces and drinks on tables were a consistent theme. One was clearly taken in Australia. It showed a younger Stella, looking less sophisticated, with her arms around an older Italian-looking couple, presumably her parents. She was taller than both, but the resemblance was clear.

In every photograph Stella looked good. The camera clearly loved her. Dark, straight hair – usually to her shoulders but sometimes longer – clear green eyes and smooth olive skin. And her mouth was very alluring. Something about it held Jack's gaze. Was it the shine on her bottom lip or the shape and line of her upper? Whatever it was, he found it extremely sensuous. Some people have come-to-bed eyes, he thought, but Stella has come-to-bed lips.

There were no other clues as to her whereabouts. Nothing that might confirm a planned trip to Hawaii. But the more he thought about it, the more it made sense. Halfway between Australia and the US, it would be a logical choice for a vacation with her family. And the island location fitted perfectly with the background noises he'd heard when they'd talked on the phone on Thursday. He'd been to Hawaii once and he could picture seagulls and lazy shoppers and slow drivers cruising down a colourful shopping strip while Stella talked of conspiracy into a payphone.

He took the photo of Stella with her parents plus a more recent shot. One without Dave in it. Just looking at O'Reilly and thinking of that body bag being hauled out onto 4th Street made his skin crawl. He considered – but rejected immediately – the idea of telling

Detective Robertson about the call from Hawaii. If Stella wanted to be left alone to work on her puzzle, he wasn't going to be the one to bring the police crashing down on her. Besides, the hotel denied she was even there. If the authorities found her by their own devices, good for them. He wasn't going to betray her trust.

Back in his office, the view that had so recently inspired him now felt gloomy and oppressive. The weight of the city, with its filth and death and ashen ruins, had become suffocating. Jack knew he had to get out of New York, and he knew he had two choices. He could go to London, where old friends and pubs and Peta's genuine affection would distract him while Stella's drama played out, hopefully without any more deaths. Or, he could fly halfway across the Pacific Ocean on the off-chance that his mystery caller had indeed been Stella and that she might still be found at the hotel where she might have been staying a few days earlier.

He found the decision remarkably easy to make.

34

Shannon Winters stopped for a bagel and coffee on Broadway before heading back to the FBI Field Office at Federal Plaza. There was plenty of activity in the building, despite it being the weekend shift, but not so much in the White-Collar Crime Division, where the crime fighters tended to follow the same business hours as the criminals.

Her desk and those around it were hidden in dark shadow until she flicked a switch on the wall and watched the fluorescents in the ceiling flicker to life. Only then did she notice the light that was already on in her boss's corner office. The door was open and Agent Winters made a beeline for it, her jaw set firmly.

Special Agent in Charge Nathan Beardsley was behind his desk, his white shirtsleeves rolled up and both hands gripping bundles of loose papers. He did not look up when Winters hovered at the door.

'What are you doing here?' she asked.

'Working, Winters, as you can see. The paperwork does not do itself.'

'Is there some special reason why I had to come all the way into

Manhattan on my day off to attend a pointless meeting a few blocks from here when you were going to be working anyway?'

Beardsley looked up from his papers. 'You know,' he said with a wry smile, 'you've got a real insubordinate streak, Winters. You think I wasted your Saturday morning? Well, boo hoo for you. Who gave you the impression the Bureau doesn't work weekends?'

'I wouldn't mind if it was a real case,' Winters said defiantly. 'But why were we at that meeting in the first place?'

Her boss shrugged his shoulders. 'Computer coughed it up,' he said. 'The cops put Daniel Cross's name in the system last night and it raised a flag in the Bureau's database. It got routed to me and I handpicked you to check it out.'

He carefully placed the papers in his hands in separate piles on the desk and contemplated them for a second. Then he turned to his computer and brought the monitor to life.

'Not much detail in here. Something about allegations of corporate corruption back in the 1960s. Involving a defence contract, looks like. There's a file reference.'

He read out the number and Shannon Winters copied it down, suddenly more interested.

'The meeting today,' she said, 'there was a witness who had a theory about Daniel Cross knocking people off to protect some evidence or something. The point is, he said it all came back to this old Pentagon deal. And then there's this poem, "The Virgin's Secret" —'

'What the hell are you talking about, Winters? A virgin's what?'

'Secret. But, the point is, it was written in —' she stopped to examine her notes, '— 1967. It all comes back to something that happened almost forty years ago.'

Beardsley stared at the computer screen, as if willing it to spit out some more information. A veteran of more than twenty years, he'd seen enough to know that digging around in the Bureau's older files could have unforeseen and unpleasant consequences. Career consequences. And the chances of achieving a conviction for a four-decade-old corporate fraud were miniscule at best.

Winters was watching him, and seemed to be following his train of thought.

'According to this Jack Rogers guy,' she said, 'people have died this week and he believes Daniel Cross is responsible.'

Beardsley thought a moment more and slowly nodded his head. 'Yeah, I guess you're right,' he said. 'Okay, Winters, you better go ahead and order up that file.'

35

It's a long way from New York to Honolulu – Jack had forgotten how far. But he did it in style and comfort, spending $2400 on a one-way, first-class seat that left Newark at ten after eight Sunday morning. Newark was a trek but the fare was $400 cheaper than flying out of Kennedy, so he took the ticket just to prove to himself that he wasn't completely stupid with money.

From the moment the plane's undercarriage lost contact with the runway, he felt himself relaxing. And every mile that accumulated between the aircraft and New York City added to the sense of well-being. For the next half day he was stuck in an airline seat, albeit a very comfortable one. There was nothing he could do, even if he wanted to. At last he could sleep.

As he began to doze, he wondered if he was actually on an expensive wild goose chase. What would he do if Stella was nowhere to be found? A few days in the islands would be pleasant, he thought, and he summoned up a mental image of perfect waves crashing on clean white sand. But he knew at once that no amount of sun-soaked tranquillity would cancel out his concern for Stella's wellbeing. If he couldn't find her, he would have to go back to New York to try to pick up her trail some other way. But the distaste he felt at the thought of returning to the city was a real worry. I'm sure my love for the Big Apple will come back soon, he told himself.

Then he felt a sharp pang of guilt as thoughts of the city led naturally to thoughts of Peta. Whenever she came to mind now, guilt always followed. Guilt for the loss of their home, for putting her life in danger, for not wanting to go to London or have babies. Guilt for not loving her enough.

And now guilt for flying west rather than east, for caring more about Stella's wellbeing than hers, for not even missing her. No doubt Peta had plenty of cause to feel disappointed in the relationship. Well, that's just tough for her, he told himself, but immediately felt guilty for even thinking that. The easier course was not to think about her at all, to trust time to heal her hurts. So he retuned the channels in his head and recalled the fantasy beach scene. By focusing on the rolling blue waves as they curled and foamed and sucked across the beach, his mind was soon drifting away and Jack fell into the deepest sleep he'd had in days.

American Airlines' connecting flight from Los Angeles to Honolulu arrived a little early in Hawaii, at three in the afternoon local time. Jack was greeted by balmy breezes and air warmed to about 85 degrees. It felt good after the autumnal coolness of New York. His only luggage was a small roll-on suitcase, purchased – like virtually everything in his possession – during a Saturday afternoon shopping spree in Manhattan. His once-splendid wardrobe now consisted almost entirely of summer vacation wear. More shopping would be required when he returned to the mainland.

A taxi delivered him to the front entrance of the Outrigger Hotel in less than thirty minutes, and Jack found the hotel perched right on top of Waikiki Beach. The exterior had a boxiness to it that reminded Jack of the Gold Coast back in Australia, where – to his eyes at least – the developers had worked hard to turn something beautiful into some-thing truly ugly. At only twenty storeys or so, at least this tower block did not dominate the way the buildings at Surfer's Paradise did. And the location was certainly a holidaymaker's dream, with access directly onto Waikiki and views across blue water to Diamond Head.

Eschewing the attention of polite, smiling staff who could not understand why he wasn't checking in, Jack wandered through the massive lobby of the hotel, hoping to get lucky and see Stella. But it was a hopeless task. There were busy bars and restaurants, an enormous pool surrounded by sun beds and then there was the beach itself, just a short walk away. Stella could be anywhere, if she was here at all.

Making his way back to the front entrance, still pulling his small suitcase behind him, Jack was quickly attended to by another friendly man in white trousers and a floral shirt, offering to call up a cab.

'Did you enjoy your stay, sir?'

'Actually, I've only just arrived,' Jack said. 'I was hoping to surprise my fiancée, who's been staying here with her family, but I can't seem to locate her.' He pulled the pictures of Stella from his pocket, along with a ten-dollar bill, and showed them to the bellhop. 'Have you seen her by any chance?'

'Sure!' the man said. 'You don't forget a hottie like that in a hurry. Oh,' he added, when he realised what he'd said, 'I'm sorry, sir. I didn't mean . . .'

'It's okay,' Jack said with a smile. 'I'm used to it.'

'She's been around all week,' the bellhop said quickly. 'I often saw her over there by the payphones. The older lady, I seen her too. But I think you missed them. I'm pretty sure they checked out yesterday.'

Jack slipped him the ten dollars and reached into his pocket for another bill. 'Any idea where she went?'

'No, sorry, but I could ask round the other guys, if you like.'

With a practised move of his hand, Jack passed over the second tip with the more recent photograph of Stella. 'I'd really appreciate that.'

Oh God, Jack thought, as he watched the bellhop scurry away towards the small group of men in identical dress gathered near the front entrance. She's gone. She's probably heading back to New York. I probably passed her in the air. But then he saw the smiling bellhop returning, with another smiling man in tow, and he reached into his pocket to peel away some more greenbacks from his dwindling wad of cash.

'Sonny here says they took a cab to the airport yesterday,' the first bellhop said.

'Sure,' the slightly built Sonny said, passing the photo back to Jack. 'I brought their bags down. Nice ladies from Australia.'

'They say where they were heading?' Jack asked, fingering a twenty-dollar bill.

'Maui,' Sonny said, his bright eyes drawn to Jack's hand. 'Kapalua Bay Resort. I asked them, you know, making conversation. The lady in the photo didn't say much, but her mother and her sister, they never stopped talking. The sister wasn't so happy to leave, you know? She liked the shopping here in Honolulu.'

'Yeah,' Jack said knowingly, 'that sounds like her. How long does it take to get to Maui?'

'It's just a thirty-minute flight, sir,' Sonny said. 'You want Island Air – they fly direct into Kapalua. They have flights, like, every hour or so.'

'Thanks, guys,' Jack said, giving them each a twenty. 'You've been a great help. Reckon you could rustle me up a cab?'

'Yes, sir!' They responded in unison and then bolted away. By the time Jack had made his way to the driveway, a taxi was waiting, it's back door already open.

Back at Honolulu International, Jack reserved a seat on the last flight of the day to Maui's Kapalua Airport, leaving at 4.30, and while he was waiting he studied a simple map provided by the helpful airline staff. He saw that Kapalua was perched on the north-western coast of the figure-eight-shaped island. The Kapalua Bay Resort was marked and appeared to be surrounded by golf courses. Would he find Stella there, he wondered? Maybe she'd left her sister and mother at the airport and they were continuing their vacation alone while she headed back to face her demons.

Don't worry, he told himself and smiled. This investigative stuff was fun. Tracking your quarry halfway around the world while hopping from one island fun spot to another. What a lark! And what a surprise he would give Stella if he found her there among the fairways and palm trees. How would she react? When his flight was called he jumped up with all the enthusiasm of a genuine holidaymaker.

The aircraft he was directed to was smaller and noisier than anything he normally flew in, but that just added to the sense of adventure. And once in the air he found the views of spectacular coastline, sweeping green fields of cane and pineapple and deep blue Pacific Ocean were so much better from a small plane, with wings overhead and an altitude not too lofty. He spent the entire flight glued to the window.

Thirty minutes later, the little plane was circling in a steep descent towards a primitive-looking airstrip perched on a ridge above the one major road that hugged the coast of Maui. As they came in to land, he thought he could pick out the Kapalua Bay Resort. It looked like a broad sea of manicured fairways with an accommodation block pushed discreetly off to one side close to the water, where it would be out of the way of the golfers.

With a thump and trundle, the aircraft rolled down the simple runway and pulled up next to a brown shed, which was more large rain shelter than terminal building. Inside the shed, there was a row of phones offering instant connection to a slew of car rental establishments. Jack picked Alamo for no particular reason, and within a few minutes, a van turned up to carry him to the depot, about a mile south along the Honoapiilani Highway, which, after a couple of attempts at pronunciation, Jack resolved to refer to simply as 'the highway'. At the depot he was issued with a metallic blue Chrysler convertible that looked like it had seen a few miles.

The young guy with the car keys saw the look on Jack's face and said, 'It's all we got left right now. If you want something fancier you should book ahead next time.'

'It'll do fine,' Jack said, taking the keys.

'Where you staying?' the Hawaiian guy asked. 'You need directions?'

Jack shook his head. 'Just like the car, I didn't book ahead. I was thinking about the Kapalua Bay Resort. I've heard it's pretty nice.'

'Sure, I guess, if you like that kinda place. Pricey though. Look, if you got that sort of cash to splash, I can get you a whole house for a week. You know, private, great views, plenty of room.'

Jack looked closely at the young man and saw a friendly eagerness. 'Really?'

'Sure! My mother-in-law's a realtor in Lahaina, right down the coast there. She's got some great vacation rentals on her books. Want me to give her a call?'

Jack thought for a moment and quickly decided that a place of his own was much more appealing than another sterile hotel room.

'You think she has something close to the resort?'

'You wait there and I'll find out,' the rental guy said, and he took off towards the office at a run.

Jack put his suitcase in the trunk of the convertible and was checking out the car's controls when the bright white smile of his new friend appeared at the window. 'You want the roof down? I'll show you how to do it.'

'Sure, why not?' Jack said.

While demonstrating the correct way to retract the soft top, the young guy said, 'You're in luck. She's had a cancellation on a great place in Napili, real close to Kapalua Bay. Two bedrooms, right on the coast. You can have it for the week for a thousand bucks. You'll rack that up in four days at the resort. The agency's closed now but she'll meet you there in ten minutes if you're interested.'

'Sounds good. Thanks for all your help.'

'Hey, no problem. I get brownie points with the wife when I get her mother some business.'

Jack smiled, thinking to himself that the kid didn't look old enough to be married, and listened to the simple instructions on how to get to the realtor's office. With the light breeze ruffling his hair, he pulled the convertible out on to the highway and headed south, waving his thanks to the beaming Hawaiian as he left.

Although Maui was quieter than Waikiki, there was still a steady stream of traffic moving in both directions along the highway. Resorts and shopping complexes along the beach side of the road apparently met every vacationing family's need to have their favourite stores and fast food outlets close by, even when they were thousands of miles from home. The busy little harbour town of Lahaina, squeezed between the highway and the water, was more quaint and Jack found the mother-in-law's agency easily. Barely fifteen minutes later he was back on the road, heading north this time.

Impulsively pulling into a shopping centre, he paid a quick visit to a supermarket to pick up a few supplies and a map. He then headed further up the coast, back past the Alamo depot and the airport. The air was still wonderfully warm and he loved the sensation of wind in his face and hair. The left side of his body felt the persistence of the sun, now dropping low in a pale blue sky out to the west. The car radio spewed out the same songs they played in New York. And London and Singapore and Sydney.

Finding the peninsula where his vacation home was located was easy enough. It was at the end of a side street running west off the old highway, which wound its narrow way around the contours of Maui's jagged coast. The area was densely populated with small- and medium-sized family vacation destinations, most utilising the word 'resort' somewhere in their advertising. Around and in front of the low-rise buildings, dense green jungle-type foliage projected the illusion of an untouched paradise.

The house Jack had rented was in a gated community perched right along the cliff top. At the end of the jungle-lined side street, a solid metal gate painted a pale rust colour slid open when he waved an electronic key at the control box. Once inside the gate, a slender asphalt road ran in both directions, but neat signs informed him he was to travel in one direction only, to the right. He followed the road around, looking for numbers on the small, almost identical houses lining both sides.

Most looked like they were occupied by permanent residents, and a quick survey of decor and vehicles suggested the average age of Jack's temporary neighbours was somewhere over sixty. After five or six houses, the road turned sharply left towards the sea, and then left again to form another street of homes, half of which looked directly out over the water. This was where the big prices must have been paid back in the eighties when, Jack guessed, the development had been constructed.

He was gratified to find that the house he'd been allocated was on the right as he drove up, perched on the very edge of Maui. Like all the others, it was a low bungalow, with a concrete carport dominating on the street side. Well-maintained shrubs and plants hugged the walls and lined the path and the rest of the ground was covered in the thick-leaved, always-green grass usually found in the tropics.

Inside was a compact but comfortable two-bedroom residence with slate floors in the living areas and a reasonably modern kitchen looking out to a casual living area and then beyond. And the beyond was spectacular. Through sliding glass doors, across ten feet of paving and another twelve of well-mown turf, Maui dropped away and the Pacific Ocean took over. Across maybe a mile or two of blue water flecked with white, another majestic Hawaiian island rose up – Molokai, according to Jack's map – framed at that moment by the setting sun. It was picture-perfect postcard stuff.

As he imagined every other first-time guest had done, Jack hurried through the building and out onto the grass at the edge of the cliff. The view was awesome. Looking north up the coast, a white collar of foam between the dark blue ocean and the land outlined small bays and points. The bays appeared to be sandy beaches and the rocky points were dominated by man-made structures. Across two bays, on one of those outcroppings of land – not much more than a half-mile from where he stood – lights in the grounds of the Kapalua Bay Resort were being switched on. He could just make out the main buildings of the resort, but he'd seen enough resorts in his time to have a pretty clear image of the layout. He could also imagine Stella there, preparing for an evening of fun and reminiscence with her sister and mother. Unless she was back in the cold night of New York City.

At that moment it didn't bother him either way. The sun was sinking behind Molokai, whose long, gently sloping sides were turning gold in the last rays of celestial light. A line of clouds close to the island's peak made it look like a smoking volcano, with the setting sun a giant fireball earlier ejected. Jack watched with contented awe as nature put on a show worthy of any opening night.

Looking around, he could see his vacation home was attached to an identical residence on one side. Beyond that, there were four or five duplexes to his immediate north and about the same to the south, although the shape of the land didn't afford him an unfettered view in that direction.

He was amazed to be the only person out in the backyard enjoying this incredible sunset. Spectacular natural wonders like this must be commonplace around here, he thought, or his neighbours were either absent or dead. Still, it suited him just fine. Here, the solitude was invigorating, compared to the sad isolation he'd experienced the last two nights in a Manhattan hotel room. He felt healthy and sharp, free of all the burdens that had plagued him in New York – and strong enough to face what was to come.

36

After a long day of travel, a shower, shave and change of clothes felt like both a necessity and a luxury. As soon as these requirements had been met, Jack could not resist the urge to continue his search. No longer fearing Daniel Cross, who was hopefully fending off a police investigation, Jack's primary motivation was simply to see Stella.

When he stepped outside, shortly after 8 p.m., he was enveloped by an intensity of darkness, never experienced in the big city. Without bothering to work out the best way to reinstate the roof of his rental car, he made his way back out to the old highway and turned left, driving slowly into the impenetrable gloom. A few minutes later he found himself surrounded by the manicured lawns of the Kapalua Bay resort, rolling over man-made hills and depressions aimed at thrilling the golfing fraternity. Then he saw a complex of tennis courts and finally the main buildings of the hotel came into view, cascading down sweeping slopes of grass – dotted with tall palms – towards the sound of waves hitting the shore. Parking the car in the large lot at the top of the rise, he chose to take a cross-country route, strolling past the southern wing of guest rooms, across manicured lawns and eventually joining a concrete path delineated by discreet lighting. Dressed in linen slacks and a Hawaiian shirt purchased, ironically, at Barney's in New York, he thought he looked the part, if a little pale-skinned.

Walking down the slope towards the beach, he looked up to his right at the five levels of hotel arranged in blocks descending, step-like, towards the coast. It was a big place, with hundreds of rooms. The architecture was uninspiring but relatively inoffensive, the whole complex painted a dark khaki colour.

Each suite on Jack's side had a large balcony facing south, making the most of the view. Although many of the rooms were illuminated from the inside, affording Jack a glimpse of crisp, white decor, the few people he could see didn't fit the description of two youngish Australian women and their mother. From the outside, the resort was eerily quiet. Palm fronds rustled and a few insects were beginning to stir into chorus, but apart from that the only noise was the gentle collapse of waves over rocks in the distance.

Following the narrow path almost to the shoreline, where it branched in several directions, Jack chose to turn right, taking him around the end of the building and then past a large, butterfly-shaped swimming pool forming the central feature of the elaborate landscaping between the two main wings of the hotel. He could see that each wing sported rooms facing both in towards the pool and out to sea, making it out of the question to locate Stella by the Peeping Tom method.

He made his way back up the hill, through the middle of the resort, along more well-ordered paths and past more beautifully kept gardens, including a trickling man-made stream that flowed out from a pool located inside the main building itself. When he reached the central block, he climbed a set of outdoor stairs to one of many doors accessing the main entrance to the hotel. He walked casually across the white-tiled lobby, which was suspended on one side over a glass-walled atrium looking out to the gardens and, in daylight, the ocean.

Beyond the concierge's desk, he found an alcove with telephone cubicles. Picking up a house phone, he followed the instructions on a card fixed to the wall and dialled '9' to talk to the operator. But as expected, when he asked to be connected to Ms Sartori's room, he was told there was no guest at the hotel by that name.

Shrugging his shoulders, Jack saw the bar situated across the lobby, in the large balcony formed by the mezzanine level. It was called the Lehua Lounge and just the thought of food was enough to make his stomach rumble. It was a good spot to observe the comings and goings so he found a table with a clear view of the lobby and a partial view of the restaurant on the ground floor below. There were more people around him now, and more noise. The lounge was about a quarter full.

On the recommendation of a waitress with the healthy, sun-drenched look of a local, he ordered a lobster salad and a beer, both of which arrived quickly and were consumed just as rapidly. Then he ordered another beer and relaxed back into his seat, beginning to sense a delightful feeling of vacation complacency. Lazily scanning the faces of the other occupants of the lounge, he felt his eyes droop and the thought of a long sleep was appealing. Tomorrow, he thought, I'll come back and check out the pool and the beach. Surely the three Aussies would not be far from one or the other. He turned his head back towards the lobby, and saw three women lined up at the concierge's desk, right opposite where he sat. He failed to register them at first, then he looked again, and his eyes widened. They had their backs to him but he was in no doubt he'd found his quarry.

On the right, Stella was the tallest, at about five eight or nine, and the most slender. Her sister was two inches shorter and about ten pounds heavier and their mother was a further two inches in arrears and rounder again. Angie and Stella both wore their hair out – straight and shiny and almost black in this light. Mother's hair was artificially frizzy and dyed reddish-brown. They were casually but elegantly attired in summer dresses. Stella's was cream silk – simply cut and cinched in at her small waist – and a striking contrast to her rich tan. In fact, Jack noted, all three women were well tanned already, and he felt a familiar envy for those with olive skin.

Jack stayed still, keeping his face in the shadow of a potted plant. It would not be fair to Stella to surprise her out in the open, he decided. Let her have one last night of peace. Any conversation she was making with the concierge was inaudible, with piano music and the burbling of an unseen water feature rising up from the level below. Then two rotund men came and stood uncertainly at the threshold of the lounge, blocking his view of the women. The men waved off the hostess who approached them, seemingly undecided about the venue. Annoyingly, they continued to stand in Jack's line of sight, but he could see enough to know Stella was still at the counter across the lobby. The concierge was on the phone.

The two men continued to stand there. Jack decided they had to be new arrivals on the island, like him. Pasty skin and brown hair showing no sign of sun bleaching. They were clearly big strong fellows, if a little soft in the middle, both around forty years old. Golfers? Maybe, but the longer Jack looked at them, the more out of place they seemed.

Then his paranoia kicked in. From where he was sitting it seemed increasingly clear these two guys were primarily interested in Stella and her party. They weren't looking into the cocktail lounge, they were watching the three women. Were they just hoping to pick up or did they have a more dangerous purpose? Jack's senses came into sharp focus and he sat forward in his chair. He had little doubt Stella and her sister would normally attract more than their fair share of male attention, but if these guys were looking for romance, they were going about it in a strange way. Maybe they were just enjoying the view – most men could be found guilty of that.

The acid test came when the three women turned away from the concierge's counter and came back into view, walking away to Jack's right across the lobby, towards the southern wing of hotel rooms. They looked pleased with themselves, waving brochures about and giggling.

In contrast, the two large men didn't behave innocently at all. First they looked away, keeping their faces hidden from the women. Then they exchanged a few words and moved back into the lobby, trailing behind Stella and her family. Jack couldn't believe it. It was a professional tail, he was sure of it. Stella was under observation. So much for one last night of peace. This changed everything.

He threw some cash on the table next to his empty plate, making the assumption that, even at resort prices, fifty bucks would cover the tab. Trying to move casually but quickly, he negotiated his way around cane furniture and glass tables and back out to the main part of the lobby. Away to his right he could see both men at the far end of the long room, but the women were already out of sight. Then one of the men stopped suddenly, hanging back while his companion continued down the hallway leading to the guest suites. They appeared to communicate with small hand movements. The one who stayed back flicked open a cell phone and pushed the buttons. Jack thought about moving close enough to hear the conversation, but this seemed too risky.

He'd set out from the lounge with the intention of following the men, but halfway across the lobby he had a crisis of confidence. If his amateurish efforts alerted Stella's watchers and forced their hand, he might well regret the consequences. He threw a U-turn in the centre of the lobby and walked over to the concierge's counter. A doorman standing inside the main entrance was watching, but was too experienced to reveal what he was thinking.

It was the Sunday evening shift, so there was a young guy on duty rather than a person of age and experience Jack would normally expect to find as concierge in an expensive hotel. It was the same man who'd served Stella's group, but Jack knew better than to ask about the other guests.

'Good evening, sir.'

'Good evening. I'd like some information about playing golf.'

'Are you a guest at the hotel, sir?'

'Do I need to be to play golf?'

'Not at all, sir, but there are different packages available to hotel guests.'

'Well, I'm just a visitor.'

'Let me get you some brochures.' He bent down to open one of the drawers under his counter.

This was the sort of thing Jack was hoping for. He leaned over the counter and scanned the few documents that lay there. A couple of brochures for mud bath beauty treatments, one advertising bike rides down the side of Maui's giant volcano and an order book – one of those pads that produce multicoloured copies. He looked for names and room numbers, reading upside down. The young concierge's head was already coming back up.

'While you're there,' Jack said, 'I'd really appreciate a map and some information about the hotel. It looks like a beautiful place.'

The concierge squatted again, muttering a polite word or two. Jack could now see the last two orders made in the book on the counter. The last was a massage for a Mrs Jones in room 243. The second-last was a manicure and facial for a Mrs Parisi in 152. It was the reservation book for health and beauty treatments. Jones 243, Parisi 152. Jack repeated the names and numbers to himself to lodge them firmly in his brain.

The helpful concierge was upright now, pointing out features on various brochures and maps. Jack tried to look interested but it wasn't easy. When the young man was finished Jack thanked him and retreated back to the telephone alcove around the corner.

Glancing back before he stepped inside, he noted that the second man following Stella had gone too. With his heart beating rapidly, he picked up the phone and tried to decide which room number to call. Although Mrs Jones had the last booking, he was uncertain. Parisi seemed a much more likely name, given Stella's Italian heritage. And the concierge had been on the phone while the women were at his desk. Maybe he took a reservation from Mrs Jones after Stella's sister was already in the book. Jack's gut told him to go with Parisi and he dialled room 152.

'Hello?'

'Hello, my name is —' he began, but then baulked at the thought of giving his name too soon, '— uh, John. I'm trying to contact Stella Sartori.'

'Who?'

'Stella Sartori.'

'My name is Parisi. Who is this? What do you want?' The lady's accent was distinctly North American, and distinctly grumpy.

'I want to apologise. I must have the wrong number.'

Mrs Parisi hung up and Jack admonished himself for trying to be too clever. He'd just have to hope Stella's sister married a nice Welsh boy. If not, he was back to square one. A woman also answered the call to room 243, which was a start, but not much more.

'Hello?'

'Hi, is that Mrs Jones?'

'No. I am her mother.' This time the accent was heavy, like that of someone whose English had been learned late in life.

'And your daughter is Angela Jones?'

'That's right, can I help you?'

'I hope so. My name is Jack, Jack Rogers. I'm actually trying to make contact with Stella Sartori.'

Jack sensed rather then heard the phone changing hands but nobody spoke.

'Stella? Is that you? It's Jack, Stella. Are you there?'

A long pause, then a sigh.

'Where are you?' Stella asked.

Her voice was music to Jack's ears. 'I'm here,' he said excitedly. 'Right here at your hotel.'

'How the hell did you find me?'

'It's a long story and we don't have the time —'

'What the hell are you doing here, Jack?' Stella kept her voice low. 'Who else knows you've come here?'

'Nobody, I promise. I didn't even know for sure you were here until about ten minutes ago. I was down in the bar when you were talking to the concierge. I was having a drink not forty feet away from you. By the way, you look great in that cream dress.'

'Jeez, you've been spying on us. How long have you been in Hawaii?' She sounded stunned, as if he'd totally knocked the wind out of her sails.

'I just got to Maui this evening. I've got a lot to tell you but I really didn't plan to bother you tonight. When I was in the bar I saw two guys behaving like they were following you. I'm sorry to have to tell you this, but I don't think I'm the only one to work out where you are.'

There was a sharp intake of breath. 'You're kidding! Are you sure?'

'Not a hundred per cent. But two guys set out to follow you, I'm pretty sure of that. Maybe they just want a date, but, without wanting to sound snobby, they didn't look like they fit, you know? Cheap buzz cuts, bad shoes, big guys. Could easily be employees of a dodgy security company.'

'Angie, make sure the door's locked and bolted,' Jack heard Stella say to her sister urgently. 'And close the balcony door, you can smoke inside.' To him, she said, 'Jack, are you truly on the level?'

'What, you think I'm trying to flush you out or something?' It was his turn to get a little riled. 'You have no idea what I've been through in the last few days, Stella. The things I've seen —' He stopped.

'What? What's happened? I tried to call you.'

He was sorely tempted to spell it all out for her. The robbery and chase, the shootings and the torture of her lawyer, the fire and death of her husband on 4th Street, all of it, but he stopped himself. Sharing the burden would have to wait. Right now he didn't want to distract either of them from the issue at hand.

'I'll tell you everything later, Stella. Soon, I promise. But we should talk face to face. And the most important thing is to get you out of here. How on earth did you think you'd get away with keeping the same vacation plans you had before the Cross thing blew up?'

That elicited another sigh from Stella. 'Well, I knew it was a risk but I didn't think it was a big one. Angie made all the arrangements, everything's in her name. And she was so excited about it. She did such a great job. David didn't want to know anything about it after I told him he wasn't coming, and I don't talk about private stuff with people at work. I couldn't think of anyone who knew. Not in the US.'

'But they found you anyway.'

'So you say.'

'Are you prepared to risk it? If you don't think they're watching you, I could just come around to your room now. Or you could come to the bar for a drink if you like. Maybe we'll see those two guys again and I can ask 'em what they're doing here. If it turns out they're two vacuum-cleaner salesmen looking for a good time, we can all relax. Even so, I'd still recommend you move hotels. After all, I managed to find you, didn't I?'

'Mmm,' was all he heard from the other end, while Stella thought about her situation.

Of course, she was loath to upset the great vacation she had planned with her family – Jack would be too. But he didn't think she had much choice. If Stella wanted to be confident she was operating beyond the clutches of Daniel Cross, she needed to get away and she needed to do it soon.

'So?' he said impatiently.

'So,' she answered, 'we need a plan.'

37

Monday morning in Manhattan found Agent Shannon Winters in a foul mood. With her right hand, she was holding a telephone to her ear, listening to the blandest of muzak. With her left hand she tapped a pen on the desk, counting down her ebbing stores of patience. A voice came on the line.

'This is Supervisor Gail Saunders. How can I help you, Agent Winters?'

'I ordered up a file on Saturday and it only just arrived —'

'Look,' the supervisor said bluntly. 'You have to understand, a file that old has to be located and then scanned. It takes time —'

'No, no,' Winters interrupted, 'I knew it would take a day. That's not my problem. As I was trying to explain to your clerk, my concern is that you didn't send the original file.'

'What do you mean? You don't get the original documents any more; we scan all our files.'

'Yes, I know, but the documents I received have been doctored. There are whole sections blacked out. Did someone down there decide I don't have the necessary security clearance or something?'

'Hold the line please.'

'Wait!' Winters said, but the muzak was back on the line.

A minute later, the uninterested voice of the supervisor returned. 'There were no special security tags on that file,' she reported, 'and it's old enough to fall outside most legislative protections. My staff have assured me you were sent the entire file as it exists in the archive.'

'You're telling me the FBI archive doesn't hold the original file on this case?'

'No, I'm telling you that you have the official FBI file as specified in your file request. Any markings or deletions in the documents must have been on the originals when the file was created.'

'I'm sorry, but that just doesn't make sense. These are all FBI documents in this file. Transcripts of interviews, background and investigative notes. It's all stuff created inside the Bureau. There must be an uncensored version of these papers somewhere, surely?'

The supervisor said nothing.

'Oh, come on, Gail,' Winters softened her tone. 'This is highly unusual, isn't it? I mean, either somebody has doctored the original file or this isn't the original, right?'

The supervisor dropped her voice. 'Actually,' she said, 'I've seen something like this before. Twice.'

'Seen what?'

'Old files like this, all marked up in the archive.'

'And?'

'And in those cases, we concluded that most likely another file existed at some time. A special file.'

'A special file? And where would such a special file have been held?'

'In the Director's office.'

It took a moment for Winters to absorb the significance of that statement. 'The Director? But . . . you mean J. Edgar Hoover's office? Are you saying this is one of his famous secret files?'

Supervisor Saunders reverted to a more brusque tone. 'All the FBI's files are treated as confidential, Agent Winters. And the only thing I'm telling you, officially, is that you have the complete archive in front of you. Now, unless there's something else my department can do for you today . . .'

'Right, okay, no, I guess not,' Winters said, as she tried to get her thoughts straight.

The supervisor disconnected the call immediately.

Winters put the phone down and looked at her computer screen. Although the scanned documents were clearly legible, she felt the need to hold them in her hands so she sent the file to a nearby printer. She collected the papers and took them to a small meeting room, sliding the sign on the outside to 'occupied' before she closed the door.

Chronologically, the first document on the file was the typed transcript of an interview recorded at the Washington DC Field Office on Friday, 30 October 1967. The participants were Special Agent Peter Sedgwick and the Chairman and President of Collins Military Systems, Gilbert Collins. Winters' eyes skipped over the preliminary information and settled on the meat of the interview.

PS: *What can we do for you today, Mr Collins?*

GC: *I thought I might be able to meet with* ███████ ▪
███████████████████. ███
██████████████████████
██▪

PS: ████████████████████. █
████████████████████. *I hope that will be satisfactory.*

GC: *Well, I suppose so, but this is a highly confidential matter.*

PS: *Of course, sir. Now, what is it you want to talk about?*

GC: *There's a contract between my company and the Pentagon. It took effect in January 1964. It's a contract for the supply of electronic detonators to all branches of the military. In the past three years, it has more than trebled the revenues of the company.*

PS: *Good for you, sir.*

GC: *Well, yes, it certainly has generated enormous growth. We're about to open our first office in Britain. I'm flying there tomorrow for the official opening and a meeting of the board. None of that would be happening without the contract.*

PS: *What's the problem?*

GC: *The sale was negotiated by my son, Ewan, together with Daniel Cross, a brilliant young man Ewan met in graduate school. Now I'm about to retire and Ewan and his advisers will be taking over officially. This meeting in London is to be my last as the head of CMS.*

PS: *Sounds like you're leaving the company in good shape.*

GC: *Financially, that's certainly true, but there is more to a great company than the bottom line, Agent Sedgwick. A company and its leaders also need to exemplify strong core values: honesty, integrity, professionalism. It is those values that my father embodied and I have tried to maintain. Until recently they were at the heart of our success.*

PS: *And you think your son won't carry on the tradition?*

GC: *I am beginning to wonder if my son has the slightest idea what honesty and integrity mean at all.*

PS: *Because of this contract you mentioned?*

GC: *The contract, yes. But not just the terms of the contract, you understand, it's the way it was won.*

PS: *Are you implying graft? Corruption?*

GC: *Yes, corruption, and worse. I'm pretty sure people died.*

PS: *What people? Government people?*

GC: *I think so. Look, I'd better start at the beginning.*

PS: *That makes sense.*

GC: *When Ewan and Daniel first came back from Washington with the deal, I was just as pleased as everyone else. They'd been at it for over a year, but they'd finally succeeded. And against some strong competition, too. When I saw the terms of this new contract, I was truly impressed. The price agreed was at the high end of our expectations; there were automatic renewal clauses like I'd never seen before. And there was a research subsidy clause with a cumulative effect built in, which is going to net my company untold millions of taxpayer dollars for decades to come, without any clear obligation to deliver any extra value in return.*

PS: *A good deal indeed.*

GC: *That's what I thought at first. I convinced myself that the military must need our detonators more than I thought. But then, after a while, I sensed that our long relationship with the Pentagon had really suffered from the deal. People weren't returning my calls, some of my oldest acquaintances were cold towards me. I no longer received invitations to industry briefings and when new contracts came up, we weren't invited to tender. I couldn't even get officials to accept my invitation to a simple lunch. When I pushed for answers, I discovered that my company is now regarded as a toxic entity. Pentagon personnel, military and civilian alike, want nothing to do with us.*

PS: *They feel like they've been duped?*

GC: *It's more than that. More sinister. It's taken me many months to tease out the information. People were very unwilling to talk, still are mostly. So I'm sure I don't have all the facts, but I have most of it, I think.*

PS: *You don't appear to have any notes or documents, Mr Collins. Do you have —?*

GC: *Oh no, it's all in my head. I'm not one for writing things down. You never know who will see it.*

PS: *I see. Please, go on.*

GC: *Well, this is what I think happened. When the Pentagon is going to make a decision like this, they establish a panel to evaluate the tenders. There are representatives of the various branches of the military, scientific advisers, other senior supply officers and so on. And each of those men has others advising him. But in the year or so our contract was under consideration, strange things began to happen to the people associated with the panel. With the benefit of hindsight, patterns begin to emerge. There were personnel changes, which are not unusual in the military, of course, but a number of officers got surprise postings, and they were all, according to my sources, people opposed to our tender. All the signs of manipulation were there, and I've seen them before. Lobbyists and politicians have been known to exert undue influence, but this must have been someone with very powerful friends.*

PS: *Hard to prove that sort of thing.*

GC: *I agree. Hard to prove the cases of graft and extortion too, but the rumours persist. Key people changed their minds very suddenly and our detonator became a front-runner. I was told that a captain in Army Purchasing rolled over for a Harley-Davidson. And a naval lieutenant changed his mind about our detonator after he was shown photographs of himself and his secretary in a motel room during the lunch hour.*

PS: *I don't suppose you can prove any of this.*

GC: *Not directly, no. Most of it is hearsay. But I've been trying to follow the money trail. You see, I'm pretty sure that CMS paid for all this. Ewan and Daniel spent a fortune that year, and they claimed it was all for attorneys and consultants. But I've been advised by my bank that, although various accounts were used, all those fees effectively went to one man – Tony Castle.*

PS: *Tony Castle. And what's his story?*

GC: *I've only met him once. He's a foreigner, European I think. Young too, but Ewan assured me he has good qualifications. Told me he was the top student in his class at business school. And that's all I really know about him, except that my company paid him well over $100,000 over the course of '62 and '63. My son assures me his work was critical to winning the contract and I believe him. But I think he did more than just give Ewan business advice.*

PS: *You think he was paying off the officials?*

GC: *Yes, but when they couldn't be paid off or leaned on, I think he also arranged for them to die. I think the first one was Colonel Robert Shroud. He was a decent man – I knew him personally. He flew in Korea and had a wife and three kids. I knew he wasn't a fan of our detonator because he was always honest with me. Then, one evening in March '63, he was killed in one of the car parks around the Pentagon when he was walking to his car. They said it was a mugging that got ugly when he fought back. He was stabbed through the heart. I didn't think there was any connection to Ewan and the contract at the time, and not for a long time after. But much later, once I'd found out about the others, it was suddenly clear. He was killed for the contract.*

PS: *The others?*

GC: *A civilian scientist who didn't like our design disappeared. Just disappeared. And one of the aides to the admiral who would make the final call for the navy, a young lieutenant regarded as a rising star, was found dead in an alley in one of the worst parts of Washington. My sources tell me that he, too, was against awarding us the contract.*

PS: *And you believe these deaths were all organised by this Tony Castle?*

GC: *I've cross-checked the dates with our accounts. Close to the time each of these men met their end, payments of exactly $10,000 were made to Mr Castle, one way or another.*

PS: *And that's the extent of your proof?*

GC: *Well, yes, but I'm not ▮▮▮▮▮▮▮▮▮. Surely, with your resources you can investigate, interrogate. Get to the truth of the matter.*

PS: *I wish it were so easy. ▮▮▮▮▮▮▮▮▮ only act on the basis of clearly established evidence. All you have so far is an interesting story. One worthy of investigation, perhaps, but still just an unproved theory.*

GC: *So, what do I do? Just hand my company over to a group of immoral criminals prepared to murder anyone who gets in their way?*

PS: *The first thing you need to do is prepare a proper statement, a signed deposition. Put in as much detail as you can, including the accounting information, the names of your contacts at the Pentagon and as much information as you can pull together on Daniel Cross and Tony Castle. Even your son, sir, anything that may be relevant. Dates, amounts, everything.*

GC: *I don't know about that. Like I said, I don't like putting things in writing unless it's really necessary.*

PS: *I assure you, Mr Collins, it is really necessary. If you expect the Bureau to conduct an investigation, we will need something substantial. Without that, there's nothing much we can do.*

GC: *All right, I'll give that some thought. But you will look into Tony Castle, won't you? Surely a man like that must be known to the FBI. And Daniel Cross. He's the puppeteer, and my only son is the goddamned puppet.*

PS: *I will make some enquiries. But really, sir, I'm going to need more detailed information.*

GC: *I understand.*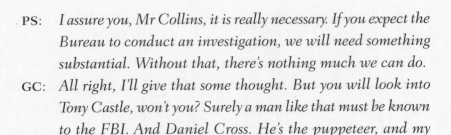

PS:

GC:

PS:

Interview terminated

The next document was dated two days later. It was a handwritten file note in the disciplined copperplate of Agent Peter Sedgwick.

I received a telephone call from Gilbert Collins, President of CMS, shortly after 4 p.m. Washington time. Being a Sunday, the call was patched through to my home. Mr Collins was calling from London, England, and the connection was not very clear. However, it was apparent that he was very upset. He said that everything he had told me on Friday was insignificant compared to what he had learned that evening in his London hotel.

He was staying at the Savoy, in the Presidential suite, which he was sharing with his son Ewan during the board's stay. After the long journey, Mr Collins decided to take a nap in one of the bedrooms. After some time he was woken by the sound of voices. Ewan Collins, Daniel Cross and Tony Castle were talking in the suite's lounge room and were clearly unaware of his presence. Apparently Mr Collins was expected to travel by ship but had changed his plans in order to meet with me in Washington on Friday. By flying, he had arrived two days earlier than his son expected.

Thinking they were alone, the three men talked with no inhibition. Mr Collins said the men spoke of celebrating their reunion — the first time they had been together since ▉▉▉▉▉▉▉▉▉▉

▉▉▉▉▉▉▉▉▉▉▉▉▉▉▉▉▉▉▉▉▉▉▉▉▉▉▉▉▉▉▉▉
▉▉▉▉▉▉▉▉▉▉▉▉▉▉▉▉▉▉▉▉▉▉▉▉▉▉▉▉▉▉▉▉
▉▉▉▉▉▉▉▉▉▉▉▉▉▉▉▉▉▉▉▉▉▉▉▉▉▉▉▉▉▉▉▉
▉▉▉▉▉▉▉▉▉▉▉▉▉▉▉▉▉▉▉▉▉▉▉▉▉▉▉▉▉▉▉▉
▉▉▉▉▉▉▉▉▉▉▉▉▉▉▉▉▉▉▉▉▉▉▉▉▉▉▉▉▉▉▉▉
▉▉▉▉▉▉▉▉▉▉▉▉▉▉▉▉▉▉▉▉▉▉▉▉▉▉▉▉▉▉▉▉
▉▉▉▉▉▉▉▉▉▉▉▉▉▉▉▉▉▉▉▉▉▉▉▉▉▉▉▉▉▉▉▉
▉▉▉▉▉▉▉▉▉▉▉▉▉▉▉▉▉▉▉▉▉▉▉▉▉▉▉▉▉▉▉▉

▉▉▉▉▉▉▉. *They talked about how President Johnson's policy in Vietnam was going to turn the contract into a gold mine. They toasted Tony Castle for his vision and courage and Castle pointed out that he had also paid the biggest price, hiding out in Sicily unable to contact his American friends. Mr Collins heard Daniel Cross assure Castle that his reward was not far off and, now that his old identity had been laid to rest, things had been organised for his return to the US.*

Mr Collins said that as the men talked, he finally understood the true impact of the unusual research subsidy clause in the Pentagon contract ███████████████████████████████
███

There was no doubt in his mind that Daniel Cross had manipulated his son into paying Tony Castle ████████████████████
███████████████████, *and with no motive other than pure greed. He said that he was sure a detailed examination of the CMS accounts and banking records would show payments amounting to more than $100,000 to entities associated with Tony Castle* ████████
███████████████████████████████████
███.

I asked Mr Collins to calm down and repeat everything he had told me, which he did. Then I told him that although the allegations were sensational, there was still nothing we could do without evidence. Mr Collins became very angry and asked to speak to ████
████. *I told him that was not possible, but I said that once he returned to the US I would arrange a meeting* ███████████████.
This apparently satisfied Mr Collins, but he said he would not change his travel plans, as he did not want to arouse Daniel Cross's suspicions. He will not be back for nearly eight weeks. He said that he would try to use the time to make a detailed record. He said his friend and colleague Cameron(?) Reeves would be travelling with him and would know how to prepare a signed statement. He will contact me again once he is back in Peoria, to arrange a time for the meeting ██████████████.

Shannon Winters was clenching her fists in frustration when her boss opened the door and stuck his head inside.

'How you doing in here?'

'Look at this crap!' she said, thrusting the papers across the desk.

While he examined the printouts, she told him about her conversation with the archive supervisor. When she'd finished, he whistled his amazement and said, 'So this was one of the old boy's specials, eh? We better tread carefully. If you believe the stories, his collection usually involved the reputations of some highly influential people.'

'I thought the specials were just an urban myth.'

Special Agent Beardsley gave her a look that suggested he didn't relish the idea of provoking Hoover's ghost. 'Who knows? Nobody talks about those days much any more. However, it isn't a stretch to assume that any reference to him has been blacked out, 'specially here, at the beginning of the interview, and here.'

'But that's not all, is it?' Agent Winters said. 'He's also blacked out a bunch of critical information, like whatever Gilbert Collins overheard in London.'

'What else is in the file?'

Winters shuffled the remaining papers. 'Sedgwick's few notes on the key players. Not much, really. Short bios on Daniel Cross and Ewan Collins, but nothing much more than you'd find in *Who's Who*. The stuff on Tony Castle is even vaguer. He was a prize-winning college student, but there was some scuttlebutt about his connections to the mob in Chicago. A suggestion that his name is actually Castelluzzo, a known mafia clan in western Sicily. An unsubstantiated claim that he had something to do with the death of another student at a Chicago college. And then, after 1963, no sign of him in America at all. According to Gilbert Collins he was cooling his heels in the home country.

'Then there's a note dated March 1968. By then, SA Sedgwick was curious as to why he hadn't heard from Mr Collins and tried to make discreet contact, only to discover that Collins had died the previous December, apparently of natural causes. He checked with the local cops who assured him there was no evidence of foul play.

He tried to find out if there was any record of Tony Castle returning to the US, but drew a blank.

'Then, I think he referred the file to the Director and received some instructions. But I'm just guessing, because that page is almost entirely blacked out. It's pretty obvious he was told to let it go.'

Beardsley rubbed his chin with one hand, pondering the options while he tried to imagine the words masked by the thick black lines. Winters was looking at the notes from her Saturday morning meeting. 'Gilbert Collins told Sedgwick that he might get a guy called Reeves to help him document his allegations,' she said. 'According to Jack Rogers, who was the guy you sent me to meet with on Saturday, Reeves wrote the poem I told you about.'

'The virgin thing?'

'Yeah. There must be some link, right?'

'Jesus, who knows? It's damned complicated is what it is. And it's ancient history.'

'Not so ancient if Rogers is right and Cross was responsible for more deaths last week.'

Her boss sighed audibly. 'What do you want to do, Agent Winters? Find out what's underneath those pesky blacked-out lines, I suppose?'

'Sure, but how would I do that? You don't know where Hoover's secret files ended up, do you?'

Beardsley smiled briefly. 'No, but I do know where you can find Pete Sedgwick.'

38

The sun arrived on Maui's shores six time zones later than New York, and the Jones group started the morning as if nothing had changed. Breakfast in the Gardenia Court restaurant, then Stella and her mother spent time by the pool while Angie was treated to the massage she'd booked the night before. Stella's sister expressed a little concern about leaving the resort, but she was determined to have the massage she'd booked and paid for.

Jack spent the morning in Lahaina shopping for, among other things, a new cell phone. Stella had already purchased a disposable phone with pre-paid credit and, thanks to the globalisation of technology, he was able to do the same in the tiny Hawaiian tourist town.

Late in the morning, the family regrouped to take a leisurely stroll around the grounds of the resort and do some wading along the nearby beach. During the walk, Stella had no trouble spotting her minders, even though they operated separately most of the time. Now she knew she was being watched, and with Jack's description of the two men, it was easy to detect them. Staying relaxed was the difficult part, although they'd concluded during their discussions the night before that Cross was unlikely to try anything overt at a place like this. He only needed to know where she was. As long as she stayed under observation and in Hawaii, he should be fairly untroubled. But that would soon change – Stella and Jack intended to shake him up a little.

They began after lunch – by which time, Jack hoped, the two observers would be thoroughly bored. He arrived at the hotel at two when, as agreed, the three women were back in their room. It took him a few minutes to locate Cross's men. One was on the lawn between the beach and the hotel. The other was watching the main entrance, sipping coffee in the lounge and relying on that old standby – a newspaper – as his cover. They were keeping in contact with each other using cell phones, just like everyone else at the resort.

Having pinpointed the enemy, Jack called Stella's room from his new mobile and reported in. 'Time for Plan A,' he said.

'Okay,' Stella replied, 'but before you go I thought you might like to know how Cross's goons found me.'

'Of course! Tell me.'

'We rang my dad this morning to tell him we're leaving. He told my mum that someone from Sutton Brothers called early Friday morning to ask if he knew how to contact me during my vacation.'

'Was he sure it was the bank?'

'Well, he couldn't be sure, obviously, but whoever it was knew I was officially on vacation this week.'

'Yeah, but Stella, David knew that too and we know he talked to Cross.'

'Of course!' she said. 'We shouldn't have come here after you told me about David.'

'Maybe. But if you were gone I wouldn't have found you either, would I?'

'I suppose that's true,' Stella said, sounding unconvinced by the logic. 'Anyway,' she added, 'Dad's information backed up my claim that I've been recalled to attend to an urgent work matter. I think my sister was convinced I was making it all up 'cos I was bored with them. She's got self-esteem issues, that one.'

'How did you explain to your mum and sister that I'm taking them to the airport?'

'I told them our client's businesses include a pineapple plant on Maui. I said I needed to take my sister's rental to go to a meeting at the company's local headquarters. You're here working for the same client, but you're not needed at this meeting so I've asked you to take them.'

Jack couldn't help chuckling.

'I know,' Stella said, laughing too, 'it's a bit of a stretch. But they really have no idea what I do at work so I'm pretty sure they bought it. Just don't say anything to screw it up.'

'I'll try,' Jack said, consulting his watch. 'We'd better get started. We don't want them to miss the flight.'

At 2.45, teary farewells complete, Stella left her hotel room, carrying only a shoulder bag and dressed appropriately for a business meeting on a tropical island. By this time, Jack had moved out to the front of the hotel, taking up a position where he could observe her departure.

When she appeared at the main entrance to collect her rental car, which was being brought around by a valet attendant, Jack could see one of her stalkers hanging back, talking urgently into his phone. A young man in uniform drove up in the red compact Angie Jones had hired from Avis and Stella gave him a tip as she settled into the car. She took her time before moving off, and Jack thought she was being clever, giving her pursuers time to get organised. In fact, she was just getting her head around the unfamiliar automobile. Her departure was smooth and unhurried.

By then, the stalker had retrieved his car, a blue Ford that had been parked in the main visitors' car park. Not long after Stella had driven away, the Ford was pulling up in front of the hotel, where the other thug was puffing after his run from the other side of the complex. He jumped in the passenger side and they took off in pursuit of Stella's red car.

Jack watched them go with a sense of unease. He thought this was the riskiest part of the plan, and he'd repeatedly cautioned Stella to stay in crowded places where she wouldn't present a tempting target. But for Stella, the highest priority was the safety of her family and she'd insisted on leading a controlled chase while Jack spirited Angie and Freda away.

A few minutes later, he was knocking at their hotel room and meeting them for the first time. Close up, he saw that good looks were something all the Sartori women had in common and age's influence was to mellow rather than diminish that beauty. Each of them had points of striking similarity and other features that were unique. Stella's incredible mouth, for example, must have been inherited from her father, because Angie and Freda were identical to each other – but quite different from Stella – in that department.

And they also presented a stark contrast to Stella in their personalities. Jack had become used to Stella's focused, businesslike approach, full of intelligence and humour but quiet and determined. Angie and Freda, on the other hand, were a whirlwind of noise and disorganised activity. Talking and laughing constantly, they didn't appear at all disconcerted about Stella's early departure. Work had always come first for her, they said, and they were philosophical about the foreshortening of their time with her.

'At least we got to see her in Waikiki,' Angie said. 'That was fantastic. We got three days with her we didn't expect and we had a great time, didn't we, Mum? Besides, she's been so distracted with this work thing she wasn't really with us most of the time, eh? She just couldn't relax a hundred per cent. But it was still fun. We shopped 'til we dropped. And it's not over for us yet, is it, Mum?'

Angie beamed at her mother. She had an accent that turned every sentence into a question. Freda Sartori often talked at the same time, usually agreeing and expanding on the story, but with a lyrical mixture of accented English and some Italian dialect.

They continued talking non-stop – and asking questions without really listening to the answers – all the way to the lobby, where they stopped just long enough to check out. They were happy, optimistic people, seemingly oblivious to any peril, and Jack couldn't help feeling at ease in their company. And they seemed to accept him as if he was one of Stella's oldest and closest friends.

The hotel had been told a family emergency necessitated the early departure and the staff were very professional about it. A porter appeared with a trolley of luggage that made Jack wish he'd rented a family sedan instead of a compact convertible. However, between the surprisingly roomy trunk and the back seat, they managed to find space for everything.

When she saw they'd be travelling with the top down, Angie giggled like an excited schoolgirl. 'This is so great. I always wanted a go in a convertible,' she said, giddy with glee. 'Can I get a photo?' She pulled a camera out of her handbag.

'Sure,' Jack said, amused but worried about the time. 'What, you don't have convertibles back home?'

'Of course we do, silly! But they're not real common in Melbourne, are they, Mum? And they're real expensive, too. Danny Fiorelli had one. His dad bought it for him. They're really rich. But I never drove in it.'

Jack took three photos of Angie, her mother and the car from various angles, and the doorman took one with Jack in the picture, at Angie's insistence. Then they climbed aboard, Angie nursing shopping bags on her lap in the front passenger seat and little Freda squeezed into the back next to Stella's suitcase and carry-on.

Jack hit the road, knowing they had a long drive – by Maui standards – to the main airport at Kahului, on other side of the island. As they picked up speed on the highway, Angie hooted like she was on a rollercoaster and shook her hair in the breeze. She and her mum were heading back to the bright lights, beautiful bodies and shopping malls of Waikiki. It turned out Angie's priorities on vacation weren't so much beach and pool, but rather shopping and nightlife. The Kapalua Bay Resort was too expensive and too far away from the action as far as she was concerned. She said she'd been 'bored shitless' after just one day at the fancy establishment, which made it a little easier for Jack to understand why she seemed so excited about leaving.

As they whistled past Lahaina, Jack's thoughts turned to Stella, who was in the harbour town somewhere, doing her best to keep two professional hoodlums distracted while he spirited her family away. He went over the plan in his head one more time, then pushed down on the gas, eager to get back to where he could be of some use in case things fell apart.

At that moment, Stella was in the Pacific Whale Foundation shop, browsing the racks of postcards and trinkets. She had more than ninety minutes to kill and was taking her time, ensuring she wouldn't run out of shops to explore. Not a fan of browsing, she found the charade mind-numbing, but that was part of the plan. If it was tedious for her she knew it would be doubly so for the men tailing her.

She'd seen the two men together only once since she parked the car, and she nicknamed them Blue and Green, after the predominant colours of the Hawaiian shirts they were sporting. As she strolled the streets looking for the whale shop, which she'd seen advertised in a brochure at the resort, she saw Green twice briefly but Blue had disappeared – maybe staying close to the car, she thought. And, despite his size, Green wasn't easy to spot either. He was obviously experienced, melting easily into the milling groups of middle-aged tourists in bright clothing.

She tried to relax. She bought key rings and postcards from the Whale Foundation, then strolled back up the street towards the main avenue of shops along the foreshore. Staying close to other people, she dawdled and browsed and concentrated hard to resist looking around for her minders. It was important that they believed she was unaware of them. If they thought she had no reason to run she would be able to lose them when the time came. They might be watching her car, but she had no intention of returning there.

For Jack, it seemed like a frustratingly slow drive to the central north coast of Maui, albeit a picturesque one. Traffic was moderately heavy in both directions and intensified as they approached what turned out to be a substantial modern airport. Each mile of highway leading away from Lahaina added to his state of nervous anxiety and he was itching to get back on the road in the other direction. Even so, he found it oddly moving bidding farewell and bon voyage to Freda and Angie, though he'd known them for barely an hour. Freda actually cried a little, between laughs, and made him promise to look after Stella.

'But you remember she is married lady,' she said, wagging her finger at him with a cheeky smile.

Not any more, Jack thought.

Sunlight sparkled on the deep blue water beyond a low wall across the other side of the road. On the side where Stella ambled, food and drink outlets abutted shops selling a wide range of items useful only to tourists or those with excess disposable income. Expensive ocean-themed works of art – sculptures, paintings and jewellery – competed with cheap T-shirts and beach apparel. Stella saw almost nothing to her taste but purchased a few small items with children in mind, like Ben Fisher's kids and her own nieces and nephews. Inside the shops she was fairly relaxed but as she moved along the sidewalk, she felt more vulnerable, even though Green was keeping his distance. She never saw him glancing in her direction and had to remind herself that she was being observed.

She looked at her watch again. Still forty-five minutes before the arranged meeting time. By then she had to be free of her minders and at the northern end of town where Jack would pick her up. She had to time it so she wouldn't have long to wait. Then they would disappear to the hideaway Jack had promised and she would post her rental car keys back to Avis, telling them their vehicle was parked just around the corner from their Lahaina office. Her family would be safely away and she would disappear once more – and this time Daniel Cross wouldn't be able to find her.

The sun was in Jack's eyes as he drove back along the highway that snaked its way around the base of Maui's gargantuan volcano. The road was thick with cars, moving at Hawaiian pace. Normally Jack would have been content at this speed, with the sun and warm wind in his face, but now the rear end of the pickup he was following began to annoy him intensely. The clock on the dash was moving way too fast and his fingers tapped the steering wheel as he waited impatiently for a chance to overtake a few of the cars in the queue.

The long conga-line of vehicles finally hit the west coast but, to Jack's frustration, most of the cars were heading north, like him. The sun was out of his eyes now, but the clock was streaking forward and each mile to Lahaina seemed longer than it had been going the other way. 'Come on!' he shouted aloud to the drivers ahead of him. Shit, he thought, I'm going to be late.

39

Five o'clock was approaching when Stella found herself at the southern end of the shops along Lahaina's shorefront. A small shopping complex called the Wharf offered a few levels of shops, but they weren't really good browsing material and Stella soon found herself back on the sidewalk out front. By her calculations, she had just a few minutes to go before it was time to make her break, and the little mall seemed ideal for her purposes. She would head back inside, find a rear exit and jog calmly the mile or so to the Cannery, the agreed rendezvous. It was another shopping complex at the northern end of town, one with a huge parking lot with easy access for Jack. She was confident Green would stay out on the street, as he had every other time, and it would be many minutes before he twigged to what had happened.

Two beeps sounded in her shoulder bag. She dug out her cell phone and looked for a message. It had to be from Jack, the only person who had the number. The message said, 'Will be bit late' and Stella muttered, 'Shit!' under her breath as she realised she'd have to string Green along a little longer.

She was hovering close to a group of six or seven young people and, when they set out to cross the street, she stayed with them. They headed for the harbour, across a small park dominated by an enormous banyan tree, towards the sea wall where brightly coloured signs advertised whale-watching and diving cruises. As she passed into the shadow cast by the ancient-looking, gnarled tree, Stella glanced back and felt a jolt of panic. Green was much closer than before, also walking towards the harbour. If he kept his line, they would meet by the sea wall. She moved closer to the group of friends, trying to keep her face calm and her pace casual.

It was late in the day so none of the stands operated by the cruise companies were manned. Racks of brochures were available for the curious and Stella picked one up and started reading and looking at pictures of giant humpbacks breaching and blowing fountains of white ocean into a blue sky. When she looked up she was stunned to find that she was alone. The group she'd been following had kept going, down the steps to the dock to join a twilight fishing cruise. She was exposed, and Green was only fifteen feet away, mimicking her brochure browsing.

She looked around the park. It seemed deserted. The nearest tourists were way back, across the park and on the other side of the street. Stay calm, she told herself. Look for the quickest, safest route back to the security of the crowd. Her heart was pounding. Then, from behind and beyond the banyan tree, she saw a man getting out of a car. A blue car. A man with a blue shirt. Instantly she knew that her deliberations with Jack the previous night had been totally wrong. These guys weren't going to be content just knowing where she was. If they got the opportunity they were going to snatch her.

A quick glance back at Green made Stella's skin crawl. He was looking right at her and there was a small smile curving his lips. She had played right into their hands. Not only had she removed herself from the natural shield provided by her family, she'd also backed herself into a corner, with the ocean behind and two large and determined enforcers in front.

Blue was walking through the park, towards their position. He shouted a casual greeting to his friend in green, maintaining the fiction of two innocent buddies on vacation. Green waved a fleshy palm in the air and moved closer to Stella, apparently advancing to meet his friend. She could see the trap closing. She was right between them. Green was barely ten feet away.

She decided her only chance was to attack. Maybe she could still surprise them. She shifted her weight in preparation and when Green was a few steps away she launched herself forward and swung her leg up in a kicking style learned from her soccer-hero brother. Her sneaker-enclosed foot hit its target with great force and Green doubled over in agony, clutching his testicles and gasping for breath.

Stella ran as fast as she could. She'd worn tight, tailored pants, not really designed for sprinting. In her right hand, she clutched her shoulder bag and three plastic shopping bags containing cheap souvenirs. Blue was running around the massive trunk of the tree and Green was struggling to straighten up. She'd almost made it to the line of cars parked along the street when she heard a shout from behind and a popping sound. With a loud crack, a hole appeared in the side window of the car she was fast approaching. An involuntary squeal escaped her throat as she realised they were shooting at her. She kept running, ducking and weaving.

She heard more pops. Her heart was in her mouth as she ran, instinctively staying away from other people to avoid any innocent bystanders being shot. She crossed the street, heading north for the Cannery. With luck, there'd be a spot where she could hide until Jack arrived.

Blue and Green had stopped chasing Stella. They tucked their firearms into holsters strapped under their floppy shirts and ran back to the blue Ford.

'Head back to her wheels,' Green instructed through gritted teeth.

Blue pushed his way into the line of traffic slowed by the confusion over the gunshots. Somebody on the sidewalk was pointing at them so he accelerated out into the opposite lane, passed four almost stationary vehicles and hurled the car around the next right-hand corner, scraping the nose of a rusty delivery van. Two blocks over and two north, they screeched to a halt by the small parking lot where Stella's red compact sat unattended. Cursing, Green climbed gingerly out of the car and walked to the corner. He waved frantically to his partner to come pick him up. 'There,' he said, pointing up the street as he got back into the car.

In the distance they could see a figure running. 'She's headed for that mall by the highway.' Blue pushed his foot down on the accelerator.

Jack whooped with triumph as a break in oncoming traffic opened up and he floored his convertible past the pickup to a stretch of clear highway. Ignoring the speed limit, he pushed the little car hard and the wind roared around his head. Barely two miles up the road, he found himself staring at the rear end of another slow-moving pickup and the stream of cars was back to full flood.

He reached for his cell phone to send Stella another message but before he could pick it up, it started ringing. When he answered the call, all he heard were short, rasping gasps of air.

'Stella? Is that you?'

'I'm in trouble, Jack.' Her voice was shaky and punctuated by more heavy breathing. 'They were going to grab me. They shot at me out on the street!'

'What's that? Where are you? Are you okay?'

'I'm at the Cannery shopping mall – where the hell are you?'

'God, I don't know!' Jack said, banging the steering wheel in frustration. 'I'm still a few miles away, I think. The traffic is terrible. Why don't you call the police?'

'I thought about it but I really don't want to explain all this. And I've lost them for the moment. Just come and get me as fast as you can.'

'Of course! Stay out of sight. Go to the bathrooom or something.'

'I'll be all right,' she said, her breathing settling. 'When you get here, try to get close to the front of the big supermarket. Honk your horn four times so I know you're there. I'll stay out of sight 'til then.'

'Be careful.'

Stella disconnected and Jack contemplated the line of vehicles in front of him.

'Get the fuck out of the way!' he bellowed into the wind.

Stella washed her face and brushed her hair in the bathroom at the Cannery but rejected it as a hideout – it was a logical place to search and it would be a trap with no escape if Blue and Green discovered her there. She made her way to the supermarket, where there were more people and more exits, and pretended to shop. She pushed an empty shopping cart up and down the aisles, but realised how odd her behaviour must look and started putting a few items in the cart. Her senses were desperately tuned to the sound of four blasts of a car horn.

She picked up a large can of olive oil because it was Italian and looked big in the cart. She threw in some toilet rolls and four boxes of Kleenex. She checked her watch again and looked around. She found herself in the pet food section. A blast of a horn made her heart leap then fall. It wasn't Jack. Looking up the long aisle she saw household cleaning goods and more pet accessories and an old lady pushing a cart. And then she saw Blue.

He walked calmly past the old lady towards Stella, one hand tucked under his shirt. Instinctively she moved away toward the front of the store but, when she looked up, she saw Green step into view, blocking the way. Two other shoppers were dawdling towards his end of the aisle but Stella would soon be alone between two armed and dangerous men.

She was eerily calm, despite the adrenaline pulsing through her system. She pushed her cart in Green's direction. As she passed the pet food shelves, she tossed three enormous bags of dog chow into her cart as if they were feather pillows, all the time watching Green. She knew Blue would be advancing down the aisle behind her and she just had to hope he didn't pull out his gun. Surely, she told herself, they'd prefer me alive rather than dead.

Her shopping cart had become weighty. She pushed it a little faster, aiming to overtake a short, middle-aged Asian woman struggling with her own trolley. Green could see her coming, and probably guessed what she was planning to do, but looked confident. He widened his stance and set his feet firmly on the floor. Stella rushed at him with such fury it made the little Asian lady shriek. The front of the cart looked more and more menacing as it sped towards him and, at the last second, Green lifted his right leg to fend off the attack. The heavy cart smashed into his leg, toppling him backwards and then crunching into his left shin as he fell, screaming in pain and shouting abuse. The terrified Asian woman was hugging the shelves as if she wanted to climb over them. Blue was running and Stella could hear the pounding of his footsteps. Then a car horn blasting – one, two, three. She didn't wait for four.

In one hand, Stella still carried her souvenirs and her shoulder bag. With the other, she reached into her shopping cart and grabbed the gallon can of olive oil by its metal handle and swung it over her head. As Green struggled to his feet, she brought the can down in a great arc, catching him under the chin. There were two nasty noises: one as Green's jaw fractured and the other as the back of his head hit the floor. Stella jumped over his prone body, dropping the can with a loud, metallic clatter.

She sprinted towards the checkouts. Two of the supermarket staff moved to intercept her but most other people moved away, concerned for their own safety. Blue was not far behind Stella and as she glanced around she saw him pull out his gun. Screams rang out. The employees looking to stop Stella left her alone as they realised she was the gunman's target.

But he didn't shoot. Maybe there were too many witnesses. He dropped the gun to his side and ran after her out of the supermarket. The onlookers parted to let him pass and he traced her route out through the mall's automatic sliding doors, down a ramp and into the expansive parking lot. He expected to see her running away through the parked cars and was determined to follow. But he stopped in confusion when he couldn't see her anywhere. The parking area looked remarkably normal. Unsuspecting shoppers loaded their cars with groceries or trawled around in their cars, looking for the best parking spot. Blue could see a family driving away in a green Buick and a guy in a blue convertible calmly waving another driver on so he could pass.

Green limped down from the supermarket, one hand clutching his head. He tapped his partner on the shoulder, unable to speak. Blue spun around in fury, but relaxed when he saw the bleeding face of his buddy.

'Jesus Christ!' he said. 'Look at you! Man, for a skinny bitch she packs a punch, don't she?'

Green looked around and grunted, wincing in pain, but his partner understood the question nevertheless.

'I don't know,' Blue said. 'She just disappeared. She musta jumped into one of these cars.'

He waved his hand at the packed parking lot and grimaced as he examined his partner's shattered jaw. 'Shit! I guess it's gonna be me has to call the fuckin' boss, right?'

40

'Wow! Did you notice this before?'

Jack was examining Stella's shopping as they moved her luggage from the car to the house. He pulled out a small paper bag containing a wad of postcards and held them up. Punched through the middle was a neat round hole. 'Look, a bullet must have gone right through the bag.'

Stella took the postcards and turned them over in her hands, realising how close she'd come to serious injury or death. She looked at him. 'I was pretty lucky, wasn't I? You sure they can't find us here?'

He nodded. 'This place is pretty isolated, and I have enough provisions for a week. We don't need to go out.'

He was watching her closely for any signs of shock. Stella handed the damaged souvenirs back to him and said, 'So where do I sleep? I really want to get out of these clothes.'

Jack pointed down the hallway and Stella wheeled her suitcase in that direction. In quick time she returned to the living room looking relaxed in a cotton dress and bare feet. She came over to where he was sitting on the sofa.

'Stand up,' she instructed and gave him a long, tight hug. 'Thank you for everything. I'm so glad you came to Hawaii. I wasn't at first but I'm very grateful now.'

Jack put his arms around her and hugged back. She felt good, strangely familiar, and he was briefly confused by sensations he normally associated with Peta. He found himself unable to let go and she held the embrace, her head on his shoulder, her stress eased by the strength of his grip. Eventually she moved her head and he released his hold, as if awakened from a dream.

'We need to talk,' she said.

He nodded grimly. 'Let's go outside and watch the sun go down.'

He made strong gin and tonics with plenty of ice and lime and brought them out to where Stella sat, on a sunlounge on the paved lanai. He handed her the drink and sat on the other lounge, glancing out towards Molokai. He looked back at Stella, her tanned face glowing in the soft light of late afternoon. He raised his glass and she did the same, taking a sip before she said, 'Okay. You go first.'

Jack swallowed a mouthful of his drink and put his legs up. He told his story, talking slowly, including every detail – drawing it out to delay the inevitable. Stella listened with a look of awe as she heard for the first time the terrible scale of events she'd unwittingly set in motion. She was horrified as he told her of the shooting at Bloch and Lieberman and the torture he'd interrupted and couldn't believe it when he told her about his home being destroyed by an incendiary device.

'My God, I had no idea what a ruthless bastard Cross is,' she said angrily. 'All I've been doing is sitting in the bloody sun, contemplating the stupid poem, while you nearly get yourself killed and the prick burns your house down. And poor innocent Alex, tortured, for God's sake! I'll never forgive Frank for trusting that arsehole.'

'Stella,' Jack said, calmly taking a deep breath, 'there's something else.'

'What?'

'After the fire at my house. In the ruins. They found a body.'

'Oh, Christ, no! Not another one. Bloody hell, Jack, it wasn't your wife, was it? Please tell me it wasn't your wife.'

'I'm not married,' Jack blurted out automatically. 'At first I did think it was Peta. You can imagine the guilt I was feeling. The next day I found out she was safe. She'd gone to London. The body was a male.'

'The intruder?'

'That's what the authorities think. They think he must have accidentally set off the device. There wasn't much of him left.'

'Was it Hollis or Hoyle?' she asked. 'No, it couldn't have been. They were with you at the law firm, right?'

She was searching Jack's face for the answer.

'When I left New York the body hadn't been positively identified, but from the remains, they can tell it was a slight man. He was wearing a blue-faced TAG Heuer watch.'

'David!' Stella said breathlessly.

'I think so. I can't be sure. I'm very sorry.'

He moved over to sit next to her, putting his arm around her shoulders but she seemed oblivious. She sat very still, her face in her hands. She didn't cry, she stared at the ground.

The sun began to sink behind Molokai and the layers of cloud turned the sunset into an even more colourful and spectacular sight than the night before. Jack looked away to watch the earth, sea and sky take on a changing palette of golds and reds while he waited for Stella to speak.

She leaned against him, but her face stayed in her hands for many minutes. Eventually she shook herself free and Jack's arm fell from her shoulders.

'I can't believe it,' she said. 'The little shit burned your place down. And he couldn't even get that right!'

They were harsh words, and for Stella it was too much. As soon as she'd finished speaking, she was overwhelmed by a sudden surge of grief. She tried to hold back the tears with her clenched fists but they were unstoppable. She jumped up, sobbing as she stood. She ran inside towards her bedroom. Jack instinctively leapt to his feet, but with a sigh, he sank down on the lounge and drained the rest of his drink.

About twenty minutes later, Stella reappeared at the sliding doors. Her eyes were puffy, her cheeks red and she was holding a Kleenex to her nose. She sat down next to Jack and reached for one of the drinks he had refreshed. In a gentle voice she talked about her husband as if she felt the need to explain.

'David and I have been living a lie for a few years now,' she said. 'I think we both knew the relationship was finished – it was probably doomed from the start. I suppose it was up to me to do something about it. I have the income and the assets, and David was unlikely to make the first move – he's always been pretty helpless with things like that. And his gambling had become chronic since he got so bored with life. I should have paid him off and sent him home years ago.'

'You seem very different from each other,' Jack observed quietly.

'We are – were. We met in high school; he was, like, my second ever boyfriend. Everybody got so used to us being together they all assumed we'd get married some day. Maybe I wasn't totally sure but who is at that age? And at first it seemed to work fine. I moved to Sydney to go to university and David came with me and got a good job with a locksmith. The differences between us didn't seem to matter so much. We got married during my last year at uni – mostly to please my mum, who didn't like us living in sin.

'When I started working, it got tougher. Soon I was earning more money than David, then a lot more. He didn't like it, didn't like the whole business I was in, couldn't relate to the people. But at least he had his job and his mates. When the opportunity at Sutton Brothers came up, I knew I was going to New York, whether he joined me or not. In the end he decided to come – I think he thought I'd make enough money to set him up in business back in Sydney and then I'd settle down and be more like the wife he expected. Or maybe he'd just gotten used to the free handouts.'

'Or maybe he still loved you.'

'Huh, maybe. I suppose I still loved him then, too. But when it started to dawn on him I was in no hurry to get back to Australia, things started to go sour. He started drinking more and gambling more, and demanding more money. We stopped talking, started to do more shouting instead. For the last year, we've been like room-mates rather than husband and wife. I think he even had an affair last summer. When I realised that I didn't care, it was obvious the relationship was dead in the water. I knew I'd have to sort it out, but I'm a busy girl and it was easier to ignore the problem.'

After a long pause, she added, sadly, 'I guess that particular problem's gone away.'

'We have plenty more,' Jack said, knowing it couldn't wait any longer. 'Like Ben.'

'What?' Stella said, her tears forgotten, 'What about him?'

'Frank was concerned because he didn't turn up to work on Thursday or Friday.'

'No!' She jumped to her feet. 'Jesus, Jack, if anything happens to him, I will never forgive myself.'

Jack followed as she went looking for her phone. For the first time that day he saw real panic on her face. 'Be careful what you say,' he advised. 'If Cross has him he may have his phone, too.'

'Oh God,' Stella said as her knees gave out. She collapsed on the sofa, dialling Ben's number quickly. 'If he has him we know what he's going to do, don't we?'

Jack tried to adopt an optimistic tone. 'He wants this merger badly, Stella. He's not going to get it if he kills off the guy who's supposed to be writing the recommendation, is he? Maybe Ben's been ill and took a couple of days off.'

The look she gave him was a combination of hope and disbelief as she held the phone to her ear. Then she closed it with a snap and said, 'Voicemail. I didn't leave a message. Shit, shit, shit!' Tears appeared. 'I should call his wife.'

Jack sat down beside her. 'It's the middle of the night in New York, Stella. Let's not assume the worst until we have to. If we do that we'll be paralysed.'

With an anguished sigh, she fell back into the soft cushions of the sofa. 'What the hell did I do, Jack, when I started asking about that bloody contract?'

'It's not your fault, Stella. There's no way you could have known. Let's not forget who the bad guy is here.'

She nodded. 'You're right. Damn, I would love to bring that monster down.'

'Me too,' Jack said. 'Let's do it. I'll throw together some food while you tell me the whole story. We can decide together how to skewer the fucker.'

Jack busied himself in the kitchen, searing chicken breasts in a pan before transferring them to the oven to bake for a few minutes while he steamed some vegetables and made a cream sauce flavoured with herbs and a little flaming gin, in the absence of brandy. Stella helped as she retold the story she'd written down for her disastrous packages.

By the time they sat down to eat, she was up to her flight from

Peoria. 'As you probably guessed, I decided to surprise Angie and Mum in Honolulu. I got to Hawaii a couple of days before them. But while I was on my road trip around the Midwest, I got Ben to dig out some information for me.'

She winced as she said Ben's name and put her cutlery down, her appetite apparently gone.

'Yeah, I know, a list of names and addresses,' Jack said, between mouthfuls.

'So you got your hands on that too, did you? You must be a persuasive bloke.'

'Ben and Jodie are very loyal but they're worried about you, too. I managed to convince them I'm on your side. Tell me about the names.'

'Okay, this is how I think it went down. We know Campbell Reeves, who was then VP Finance at CMS, penned the poem on 8 December 1967. The poem refers to two women, the "Virgin" and Beth. I'm certain that Beth was his wife. Obviously Campbell thought his wife would be able to understand the poem and its cryptic clues but she never received it. With me so far?'

Jack nodded and Stella continued. 'Campbell tells Beth that if he doesn't make it home, she should find some allies she can trust and go after the secret. And the secret seems to be information that will deliver "truth and justice", in Campbell's words. Truth and justice relating to some past deed or deeds committed by Daniel Cross. You've seen the poem. It talks about "a past of death and murder vile".'

'Yes, all very melodramatic.'

'A deadly melodrama. Campbell Reeves died on 9 December 1967 in Long Beach, California. One day after he wrote the poem. He didn't make it home, as he predicted.'

She sat back in her chair, looking a little happier, watching Jack's reaction. His eyes were wide with surprise. 'You think Cross killed Reeves too?'

'I think he did a lot more than that. When you put it together it only makes sense one way. The contract with its bizarre clauses, the poem in the contract's file, Campbell's death, Gilbert's death, the way Cross has controlled that family for decades, maybe even Ewan's so-called suicide in 1980. Clearly he was prepared to kill to get that deal with the Pentagon. We know he's capable.'

'Well, yeah, but we'd have a better chance of proving his responsibility for these latest deaths, wouldn't we? Reeves died thirty-five years ago.'

'But that's not the point, don't you see? Campbell left a trail for his wife to follow. It must lead to some information that can be used to bring Cross to justice, otherwise there'd be no point, right? I've thought about this a lot. Whatever Campbell left behind for Beth would be enough to give her protection. It would have to be good, don't you think?'

Jack look thoughtful. 'Whatever you might read into the poem, Stella, I figure it has to point to something sensational. Why else would Cross be so determined to stop you? What I don't get is how you intend to find this secret treasure trove of evidence. Like you said, the poem is a set of clues only Beth Reeves could understand. And it all happened a long time ago, for Christ's sake. How could anything still be there? Wherever "there" is.'

'I don't know,' Stella admitted, 'but I feel it here.' She put a hand to her heart. 'I can't rest until I've chased down all possible leads. If it goes nowhere, we can try to nail Cross for the deaths in Chicago or for Alex. Or poor Ben.'

'What other leads are there?' Jack asked, determined not to be distracted. 'Do you know who the virgin is, or was?'

'No, not yet. I've managed to track down very few senior CMS employees from the sixties. Most of them are dead of natural causes as far as I can tell. I did find one or two who knew Campbell Reeves. That's why I needed the names and addresses. It was a bit naughty, but I got the guys in Peoria to pull the current or last known address for every name on the company's organisation chart – the one in the second package. That's why they had to extract them from the company's pension plan files. Not very kosher, was it?'

Jack shrugged. He wasn't about to pass judgement.

'Anyway,' she continued, 'I spoke to a few surviving spouses and to one guy who reported directly to Campbell for twenty years or more. In those days people stayed with the one firm all their life. This guy – his name was Randy, or Rudy or something, I'd have to look at my notes – he said Campbell was a great guy to work for. He hated the guy who took over.'

'Did he remember anything about Campbell's death?'

'Not much, except that it was sudden. And his boss, Gilbert Collins, the president of the company, died a few days later.'

'Did Collins die in Long Beach too?'

'No, he died in Peoria.'

'In suspicious circumstances?'

'Nobody seemed to think so. Gilbert Collins and Campbell Reeves were both in their late sixties when they died. That wasn't unusual in those days. Apparently Collins and Reeves were great friends, though. They worked together for more than forty years.'

'And where was Reeves when he wrote "The Virgin's Secret"? Do you know what he was doing in California?'

'No.'

'And you don't have any lead on who this virgin was or what she might have done with her purse?'

'Nobody could remember any girl who might have fit the name, either at the company or among the community of CMS families. Women employees were mostly secretaries back then. Campbell's assistant was called Rose. And she was married with kids, so we can assume it probably wasn't her. The pension records show she died in 1974.'

'But the virgin is the key, right? The poem says the virgin is the one holding the secret or the one with the directions to find it. Without her, we're blind.'

'I think maybe the virgin might be a code name – you know, like a name only Campbell and his wife would understand.'

'Okay. We're back to the cryptic clues only Beth Reeves can interpret. What do you propose to do about that?'

Stella gave him a cheeky look. 'I propose to ask her.'

'She's still alive?' he said, incredulous. 'She must be ancient.'

'Well, she's elderly now but, luckily for us, Campbell married a much younger woman. She's still getting a pension cheque from the company every month. She lives in San Francisco.'

'You've tried contacting her?'

'Yes, but she has no phone listing. I really need to see her face to face.'

'That was your next step?'

'Yep. I was planning to pay her a visit. On the way back to New York.'

'So now it's *our* next step.'

'I guess so.'

She rose from the table and stretched languorously to ease away some of the stress in her limbs. Then she moved over to the window, looking out at the lights sparkling further up the coast.

'It's a shame we have to race off, isn't it? It's so beautiful here.'

'We can always come back,' Jack said, 'when this is all over.'

She turned to face him and gave him a quizzical look. Only then did Jack realise how many assumptions were wrapped up in his words and he blushed.

Stella smiled, but it was a little sad at the edges. 'We might as well enjoy it while we can,' she suggested. 'It's still warm out. Want to sit on the grass and listen to the sea for a while?'

'I guess there's nothing else we can do tonight.'

'I checked with American Airlines while I was killing time in Lahaina. They had plenty of seats on flights to San Francisco tomorrow.'

'Right, then,' Jack said as he stood up. 'Fancy some wine?'

'Red, please.'

Jack spread a rug on the grassy cliff top while Stella carried the wine bottle and glasses. When they lay back on the rug, Jack was momentarily startled by the night sky. The clouds of sunset had been blown away to reveal a shimmering fog of stars; more stars than he'd ever seen. And just as startling as the brightness of the stars was the density of blackness everywhere else. It was as if living so long in the city had erased his memory of open, dark landscapes and the starlit heavens. This scene was so unfamiliar it was almost disconcerting.

'Jesus, look at the stars!'

'Aren't they just beautiful?' Stella's voice sounded calm. 'It's like being out in the bush back home.'

They lay there a long time, a respectable distance between them, just looking out at the universe and pondering its hugeness. Stella willed the stars to align to save Ben, while unseen insects and amphibians serenaded them and the surf washed below with a rhythmic certainty.

In a quiet voice, appropriate to the awed mood, Stella asked Jack about Peta. He answered frankly and asked her about her family and growing up in suburban Melbourne. She asked him about his university days in England and he asked her how she got noticed by Sutton Brothers. And they continued, asking each other questions, listening to the answers – exploring.

Some time after midnight the sea breeze picked up and Stella said she was chilly. She asked if it would be okay if she moved a little closer to him.

'Do you want to go inside?' he said.

'No, no. I like it here, listening to you and the ocean. I'll just snuggle up, if that's okay. We know each other well enough by now, surely.'

Jack was lying on his side, his left arm propping up his head. Stella rolled over and backed her way into the curve of his body. They were spooning, like lovers, but at least she was out of the wind. Jack struggled for a moment with where to put his right arm before letting it drop to his hip.

Stella kept talking. Jack tried to listen but found it hard to concentrate. It was dark and Stella was barely touching him, but he could sense every inch of her, from head to toe. Her hair wafted into his face, tickling his nose, and he took in her exotic scent. Coconut and jasmine. Tea and sandalwood. He felt like he was heading for serious trouble. It was as if tiny, tingling sparks of electricity were jumping from her body to his.

Blood rushed to his groin and he was mortified. If he backed away it would be too obvious, so he stayed still, cursing his loose shorts and trying to recall the name of every English cricket captain of the twentieth century.

It didn't work. And Stella, either teasing him or oblivious, kept talking. He talked back, struggling against the dulling effect that an erection has on a man's ability to think about anything else. He was embarrassed but also amused, and the sensations he was feeling were delicious.

Eventually the coolness of the air and the firmness of the ground prompted them to move back inside. By then Jack's embarrassment had waned. He moved to clean up the mess he'd made earlier in the kitchen and Stella lent a hand. She seemed unaware of the sexual tension he was feeling and when they were done clearing up, she said she was exhausted and heading to bed. They exchanged quick, clumsy kisses on the cheek as she said goodnight and Jack watched her go with a strange mixture of relief and regret.

Before long he was naked between clean, crisp sheets in a dark and silent house, listening to the sounds of the sea through an open window. His thoughts turned to Stella and he was hard again. He considered doing something about it but found he was too tired and too lazy. The wine and the soothing sounds of the island worked their magic and he drifted away to sleep.

41

Jack woke with a start, sensing something was wrong. He was face down on the bed, uncovered from the waist up and twisted up in his sheet from the waist down. It was dark. Someone was in his room. He could hear breathing.

Without moving, and with a sense of dread underscored by a loud thumping in his chest, he said, 'Stella? Is that you?'

'Yes.' It was a husky whisper. 'Sorry if I scared you.'

He relaxed, but felt completely awake as he wondered what she was up to. He didn't move. He felt her sit down on the side of the bed. Then he felt a light touch as a fingernail ran slowly up his leg and over his sheet-covered backside onto the bare skin of his back. Sensuous ribbons of pleasure radiated out from that moving spot to all the best parts of his body. His eyes snapped open, then closed in delight as her other fingers joined in the dance on his back. He groaned, low and guttural, and turned over, not because he wanted her to stop, but because he needed to see her face.

'What are you doing?' The question was more dreamy than accusatory.

'What do you think?' She moved closer, fully on the bed now.

'Do you think this is a good idea?'

He was holding her right hand, but her left was still making mischief, moving up and down the sheet covering his left thigh. In the dim light he hoped she wouldn't see the tent that had formed – or maybe she would.

'You don't think it's a good idea?'

Stella bent over and licked his left nipple. He let out an involuntary sigh of pleasure.

'Well,' he said softly, pulling her closer, wanting to feel her hair sweep across his chest, 'I am sort of on the rebound.'

'Yes,' she said, straddling one leg across his stomach and pulling off her T-shirt. 'And I've just lost my husband in a terrible fire.'

Jack could feel her wetness on his belly and it sent flashes of erotic anticipation to his brain. 'So,' he said, pulling her down to feel her breasts press against him as he gently nibbled her neck while his hands explored her back, 'we're both kinda vulnerable at the moment, right?'

'Right.'

Her voice was throaty with passion. She kissed him hard on the mouth, exploring his lips with her tongue. She sat up and reached behind, gripping him through the sheet. Jack gasped again, thrilled by her audacity.

'What do you think we should do?' she said, squeezing him hard and daring him to say no.

He had no intention of saying no. Couldn't have said no, even if he wanted to. There was too much tension in the air.

'I don't have any, uh, you know . . .' It was so long since he'd needed to worry about safe sex.

'Jack,' Stella said calmly into his ear, 'how long is it since you slept with someone other than Peta?'

'At least eight years. I'm a good boy like that.'

'And I've been, was, married to one guy for fourteen years. He was my first and only, as embarrassing as I find that now. In the circumstances, I'm prepared to take the risk. What about you?'

Jack felt a slight, familiar panic. 'I'm not worried about disease, Stella. It's just that —'

She put a finger to his lips and said, with a tinge of sadness. 'You don't have to worry about that, Jack. I can't have kids. I went through all the tests with David.' She was still holding him. 'Oh,' she said, 'you just got even harder.'

In the darkness she couldn't see the grin on his face but she could feel the passion in his hands as they explored her body, resting on her buttocks as she straddled him. In a teasing voice, he said, 'Are you seriously telling me you've only ever been with one man?'

'Okay, don't rub it in. I never had the time or the urge to cheat, even if we weren't happy. It's not cheating now, is it?'

'No, it's not,' Jack said, his conscience also clear. Stella's embrace felt completely right and natural, in a way he hadn't felt with Peta for a long time.

He kicked off the sheets and rolled her gently onto her front. He started by patiently exploring her body with his lips and tongue while Stella signalled her appreciation with deep moans, encouraging him to continue.

The first light of dawn found them lying with heads at opposite ends of the bed, glistening in the afterglow of two long lovemaking sessions. Jack hauled himself off the bed to fetch water from the refrigerator.

'You know, Jack,' Stella said dreamily as he returned, carrying a bottle of water to share, 'that was a lot of fun but if it's going to take that long every time, we'll never get any sleep.'

He laughed, satisfied and smug, and the praise, combined with the sight of Stella's inviting curves draped across the bed, sent his blood rushing south again. This time he wasn't embarrassed.

'Slow is good,' he said, emulating the sleepy sensuousness of her voice. 'But quick can be good too.'

The tone of his voice caused Stella to look up.

'My God, Jack! How old are you, anyway?'

He looked down at himself. 'Today it seems I'm eighteen again.'

A few minutes later they were panting for breath, coming down from the most intense high. Like exhausted puppies at the end of a long play session, they fell asleep where they lay, their limbs intertwined. The sun climbed up into the sky and filled the bedroom with light. Despite the warm air, they moved closer together in sleep, undaunted by the stickiness of their skin and the lingering odour of sex. It was as though their bodies were melting together, fusing like precious metals in a furnace.

Hunger woke Stella at eight and she volunteered to make bacon and eggs, which they ate in bed, accompanied by buttered toast and tall glasses of ice-cold milk. When breakfast was over, they pushed the tray to one side and, oblivious to the crumbs, cuddled up tight, their naked bodies folding together naturally.

The dreamy reverie was shattered by a shrill ring from the telephone next to the bed. Jack was astonished by the sound and sat up in shock, pushing Stella to one side. She looked up at him with concern. He shrugged his shoulders and said, 'It has to be the realtor, I guess. Who else could it be?'

He reached for the handset as she watched. 'Hello?'

'Hi, Jack. How's the weather over there in London?'

The voice dripped with sarcasm and Stella sat up too when she saw the look of shock on Jack's face.

'Detective Robertson!' he said. 'How are you?'

He looked at his watch, next to the phone. It would be 3 p.m. in New York and the thought of cold, grey skies over the concrete city made him feel chilly.

'And tell us, how's Stella Sartori?' This time it was the voice of the FBI agent, Shannon Winters, coming down the line.

Jack was flummoxed, unable to speak for a moment. Stella was watching him. He looked around the room frantically, imagining they could see in somehow.

'You shouldn't be surprised, Jack,' the detective said. 'You've been using your credit cards all over the place. Airline, car rental, realtor, phone company. You've been spending up big.'

'And then we found Stella Sartori in the airline records,' Agent Winters chipped in. 'Same destination. Surprise, surprise.'

'You had no right,' Jack said indignantly, feeling a little foolish.

'You took off,' Robertson said accusingly, 'and your girlfriend said you'd called to say you weren't coming to London. What was I supposed to think? Don't worry, we did it all legally. The FBI's great at that.'

Jack heard the cynicism in his voice and wondered if Agent Winters was enjoying working with the gruff New York cop. Robertson said, 'You shoulda kept in touch. What if Cross had found you first?'

'He did!' Jack said, and told them about the two men who'd tried to kidnap Stella. He was asked for detailed descriptions of the men and he did his best. Stella was dressed and looking serious.

'Why didn't you tell me you knew where Stella was?' Robertson demanded.

'I only worked it out after I left you,' Jack said defensively. 'And it wasn't my place to upset things for her. I was planning to get in touch with you once she and I made contact. But I've had my hands full since I got here.'

He gave Stella a wink and the smile returned to her face.

'We can't argue the rights and wrongs of that now,' Agent Winters interrupted forcefully. 'There have been some developments.'

'Wait,' Jack said.

There seemed little point in keeping Stella out of the conversation. He indicated that she should join the discussion from the phone in the kitchen. Introductions were tersely exchanged.

'Has Ben Fisher turned up?' Stella demanded.

'No,' Robertson said. 'I understand his wife filed a missing persons report with the New Jersey police. He was on the flight from Peoria to Chicago but missed the connection to La Guardia Wednesday night. Unfortunately that's all we know.'

The news rattled Stella, who leaned against the kitchen bench for support.

'That's my fault,' Jack said. 'I told Cross that Ben had been talking to Stella before I knew his capacity for violence.'

'A lot of people have been surprised by Cross,' Agent Winters said, 'including his own guys, as it turns out. William Hoyle was dragged out of New York Harbor last night. He'd been shot in the back.'

'Oh no!' Jack said. 'Without him we've got nothing.'

'Hang on, let me finish,' Winters said impatiently. 'The big lug is still alive. Apparently the cold water and the drugs in his system kept him going. The bullet came right out his chest but he'll make it. And he's not too impressed with his former boss, who tried to permanently sideline him.'

'Well, that's better news,' Stella said. 'We got him then, right?'

'I wish it was that simple,' Agent Winters said. 'William Hoyle isn't the most impressive witness, and his instructions usually came by phone or from Hollis, the dead one. The link to Cross is tenuous. We'd like to have more. Chicago PD is looking into the deaths of Harding Collins and Maria Petrillo, but the pickup that hit Maria was found abandoned and swept clean. It had been stolen the same night. The handwriting on the suicide note found at Collins' office is being re-examined, but no obvious flaws have been found so far. And Daniel Cross is still a very well connected businessman. I finally got permission from my superiors to interview him after we fished Hoyle out of the harbour, but he'd already left the country. He's been in London ever since, according to his secretary, and he's not returning my calls.'

'We've got him stirred up a little,' Jack said.

'You could say that. And your little stunt in Hawaii will have stirred him up some more. Why the hell didn't you contact us when you first saw those two guys? If we'd picked them up, we might have had three unreliable witnesses instead of one.'

Neither Jack nor Stella proffered an answer because they had none. The frustrated FBI agent was forced to move on. 'The point is, we need some better evidence if we hope to go any further with this. Now, what about this poem? We've reviewed the documents Jack took from O'Reilly, including the poem. But we're not sure what it means. I'm hoping you all can tell us it points to some unimpeachable evidence we can use against Daniel Cross, 'cause if not, we're going to have trouble making anything stick.'

'We hope so too,' said Stella. 'It has something to do with how CMS won that unbelievable contract, but we still have some unravelling to do.'

'What sort of unravelling?' Agent Winters asked crisply.

Jack leaned out of the doorway to his bedroom so he could see Stella's face as she stood behind the kitchen bench. She looked at Jack and held a finger up to her lips, before continuing, 'Just cross-checking information, building a timeline of Cross's career so we can see what he was up to at the time "The Virgin's Secret" was written, that sort of thing.'

There was a pause, and Shannon Winters said, 'What about Elizabeth Reeves?'

'Who's she?' Detective Robertson asked.

'The widow of the guy who wrote the poem,' Winters explained. 'Her name's in one of the documents.'

Jack saw Stella frowning, and wondered why she was so determined to keep the FBI and police out of the picture. Then he heard her say, 'We're not ready to talk to her yet. I don't want to upset her unnecessarily.'

She gave Jack a questioning look, as if to say, do you think it sounds convincing? He just raised his eyebrows and waited for Agent Winters to react. Her irritation with Stella's guarded responses was clear.

'Ms Sartori,' she said, 'you must understand that this is now an FBI investigation. I won't tolerate any more amateur sleuthing by you or anyone else. I need you, and all the documents you've collected, back in New York immediately. This is my case and you two are key witnesses. I need detailed statements from both of you and your assistance in solving the puzzle of "The Virgin's Secret" may well be critical. I need you to do it with me, under my direction, understand? And if and when it's time to talk to Elizabeth Reeves, I or one of my colleagues will conduct the interview, even if you're asked to be present. Is that clearly understood?'

She waited until she heard sounds of grudging acknowledgement. 'Good.'

Detective Robertson tried to put things back on a man-to-man basis. 'Bottom line, Jack, is we need you two back here ASAP. I need you to identify Hoyle, and after what you've been through in Hawaii, it's pretty obvious you're gonna need police protection until this whole shebang is resolved.'

Stella's expression made it very clear what she thought about being restricted or, worse, confined – even if it was for her own safety. She was pacing up and down the kitchen, as far as the telephone cord would allow.

Agent Winters spoke again, still peeved. 'Can we trust you to get back to New York under your own steam or should I arrange an escort?'

Stella stopped pacing and said, 'We're grownups, thank you, we can make it on our own.'

Winters ignored the defiant tone. 'Send me your flight details and I'll arrange for you to be picked up at the airport. I'm meeting with Frank Spiteri tomorrow morning so I'll let him know you're cutting your vacation short. You still have my card, Jack?'

'Yes.'

'Call me when you've got your bookings.'

'Okay.'

Stella was stony-faced when the telephone conversation ended. Jack went out to the kitchen and put his arms around her, but she was unresponsive. 'You know,' he said, 'it's a good thing the FBI's involved, Stella. We could never hope to bring down Cross on our own.'

'What's it got to do with the FBI, anyway?' she countered, pulling away. 'Who called them in?'

'What do you mean?'

'I mean, don't they need to have a reason? Murder is a local issue, like your cops in New York, each to their own precinct.'

'I guess it must be the Pentagon connection.'

'Exactly! It comes back to the contract. That Winters woman knows something we don't.'

'She has your second package. She has your analysis.'

'Not enough,' Stella said. 'She wouldn't be interested unless she had some other information to back it up. There has to be something else.'

'Good! It's nice to think the FBI might be ahead of us on this, don't you think? People have died, Stella.'

She gave him an apologetic look. 'I know,' she said, 'but it's too soon. We haven't solved "The Virgin's Secret" yet. And it's not that FBI woman's puzzle to solve, it's mine!'

'Look, she's not going to exclude us. She needs us. Besides, you were nearly shot yesterday. I'd hope that working with the FBI is going to be a bit safer.'

Stella brushed the concern aside with a wave of her hand, but she returned to Jack's embrace, backing up to his chest so his arms were intertwined with hers at her waist.

'The only reason to work with her,' she said as she leaned back into him, 'is because she knows something I don't.'

Jack smiled into her hair. 'Fair enough. What do we do next?'

She stroked the dark hair on his arms gently. 'I suppose we book our flights.'

'New York, here we come?'

'Yes,' she said, raising and turning her head to show him sparkling eyes and a sly grin, 'via San Francisco.'

42

Shannon Winters hailed a cab outside Robertson's precinct building on 14th Street and gave the driver an address in Brooklyn. Thirty-five minutes later she was standing outside the Bracken Ridge Retirement Home.

Bracken Ridge was unlike any old people's home Winters had ever seen. It was clean, almost luxurious and completely lacking the hospital smell of her own grandfather's community residence in Jersey. Following directions from a smiling receptionist, she took an elevator up two levels and knocked on a door at the end of a long corridor elegantly decorated with original works of art. The knock was answered by a thin, craggy-faced man with steel-grey hair.

'Beardsley wasn't lying when he said you're a looker, Agent Winters,' he said as he invited her in. 'I guess he thought I needed some extra motivation to meet with you but, truth be told, these days I'll take a visit from anyone.'

'I really appreciate you seeing me, Special Agent Sedgwick.'

'Oh, please, call me Pete. I've been retired for years.'

Inside, the room was like a spacious five-star hotel suite but the most impressive feature was the view.

'Amazing, isn't it?' Sedgwick said. 'I can see right across Sheepshead Bay to Rockaway Point. In the summer the water is full of yachts and other small boats.' He gestured to the armchairs. 'Who knew there were places like this, huh? I had no idea myself 'til six months ago. When I moved back to New York all I could afford was a crappy little apartment looking out onto an alley, but my nephew moved me here.'

'Nice when the family comes through for you.'

'Sure, he's a good kid. Twenty-five years old and he sold his software company for fifty million. That's two mil for every year he's been alive! And after forty years of public service all I could afford was a shoebox with a roach problem. It's a mixed-up world, Agent Winters, I'll tell you that for nothing.'

Winters sat down and reached into her briefcase. 'I was hoping you might be able to help me with one of your old files.'

Sedgwick picked up a pair of spectacles from the bedside table before sitting down opposite her. 'Wanna test an old man's memory, do you? You know how many cases I worked on at the Bureau?'

Winters handed him a manila folder. 'I know, it's asking a lot, and this was one of your early ones.'

'This is the whole file?'

'I'm afraid so.'

'Christ, you really want me to look foolish, don't you?' Sedgwick gave her a good-natured smile and looked at the documents in the folder. After a few seconds, he closed the folder and placed it on the table in front of him. His face was a shade pinker.

'What is it?' Winters asked.

'I remember this one,' Sedgwick said, 'like it happened yesterday.'

'Really? Why? There's so little in the file.'

He turned his head to study the grey-green waters of the bay, his mind replaying the memories of many years earlier.

'The file is censored,' Winters pointed out. 'The original documents aren't in the official record. I was hoping you —'

'Hoover kept the originals,' Sedgwick said.

'We thought that might be the case. And was he also responsible for the censorship?'

'I told him I wanted to put a flag on the file in case any of the names came up again. Cross, Collins, Castle. The three Cs. I've never forgotten. The Director said only a doctored version of the documents could go into the system and his word was law, even then, when the old bastard was . . . well, I guess he was about the age I am now. Hell, he seemed so ancient to me then.'

'You even remember the names,' Winters observed. 'That one meeting with Gilbert Collins really had an impact on you, didn't it?'

'Yes, of course. I thought it was going to be the case of my career. But then Collins died and all the information died with him. Local cops and coroner had no suspicions, and he'd been cremated before I even found out he was dead.'

Winters shifted to the edge of her seat in frustration and anticipation. 'Information about what, Pete?' she said. 'What did he overhear in that hotel room in London?'

Sedgwick brought a thumbnail to his mouth and tapped it on his teeth, unsure of how to proceed. 'Hoover had his reasons for blacking out that file, Winters. I'm not sure I should be the one to decide . . .'

'If you don't fill in the gaps,' she said, 'it will be lost forever.'

'Maybe that would be best,' he said, standing up. 'I just realised what a lousy host I am. Would you like a cup of coffee, or maybe a cold drink? I think I have some juice.'

'Your flag worked,' Winters said. 'The file popped up again when

Daniel Cross's name came up in connection with two deaths in the city over the weekend. And he may be responsible for two more in Chicago last week. The story is that he's trying to shut down an investigation into something he did in the sixties. Something to do with that contract.'

Sedgwick stood at the window, transfixed by the boats on the glistening water. 'A Bureau investigation?'

'No, it started with a Wall Street consultant who stumbled onto something while analysing CMS as part of a merger. She's now on the run. And if it's true that Cross is responsible for these other killings, he has to be hiding some serious secret. He's been a legitimate and successful businessman all these years. What would make him lash out again? It must be something sensational.'

'Sensational, yes,' Sedgwick muttered. 'A sensational secret.'

'The way I figure it,' Winters persisted, 'he can't be worried about the people Gilbert Collins claimed were killed or corrupted to get the contract. That's all just unsubstantiated rumour and closed police files. It has to be the other stuff, the blacked-out stuff. He's determined nobody links him with whatever was in that file. My guess is he killed a Member of Congress.'

'Cross didn't have the muscle,' Sedgwick said, 'not back then. Tony Castle's the one in that trio who thought killing was an effective negotiating tactic. He was charged with murder twice before he turned seventeen, back in the old country. Got off both times due to a sudden lack of witnesses. Growing up Mafia in Sicily certainly gave him a warped sense of what's reasonable in the course of getting what you want.'

'None of this is in the file.'

'I never forgot this one, I told you that. Did as much research as I could in my spare time after the Director shut it down. Nothing official. I figured out that Castle's real name was Castelluzzo. His family's been part of the ruling underworld in Sicily for generations. But the claim that he was in London in 1967 is the last trace of him I ever found. I don't suppose he's shown up again?'

'No. He's probably dead, a man in his profession.'

Sedgwick shook his head. 'He worked hard to graduate from a good college. What wise guy bothers to get a Masters degree? Not so he can grow up to be a workaday killer. The story was he wanted more than the mob could ever give him. He wanted respect; he wanted success and recognition in the legitimate business world.'

'He could be anywhere.'

'Or anyone,' Sedgwick added.

'What about Campbell Reeves?'

'The guy Collins was going to dictate his confession to? Turned up dead too, didn't he? Just like his boss. Too coincidental but there was just no evidence. No autopsies, no bodies, no police investigations. They were old, I thought. Christ! Now I'm older than they ever were. The Director told me to drop it.'

'Because of the sensational secret.'

Sedgwick turned back from the window and sat down. 'I don't think he wanted it out there any more than Daniel Cross or Tony Castle did. He had his reasons.'

Winters spread the papers from the file across the table and pointed to the transcript of his interview with Gilbert Collins. 'Some of these are pretty obvious,' she prodded, 'these first blacked-out sections. They're references to Director Hoover, right?'

Reluctantly, Sedgwick lowered his eyes to look. 'Yeah, Hoover didn't want any connection to these documents. Gil Collins was introduced to him by the senior senator from Illinois and was hoping to meet Hoover personally. Any mention of Hoover or the senator were wiped.'

'And here?' Winters asked hopefully, pointing to the record of the telephone call from London, but Sedgwick was staring out the window. 'Look,' Winters said, 'that consultant I told you about. She found this weird poem. It was written by Campbell Reeves just before he died. His wife was meant to receive it but never did. It's cryptic but it seems to be pointing to some hidden evidence, something that can bring Cross to justice. It has to be the deposition Collins was going to make, don't you think?'

The retired agent didn't seem impressed. 'Oh, I'm pretty sure the deposition was prepared,' he said sourly. 'The way Collins sounded during that last phone call, I'm sure he wanted to see it through, even if it brought down his own company. And he had the time. He and Reeves were travelling together for, like, six weeks after that call. But, at the end of it, Reeves was dead, Collins wasn't long for this earth and there was no deposition. Nothing arrived in the mail. And who had control of all the paperwork? Ewan Collins and Dan Cross. If the deposition was ever written, it was lost or destroyed. And now, nearly forty years on, you think you're going to find it?'

'No, of course not, but it doesn't matter, does it? As long as Cross believes the threat exists he's going to keep killing people. And I'd really like to understand what it is that's motivating him, Special Agent Sedgwick.'

She fixed him with a stare, which he held for a long moment. He blinked. 'All right,' he said, 'but don't say I didn't warn you.'

Winters didn't respond, but sat back and adopted sympathetic body language.

'It wasn't a congressman,' Sedgwick said slowly. 'It was a president.'

'Of what?' Winters asked, automatically, but she felt a knot forming in her stomach.

'Of the United States,' Sedgwick answered. 'According to Gilbert Collins, at Daniel Cross's urging, his son Ewan paid Tony Castle to arrange for the assassination of John F. Kennedy.'

43

Later that evening Tony Castle was standing over Daniel Cross, who was slumped in one of the high-backed leather armchairs in Tony's study, a heavy crystal goblet of dark liquor in one hand.

'What are you telling me? You lost her again? Who the hell are these people you've got working for you?'

'Bitch, bitch, bitch!' muttered Cross. 'She smashed my boy Justin's jaw. And I had to get 'em out of there fast. The cops were all over the place. She abandoned her car and got her family away from the resort. How did she do all that? My boys are good, I don't care what you say, Tony. She gave no hint that she was onto them. Who the fuck is this woman, anyway?'

Tony turned away with a sigh. 'I suspect she had some help.'

'You serious? Who?'

'Jack Rogers. I think he tracked her down.'

'Oh Christ, another loose end.'

'What the hell did you think he'd do, Daniel, after you burned down his fucking house and nearly killed his girlfriend? You've made this personal for him now, too.'

'Why didn't he tell you he'd found her?' Cross asked, looking up quizzically.

'I don't know,' Tony said, after a long pause. 'Maybe he doesn't trust me any more.'

'You're losing your touch, old pal. Loyalty used to be your stock in trade.'

'Oh, I think he's loyal. To the bank and to me, too. But not as loyal as he is to Stella right now. She has that effect on people.'

Cross bristled and straightened up in his chair. 'You know, Tony, I'm really getting pissed at your unfailing admiration for that woman. She's hell-bent on bringing me down and all you can do is coo about her like she's your own flesh and blood. You haven't forgotten what's at stake here, have you?'

Tony sighed again. 'No, Daniel, I haven't forgotten. And now she's teamed up with Jack, the risk is even greater. They're two of the smartest people I know.'

'And,' Cross said darkly, 'they both have to go.'

Tony nodded sadly. 'Yes, they both have to go. But it has to be done right. There can be nothing left behind to implicate us further. I don't want any more "virgin's secrets" popping up. And that's the last I want to hear of your dumb thugs, Daniel. From now on we use only my people.'

'I can live with that. How do we find your Sutton Brothers runaways?'

'We know they're trying to decipher something written by Campbell Reeves just before he, uh, died. Let's start with what we know about that poem and the man who wrote it.'

Cross leaned his head back against the soft leather of his chair and closed his eyes, forcing his memory back to a time he had long forgotten.

'We kept an eye on them pretty well, didn't we? And then the

Nicolisis tracked their every move after they came on board. Old man Collins spent most of his time in the smoking lounge, remember? Reeves, too, when he wasn't strolling the deck. They played cards, drank like fish and smoked like chimneys. We didn't see them do anything suspicious. We searched their cabins when they were out and about. We intercepted everything they wrote or said, but there was nothing.'

'They had plenty of time before we came on board. Plenty of time for Gil Collins to tell Reeves about London.'

'London, yes, I remember London. The Savoy Hotel, wasn't it? Our big reunion. I hadn't seen you and Ewan for years.'

'Yeah, well, what we did was a big deal. You had to lie low for a time and I had to build up some influence with the bankers to smooth the way for your return.'

Tony chuckled. 'We were still kids, when you think about it. Amazing, the balls we had. Bossing the old farts around, giving orders to the snooty bankers and the board. We weren't even thirty.'

'We were good,' Cross said.

'We weren't so smart at the Savoy. Shooting our mouths off before we checked the suite.'

'We were drunk. We'd been celebrating all afternoon. Even Ewan was in a happy mood, remember? And he started it, all that bragging and boasting. The little prick was such a coward, but once he thought he'd gotten away with something, he could get mighty cocky.'

Tony shook his head. 'It wasn't all his fault. I hadn't talked to you in ages. I didn't get much news hiding out in Sicily. I was asking plenty of questions. About Oswald and Ruby and the FBI investigation and that case in New Orleans.'

Cross sneered. 'Yeah, and Ewan gabbed on about it all like it was his favourite topic when I know the whole thing terrified him. He spent the rest of his short life trying to forget he had any part in it.

But on that day when he thought he'd finally found a way to impress you, he couldn't shut up to save his life.'

'Until he asked about my friends in Chicago,' Tony said with a smirk. 'Then I shut him up.'

'Right,' Cross said. 'And that's when he put his pout back on and went to grab the best bedroom before his father arrived. Typical. About the only way he could ever best his dad without my help.'

'And then he found his old man was already there, in the best bedroom, with the door ajar.'

'Sleeping, he said. "Not used to the sudden change in time zones you get from flying." Bullshit! In all the time I was at CMS I never saw Gil Collins tired.'

'Except on the ship,' Tony reminded him. 'It was clearly weighing him down by the time we saw him in Rio.'

'Well, I suppose it would,' Cross said with a dismissive shrug. 'He'd been asking Ewan some ugly questions even before we came to London.'

'Yeah, but I doubt he'd have sacrificed the good name of the company for the early stuff. As long as it couldn't be proved he would've turned a blind eye. But after he found out about the big one . . .'

'It only meant we had to bring our plans forward, Tony. We always knew his silence would have to be guaranteed.'

'Except we discovered he was going home the long way and Campbell Reeves was going along as his companion. Reeves, the man who wrote everything down.'

'But he didn't,' Cross said. 'We searched. We watched. He sent letters home, but they were all innocuous. Except the last one.'

'Exactly. Except the last one. "The Virgin's Secret". It suggested there had to be something else. Come on, Danny, you read it. You must remember something.'

Cross closed his eyes and concentrated. 'I just glanced at it. One of your Sicilians brought it to me just before we went down to deal with Reeves in his cabin. It didn't make any sense to me and I knew it didn't matter. We had the poem and Reeves was about to die.'

'You just wanted to use it to make Reeves squirm, didn't you?' Tony said, with a hint of accusation. 'You produced it, like a rabbit from a hat, loving the look of horror on his face.'

Cross had a clear image in his head. He could see a first-class cabin. He was standing inside the doorway, facing two single beds separated by a nightstand. Campbell Reeves was sitting on the bed furthest from him, the one closest to the porthole. Behind Reeves stood the wiry Nicolisi men, exuding menace. One of them was carrying a wooden case. Near the dressing table and mirror, on the wall to Cross's left, a young Tony Castelluzzo was dazzling in his dinner suit.

As he played the scene in his head Cross knew that he was holding a document file. The contract. It was his favourite prop back then. It gave him strength and sustained his ego. He carried it everywhere. The memory of the file triggered another. Reeves, the dried-up, outgoing head of finance at the company that would soon be his to rule, mocking him as he sat on his bed.

'Your sick obsession with that obscene contract has turned you into a monstrous parody of what you might have become, Daniel. You had such promise when you first came to the company. I thought, with your guidance, Ewan might take the company to new heights. But your moral decay and your fixation on that contract will only destroy everything a great family has built.'

This was the memory Daniel Cross had locked away, but the voice of the dead accountant was as vivid as if the words had just been spoken.

'What will your parents say, Daniel, when they find out what you've become? So young, yet so completely destroyed. You think they'll be proud that you count mobsters as your only friends? That you would murder innocents and violate a society to close a business deal? And they will find out, Daniel, believe me. You will not get away with this.'

The mention of his parents had penetrated the defences of the younger Daniel. The older Daniel sucked a large mouthful of bourbon and swallowed hard, as memories of that night came flooding back.

'How dare you lecture me, old man! This contract,' he had waved the precious file, 'has secured the future of the company. A future you will have no part of. And whatever it is you think you know about my business dealings will all go with you to the grave. Sooner than you think!'

Cross had a visceral recollection of the disappointment he'd felt at the lack of fear or surprise on the face of Campbell Reeves. But he had one more trick to play.

'But wait,' he remembered saying theatrically, 'is there some reason you might be so confident about my upcoming disgrace? Perhaps you think somebody might look into your sudden demise and conclude that it wasn't just the natural end for a drunken old has-been? Who would do that, do you think? Your dear wife, perhaps?'

Reeves had stopped looking calm and Cross had felt a ripple of pure pleasure. 'I wonder if this might have something to do with your misplaced sense of self-confidence.'

He had reached inside the front cover of his precious contract file and slowly taken out a white envelope and showed it to Reeves, who was looking pale. To heighten the old man's sense of anxiety and failure, Daniel gently teased open the envelope and pulled out the distinctive page of notepaper covered in neatly formed verses.

'What do we have here? Another love poem to that young wife of yours? This seems a little different. A virgin, Campbell? That's a bit saucy. And it speaks of Danny Boy. Could that be me? Why would Campbell write to his wife about me, Tony? We'll have to keep a close eye on Elizabeth Reeves when we get home, won't we?'

And then the memory collapsed into chaos. One second he'd been feeling almost omnipotent but, in the next second, the old man had surprised them all by charging across the narrow bed and smashing into Daniel, trying to get his hands around his throat.

Instinctively Cross raised his left hand to his cheek at the memory. He shook the image from his head, turned to Tony Castle and said, 'I know how the fucking poem ended up in that file.'

Tony nodded his encouragement.

'Reeves attacked me.'

'God, that's right. He cut your cheek, didn't he?'

'The old fucker nearly strangled me before your boys got him off me. And the file, Tony, remember? It flew apart. The contents went everywhere. I was so pissed. I grabbed all the pages, stuffed them into the folder and gave it to my secretary to sort out.'

'We all forgot about the poem, didn't we?' Tony said. 'Me and Vincenzo were busy pinning down the old goat while Carmelo got his suitcase opened. And you were bleeding so I told you to get out of there. But why didn't you notice it later, Daniel? You never used to go anywhere without that damn file.'

'Not after that night,' Cross said quietly. 'I told them to lock it away after that night.'

'And the next day we were all busy with Gil Collins. Getting him off the ship in a wheelchair, keeping him drugged up until we could get him back to Peoria for his own appointment with the end of his life.'

Cross snorted into his glass. 'And the fucking poem sat there all these years, locked in a safe until your protégé comes along to find it.'

Tony was suddenly aware of vivid memory of his own. 'That last night on board was when I picked my new name,' he said. 'After you told me you'd swung me a position at Sutton Brothers. This woman I banged that afternoon, her husband was Maltese and his name was Spiteri. That was the night I began my transformation.'

Cross allowed Tony just a moment to relive the past before returning him to the present. 'What do we do now?'

Tony looked at his friend. 'Based on what we know about the poem and Campbell Reeves, there is only one place it could lead Stella and Jack.'

Cross's blue eyes first narrowed, then opened wide. 'Back to the ship!'

44

When Special Agent in Charge Beardsley entered his office at 7.30 on Wednesday morning, he found Shannon Winters sitting in the visitor's chair.

'What the hell are you doing in here, Winters?'

'I tried to call you last night,' she said.

'This morning, too,' her boss noted. 'I decided nothing you were working on could possibly justify interrupting my son's eighteenth birthday celebrations. Or my breakfast, for that matter.'

'I wouldn't have called unless I thought it was important.'

'When you have my job, Winters – and I'm sure you will before long – then you'll get to decide what's important. But if it's about that forty-year-old mystery and your meeting with Pete Sedgwick last night, I'm pretty confident another few hours aren't going to make all the difference.'

'I'm not so sure about that,' Winters said. 'If you knew what Daniel Cross is trying to hide, you might understand what a dangerous man he is.'

Beardsley gave her a look of scepticism as he took off his suit jacket and sat down at his desk.

'Go on then, surprise me.'

As Winters explained, Beardsley's face began to take on a new expression, a combination of awe and concern. His next reaction was to close the door to his office. 'My God, Shannon, what have you done?'

'What have I done?' she said, taken aback. 'I haven't done anything except my job. Aren't you interested in getting to the truth about the Kennedy assassination?'

'Oh, please, don't be naive,' Beardsley said. 'Who do you think wants that can of worms opened up?'

'The American people —'

'— will not be happy to learn that their president was taken down so a few crooked businessmen could make a bit more money. Where do you think we can go with this hearsay? No, no, Shannon, this is not something you want to tie your career to.'

Winters shook her head with astonishment at the suggestion.

'Okay,' she said, 'so forget about the Kennedy stuff. I agree, without that deposition, there's little we can do.'

'Even with the deposition.'

'Putting that to one side,' she persisted, controlling her anger, 'we still have a ruthless man out there who's prepared to kill to keep his secret safe. We can't ignore what that secret is, can we?'

'Think about the embarrassment to the Bureau, Shannon, if this has been in our files the whole time,' Beardsley said, in a fatherly voice. 'Imagine the lawsuits if sensational allegations are made about wealthy, high-profile people like Cross, especially if they can't be proved. And imagine all the conspiracy theory nuts coming out of the woodwork.'

'Well,' Winters observed dryly, 'this is one conspiracy that might be more than just a theory.'

'Yeah, well, you can say that. But I doubt our political masters would appreciate the massive distraction, not after 9/11.'

Winters shook her head in disbelief. 'When do you think a good time would be, exactly, Nathan? You can't choose the timing. It's out there. We have it. It's not going to just disappear. And Cross isn't going to stop until he's certain he's safe. Doing nothing is not an option, boss.'

Beardsley sighed and leaned back in his chair while he thought about the position in which they found themselves. 'It would be pretty amazing to see that deposition, wouldn't it?' he said at last. 'How much did Collins know?'

'He overheard a lot, according to Sedgwick. There were names, including Oswald's handler and one of the other shooters, who apparently wore a police uniform. You know, the mystery guy on the grassy knoll? He also heard them talking about Jack Ruby and the Chicago mobsters who set it all up.'

'It could just be a lot of talk, couldn't it? Maybe they made it all up to give the old guy a scare. It could all be bullshit.'

'Maybe, but it could be cross-checked. There'd have to be enough in a deposition like that to kick-start a pretty thorough investigation. We can't just ignore the possibility that it still exists, can we? Especially with Daniel Cross behaving like it certainly does. Come on, boss, grow some balls!'

Beardsley's furious glare was quickly eclipsed by the awesome implications of the decision he had to make. He was silent for a long time, but the struggle to reach a conclusion played out across his face, to the point where Winters found herself resisting the urge to give it a slap.

He refocused his attention on her and said, with a distinct tone of uncertainty, 'I really don't want to do this, and it could blow up in our faces, but I guess we don't have much choice.'

'What?'

'Call the Director.'

45

'Try to stay calm,' Jack said, his eyes flitting across the faces of fellow travellers waiting to board the 12.30 p.m. flight direct from Honolulu to San Francisco, 'but I think we're being followed.'

Stella's eyes didn't move from the magazine in her lap. 'You mean the guy with the Mets cap and the torn jeans? The one who keeps moving around all the time?'

'Yes, him and another guy, wearing a blue suit. He's sitting two rows behind us. I saw them talking and laughing with each other when we arrived at the airport on Maui.'

'I noticed them too,' Stella said. 'They were such an odd couple.'

'But now they haven't acknowledged each other, and I've been watching. Not even a nod. Even if they were just sharing a smoke and a joke outside the terminal, they'd at least say hello. I mean, they both ended up on this connecting flight and there's only one other person from that flight going this way. It doesn't smell right.'

Stella closed her magazine. 'Maybe we're being paranoid,' she said, 'but let's test it. There are two of them and two of us. If I go for a walk, one of them will have to follow.'

'I don't like the idea of letting you out of my sight. It didn't go so well last time.'

'I'll just go far enough so one of them is forced to come after me. As soon as you know, text my number. I'll come straight back.'

Stella took her phone and wallet from her bag and strolled away. Jack fumbled for his phone and quickly punched the buttons so that a message was loaded and ready to fire. He kept watching the unshaven slob in the baseball cap, who was hovering close to the gate, where tired-looking staff were dealing with a line of passengers with problems. He showed no apparent interest in Stella's departure.

Feeling like a ham, Jack stood and stretched, feigning fatigue to allow him a chance to turn around and look in the direction Stella had taken. His eyes flicked to the spot where the man in the suit should have been sitting. He saw lines of bored tourists and restless children sitting in rows, but the spot where the man had been earlier was conspicuously vacant.

Jack's muscles tensed as he looked out across the wide terminal building, trying to spot Stella among the crowds. There she was, already further away than he liked. And then she was gone, around a corner, and Jack's eyes settled intuitively on the shape of a man in a blue suit, hurrying after her. Jack punched at his phone, his heart in his throat, and was relieved to see Stella's face reappear. He smiled as she passed by the suited man, who had propped himself in the middle of the milling crowd to tie a shoelace. As he sat down again, Jack glanced at the guy in the cap and registered his look of concern.

When Stella returned and sat down, she opened the magazine and pretended to be reading it. 'Nothing we can do about it. We'll have to lose them in San Francisco. Stop tapping your foot!'

Jack pushed down on his leg, trying to still the nervous energy in his muscles. 'We get in at 8.30. It'll be dark.'

'We should rent a car,' Stella said, 'something ordinary. We should be able to shake them.'

Jack pulled out his phone. 'I'll book it. Maybe we can agree on a spot where I can pick you up. In one of the car parks or something.'

'Let's not get too fancy. Better to stay where the people are. We should be able to lose them on the road, even if they're able to track us to the car. I'll drive.'

'You know San Francisco?'

'No, but I'm Italian,' Stella stated, as if the logic was unimpeachable. 'I drive fast.'

Jack smiled. 'And we should find a different hotel,' he suggested.

'Agreed. Somewhere large and busy.'

'And fancy enough for the Mets fan over there to stick out like a pimple on a supermodel.'

'Naturally,' she said, and reached out to squeeze his hand. 'I'm glad we're doing this together.'

'Me too,' he said.

The flight lasted almost five hours, but Stella's tortuous path into the city from the airport took another hour, including two dummy stops at landmark hotels, before finally handing the car to a valet at the very grand Fairmont Hotel in Mason Street. The two suspicious men hadn't been seen by either of them since the departure lounge in Hawaii and Jack was beginning to wonder if they'd imagined the whole thing.

The next morning, Jack parked the rental across from a handsome wooden row house clinging to the side of one of San Francisco's steeper hills. Built, he guessed, after the infamous 1906 earthquake, the peaked, three-storey residence was in immaculate condition, painted pale lemon with white highlights on the mouldings.

'Should we be doing this?' Stella asked, as she watched Jack switch off the engine and pull on the handbrake. 'Everybody who gets involved with this mess is in danger.'

'I know, but we don't have much choice, do we? When we get back to New York tonight, I'll ask Shannon Winters if they can do anything to keep an eye out here.'

According to the pension records, Elizabeth Reeves lived in the downstairs part of the large building, but they found nobody at home. Stella immediately marched up the steps leading to the front door of the main house and rang the doorbell. The woman who came to the door looked around fifty. Tallish, square-shouldered and large-breasted, she was wearing a simple but elegant blue dress.

'We're looking for Elizabeth Reeves,' Stella began, having first offered a dazzling smile. 'We understand she lives downstairs.'

'She's up here,' the woman said, as if it should be obvious. 'She's my mother.'

Stella turned on all her charm, starting with introductions then telling enough of the story of 'The Virgin's Secret' to get them invited inside. Heather Mortlock, as she introduced herself, was clearly unnerved to find two strangers on her doorstep talking about her father's death.

When she finally asked them inside, they followed her down the first ten feet of a much longer hallway and into a comfortable living room looking back out to the street through a bay window. There was no sign of an older woman, and Heather didn't explain, preferring to understand their intentions first. Stella's tense impatience was palpable to Jack, but had no apparent effect on Heather Mortlock.

Stella showed her the original piece of her father's stationery, and the poem. Heather read it but it meant little to her.

'He used to do this all the time,' she said, smiling sadly and handing the page back to Stella. 'They loved crosswords and puzzles, the pair of them. He'd leave presents and love letters for her around the house and she'd have to solve the clues to find them. It was like their secret language – so they could keep stuff from us kids, I used to think.' A tear moistened the corner of her eye.

'Do you think your mother could interpret this for us?' Jack asked, as gently as his gnawing anticipation would allow. 'We think it may have something to do with your father's death.'

'Oh, once she could have. But she's an old lady now. She turns eighty-seven soon and she's . . .'

She trailed off, seeming flustered, but then stood up. 'Well, I suppose the easiest thing would be for you to meet her.' She indicated the doorway leading back to the hall. 'It's good for her to have visitors, anyway.'

They walked behind Heather, through the darkness at the centre of the old house and out to a sunnier room at the rear. At first Jack didn't see the old lady propped up in a wheelchair next to a round kitchen table, where a drink and a sandwich sat untouched. She looked tiny in the chair, shrivelled and thin, her mouth moving as she muttered something indistinct. Small china-blue eyes wandered around, never seeming to fix on anything for long.

Heather bent down to give her mother a quick kiss on the cheek and tell her she had visitors. It made little difference to Elizabeth. She exclaimed, loudly enough to make Jack start, 'When's Adam coming round?'

'Later, Mom.'

Heather spoke the words as if she'd said them a thousand times before, but with a gentle voice. She explained that Adam was her mother's long-dead brother. 'She's been going downhill rapidly, I'm afraid. Birthday before last, she was bright as a button. Made a speech at her party and everything. Now, she hardly recognises me most of the time. She can't recognise her grandchildren at all.'

She wiped her eyes with the back of her hand. 'She was never happy again after Dad's passing. Came out here to get away from Peoria. She hated it there after he was gone. She decided to live where she could see the sea. Bought this house and we all went to college here, made a good life for ourselves. But for her it was never the same without Dad. They were so much in love.'

Heather was stroking her mother's head tenderly and Jack's heart went out to her, but he was bitterly disappointed. Dementia had claimed their star witness. The woman who was supposed to solve the puzzle of Daniel Cross's ugly past was incapable of forming a complete sentence.

He watched Elizabeth playing contentedly with a cluttered charm bracelet strung around her scrawny left wrist, and felt a tremendous sense of loss. After eighty years accumulating all the experience and memories of a romantic, passionate, successful life, it was all gone. From her consciousness and therefore from existence.

'Does she remember anything at all about the past? I mean, isn't long-term memory the last thing to go?' Stella winced as she spoke, realising it sounded a little tactless.

'Sometimes,' Heather said, not offended. 'It's very unpredictable. Would you like to try talking to her?'

Stella pulled a chair next to Elizabeth's wheelchair. She talked softly in the old lady's ear for several minutes but got little response other than a smile and a giggle. Heather seemed pleased Stella had achieved that much. And when the letter with the last words her beloved husband ever wrote was presented to her, Elizabeth couldn't or wouldn't look at it.

Heather sat down and Jack followed suit, taking the opportunity to find out what she knew about her father's death.

'I was nineteen at the time and a bit young for my age,' she recalled. 'I grew up pretty fast after that. Mom and I had my two younger brothers to contend with, and Dad had always been the disciplinarian.'

'You weren't, you know . . .' Stella began, and Jack almost blushed as he realised what was coming next. 'Back then, when you were young . . . I mean, sorry, but your father titled his poem "The Virgin's Secret". Is it possible he was referring to . . . ?'

'Me?' Heather struggled to look calm, but her cheeks flushed and her fingers went to the pearls at her neck. 'Well, no. I mean, I don't think . . . and even if it were true, my father would never know about, uh, we never talked about that sort of thing.'

'I'm really sorry,' Stella said, 'that was a stupid question. It just popped into my head and I opened my mouth. I'm just worried about solving your dad's puzzle. It's more important now than ever. Our futures depend on it.'

Heather turned towards Jack, with a look suggesting she thought Stella was slightly mad.

'It sounds melodramatic, I know, but it's true. We were really hoping we could get your mother's help today and well, we're a bit, you know, disappointed that she . . .' Jack said.

'If you can give us any insights into how your dad used to think,' Stella added, 'it would be an enormous help.'

'Well,' Heather said, 'we were brought up strict Catholics. In our house, the Virgin only ever meant one thing.'

'The Virgin Mary,' Jack and Stella said in unison.

'That's right.'

'Mary,' Stella said. 'The Virgin Mary's secret. Mary's secret.'

'Did you know many people at CMS in those days?' Jack asked. 'Do you remember any Marys?'

'Sure. All the kids went to the same school. The families of executives got together on weekends. There was bound to be a Mary or two, although none spring to mind.'

'Do you remember a man called Daniel Cross?' Jack asked.

'No. Should I?'

'He was a rising star at the company back then.'

'There were lots of rising stars in those days. The company was doing well, expanding and employing people all over the place. I worked there for a year myself, in the typing pool, while I decided on a college.'

'Why was it so busy?'

'You never heard of the Vietnam War?' She looked at Jack with gentle disdain. 'The company had big contracts from the Pentagon, and also from the British Government. There was a big push into the British market. I remember that because Dad had to go over there twice before the big meeting.'

'What big meeting?' Jack said.

'Sorry?'

'You said he had to go to London for a big meeting. What was the big meeting?'

'The CMS board met in London to mark the opening of a branch office there, or something like that. I'll always remember it because that was the trip Dad never came home from.'

Stella had been listening intently to the conversation. 'I thought your father died in Long Beach.'

'He did. At least that's where the death certificate was issued. But he was on his way home from London.'

'He came home from London via Long Beach?'

'He didn't like to fly. Many older people didn't like to fly in those days. For my father, passenger jets were a new thing. He was born in 1900. He liked to go by sea. So did other members of the board – it wasn't unusual back then.'

'Slow, though,' Jack commented.

Stella was distracted. Jack saw that she had a look of intense concentration on her face. 'And your father got off the ship in Long Beach?' he asked.

. 'He was taken off the ship at Long Beach,' Heather said with a touch of disapproval. 'He died at sea.'

'Oh, I'm sorry. Was he unwell before —?'

'Unusual destination, Long Beach,' Stella interrupted, 'for a ship leaving England.'

'Yes, it was. But it was an unusual trip. You see —'

'Don't tell him!'

Stella held up her hand and turned her green eyes on Jack.

'It was an unusual trip because it was the final voyage of a great liner, right?'

Stella was looking at him, but the question was for Heather, who nodded. A cog went 'clunk' in Jack's brain.

'So Jack,' Stella said, 'Campbell Reeves spent his last few days alive aboard a great ship heading for Long Beach, California in 1967.'

She paused for effect.

'He died aboard the *Queen* —'

'Mary!' Jack said in a rush. 'The Virgin is the *Queen Mary*!'

46

The remains of lunch littered Heather Mortlock's round kitchen table. Beth Reeves was flanked by her daughter on one side and Stella on the other. Jack sat next to Heather, who listened closely as Stella slowly read the poem aloud:

The Virgin's purse a secret hides
riveted by her metal sides.
Her drawers reveal a hidden box
four by two the key unlocks

'What part of a ship is the purse?' Heather asked.

Stella furrowed her brow. 'He has to mean the purser, wouldn't you say?'

Heather thought about it and then nodded in agreement. 'Of course,' she said. 'So the *Queen Mary*'s purser was hiding the secret.'

'In a hidden box,' Jack added.

'Or in a box hidden in the purser's drawers,' Stella said.

'You don't mean his boxers?' he suggested with a smile.

Stella gave the joke all the due it deserved. 'That's an English expression, Jack, not an American one.'

'I understand it,' Heather said defensively. 'It's used in America.'

'I don't think your father meant he hid the secret in the purser's underwear, do you?'

'I guess not.'

'Then it has to be one of his official drawers – one in his office or whatever space he had on the ship.'

'One with a key,' Jack said.

'Yes,' Stella said, 'a specific box with a specific key. Four by two. A numbered drawer, perhaps.'

'Like a safety deposit box?' Heather said tentatively.

'Exactly!' Stella said, and Heather looked pleased.

Elizabeth chewed slowly on a bite of her sandwich but was still in a world all her own. Stella continued with the poem:

> A past of death and murder vile,
> Oh Danny Boy, all style and guile.
> The Virgin, innocent and serene
> bore witness to the awful scene.
>
> Thus in her heart you'll find the truth,
> don't forget to check the roof.
> A lesson learned, amid the gloss,
> death stalks the man who crosses Cross.

Heather was caught up in the puzzle now. 'So this Danny Boy, that's Daniel Cross, the man you asked me about earlier?'

'That's right,' Jack said. 'We think whatever your father left behind reveals some dark secret about Cross. At least we hope so.'

'And you seriously think he killed my dad because of it?'

'It seems highly likely.'

'Do you know who else travelled with your father on the *Queen Mary*?' Stella asked.

'Well, he was travelling with Gilbert Collins. They were pretty much inseparable. Best friends.' Heather was again fiddling with the pearls around her neck.

'And Gilbert also died, soon after?'

'Yes, a week or so later, back in Peoria. Everybody said the long journey had been too much for them. It was very hot and humid for most of the trip. I remember being told they'd lost one of the ship's cooks during the voyage too, and he was a much younger man than my father.'

'There was nothing at all suspicious?' Jack asked.

'Did they do an autopsy?' Stella interjected.

Heather looked at Jack first. 'No, there was nothing suspicious. The ship's doctor told my mother Dad passed in his sleep on the very last night of the cruise.'

She turned to Stella, the tightness around her eyes revealing her distress. 'And no, I don't believe there was an autopsy. They weren't so common in those days and, given his age, his general state of health and the lack of any evidence of foul play, there was no need for one. At least, that's what Mom said. I don't think she could bear the thought of him being cut up.'

She wiped a tear from her cheek and Jack gave Stella a look and a gesture, encouraging her to ease up a little. Stella looked back at the paper in her hand. 'I wonder what he meant by "Don't forget to check the roof",' she said, almost to herself.

'Maybe the purser's office was at the top of the ship,' Jack offered, but didn't sound convinced.

Stella read on.

If I fail to make it home,
don't hesitate, pick up the phone.
Choose your allies carefully,
solve the puzzle, use the key.

The Virgin's path will lead you there,
down curving hall and sloping stair.
Truth and justice will be your gain
Or else my death will be in vain.

I love you truly, Beth, you know,
so for my sake take care, go slow,
tho' your loving arms I can't replace,
The Virgin may have my last embrace.

'Truth and justice will be your gain,' Stella repeated quietly. 'God, I hope so.'

'He's telling her to be careful who she goes to,' Jack said. 'He wants her to know Cross and his cronies aren't to be trusted.'

'At least we know what the halls and stairs refer to now,' Stella said, tapping her fingers on the table in thought.

'Does she still exist?' Jack said.

'Who?'

'The *Queen Mary*. What happened to her?'

'Oh, she's still there,' Stella said, 'in Long Beach. When you fly into LA from Australia you sometimes see her. I think it's a hotel now.'

Heather nodded. 'Yes, it's a hotel. We stayed there once, Mom and me. About fifteen years after Dad's passing. It was still quite beautiful but we didn't stay long. It was too much for her.'

She nodded in the direction of Elizabeth Reeves, who was muttering unintelligibly to herself.

'Really?' Jack said, new hope rising. 'The ship's still there? What sort of shape is she in? Did they gut her completely?'

'They took out the engines, as I recall,' Heather said. 'We did a tour. Most of the first-class cabins they kept as hotel rooms. And many of the public rooms were still on display.'

Stella jumped in. 'What about the purser's office? Do you think they kept the safety deposit boxes?'

'I have no idea,' Heather said. 'I don't remember seeing anything like that.'

'And what about the key?' Jack asked. 'In the poem, he says "use the key", as if she should have it. Do you think he planned to send it with the letter?'

Stella thought for a moment before replying. 'Maybe he put it in the envelope with the poem, but I don't think so. It doesn't make sense. The poem to Beth was written as a backup, just in case he didn't make it home. He couldn't be sure he'd be killed.' She gave Heather an apologetic glance. 'He wouldn't send the key off the ship because then he couldn't use it himself.'

'So what do you think he did with it?' Jack asked Heather.

'How would I know?'

'Weren't there any personal effects returned to the family?'

'I remember his luggage being returned. I know Mom was very upset but she insisted on going through it all herself.'

'What about his wallet or his house keys or a briefcase or something like that?'

'Yes!'

Heather leapt to her feet and raced out of the room. She returned a minute later, with something in her hand. 'His wallet,' she said breathlessly. 'I remembered seeing it in Mom's drawer when we moved her upstairs. Here, you look.'

She thrust the brown leather wallet into Stella's hands, and Stella opened it up. Jack leaned in closer, holding his breath, and saw a photograph of a young woman behind cloudy plastic. On the other side, some business cards and an antique Diner's Club card. In the slots for cash, nothing at all. Stella poked her fingers around inside, the disappointment visible in her face. She carefully pulled the photograph out from its tight pocket and found another behind it, this time showing a young Elizabeth Reeves with her proud husband.

Heather sighed. 'She was so beautiful.'

'Yes,' Stella said. 'Your father was a handsome man, too.'

'Such a lovely face, such a gentle man,' Heather said, with a sad smile. 'What is it?' she added, when she saw Stella looking at the photographs at a flat angle, turning them in the light.

'I might be imagining it but I reckon there's an impression in these photos, like there was something lumpy behind them. See?'

Stella handed the photos to Jack who examined them and agreed. 'It was actually tucked between the photographs. The lump goes in on the bottom one and out on the top. Could be the shape of a small key.'

'Key!' Elizabeth Reeves grunted, shaking her left fist violently.

They all looked at the old lady, surprised by her sudden outburst. 'Please, relax, Mom,' Heather said soothingly, stroking Beth's right forearm and the top of her hand, the fingers of which still clutched a piece of bread.

'The key would be very useful,' Stella said, willing Heather to remember it. 'I reckon whoever possesses the key would have a legitimate right to ask the current owners of the *Queen Mary* to take a look at the safety deposit box if it still exists. And as your father's heir you'd have a legal right to whatever's in the box, wouldn't you say? Think, Heather, where would she have put that key?'

'Key! A key!' Beth Reeves cried out. The charm bracelet on her wrist clattered against the table.

'Mom, please!' Heather said with concern. She gave Jack a sad look. 'She seems a little distressed. Maybe I should take her through to the other room. She needs a change of scenery.'

She stood up, ready to push her mother's wheelchair back from the table. The old lady was now holding her left arm straight up, as if seeking permission to go to the bathroom. Maybe that's what she needs, Jack thought, but then he noticed Stella.

She was staring closely at the old woman's tiny arm, transfixed by the bracelet on the arm Beth Reeves was turning back and forth under the kitchen light. Because the old lady's arm was so thin, the bracelet had fallen back, almost to her elbow. It was right at Stella's eye level. She reached out and gently held the skinny limb still, all the time staring closely at the charms hanging from their silver chain.

'Key!' Beth muttered.

'Key,' Stella repeated, still staring.

Then she broke the gaze to look over to Heather and Jack. 'There's a charm here that looks like a tiny key,' she said, almost whispering. Her slender fingers reached out to touch the bracelet, and she thought she saw the letter 'M' stamped on the little charm. 'Yes, it is,' she said breathlessly, as if she'd discovered a priceless diamond. 'Jack, I think we've found the key!'

47

The euphoria at finding the key soon passed as Stella and Jack realised that their problems were far from over. Their tiny prize lay on the table in front of them – Beth had given it up cheerfully, as if she'd always known it would be needed some day – but solving the puzzle of 'The Virgin's Secret' presented a new set of problems.

'Well,' Jack said, 'I suppose we go to the *Queen Mary*. We may as well find out if the safety deposit boxes still exist.'

'Even if they do,' Stella said gloomily, 'surely they would've been cleaned out by now. Wouldn't they have checked through them when the ship was refurbished?'

'Probably.'

'So even if we find the right box, it will most likely be empty.'

'Most likely.' Jack couldn't contain a small sigh. 'But that doesn't mean we give up, does it? We have to see it through.'

'Yes, of course,' Stella said, 'but I wish we could do more.'

'More?'

'Yes, more.' Stella looked at him. 'Assuming we don't find a secret cache of evidence hidden on the *Queen Mary*, how do we get some leverage against Daniel Cross? If the box is empty, we're screwed.'

'If the FBI can get that guy Hoyle to talk they may have a case against him already. Surely that would clear our names.'

'Maybe,' she said, 'but it's not about our reputations any more, is it? It's about saving Ben, if it's not too late. It's about bringing Cross to justice. We need him to admit he was involved in the death of Harding Collins. We need him to admit he sent David to firebomb your place. And anyway,' she said, 'according to Agent Winters, he's in London. Even if we dig up something against him, we'd have to get him back in this country to be arrested.'

'And how do you propose we do all that?'

A vague plan popped into Jack's head, but he was hoping Stella had a better idea. She hadn't.

'We could set a trap.'

'And the bait for this trap would be?'

'Well, us of course!'

'You really think Cross would risk it all just to get at us? He'd never expose himself. He'd send a team of goons.'

'If he thought we'd found something Campbell left behind, he might come himself.'

Jack looked over to Heather to see if she shared his discomfort with where this was going. The only hint she gave was a furrowed brow. Turning back to Stella, he saw excitement in her emerald eyes at the thought of a daring sting operation.

'You're out of your mind,' Jack said. 'You propose the riskiest possible approach when we don't even know if the safety deposit box is empty, or even if it exists. It doesn't make any sense.'

She turned away, a little hurt, but was quick to bounce back. 'You're right, Jack,' she said, 'I'm getting ahead of myself. If by some miracle we do find something the authorities can use against Cross, we wouldn't need to set a trap. And if we don't find anything, I suppose we could still try to lure him out, pretend we found the jackpot.'

'Anyway, then it would be the FBI's problem, right? Solving the clues in the poem was as far as we can take this, surely.'

Stella gave him a disdainful look. 'You still don't get it, do you, Jack? If the box is empty, the FBI will lose interest. They're not going to push it, not on the strength of William Hoyle's testimony. Not against a man like Cross. And certainly not just because we want them to.'

Heather was silent in her armchair, uncomfortable with the sharpness of Stella's tone. Jack pushed a thumb against his temple, which was beginning to pound.

'So we'd better hope there's something still to be found on the *Queen Mary*,' he said.

Stella nodded, then gently picked up one of his hands with both of hers. Her voice was soft again. 'And if there isn't? Will you help me try to get Cross anyway? Help me find Ben and clear my name?'

'Of course I will, Stella. We're in this together, to the end. But let's take it one step at a time – agreed?'

'Agreed.'

Stella asked Heather to pen a short letter, authorising them to act as her agents in recovering any property that might still be found in the safety deposit box. Before they left, Jack and Stella each gave Elizabeth Reeves a gentle kiss on the cheek while she sat up in bed. She seemed to enjoy the attention. She gave them a toothless grin and flashed her blue eyes as they exited the bedroom. This woman had meant so much to Campbell Reeves, yet Jack found himself wondering if she retained any memory of the man at all in the jumble that her mind had become. On the other hand, as far as Jack was concerned, she was a champion. She'd delivered the key. And he was sure that, somehow, it was a deliberate endeavour on her part. An act of determined concentration to understand what they were looking for and communicate with them. He just hoped they could do her effort justice.

Heather said her goodbyes on the front porch and wished them luck. Stella promised to call as soon as there was something to report. As they walked down the steps toward the street, a flash of sunlight from the window of an opening car door caught Jack's eye. He turned to look down the street and gasped.

'Oh, fuck!' he said.

Stella froze, her eyes following his gaze to where a man was standing on the sidewalk beside a silver car. A scruffy man, with a three-day growth and a dirty Mets cap pulled down low. And coming around the car to join him was the man in the cheap blue suit. His eyes were riveted on Jack and Stella as he strode towards them, his right hand was moving, disappearing inside the jacket of his suit.

'Heather!' Jack hissed over his shoulder. 'Get inside, now!'

48

Jack heard the click of the door closing behind them, but his eyes remained fixed on the suited man, whose hand was reappearing. Instinctively, Jack reached out to pull Stella behind him, but she was firmly planted on the stairs, shoulders squared and face defiant.

There was something dark in the man's hand but it didn't look like a gun. As he came closer, stopping at the bottom of the stairs, Jack could see that he was holding up some sort of identification.

'Harrison, FBI,' he said, then, pointing to the Mets fan, added, 'and that's Agent Ken Sanchez.'

'Kenny,' the other guy said, casually tipping his cap. 'How're you folks doing today?'

Stella turned to look at Jack with an amazed expression, and their tension snapped with a burst of spontaneous laughter.

'Thank God!' she said. 'We thought you were Cross's guys.'

'No ma'am,' Harrison said seriously. 'We were assigned to make sure you come to no harm.'

Stella chuckled again. 'Hey, look, I'm sorry about losing you guys last night. I had no idea.'

'No problem,' Kenny said with a sly grin. 'We're glad you picked the Fairmont. We don't get to stay in fancy hotels like that too often.'

'Wow! Good for you. I thought I was pretty sneaky.'

'You were mighty sneaky but we know the streets better than you. Don't feel bad.'

'You're from San Francisco?'

'LA, but we get up this way a lot.'

'We need you to come with us,' Agent Harrison said. 'Agent Winters is waiting for you.'

'She's here?' Jack said.

'Yep. She said she knew you'd end up here.'

Jack and Stella exchanged a glance as they started walking down the stairs.

'Not very trusting, is she?' Stella said, and they shared a smile.

'We have a car,' Jack said.

Harrison nodded. 'Sanchez will bring it.'

He drove them to an office building in the flatter part of the city, near Market Street. They entered through a basement car park where an elevator took them up six floors to a nondescript collection of offices beyond a reception area branded with the FBI seal.

Agent Winters was waiting in a meeting room. Her face looked drawn and her blonde hair was pulled back in a severe ponytail. As soon as Stella saw her, she bristled, and Jack sensed the tension as he introduced them and watched them shake hands coolly.

Winters dismissed her two colleagues and closed the door before gesturing to the chairs. 'You must think I'm pretty dumb, Jack,' she said, with the tone of a disappointed parent. 'As if I wouldn't check to see what flights you booked.'

Jack sat down at the table and made a gesture of indifference. 'Then you know we're booked on a flight to New York tonight. That's not unreasonable, is it? We're not under arrest or anything, are we?'

Stella remained standing. 'Why are you interested in us in the first place, Agent Winters? Surely you're not planning to prosecute Daniel Cross for fraud on a Pentagon contract he won forty years ago, do you? What's your jurisdiction here?'

Winters pursed her lips as she sat down. 'Actually, I don't think it's your place to question the FBI's jurisdiction,' she said. 'What's your jurisdictional knowledge based on anyway? TV shows?'

Stella said nothing, not wanting to admit the agent had hit the mark.

Jack tried to ease the hostility in the room. 'Look, Shannon,' he said, 'we just wanted one more day to finish our research. That's the type of people we are. We like to see things through.'

Stella held up the letter Heather Mortlock had written. 'We've been authorised by Campbell Reeves' heir to investigate and recover his property,' she announced.

'You don't have the authority to investigate squat!' Winters responded angrily. 'I should charge you with obstructing justice.'

'Hey, hey, hang on,' Jack said. 'Please, I think we all want the same thing here. We all want to solve the puzzle, maybe even solve a crime, right?'

'It's not your job to solve crimes,' Winters said.

'And it's not yours to tell me how to protect my professional reputation,' Stella shot back.

'Frankly, I don't give a damn about your reputation.'

'Oh really? I would never have guessed! But you have no idea what this is all about. And you won't be able to solve a damn thing without my help.'

The agent's face was grim, pink flushing her alabaster cheeks. 'Actually, Ms Sartori,' she said, 'it's you who has no idea what this is all about. And your assistance will be provided if we need it, either voluntarily or at the order of a judge.'

Stella closed her mouth on the zinger she was about to deliver. Damn, she thought, she really does know more than I do.

'It's not going to come to that, Shannon,' Jack said soothingly. 'We just need to talk it through. We were going to call you as soon as we got back to the hotel, right Stella?'

Stella's face remained impassive, unwilling to confirm the lie just to make the FBI agent feel better.

'We were planning to fill you in on our visit to Elizabeth Reeves and her daughter,' Jack persisted. 'We made quite a find.'

He pointed to a chair and, reluctantly, Stella sat down. Winters turned her gaze towards him and said, 'I should've been there for the interview with Mrs Reeves.'

'Mrs Reeves doesn't have much to say,' Stella said sarcastically. 'And I doubt you'd have discovered what we did.'

'It was hardly an interview,' Jack said quickly, 'it was just a conversation, very gentle. I think that's why Beth was able to cotton on to what we were looking for.' He went on to fill the agent in on their discoveries.

'I knew Reeves had a long journey home,' Winters said, 'but I didn't know it was on the *Queen Mary*.'

'With Gilbert Collins,' Stella said pointedly. 'I wonder what they talked about all that time.'

Winters reacted as if she'd been slapped. 'Well, something to do with that contract, I imagine,' she said, stumbling over the words.

Stella shot Jack a glance and he said, 'I think it's only fair you tell us what you've learned, Shannon. Jurisdiction or not, the FBI must have a reason for sending you out here, and assigning those two guys to protect us. The story I told you on Saturday wouldn't justify all that. What gives?'

Winters thought for a moment and then said, 'There's a Mafia connection.'

Stella and Jack sat up straight. 'Mafia?' Stella said.

'Italian or American?' Jack asked simultaneously.

'Both, perhaps. There was some suspicion, back in the sixties, that Cross and Ewan Collins partnered with an unusual Chicago mobster, originally from Sicily, to get that contract pushed through.'

'Unusual how?' Stella asked.

'Unusual because he had an MBA. His big dream was to be a legitimate businessman. Seems he used the Collins family connections to open the right doors.'

'So you think there's still a link between Cross and this mobster?' said Stella.

'I think so. Among other things, I've been looking into all Cross's known business associates since the sixties.'

'Does that include Frank Spiteri?' Jask asked.

'Of course,' Winters replied. 'His documentation checked out better than most, and I was even able to find his Maltese birth certificate. There's no record of him working with Cross until after Cross took over as CEO of the Collins company.'

'That's what he told me,' Jack said. 'He worked with Cross in the eighties. That's twenty years after the contract was signed.'

Stella nodded her agreement. 'But if this is Mafia-related, what about those idiots who attacked me? They weren't Mafia.'

'No,' Winters said. 'They worked for Cross's security firm, average ex-cons, not the professionals Antonio Castelluzzo liked to work with.'

'That's his name?'

'Or Tony Castle. But there's been no sign of him since 1967.'

'When Campbell wrote the poem,' Stella observed.

'Exactly.'

'And that's it?' Jack asked. 'You're pursuing an old Mafia connection? You think you're going to flush out a geriatric don?'

Winters looked defensive. 'That fire at the attorney's office. That was a professional job. Avoided the security systems, left no evidence. Somebody with high-level mob connections is still helping Cross.'

'Cross's thugs weren't hacks all the time,' Jack said. 'Remember Harding Collins and Maria Petrillo.'

Winters allowed herself a small smile. 'Actually, thanks to you, the FBI techs in Chicago reviewed the evidence and determined that the suicide note had been faked – put together with a scanner, a computer and some tracing paper. And they managed to raise a partial print from the car that killed Maria Petrillo. It was a match to Randy Hollis, the guy killed at the attorney's offices.'

'This is great news,' Jack said. 'All the fingers are starting to point in the right direction.'

'Yeah but it's still circumstantial,' Winters said. 'It comes down to Cross's word against Hoyle's. It'd be nice to have some solid evidence of his motive.'

'It's on the *Queen Mary*,' Stella stated, with conviction.

'You really think so?'

'It has to be. Can you help us get out there?'

Winters tightened her mouth. 'Sure I can smooth the way; get a warrant if it's required. But you still sound as if you think this is your investigation, Stella.'

Stella sighed with frustration. 'Look, we each have our own investigation, okay? I need to close the loop on "The Virgin's Secret" and prove it has some connection to my work for Sutton Brothers. You want to flush out a Mafia guy. We both need to find Ben Fisher, hopefully alive. If I succeed, you will probably succeed. But I have to be a part of it, don't you see?'

Agent Winters chewed her lip and looked away.

'What?' Stella demanded. 'Is there something you're not telling us?'

'No,' Winters said. 'Nothing else.'

'We're planning to go down there tomorrow and stay the night,' Jack said, sensing the time was right. 'We don't even know if the safety deposit boxes still exist. When the ship was turned into a hotel, they must have pulled out a lot of the old fittings.'

Winters shook her head. 'I don't want you doing anything until we've followed proper procedure,' she said. 'If some sort of evidence is found I want it taken legally and with no possible suspicion that it might have been planted or tampered with.'

Her words hung in the air like an accusation and Stella gave Jack a sour look. Winters interpreted it as defiance. She said, 'I could still have you arrested, you know.'

'On what charge?' Stella said boldly. 'Obstructing justice would never stick. We've told you everything we know.'

'Oh, don't get me started,' Winters said. 'At the very least I have grounds for taking you into protective custody. By the time your lawyers have you out, I'll have all my paperwork in place.'

'Relax, Shannon,' Jack said soothingly. 'We're not about to screw this up for you. But you've got to let us go down to the ship and have a look around. Surely we've earned that right. And we have written authority from the legal heir. It gives us the right to see what's in the box. We're not planning to break in or anything, as far as I know.' He gave Stella a questioning look and she shook her head and smiled. Even Agent Winters smiled, briefly.

'If we find someone down there who can give us access, why not go for it?' he went on. 'You can come and observe if you like. Nobody's going to be planting anything.'

There was a long pause while Winters tapped her pen on the table. At last, she said, 'Okay, you can go to the ship. Stay in a nice room. Take a look around. But don't do anything else until you see me or talk to me. No contact with the staff and no attempt to get at the safety deposit box, even if you find it, understand? Just keep a low profile.'

'You're not coming with us?' Jack asked, a little surprised.

'Harrison and Sanchez will be keeping an eye on you. And I'll be there too.'

Stella was looking hard at the FBI agent. 'There's something else, isn't there?' she said, shaking her head. 'I've got that feeling in my gut, like I get when there's something off about a deal. Like I'm missing some vital piece of information. Why do I feel like you're cutting me out, Shannon?'

Winters tossed her head and ignored the question as she stood. 'I'll get Harrison to drive you back to the hotel. Don't try to lose them again or all bets are off and you'll never get anywhere near that ship.'

'Our car is downstairs,' Jack said.

'Right, good,' Winters said, avoiding Stella's eyes. 'I'll tell Harrison you're ready to go.'

Thirty minutes later, back in their suite at the Fairmont, Jack used his cell phone to change their flights and book a car in Los Angeles. When he was done, Stella said, 'We should call Frank.'

'I guess he deserves to know what's going on,' Jack said. 'After all, he's still paying us.'

Stella nodded. 'And I'd better get back on his good side if I want to keep my job. Especially if we don't find anything on the *Queen Mary*.'

It was already after normal business hours in New York but Spiteri was still in the office.

'Stella, my dear girl! It's so good to hear your voice.'

'I'm not a girl, Frank,' Stella said through her smile, and he chuckled, as if they were back on familiar territory.

'It's so good to know you're okay, and that Jack has found you. Clever boy.'

'He's been fantastic,' Stella said, glancing suggestively at Jack. 'I'm so glad you asked him to find me.'

'He will be rewarded,' Spiteri said. 'You both will. Now, tell me what's been happening.'

Stella told the story, with Jack adding details along the way. Their boss said little until they'd finished. Then he apologised. 'I can't believe that I questioned your actions at the start, Stella. That was very stupid of me. I should've known your instincts are impeccable. And it's unforgivable that I allowed you both to get into this position. But Daniel's one of those clients, you know? The ones that stand by you; support your bid to become a partner. I'm still finding it hard to comprehend.'

'You didn't know him in the sixties,' Jack said. 'It looks like he was ruthless enough to kill to win that contract and to involve the Mafia.'

'Yes,' Spiteri said, his voice sounding sad. 'So it seems. And that deal underpinned his entire career. I always knew it was important to his resumé, but I had no idea . . .'

'Even if we don't find anything on the *Queen Mary*, he's in trouble,' Stella said. 'The evidence is mounting and the cops have one of his henchmen in custody.'

'He's finished,' Spiteri growled. 'Whatever happens, Daniel's finished as a CEO. His reputation won't withstand this. And obviously the bank can't work with him any more.' In a melancholy tone, he added, 'I can't protect him now.'

'It's not our job to protect clients who turn out to be crooks, Frank,' Stella said. 'If Sutton Brothers works with the authorities to bring him to justice, we may yet emerge from this with our good standing intact.'

'Perhaps,' Spiteri said unenthusiastically.

'Are you in touch with Cross, Frank?' Stella said, a note of concern in her voice.

'No, no,' Spiteri said quickly. 'I believe he's still in London – he returned there at the end of last week – I haven't been able to talk to him since the fire at Jack's house.'

'What about Ben? Have you heard anything from him?'

'No, I'm afraid not. I spoke to his wife yesterday. She is obviously terribly distraught. She's told the children he's away on business and is just living in hope that he turns up. The uncertainty must be soul-destroying.'

There was a pregnant pause, so Jack jumped in. 'We're going down to Long Beach tomorrow to the *Queen Mary*. But we have to wait for the authorities to do it properly so it may be another few days before we're back in the office. We'll be staying on the ship tomorrow night.'

'Really?' Spiteri said. 'Do you think that's wise? Can't you leave it to the authorities now? I don't like the idea of you two being exposed to Daniel's thugs again.'

'He's lost at least two of his thugs,' Stella said. 'Besides we have three FBI agents looking out for us.'

'Is that so? I met Agent Winters this week, of course. Seemed a little young to me. But there are more?'

'Agents Harrison and Sanchez,' Jack said, flashing a grin in Stella's direction. 'And they've already had the opportunity to impress us with their surveillance skills.'

'Are they experienced enough, do you think? Do you feel safe?'

'We couldn't shake them,' Jack told Frank. 'They seem experienced enough, I guess.'

'Funny looking pair,' Stella mused. 'But yeah, I'll feel safer knowing they're around.'

'Good, good,' Spiteri said. 'As soon as you stop feeling safe, you get out of there.'

'Okay,' Stella said, smiling in response to his concern. 'Thanks, Frank. It was good to talk to you again. I'll call you as soon as we know what's going on, all right?'

'That won't be necessary, my dear girl,' Spiteri said. 'I can't possibly let you face this on your own. I'm coming out there. I'll see you both tomorrow, aboard the *Queen Mary*.'

49

Late in the afternoon of the following day, Jack and Stella were in one of thousands of motor vehicles making their way south from Los Angeles International Airport along the 405 freeway. Jack was driving, Stella navigating. Neither task was too onerous. The enormously wide band of concrete they were travelling down had many lanes, and the traffic moved steadily. The signs to Long Beach were impossible to miss and they exited at the 710 and drove west, ignoring the city, heading straight for the coast.

The approach to the *Queen Mary* was remarkably unappealing. Massive roads led to largely vacant docks, static cranes and huge, mostly empty, car parks. But when they first saw the ship, all of that was forgotten. It was truly an impressive sight. Over a thousand feet long and twelve decks high, it looked big from a distance but as they drove closer, it loomed even larger. The shiny black hull was topped by a cityscape of crisp white structures leading up to three massive orange funnels, tipped in black, leaning slightly aft as if in response to the liner's great speed.

But this thing of nautical beauty wasn't going anywhere. As Stella and Jack came alongside, they could see it sat in the water but was virtually landlocked. Later, they discovered it was permanently fixed to the shoreline with concrete, making it more peninsula than ship. The liner was also attached by a bridge to an ugly metal structure containing an elevator for hotel guests and a long series of permanent ramps and escalators bringing day visitors up for tours.

They parked the rental car and travelled up via the elevator to the reception on A Deck and were surprised to find the hotel almost full. There were to be two weddings on board that weekend. As Stella filled out the registration card, she couldn't resist asking a few leading questions. She looked up at the neat, effeminate man serving them.

'Do you happen to know where the purser's office used to be when the ship was in service?'

'Which one?' the man replied with a polite smile.

'How many were there?'

'Three. There was a purser for each class of passage.'

Stella didn't hesitate. 'First class.'

The receptionist's lips closed in a little pout. 'On the *Queen Mary*, it was known as cabin class.'

'Right,' Stella said impatiently.

The young man indicated the reception area behind him with a wave of his hand. 'It was right here. This is where the cabin-class passengers first entered the ship. The purser's office was right behind me.' He pointed over his left shoulder. 'The mail room was there.' He pointed behind them. 'And the typing room and bank were on that side.' He indicated to his right.

The man behind the desk was beaming, but Jack felt ill. The thrill of coming aboard was quickly deflating with this news. 'So you mean this part of the ship was gutted when it was turned into a hotel?'

'That's right, sir. Most of the furnishings in this area are new.

There was no formal reception desk on the *Queen Mary*, so they had to put one in. But don't worry, you can still see plenty of the original decor in other parts of the ship. As hotel guests you're free to explore all the public areas. Here's a guide map.'

Jack was handed a brochure, which he looked at blankly.

Stella persisted with her questions. 'What would they have done with the fittings removed from here during the renovation works, do you know? Surely they wouldn't have thrown it all away.'

'Oh no, ma'am. Anything unique was kept, of course, including part of the cabin-class purser's office. His desk is part of the state-room exhibits up in the bow of the ship.'

'And the safety deposit boxes?' Stella asked breathlessly.

Jack held his breath. The receptionist frowned in thought. 'I'm not sure,' he said slowly, 'I think there are some boxes behind the desk but it's some time since I've been up there. Would you like me to ask one of the guides?'

The offer was made with a tone that suggested he didn't relish the idea and Stella didn't want to wait. She said, 'It's okay, we can go look for ourselves. Thanks.'

She tapped her fingers on the counter with rhythmic impatience while they waited for the man to issue them with a key.

The immense length of the *Queen Mary* struck them anew as they entered one of the long corridors along which the guestrooms were arrayed. The floor sloped up and away from them, and the dark wood panelling and simple brass handrails on both walls appeared to stretch forever to meet at some unseen point. Low ceilings and the endless swathe of red and blue geometric carpet added to the effect.

Their cabin was right up at the front of the old liner, and down one deck from reception. It was on the right or – more correctly – star-board side, with two portholes looking out across a stretch of still water towards a marina. The cabin was furnished as it had been when the ship was last in service, with a few alterations in the bathroom and the standard modern necessities – such as a television – added to the bedroom. The narrow single beds didn't meet with Jack's approval, but they were in keeping with the original decor.

The overall effect was charming and Jack almost wished a vibration would shiver up through his feet, signalling a start to massive turbines that would power them away on a long cruise to some exotic destination. Stella wasn't caught up in the romance of the ship at all. 'Come on,' she said, as soon as they'd dropped off their few possessions. 'Let's go and see if the safety deposit boxes are still there.'

At the forward end of the corridor, just a few paces away from their cabin, there was an open door marked 'Third-Class Lounge'. Through there they found a staircase, much narrower and plainer than the elegant flights at the centre of the ship. But this stairway suited their purposes well, bringing them, in a roundabout way, up to the promenade deck and close to the bow.

In their exploration of the promenade deck, they discovered a shopping arcade glowing with golden veneers and etched glass wrapped around curved art deco fittings. There was a bar beyond the shops, splendidly representing the era with carved chrome rails and bright red furniture.

Making their way outside – although the deck was actually a covered walkway open at the side – they walked straight and climbed down several flights of metal steps, right out into the open. They were following signs to the 'Stateroom Exhibits'.

In the bow area they found a passageway – quite dark, especially in the fading light of dusk – which was lined with exhibits behind glass. There was a fully made-up example of each class of cabin on the ship, ranging from the apartment-sized staterooms of a luxury suite, with its own sitting room, to the narrow beds and exposed plumbing of third class.

Around a corner, lit up from behind as if still open for business, was their goal – or at least a reconstruction of it. Brass capital letters on a black background spelled out the words 'Purser's Office' across the top of a five-foot wide display, framed with fluted pillars that held a sheet of glass to protect the exhibit from the public.

At the front of the display was a curved counter, finished in radiant burl veneers from rare and expensive woods, which extended beyond the glass. Papers were scattered about as if the purser had just stepped out to check some detail for a passenger.

And most impressive of all, to Jack and Stella at least, was what they could see through the protective glass. Behind the curved counter there was a narrow space. Then a waist-high cabinet in pale ash – made up of sliding cupboard doors and drawers with bone handles – supporting rows of shiny stainless steel rectangles of various sizes, each with a round brass lock.

Safety deposit boxes. They looked to be in mint condition. Open pigeonholes running down the centre of the boxes were stuffed with more papers, obviously to enhance the visitor's experience. Jack was struck with the thought that these boxes must look remarkably similar to the day Campbell Reeves visited them, not long before his death.

'A couple are missing,' Stella said, and Jack could see she was right. Two narrow, black slots broke the gleaming symmetry of the display. Obviously these boxes were like drawers, which, when unlocked, would pull out completely. Somewhere along the way, two of them had been souvenired.

'I hope ours is still there,' Jack said, and from the corner of his eye he could see Stella smile.

'I'm sure it's still there, Jack. But whether it's got anything in it is another matter completely.'

'Which one do you think it is?' he asked, pressing close to the glass like a kid looking through the window of a toy store.

'I think it's that one,' she said, full of self-belief.

Jack looked at her finger, but she could have been pointing at any one of fifty boxes. He'd already calculated there were over 120 of them. 'Which one?'

'That one,' she repeated. 'Top left. I can't see the number. Four across and two down.'

'Ah, four by two. That's your theory. I thought it might be number eight.'

'Maybe, but Campbell was an accountant. He understood all about x and y axes.'

'Well, maybe they're all unlocked. You can't tell from here. They don't look like they've been touched.'

Stella's voice was glum. 'I'm someone would have gone through them, if only to look for valuables.'

'Maybe not. They'd have no good reason to assume anything of value was left behind, would they? Passengers wouldn't forget stuff that was important enough to lock away in a box like that. Unless they were dead.'

Stella put one hand flat on the glass. 'I can't wait too long, Jack. If we don't hear from Shannon Winters tomorrow morning, telling us she's arranged an official opening, I'm going to have to find a way in there. It's eating me up.'

'Me too,' Jack said. 'But we need to do it by the book.'

'Somebody on this ship must have access to the exhibits. I don't care who it is. You find me the guy with a key and I'll convince him to let us in.'

Jack smiled. 'I don't doubt it for a second.'

She returned the smile, then glanced at her watch. 'Come on, let's get away from here before it drives us nuts. It's waited thirty-five years; I guess it can wait one more night. Why don't you buy me a drink?'

They returned to the red and chrome bar on the promenade deck and Jack ordered cocktails – Campari for Stella and a Tanqueray martini for him. Through the ship's windows, they watched the sky darken and they chatted aimlessly, studiously avoiding subjects associated with their reason for being on the ship. Before returning to their cabin to freshen up for dinner, they took a stroll around the *Queen*. For a while they stood at the railing arm in arm, looking out across perfectly flat water to the lights of the marina.

After a time, Stella said, 'You know, Jack, we haven't talked about us.'

'Do you want to?'

'Not really.'

'Then let's not,' he said. 'We'll have plenty of time when this is over.'

She gave him a grateful smile and snuggled in closer. They kissed. Other people, including several couples, moved around the deck behind them, finding their own slice of on-board romance. But Jack and Stella paid them no mind, and were completely unaware of two figures moving up behind them.

'I'd say this gives a whole new meaning to the concept of team bonding, wouldn't you agree, Agent Winters?'

'Frank!' Stella recoiled from Jack's embrace like a teenager caught out by her father.

Out of the shadows stepped their boss, his face wearing a look of pleasure as he registered the guilty looks on their faces. Then Shannon Winters stepped into the light, her professional countenance broken only by an amused twist to her lips. As she came closer, her golden blonde hair formed a halo as she was backlit by the bright spotlights illuminating the ship. Spiteri was dressed in a well-tailored suit and designer tie. Winters was wearing the same tight-fitting business suit they'd seen her in yesterday.

'Jesus!' Jack said. 'Where did you two spring from?'

'We haven't been here long,' Spiteri said, smiling broadly. 'I ran into Agent Winters downstairs. She seemed to know where you'd be.'

Jack found himself looking around. Obviously Harrison and Sanchez were lurking somewhere, and doing a better job at staying inconspicuous than in Hawaii. Spiteri was looking Stella up and down. 'You don't seem to have suffered too much for your ordeal, my dear. In fact, you look positively radiant. Would it be wrong for me to give you a hug?'

'Of course not, Frank,' Stella said and she moved to embrace him tightly. Spiteri whispered into her ear while his arms were around her, expressing condolences for the loss of her husband. 'Although you seem to be coping well,' he said more distinctly as he broke the hug, nodding in Jack's direction and raising an eyebrow.

Stella flushed with embarrassment and instinctively stepped away from both men, finding herself standing next to Shannon Winters.

'Still no word on Ben?' Stella asked.

'No,' Spiteri said, with a shake of his head. 'Jennifer, his wife, called me again today.'

'We have to flush Cross out,' Stella said angrily, 'whatever we find on this ship. He has to pay for Ben.'

'Unless he's here already,' Jack said, feeling a chill of trepidation as he looked down the long, shadowy deck.

'No,' Agent Winters said. 'He's definitely in London. I saw security photographs from Heathrow airport today, showing Cross arriving in the UK last Friday. And I have all port authorities on watch for his return. He won't get into the US without me knowing about it.'

'We can relax for a while,' Spiteri said. 'Daniel won't be able to interfere, not with the FBI looking out for us. I must say, for my part, I'm certainly intrigued to see if there's anything in the safety deposit box.'

'Join the queue!' Jack said.

'Yeah, well, a warrant should be issued in the morning,' Agent Winters said with an air of authority. 'It hasn't been easy. The background material's so vague and messy.'

Stella interpreted the comment as a criticism. 'I'm sorry you found the evidence so complicated, Agent Winters. Anyway, as I've said many times, we already have the legal authority to investigate the box. I don't see why the *Queen Mary*'s owners would refuse to cooperate.'

'It's not a question of cooperation —'

'It's a question of letting the FBI do their job, Stella,' Spiteri interrupted earnestly. 'We'll have to be patient. I suggest we eat. By New York time it's well past the hour. I saw a sign to a restaurant that way.'

He extended his arms to start herding the group back towards the interior of the ship. The force of his personality was enough to overcome any resistance.

'But I'm not dressed,' Stella said.

'You look gorgeous,' Spiteri responded. 'Come – Sutton Brothers is paying!'

The place Spiteri chose was, naturally, the most exclusive in the floating hotel. And he worked his charm to its limits, trying to raise the spirits of the group, but it was an uphill battle. Stella's thoughts were with Jennifer Fisher and her kids, whom she knew well. Agent Winters behaved like a bodyguard, eating little, drinking nothing but water and constantly monitoring all movement in the restaurant. Jack tried his best to smile at the boss's jokes and stories, but his heart wasn't in it.

'Dessert?' Spiteri asked, as the half-eaten entrees were removed.

All three of his guests declined. 'Coffee, then,' he suggested and got three desultory nods.

As the coffee was being served to the despondent group, a cell phone started to ring. Shannon Winters reached into her jacket and pulled out a phone, standing up as she did so. 'I'll take this outside.'

Spiteri watched the agent with obvious appreciation as she made her way to the door. 'Her talents are certainly, uh, well-rounded, aren't they?' he said.

'Frank!'

'Sorry, Stella,' Spiteri said, but he winked at Jack.

Stella looked prepared to call him on it but stopped when she saw Agent Winters hurrying back to the table. And something was making the icy agent smile.

'That was Chicago,' she said, 'Ben Fisher has been found!'

Stella was ecstatic. 'Is he okay?'

Winters expression was ambivalent. 'Not entirely, but he's alive. He was badly beaten and left for dead. He's been in hospital for a week in an induced coma. He had no ID so it took a few days for the connection to be made. But he's conscious and seems to be improving. No memory of the beating, as yet.'

Spiteri beamed and clapped his hands. 'Thank God,' he said. 'And his wife?'

'She's been told,' Winters said. 'She's on her way to Chicago.'

The mood of the group was transformed. Smiles replaced the long faces and Spiteri insisted on ordering a bottle of champagne. Even Agent Winters took a sip to toast Ben's recovery. She leaned closer to Stella.

'I've also had a message from Detective Robertson,' she said quietly. 'Dental records have confirmed it was your husband's body they recovered from Jack's place. I'm very sorry.'

Stella kept her face expressionless. 'Thanks, Shannon.' She

glanced across at Jack, who was watching her closely. 'I think we've been assuming that already, but thanks anyway.'

It didn't kill the mood entirely, but it did return Stella to a contemplative silence. Jack wanted to get her alone to comfort her properly so he suggested they call it a night. Spiteri looked disappointed but signalled to a waiter for the bill and Winters stood up, saying she needed to check in with her team.

'I have your number, and you have mine,' Winters said to Jack. 'If you don't hear from me earlier, we'll meet at eight in the morning, at reception.'

Jack nodded and watched her depart, reaching for her cell phone as she exited to the deck. Spiteri was looking around for the waiter. 'You go ahead,' he suggested, a look of paternal compassion on his face. 'I'll take care of the paperwork and see you in the morning.'

'Thanks for the lovely dinner, Frank,' Stella said. 'Sorry if I've been no fun.'

'It's the very least I can do,' Spiteri responded, 'and there is no need to apologise. You've had an extraordinary few days.'

Jack stood up and Stella followed. Spiteri seemed to be studying their faces. As they said their goodnights, he stood to hug Stella and shake Jack's hand firmly. 'I want you to know,' he said, with the hint of a tear in his eye, 'how proud I am of the two of you. It's been a privilege – it is a privilege – working with people of your calibre.'

Stella smiled and shook her head. 'That's sweet, Frank, thanks.'

When they were out in the cool air of the upper deck, she said to Jack, 'He can be hard work sometimes but his heart's in the right place.'

'He obviously loves you.'

'He loves anyone who can make him or the bank look good, but he does invest a lot of emotion. That's just his way.'

Jack was leading the way down to the main deck, looking for the right way to return to their cabin, when Stella took his arm and said, 'You know what? I was ready for bed a while ago but now I think I need another drink. You up for a cleansing ale in that cool lounge we saw this afternoon? We can toast Ben's health again.'

'What about our minders?'

Stella made a sweeping motion with her arm. 'I guess they're out there,' she said, then she raised her voice and shouted, 'Hey, Kenny, you guys want a drink? Follow us!'

There was no response from the dark sky or the empty decks.

'Maybe it's past their bedtime,' Jack said with a smile.

Stella raised her eyebrows conspiratorially. 'Oh, no. They're out there somewhere. They're just pissed that we sussed them out in Hawaii.'

Jack saw a sign for the observation lounge and pointed the way. 'First one to spot them gets breakfast in bed.'

'Ooh,' Stella said happily, 'I reckon I can come up with a better prize than that.'

Two decks further down, Shannon Winters was also looking for her FBI colleagues. She wandered the hallways and the decks, checking the agreed observation and access points, all the while punching buttons on her cell phone and telling herself to stay calm. She made her way back to her assigned cabin in the hope that they had regrouped there. She passed a middle-aged couple in the hallway as she hurried along but was completely oblivious to their polite greetings.

By the time she reached the cabin door, her heart was beating at twice its normal rate and her nerves were on edge. Her gun was in a holster over her right hip and she reached under her jacket to take it out. With her other hand she used the key to unlock the door. Pushing the door open, she looked down the short hallway formed by the bathroom. The room was dark but for the faint light coming through the portholes. She reached a hand to the light switches inside the door and flicked them up. The quaint art deco furniture and fittings of her bedroom were illuminated and Winters relaxed slightly, still moving cautiously as she entered the hallway.

The end of the two single beds came into view and then something else that made her freeze. Two feet, shod in worn trainers, protruded from behind the end of the first bed. Pistol raised, checking the corners, she moved forward to get a better view. Both of her fellow agents were lying there in the space between the beds. Agent Harrison was unconscious but had no obvious wounds. A dark stain had formed on the jacket of his suit, but only because it was lying in the puddle of blood extending from a deep slash across the throat of Kenny Sanchez.

Swallowing her revulsion, Winters swung her pistol in a double-handed grip towards the bathroom door. She moved forward slowly and pushed the door inwards with the barrel and quickly released one hand to hit the switch. When the light came on, it reflected off the aged, white tiles of the walls and drew her eyes to the old bath, with its thick but translucent white curtain. The curtain was pulled. Was that how she'd left it? She sensed more than saw a shape in the bath behind the curtain.

Gun raised, she commanded, 'FBI – freeze!'

'Don't shoot!' a heavily accented male voice answered.

The shower curtain was pulled aside and a deeply tanned, wiry man appeared, his arms raised in surrender. Agent Winters had only a moment to register the syringe in the man's right hand before her own hand, and the gun in it, was violently wrenched to one side. A second man stepped out from behind the bathroom door and twisted the agent's arm in a painful arc up behind her back. The gun skidded across the tiles and came to rest next to the bidet. The first man stepped out of the bath and lowered his arms. His face was expressionless as he pushed the syringe into the agent's pinioned arm. Shannon Winters slid, senseless, to the cold floor.

Up at the forward end of the great liner, Jack and Stella had found their way to the observation lounge. Only a few of the red leather seats in the curved bar were occupied, and the lone waitress on duty seemed grateful for some action. They ordered beers and sat in a quiet corner of the second tier up from the bar, a small circular table between them.

The atmosphere in the lounge almost discouraged conversation, and Jack found himself admiring the extraordinary decor, which was rich in detail he hadn't noticed before. He had a sudden, strong urge for a cigarette. Looking across at Stella, he saw that she was rummaging in her handbag. As she searched, she pulled out a small notepad, a packet of tissues and a mini tape recorder and put them on the table. Then, to Jack's amazement, she proceeded to pull out a crumpled packet of Marlboros on the table, shaking a lighter from the packet on the way. She swept the tape recorder and other items back into her bag and placed it back on the floor. With a guilty smile she said, 'I don't smoke very often but I really feel like one; I stole this pack from my sister. You won't want to kiss me, will you?'

Jack answer was to light two cigarettes and hand one to her. He'd always wanted to do that. Stella eye's sparkled with wicked surprise and she smiled seductively, putting the cigarette up to her mouth. Jack was transfixed. They had barely exhaled the first puff when the waitress appeared at their table to tell them smoking wasn't permitted inside. Without the need for a discussion, they stood up to take their antisocial behaviour outdoors. When they returned to the table, Stella put the cigarettes back in her bag and raised her beer.

'Here's to Ben's speedy recovery and Alex's too.'

'And to the memory of all Cross's victims, past and present,' Jack said, taking a long swallow from his bottle.

Stella nodded sagely, then stood up. 'I really gotta pee,' she said. 'Keep an eye on my bag. It has the key in it.'

Jack's eyes followed her as she moved down to where the waitress was leaning on the bar. Having received directions, she turned and gave Jack a little wave before heading out to the far side of the bar. Jack relaxed into a gentle reverie, his head filling with thoughts of Stella's body and her eyes and that mouth, all in the genuine art deco setting of their cabin below decks. He took another mouthful of beer, deciding this drink should be their last. His eyes wandered to the chrome railings and the bizarre painting behind the bar and he looked at the other patrons – two couples and a single man – and at the bar staff.

Time always dragged for Jack when he was waiting for someone. He glanced at his watch. It's been a while, he thought, and Stella doesn't seem the type to spend an age in the bathroom, fixing up her hair and make-up. Twisting around, he attempted to look out of the windows, which faced forward towards the bow of the ship, but all he could see was black sky and a few points of light. Behind him he heard Stella's chair move and he turned to welcome her back. Sudden shock rocked him back in his chair, and his knee hit the table, knocking over the beers. His eyes stared at the person sitting where Stella should be.

'Oh, what a shame, Jack, you seem to have spilled your drink,' Daniel Cross said. 'Let me get you another.'

50

Anger and confusion ran through Jack's brain as he registered the triumphant look on Daniel Cross's face. Cross raised his finger to the waitress, who rushed over quickly to clean up the mess. He ordered two more beers and turned back to Jack. The man smiled like a genial host but his look was cold.

'Welcome to my place, Jack,' he said, making a sweeping gesture with his hand. 'I haven't seen the *Queen Mary* since her fateful last voyage in '67. But for the past day or so she's been my home again.' His stare intensified. 'I can't begin to tell you how disappointed I am in you, Jack. I thought you had the potential to be a real player.'

'Where's Stella?' Jack said.

'Safe and sound, don't worry. You'll be joining her soon.'

Jack felt his blood heating up and his hands gripped the arms of his chair. He forced himself to calm down. He let his arms drop and took a deep breath. His fingers brushed the handle of Stella's bag.

'What are you planning to do with her?'

'Relax, Jack. Don't be so impatient. Whatever fate Stella has in store, you'll be sharing it with her.' Cross flicked some invisible speck from the lapel of his jacket and then smiled up at the waitress who had returned with the drinks.

'On your room, sir?' she said and Cross nodded.

Jack thought of escape while Cross was distracted but he realised it would be futile. They had Stella.

Cross poured beer into a glass and took a sip. 'You all thought I was in London, didn't you?' he said with a self-satisfied tone. 'Only my passport travelled to England last Friday, Jack. I keep a man on my payroll who bears a striking resemblance to me, even though he's nearly twenty years younger.' With the palm of his hand he brushed his bald dome. 'Sometimes it's an advantage to have a distinctive look. People only notice your outstanding features.'

Jack glared but his mind was toying with a plan. Cross was settling in to gloat, to show off. If Jack could catch some of Cross's admissions on tape, perhaps he could turn this situation into the trap Stella had hoped for. He shifted in his seat and his fingers moved slowly towards the handbag. He was guessing the movement was out of Cross's line of sight.

'You've been here the whole time?' he said, reaching to pick up the beer bottle in front of him while his other hand reached down into the bag.

'It seemed as good a place as any,' Cross said. 'I have no recollection of that idiotic poem Campbell Reeves wrote. But I knew where he wrote it and I knew where he died. There was a good chance it was going to lead you here in the end.'

'What are you trying to hide, Daniel?' Jack said, his fingers barely touching the cool metal of the tape recorder. 'What could be so bad that you felt the need to kill Maria Petrillo and Harding Collins?'

A row of buttons teased Jack's fingertips. He tried to visualise the order of the ridged markings on the switches. Which one was the record button?

Cross was looking at him, as if deciding how much to say. 'Only people who present a real threat to me are ever in any danger,' he said, as if it was a perfectly reasonable explanation. Jack knew he had to choose a button. Cross was about to incriminate himself.

'Harding and his assistant only became a problem because of Stella Sartori,' Cross said. 'If she'd kept her nose out of things that didn't concern her, they would still be —'

'Tuesday, eighth of October.' Stella's voice floated up from the floor. 'Remember to get Ben Fisher to do a spreadsheet showing —'

Jack frantically pushed all the buttons on the little machine. There was an audible click and Stella's voice stopped. Cross leaned to one side and saw the bag on the floor. He reached out a foot to pull it closer.

'Jack,' he said, his voice deepening, 'you see that guy over there?'

He indicated a point over Jack's shoulder. When Jack turned to look, he saw a brown-skinned man wearing a scruffy suit, sitting at a table on the far side of the lounge. The man looked back at him.

'That man is a trained killer, an expert. If you do anything to threaten me you'll be dead before the thought is fully formed in your head. And Stella will be dead soon after.'

Cross took the tape recorder out of Stella's bag. Anger rippled over his face for a second. 'You really don't give up, do you, Jack? I suppose I should admire that. But how can I admire a man who throws his life away for a taste of pussy?'

Jack's eyes narrowed. 'I don't want your admiration, Daniel. Stella's the one who deserves admiration and respect, and she has mine.'

'Stella Sartori? A woman so hateful her husband was prepared to sell her out for a few lousy bucks. I think you make your choices with your dick instead of your head, Jack.'

'Her husband was a loser, Daniel. It's not surprising he was attracted to you.'

Cross laughed, enjoying the schoolboy taunts. 'You're right, of course O'Reilly was a loser. But he was an incredibly useful loser for a time.'

'You meant for him to die in the fire, didn't you?'

'It was brilliant, wasn't it?' Cross was exhilarated by his own cunning. 'I got rid of the evidence at your house and a potential witness in one easy move. I love new technology.'

'You're a cold-hearted bastard,' Jack observed dryly.

'I just don't like loose ends, Jack.'

'The FBI knows about you, Daniel. You can't possibly believe you can get rid of us without any consequences.'

'What they might think they know and what they can prove are two very different things, Jack. Witnesses are the key. If there are no witnesses and only weak circumstantial evidence, there's nothing they can do about it. It's one of the many reasons I love this country.'

Cross grinned and took another swig of his beer. He glanced at his watch, nodded to the man across the room and pulled out a cell phone. 'I think we've kept them waiting long enough,' he said, flipping open the phone. 'Hopefully this time the boys resisted the temptations that you obviously couldn't.' He winked lasciviously. Into the phone, he said, 'We come now,' as if talking to someone with poor English, then he slid the phone back into his jacket and stood up. He picked up Stella's tape recorder and pushed her bag over to Jack.

'You carry this. It doesn't match my outfit.'

Jack picked up the bag, briefly wondering if Cross was aware of the key. But he was more worried about Stella, fending off the advances of some horny thugs who knew they were beyond the law.

Cross's confidence suggested that he was in complete control of the situation on board. He and his men would know the security arrangements, the best ways to move around the ship. And there were a number of them. But where were Kenny and the sombre Agent Harrison? Jack wondered. Were they waiting for the right time to leap out and rescue him? Why had they allowed Stella to fall into Cross's hands?

'Follow me,' Cross ordered and Jack trailed him from the lounge back out to the promenade deck. There was nobody in sight but for the man in the shabby suit, who followed close behind.

Jack was conscious of the bulge in the pocket of his jeans. His cell phone was in there. They hadn't searched him. Shannon Winters was just a call away but how could he do it without being noticed? His only chance would be when they moved outside onto the dimly lit foredeck of the ship. He tried to angle his body so that the man following them couldn't see what he was up to. Cross led them down the metal stairs towards the bow. The sky was dark and starless and the deck was shadowy and deserted.

He ran through the sequence of buttons he needed to push to retrieve the numbers stored in memory, select one and place the call. Even if he couldn't speak, he hoped Agent Winters might find the call intriguing enough to investigate. After a few prods with his thumb, he was confident he'd called up the memorised numbers. There were only two names in there, Stella and Shannon Winters. All he had to do was pick one. They'd be listed alphabetically, but he couldn't remember if it would be according to their first or last names. It would make all the difference. At worst, he had a fifty-fifty chance. He took his best guess.

A few seconds later, a loud peal rang out from the bag Jack was carrying in his other hand. Daniel Cross spun around and grabbed the bag while Jack pushed a button in his pocket to terminate the call, cursing himself. He was proving to be the Mr Bean of covert action.

Cross found the phone and checked the number of the missed call. The man trailing them came forward and pinned Jack's arms behind his back with surprising force for a little guy. Jack gasped in pain and the man holding him muttered something in a foreign language and indicated with a nod of his head that Cross should look in Jack's pocket. Cross now had Jack's phone, along with Stella's. He took three long steps to the ship's rail and dropped the phones and the recorder over the side.

'Who were you trying to call, Jack? I hope it wasn't that pretty little FBI agent. She needs her beauty sleep, son, so we won't bother her. I avoid taking out officers of the law if I can, but if you drag her into this, Jack, she'll be just as dead as —'

He paused as if trying to decide. His own cell phone suddenly buzzed. After listening for a few seconds, he lowered the phone and said, 'We have forty minutes.'

The Mediterranean-looking man's expression suggested he hadn't understood a word. Cross shrugged and said, 'Come on, Jack, move it.' He strode towards the bow. Jack shook himself free of the strong-man and followed.

As they came towards the entrance to the corridor housing the stateroom exhibits, Jack saw another dark shape in a suit emerge from the shadows. This man was better dressed than the strongman and his face showed deep lines of experience. Grey flecked his thick black hair. Turning into the corridor, another olive-skinned man came into view, a young guy this time, standing next to Stella, who looked pale. She stood stiffly, her right hand crossed defensively over her chest and gripping the upper part of her left arm.

'Are you okay?' Jack said, moving forward slightly.

'Shut up!' Cross snarled and, as if on cue, the older of the hench-men reached behind his back and pulled a stubby pistol out from under his jacket, already fitted with a silencer. The other two followed suit and took a step back, positioning themselves to cover any further move Jack or Stella might make.

Jack heard his heartbeat thumping in his ears. A reassuring nod from Stella only calmed him a little. There were two men with guns in front of him and one behind. Fear gripped his belly and he wondered how long they had left.

Cross walked to the purser's office display and put the handbag down. Glancing in at the safety deposit boxes, he said, 'This seems to be what brought you two to the *Queen Mary*. It's the only part of the ship you've shown any interest in. I assume you have a key?'

Stella and Jack remained silent, their faces blank. Cross's eyes narrowed slightly and he looked to the older gunman, then nodded towards Jack. The gun in the man's hand was raised to shoulder height, pointing directly at Jack's head. Cross looked at Stella with a look of grim determination.

'So, Ms Sartori, do you have a key or not?'

She didn't hesitate. 'It's in my bag.'

'Get it then, and don't screw around, unless you want to lose another lover.'

Stella rushed to the handbag to retrieve the tiny key. When she handed it to Cross, he examined it closely. 'It isn't numbered,' he observed. 'Do you know what number the box is?'

'We have our theories,' Stella said. 'If you interpret the clues in the poem, you can develop one of your own.'

'As it happens,' Cross said, with obvious irritation, 'I never got my hands on a copy of the damned poem.' He glared in Jack's direction.

Ignoring the threat of the gun, Jack said, 'And you thought that was justification enough to burn down my home? To nearly kill my partner?'

Cross laughed derisively. 'Jesus, Jack, you can't nearly kill someone – you kill 'em or you don't.' Before Jack could respond, Cross spoke to the man holding up the gun.

'Vincenzo,' he said, 'we need to get inside.' He pointed to the purser's display. 'We go in there. You find door, okay?'

Vincenzo lowered his gun and muttered orders to his colleagues in a guttural language Jack couldn't make out. The young one took up position next to Jack, his pistol at his side. Vincenzo stayed beside Cross, his eyes on Stella. The third man disappeared and, a minute later, they heard a loud crack as a door was forced. The man reappeared and said simply, 'Is okay.'

Cross handed the key to Stella and said, 'You go with him. Do as you're told or Jack won't get to see what's in the box, understand?'

Stella shot a glance in Jack's direction as she moved away. There was fear and concern in that loaded look, as well as guilt and an apology. She disappeared with her minder, but reappeared a few seconds later behind the glass, entering the purser's office from the adjacent cabin display. The armed man used one hand to drag a wooden desk chair into the narrow space and indicated that Stella should stand on it. Now she could reach even the highest boxes.

'Can you hear me?' Cross called to Stella through the glass, and she nodded.

'Good.' He moved closer, leaning on the purser's counter like a regular passenger impatient for service. 'Unlock and pull out the drawer. Don't open it. Bring it out here. Understand?'

Stella nodded again, but then hesitated. 'I told you. We don't actually know for sure which box it is.'

Her voice was muffled by the glass partition but they could hear her well enough. She reached out and pulled at the nearest box experimentally. It didn't move. She tried the next one and it, too, was locked in place. She looked down at the key in the palm of her hand and said, 'You saw for yourself, the key isn't marked. The poem is a bit cryptic about it.'

'I'll give you five minutes,' Cross said with flinty indifference. 'After that, I'll just leave your bodies here for the cleaners to find in the morning.'

'You'd never get away with it,' Jack said impetuously. 'If we turn up dead, the FBI will know where to look.'

'They can look all they like,' Cross said, quietly and confidently. 'Witnesses, Jack, like I told you. Once you're gone, there'll be no witnesses. There are twelve respectable people in London who'll swear I've been there all week.' He nodded in the direction of Vincenzo. 'And the FBI will never find these guys. They're invisible.'

Jack could think of no adequate response. Cross turned his arrogant expression back to Stella, saying, 'Ms Sartori, you now have four minutes.'

Four minutes to live, Jack thought with alarm as he watched Stella contemplate the boxes. Whether she found the right box or not, their current life expectancy was little more than a few hundred seconds. He glanced at the gunmen, whose concentration was unwavering. He could see no way out. No final desperate move that might save them. Stella was isolated behind the glass with her own armed escort. Cross's face was cold and impassive as if he didn't care whether they found anything. Jack willed Stella to discover Campbell's hiding place soon. Apart from completing the clues in the poem, it might buy them a little more time.

Stella held the small key in her right hand and Jack watched, fascinated, as she raised it up to the top row of boxes. She wasn't following her own instincts for some reason. She was following Jack's. 'I'll try box number eight,' she said, giving him a fleeting look.

Jack's heart stopped. He felt slightly dizzy. His eyes were riveted to her fingers as they approached box number eight. The key slipped into the round brass lock. It was home. Box number eight, Jack thought, I was right. But the key wouldn't turn.

Cross looked at his watch. 'Two minutes.'

He pointed at Jack and made a gesture to Vincenzo, who nodded and spoke. The younger man raised his pistol and Jack could feel a force extending from the silencer, pressing against the side of his skull.

Stella saw what was happening. 'Jesus Christ, please! Relax! I'll find it.'

Cross was staring at the rows of silver boxes intently. 'Get on with it.'

Stella shifted the chair quickly over to the left side of the metal boxes – pursuing her own theory of four across, two down. 'Box number fourteen,' she called out, as if for the record.

The key slid easily into the lock. With a tiny noise of surprise and relief, Stella turned the key. The heavy lock disengaged smoothly and the metal drawer slid out slightly, as if propelled by a spring.

Stella gave Jack a brief look of triumph. Then she pulled the long metal box out of the wall. It was slim, barely an inch deep and four inches wide, but it was long, more than eighteen inches front to back. It had a hinged lid, almost as long as the box, to keep the contents hidden.

Stella needed two hands to lift the box down from its slot. Stepping down carefully, eyes glued to her prize, she carried it back to the narrow corridor where they were standing. Cross directed her to put it on the curved counter.

Without thinking, Jack moved forward to get a closer look, forgetting about the gun at his head. The young man kept the gun up and muttered some curse, but he didn't fire. The older one, Vincenzo, reached out and grabbed Jack's shoulder, pulling him back before he got too close to Cross. Stella was pushed beside Jack and the younger man positioned himself behind them, covering them both easily with his gun. The third guy, who had escorted Stella, moved to the end of the passageway, his pistol held at his side. Jack could see they were getting ready for an execution, but at that moment his impending death wasn't the dominant thought in his mind. Like Stella, whose eyes were fixed on the long metal box, he was desperate to know what was inside.

Daniel Cross obliged, turning the box around so the lock faced him, then lifting the long lid on its squeaky hinge. They all craned their necks to look inside.

The box was empty.

Cross put his hand inside and then felt around the lid. The box was completely empty.

The anticlimax was overwhelming. Jack looked at Stella and she looked at him and they both knew they were about to die for nothing.

Jack's muscles tensed. He felt sad and angry and embarrassed all at once. Cross turned to face him and Stella. 'It looks like we won't be needing you two any more.'

Cross glanced over at Vincenzo and said, 'Make your call.' He made a phone shape with his hand and raised it to his ear.

Vincenzo nodded and, without relaxing his pistol arm or his focus on Jack, pulled a cell phone out of his left trouser pocket.

The language the man used sounded to Jack like a hybrid of Italian and Arabic. It was a short conversation, obviously planned well in advance. Vincenzo appeared to report and then listen for instructions. Some higher authority, perhaps. Tony Castle? Jack looked over at Cross, who was completely at ease.

'Si, si,' Vincenzo said and disconnected the call. He spoke to the other two men and they said something in return. Jack's hand reached for Stella's and she gripped it. The touch sent a wave of sadness through them both.

Vincenzo took a step past Jack, closer to Daniel Cross. Jack felt a change in the atmosphere. Cross felt something too. Vincenzo mumbled a few words and raised his pistol at Jack, but the pistol didn't stop moving. With a fluid motion, Vincenzo kept swinging the gun up towards Daniel Cross's head. And then he pulled the trigger.

51

There was a soft popping noise. Blood and pieces of brain and bone splattered over the glass partition. Cross keeled forward, his long frame falling directly towards the spot where Stella and Jack were standing. Instinctively, they both jumped back as his disfigured face hit the deck with a sickening thud.

Astonishment rendered Jack momentarily senseless. He looked at the corpse in front of him, then at Vincenzo, then at Stella, his eyes wide with surprise. Stella's face mirrored his – her mouth hung open like a sideshow clown, shock painted across her face.

Jack jumped again as Vincenzo took a step forward, stood over Cross's body, and calmly fired two more bullets into the back of the head. The younger man stepped forward suddenly, eliciting another jolt of fear, but he just bent down to pick up the spent cartridge casings from the gun. When Jack looked up at Vincenzo again, his hand was reappearing from behind his back and his pistol was nowhere to be seen. His face betrayed no emotion at all as he watched Stella and Jack with the unblinking concentration of a hunter.

Was it up to the others to finish the job? Vincenzo's hand moved towards his face. Stella and Jack watched, hypnotised. The fingers curled into a salute and he said, with a heavy accent, 'Good e-ven-ing.'

He barked an order to the others and turned on his heels, straightening his suit jacket and tie as he walked down the passage, followed by the others. Stella and Jack stood stunned as the three men sauntered out into the gloom of the night and disappeared.

By unspoken agreement they let them go without any fuss. Anyone who threatened their escape had a good chance of regretting it. Besides, the man they'd come to regard as their nemesis was lying in front of them, face down, his blood splashed across their shoes.

A *Queen Mary* security guard was the first to find them. When he registered the body on the deck and the gore splashed over the glass and counter, Jack thought the poor man was going to lose his supper.

Jack and Stella were sitting side by side on the deck a few feet from the corpse, their backs propped against the glass of a cabin display. As the adrenaline ebbed away, they both felt exhausted. Fear, shock, exhilaration and anticlimax. It had been quite a ride.

Apart from checking them for weapons, the young guard seemed unsure of what to do next. He started asking clumsy questions until Stella told him to contact Agent Winters of the FBI, who was a guest on board. A few walkie-talkie exchanges later, more security staff and hotel employees showed up. After what seemed like an eternity, Shannon Winters stumbled into the corridor, flashing her FBI badge, her power suit torn where the sleeve met the right shoulder. Her hair was uncharacteristically messy and the paleness of her face emphasised the darkness around her eyes.

She leaned against the glass wall of the displays, struggling to absorb the scene in front of her – and struggling to stay conscious. From his position on the floor, Jack told her everything that had happened, then asked, 'What happened to Sanchez and Harrison?'

Winters grimaced. 'Harrison's okay,' she said. 'They're checking him out downstairs. He was drugged, like me.' Swallowing hard and looking away, she added, 'Kenny's dead. He must have fought back.'

She shook her head, as if to clear it. 'It's all my fault. They played us like fools. Harrison and Sanchez were good. How did Cross even know about them? And you're telling me it was all for nothing. The deposit box was empty?'

'Yes,' Jack said despondently, struggling to his feet and holding out a hand to Stella.

'I'm not so upset about that,' Stella said, as she pulled herself up. 'I think it saved our lives.'

'How do you figure that?'

Before she could explain, there was a shout from the group of people gathered at the end of the corridor. Frank Spiteri's face appeared over the shoulder of a security guard who was impeding his progress. Agent Winters went to usher him past the proprietary guard. When he saw them, standing with their backs to the seeping body of Daniel Cross, his face reflected confusion and concern. He rushed forward, hugged each of them and wasted no more than a quick glance on the body of his old friend.

'What happened?'

'We were just getting to that,' Winters said, her composure returning. She led them all down the corridor to keep their feet out of the forensic evidence, then turned to Stella. 'You were saying you think you're still alive because the box was empty. Tell me what you mean.'

'Okay, but let me start by saying the three guys Cross had with him were Sicilian. At least they spoke Sicilian.'

'You could understand them?' Jack said, intrigued.

Spiteri was surprised too. 'I thought your family was from the north.'

'My father is, but my mother's of Sicilian stock. My grandmother came to live with us when I was young. She could only speak her local dialect, right up 'til the day she died. It wasn't exactly the same as these guys were speaking, but it was close enough. Anyway, they weren't saying anything too complicated. I reckon any Italian speaker could've got the gist.'

Jack was impatient. 'What did they say?'

'When they grabbed me, after I left the ladies' room, they held me in a cabin for a few minutes. The guy called Vincenzo was the leader. He and the youngest guy talked while we waited for Cross to call. I think, from the way they referred to each other, that the two younger ones were brothers and Vincenzo was their uncle. They were saying something about Vincenzo being on board the *Queen Mary* before, when it was still running as a liner. '

Agent Winters held up a finger. 'No other names mentioned apart from this Vincenzo?'

Both Jack and Stella both shook their heads. Stella picked up the story again. 'After we'd all gathered here, and after I'd found the right box and put it there,' she gestured back towards the counter, 'Cross opened it and we could see it was empty.'

'Right,' Jack said. 'Then Cross told Vincenzo to make his call, like the phone call was part of the plan.'

'Yeah,' Stella agreed. 'I think what happened next depended on what they found in the box, and it was up to someone else to make the decision. Someone else had the final say.'

'Tony Castle,' Winters said, her eyes widening.

'Who?' Frank Spiteri said.

Stella shrugged her shoulders. 'All I know is Vincenzo called some-one who was obviously waiting for the call. He said something like, "It's empty," then, "Yes, I'm sure it's empty, there's nothing there." He listened and said "Yes" a few times, as if he was acknowledging instructions. Then he hung up, walked over to Cross and shot him in the head.'

Spiteri muttered, 'Amazing!'

Jack glanced back at the body of Daniel Cross and thought about his final few seconds. 'There was no hint he might have expected it.'

Stella agreed. 'No, not until just before the very end. Cross thought Vincenzo was going to kill us, I'm sure of it. He had a smug look on his face, like he was going to enjoy it.'

An image of the gun swinging up to Cross's head flashed into Jack's mind. 'Stella, did you notice Vincenzo say something to Cross just before he shot him? Did you hear him?'

'Yes I did, but I can't be sure I understood it. I thought he said something like, "The professor thanks you for your service." But that doesn't make much sense, does it?'

'Yes it does,' Winters said. 'Tony Castle was called the Professor when he was a kid because of his love of books. The bastard is still alive.'

Spiteri was shaking his head. 'I'm missing something,' he said, 'but surely none of that matters now. This unfortunate mess seems to have resolved itself neatly, except for Daniel Cross over there. I'm afraid he paid the ultimate price for mixing with the wrong people.'

'But Frank, don't you see?' Stella's eyes were shining with excitement again. 'This means there's an even more powerful conspirator out there. Someone with the power of life or death over Daniel Cross. Someone who must be secure and happy in the knowledge that he's in the clear, because Cross is dead and whatever Campbell Reeves left behind is gone. It must be the Mafia guy.'

Spiteri said nothing, so Stella took a breath and rushed on. 'I'm convinced if there'd been something damaging in that safety deposit box, we'd both be dead. Whatever it was Reeves knew, it must have had the potential to implicate more people than just Cross, wouldn't you say?'

She looked at Jack with wide green eyes and he nodded.

'And obviously Cross's partners must have decided he was a liability,' he said. 'Maybe he was marked for execution before tonight. Maybe the phone call was just to see if we should be killed too.'

'Whoever it was decided to spare us.'

Frank Spiteri was looking at the body of his client, seemingly fascinated by the shattered spot on the back of Cross's skull. 'Whether or not there's a "Mr Big" out there somewhere,' he said, 'I think it's up to the FBI now, right, Shannon? And the rest of us need to put this behind us. You two may want to take some time off, but I think the sooner we all get back to work, the sooner we'll feel better. The world keeps turning and the work of Sutton Brothers goes on.'

Stella and Jack exchanged a glance, like rebellious teenagers reacting to a pious sermon. Shannon Winters wasn't listening. She was thinking about the case, ruing the lost deposition and wondering how she was going to explain all this to the Director, who was taking a personal interest in her progress. Her boss's warnings rang loud in her ears. There had to be something she could salvage from this mess.

'Our only chance to catch Castle is to track down the Sicilians,' she said. 'That won't be easy, but I'll try to get some help from the Italian authorities. And I'll just ring through these descriptions to the port authorities and the INS. Maybe we can pick them up at an airport or at the borders.'

She walked away, using one arm to steady herself as she pulled out her cell phone. Sirens from off the port side of the ship marked the arrival of more people in uniforms. Soon cops and sundry experts were fighting for elbow room in the narrow passageway as they sealed off the scene and took charge of Cross's body.

Winters reappeared, making sure everybody present understood the

FBI was running the investigation. Jack felt sorry for her as he watched the strain of the situation play out on her face. Frank and Stella stood silently beside him in the passageway, observing the administration of a crime scene by a team of professionals. The officers appeared neither surprised nor impressed by the unusual location or situation of this homicide. Winters suggested that there was no need for them to stay, if they wanted to return to their cabins. Nobody moved. Somehow it was important to see Cross's body carried away.

Jack, Stella and Frank continued to stand to one side, keeping out of the way of the photographer and the forensic technician and the guy wrapping yellow crime-scene tape around everything. Stella took Jack's hand and gave it a squeeze.

They had to press themselves back against the glass to make room for the gurney removing the now covered body of Daniel Cross, leaving behind a gruesome mess, much to the horror of the *Queen Mary*'s management whose unhappy representatives were being held at the end of the passageway by a uniformed policeman.

Agent Winters came over to their group and said, 'That's it. We'll take formal statements in a few hours. You should all go and get some rest, or maybe a stiff drink.'

'I'm buying,' Spiteri said immediately, and he started down the corridor. 'I just have to get them to open the bar.'

Jack started to follow but stopped when he was wrenched back by Stella's grip on his hand. She stood still, looking back at the purser's office and through the bloodstained glass to the safety deposit boxes. Campbell's empty box sat on the counter, waiting to be tagged as evidence.

'What?' Jack said, and Stella replied simply, 'I've been thinking.'

The way she said it was enough to get everybody's attention. Spiteri stopped where he was and turned around. Winters looked at Stella expectantly.

'Go on,' Jack said.

She gave him a mischievous smile. 'Well, I was thinking about Campbell Reeves and his safety deposit box. If I were on this ship, trying to hide something that someone else would kill to get his mitts on, I'd try to be a bit clever, wouldn't I? I was thinking about what Campbell would have done if Cross had found out he'd hidden something incriminating. If Cross had found out about the safety deposit box. If Cross had found the key.'

Jack jumped in. 'Cross would have forced him to open the box or opened it himself, if he could.'

'Right,' Stella said. 'And if he was being interrogated about it, Campbell would have denied the whole thing. He would have said, "I haven't hidden anything. The safety deposit box is empty. I was going to use it to store some expensive jewellery that I'm planning to buy my wife." Are you with me?'

Shannon Winters looked dubious but Jack knew better than to doubt Stella's powers of deduction. He encouraged her to finish her train of thought.

'Okay, so I'm thinking, what if Campbell thought all this through? What would he have done about it? He was a bit of a prankster, remember, he enjoyed puzzles and hidden clues. How could he keep his secret safe, even if Cross found out about it?'

There was a long pause before Shannon made a suggestion. 'Have another safety deposit box? With this box acting as a diversion?'

'Maybe,' Stella said, but Jack could tell she had a more interesting theory.

'Make the safety deposit box only appear to be empty,' he offered tentatively, thinking it was obvious but improbable.

'Exactly!' Stella pointed to the rows of silver boxes and said, 'Don't forget to check the roof.'

Shannon said, 'What?' as Jack repeated, '"Don't forget to check the roof". It's a line from "The Virgin's Secret". We couldn't make sense of it.'

Stella ducked under the yellow tape strung across the passageway and strode back towards the purser's office. Winters bolted after her, saying, 'Where the hell are you going?'

'To check the roof!'

Not prepared to be left out, Jack followed Winters. Spiteri was the only one who stayed where he was.

Stella moved more cautiously as she approached the sticky spatters of blood on the floor and walls. Hopping over the main puddle of muck on the deck, she went through the door leading to the ship's displays. Shannon stopped abruptly and put out an arm to keep Jack from stepping any closer to the spot where Cross had been shot. They stood about ten feet back from the counter, craning their necks, trying to make sense of what Stella was doing when she appeared behind the gore-splattered window.

The slot where Campbell's box had resided for so many years was a rectangular black hole, barely wide enough to fit a hand. Stella was standing on the desk chair with her hand wedged deep inside the space for box number fourteen.

She shouted something, but she was facing the other way and, from this distance, Jack couldn't make it out. And he couldn't see her face through the red haze of the glass partition. He watched, spellbound, as Stella began to wiggle her arm slowly out from the slot. Her hand came out palm up and he thought it was empty. But in between her outstretched fingers, he caught a glimpse of something white. Stella pulled the object out from the long hole and, perched precariously on the old chair, held it up triumphantly. It was an envelope.

'It was stuck to the roof of the slot,' she called out. 'Campbell Reeves was one smart bloke!'

Stella hurried to where they were standing. By the time she

reached them, and much to the FBI agent's horror, she had the envelope open and a sheaf of fine paper in her hands. The pages were covered on both sides in tiny, meticulous handwriting.

She flicked through the pages quickly, saying, 'Wow, there's a huge amount of information here. Oh, and look, at the end – here's a letter to Beth.' She started to read the letter to herself and then said, 'Oh, God, this is sad.'

Winters was suffering a mild panic attack. 'Give it to me at once!' she ordered. 'And try not to get your prints all over it, please!'

Stella stopped, out of the agent's reach, suspicion written all over her face. Taking one step backwards, she looked down at the documents in her hand and started to read out loud.

'This is a deposition by Gilbert Collins, President of Collins Military Systems, prepared by Campbell Reeves, Vice President in charge of Finance at CMS. It sets out details of the criminal activities of certain company employees, in particular Daniel Cross and Ewan Collins, as well as others outside the company including, in particular, Tony Castelluzzo of Chicago, Illinois, otherwise known as Tony Castle. These crimes include the extortion and murder of government officials in Washington and, most importantly, the assassination of President John F. Kennedy.'

She stopped, then repeated, 'The assassination of President John F. Kennedy,' as if she wasn't sure she'd read it right.

Rosy red spots were colouring the pale cheeks of Agent Winters. Stella lifted her eyes to Jack's and he gazed back with a mixture of astonishment and wonder. Her face was glowing. Her head turned slightly, looking past Jack's shoulder. Jack turned too, intrigued to see the look on Frank's face.

But the passageway was empty, except for a uniformed police officer. Frank Spiteri was gone.

52

'Frank was Tony Castle,' Stella said, stunned by the notion that she'd been working not just for a mobster, but a mobster with an incredible resumé.

Agent Winters had ushered them into an office reluctantly given up by the hotel's night manager. Asserting their legal right to the Collins deposition, but suspecting their time with it would be short, Stella and Jack were poring over the pages spread across a meeting table.

'Must have been,' Jack said, also struggling to take it in. 'Now we know how Cross knew about the FBI agents. We told Frank!'

Winters was standing with a phone to her ear, but was obviously on hold, because she said, 'He had an impeccably constructed background, perhaps the best we've ever seen. And already there's no sign of his wife or daughter. His Manhattan condo is empty. He must have had an escape plan ready to go at a moment's notice.'

The agent held up a hand to indicate that someone had come on the line and Jack returned to studying the deposition with Stella.

'Look at this,' she said, pointing at the elegant handwriting without touching the page. 'Apparently Frank, or Tony, had the brilliant idea of speeding up the US commitment to South Vietnam so they could maximise the value of the contract. He did all this research on the politics of Kennedy and Johnson and their respective advisers and concluded that the Vice President would commit more men and material to Vietnam than Kennedy, and do it sooner.'

Jack shook his head in amazement. 'We always knew he was a big thinker.'

Stella grunted at the irony. 'Follow the money,' she said. 'Who'd believe it was just about the dollars? It seems so unsatisfactory.'

Their musings were interrupted by Agent Winters, who stopped talking on her cell phone and placed it next to the pages of the explosive deposition. She pressed a button.

'Director,' she said in a formal tone, 'you are now connected with Stella Sartori and Jack Rogers of Sutton Brothers.'

It was just after 2 a.m. on the *Queen Mary* and three hours later in Washington DC, but the voice of the speaker sounded fully alert.

'It's a great pleasure to make your acquaintance, Jack and Stella, albeit by phone.'

Jack smiled at the thought of the Director of the FBI, sitting up in bed, trying to sound impressive while wearing his pyjamas.

'I understand from Agent Winters that you two have had quite a night,' the Director went on, 'but I thought it was important for us to talk as soon as possible about what happens next.'

Already the one-sided conversation had the air of a negotiation. Stella licked her lips. Putting deals together was her stock in trade.

'Let me see if I can sum it up for you, Director,' she suggested confidently, 'in the interests of saving us all some time. I imagine you'd like the FBI to take full custody of the documents we discovered tonight and you probably want us to sign some sort of confidentiality agreement – am I right?'

'Something like that,' said the Director. 'Accusations like these must be handled very sensitively. I want the Bureau to have the opportunity to investigate the claims made by Mr Collins without interference from tabloid journalists and conspiracy theorists.'

'We have no problem with that,' Stella said, without hesitation. 'All Campbell Reeves wanted for that deposition was that it be placed in the hands of the appropriate authorities. I'd say you qualify, wouldn't you agree, Jack?'

'Can't think of an authority more appropriate,' Jack said with a casual smile.

'But,' Stella said, 'there's another document in this collection apart from the deposition. Campbell also wrote a letter to his wife. He doesn't mention the Kennedy assassination because I don't think he wanted her to know. He just needed her to find the product of all his hard work and get it to your predecessor or to an agent called Sedgwick. Jack and I will agree to your terms completely if you let us take Campbell's letter and deliver it to his wife, as he wished.'

There was a pause, until Shannon Winters cleared her throat and said, 'Director, sir, Mr Reeves – and Gilbert Collins too – died trying to deliver the truth to the American people. His wishes deserve to be honoured.'

'Yes, Winters,' the Director said, as if he didn't appreciate the input, 'they do. All right then, I think we have an arrangement. And I won't ask you to sign any confidentiality agreement. I'm sure, as foreign nationals, you're well aware how quickly your residency status can change. There's no incentive to upset your hosts, is there?' Without waiting for a response to his veiled threat, the Director continued, 'I want to thank you for your courage and determination. You too, Winters, good job.'

The line went dead and Winters picked up her phone as if it was a precious artefact. But it wasn't only her who was experiencing a proud sense of achievement, underwritten by words of praise from one of the most powerful men in the nation. And the shared feeling in the room had the effect of softening attitudes.

'I'm sorry for being difficult,' Stella said to Winters. 'And thanks for saying that about Campbell Reeves.'

'I'm sorry for almost getting you killed!' Winters responded, and they all laughed with relief. 'No, I really am,' she said. 'The Director wanted to keep the team small and I accepted it. I was over-confident and poor Kenny Sanchez paid the price.'

'We all made mistakes along the way,' Jack said. 'And now that we know the resources Tony Castle had access to, I doubt you stood any chance without the entire Bureau behind you.'

'Bloody hell!' Stella said incredulously, 'Imagine how the partners of Sutton Brothers are going to react when they find out that their biggest star was a Mafioso! They're going to have kittens.'

'Yeah, but imagine if you hadn't gone back for another look, Stella. It would have been business as usual for Frank Spiteri,' Winters said.

'That's what he was hoping for, obviously,' Jack said. 'Isn't that amazing? He orders the death of one of his oldest friends one day so he can return to his respectable life the next.'

Stella found herself yawning uncontrollably as the events of the day took their toll. She pointed in the direction of the cabins and summed up her needs in one word: 'Sleep.'

The new day dawned clear and sunny as Stella and Jack stood in the car park, taking a nostalgic look up at the magnificent ship, which now occupied a unique place in their memories.

Two hours later, they flew to San Francisco through a cloudless sky and took a cab from the airport to climb the hill where Elizabeth Reeves and her daughter were waiting for them.

Heather held each of them tightly to her ample bosom as they arrived on the top step, before ushering them inside to the rich wood panelling of her sitting room. Elizabeth was there, propped up in her wheelchair. She was wearing a floral day dress and a little makeup and lipstick, giving her the look of an elegant, elderly woman about to embark on a shopping trip. She seemed cheerful too, smiling broadly enough to show her dentures and flashing her blue eyes as Jack and Stella each gave her a peck on the cheek.

After the compulsory tea and cake, Heather sat enraptured as Jack and Stella told their carefully edited tale. She sighed and gasped as they explained a little of the events on the ship and when they told her about Cross's death, she said quite loudly, 'Good!'

Immediately she lifted one hand to her mouth, as if aghast at the strength of her own feeling. Jack reassured her by agreeing whole-heartedly that it was a good thing. There was no way to tell if Beth was absorbing anything they said, but her eyes followed the conversation and Jack was convinced she was trying to take it in.

At last, Stella came to the letter, which she offered to Heather. Heather looked but didn't take the folded paper. She turned to Jack instead and said, 'Would you mind reading the letter to my mother, Jack? I think it would be best in a male voice, don't you?'

Stella presented the letter to Jack in a way that gave him no choice but to take it. He didn't like the idea of impersonating a dead man just to improve the impact of a love letter. But when he looked over to Heather, she had her eyes closed, waiting, as if in prayer.

He realised that he'd be doing this small service as much for her as for her mother. She wanted to hear her father's words, and she wanted to imagine him speaking them. It was a bridge to the past, the closest she could ever get to her long-lost father.

He cleared his throat, looked down at the page in front of him and thought, This is going to be tough.

My dearest Beth,

Alas, my love, if you are reading this note, it means that I am dead. It means the life we had together – a life of love and happiness and everlasting joy in your embrace – has been cruelly cut short by ruthless and selfish men. I can only hope and pray, with my final few breaths, that the record I have made of the criminal deeds of Dan Cross and his ilk will aid the authorities in bringing them to justice.But Beth, I must admit to you that all their crimes seem insignificant to me next to the unspeakable horror of destroying our love. I am a selfish man too, Beth, and I can't bear the thought of being without you.

My great regret is that I didn't meet you earlier in my life. It seems so unfair that God should have granted us little more than twenty years together. I anticipated so much more time, time for just you and me.

And now you'll have to endure that time without me. I won't have to bear the loss of our togetherness, but you will – and I despair. How cruel it is that my final thoughts will be of the pain my death will cause you and the children. I beg you, darling, treasure our love and the time we had together but try to find some new happiness. Don't let your life end with my departure. Start over and, when you're ready, look for love again.

Deliver my report to the authorities as quickly as you can, and then forget about Daniel Cross. Let the government take care of it. But get out of Peoria, Beth – get away from the

Collins family and the company. Take the children away too. Find a place near the sea, like we always talked about. And smile, if you can – the world would be a cold place without your smile.

Tell Heather and Duncan and Cam Junior I love them and I'm proud of them. I'll be watching over you all and I won't be happy if, for one single minute, you stop looking out for one another.

It pains me to stop writing, Beth, as if the end of this letter marks the end of my life. The very thought that these may be the final words you hear from me fills me with sadness and dread. But I need to be brave, for your sake and for the sake of my friendship with Gil. Who knows? With God's help, we may yet look back on this voyage and be able to smile.

If that is not to be, then remember all the happy times we spent together and remember my love for you.

Your most loving husband,
Campbell

8 December 1967

A clock on the mantelpiece ticked loudly. Jack hadn't noticed it before, but in the thick silence of Heather's sitting room the tick-tock dominated. Stella looked as if she was a million miles away, her head tilted slightly. Heather sniffled into a lace handkerchief.

Beth's eyes were in sharp focus. Jack could tell because they were looking at him. There were no tears on her face but there was a sadness that gave him a jolt. Did she understand? Did she remember? Then the old lady did something to give him hope. She held out her hand and looked down at the letter in Jack's lap.

Jack folded the paper carefully and, leaning forward, held it out to her. Elizabeth touched his hand gently with the soft, dry skin of her fingers before taking a firm hold of her husband's letter. She lifted it to her lips, gave it a tiny kiss, and held the letter to her heart.

Her smile was all the reward Jack needed.

Later, Stella and Jack stood in the sun outside Heather's home before setting off down the hill to find a cab. They felt good, as if they'd somehow closed an important loop. And Campbell's eloquent expression of enduring love had been inspiring.

As they walked, Stella didn't hesitate to pose the obvious question. 'So, Jack, what next?'

Jack gave her the obvious answer. 'Well, I suppose I have to go back to New York and sort out the mess that was once my home. Mind you, the prospect of searching through the rubble and dealing with the insurance company isn't too attractive. Talk about coming back to earth with a thud!'

And, he thought with a vague sense of foreboding, I have to sort out my relationship with Peta. She'll be pissed that I've moved on so quickly, that I can walk away so easily. She'll say Stella's just part of my usual pattern, a convenient way to avoid real-life commitment. And the fact that it feels so right to me isn't going to matter a damn to her.

Then he looked over at Stella and forgot all the potential troubles. She smiled at him and took his hand. 'Will you stay with me in New York?' she said. 'Or is that too weird?'

Jack thought about moving into the home of the guy who died destroying his. 'Of course it's weird, but if that's where you're going to be, then that's where I'd like to be, too.'

'Aaah, you romantic fool.'

'Guilty,' he said, and gave her a clumsy kiss on the cheek as they negotiated the steep San Francisco street, all the time resisting gravity's demand to break into a run.

There was a short pause before Stella piped up again. 'And after that?'

'I don't know. I haven't thought that far ahead.'

'Do you want to go back to Sutton Brothers?'

'I don't think so,' he said, surprising himself. 'Anyway, if and when the story breaks that one of the most senior partners was a mobster, I have a feeling they're going to be downsizing.'

'Agreed. They might treat us like heroes at first, but when they realise the damage this affair will do to the bank, the partners will soon stop loving us.'

The hill flattened out a little and Stella actually skipped, twice, like an excited schoolgirl, and said teasingly, 'So what do you want to do?'

'I don't know. I certainly don't want to go back to trading, but I can hardly fall back on my track record as a mergers consultant, can I?'

She giggled. 'Not really. There's no way the Kradel deal will go ahead. So not only do you have the country's shortest track record in mergers and acquisitions, but you also played a primary role in bringing down the only deal you've been involved with. It's not going to look too good on the CV.'

'No, you're right,' he said, laughing with her. 'Who's going to hire someone who worked for a mobster, even if he was a good dealmaker? But it's the same for you, Stella. When you go for a job, who are you going to nominate for your references? How do you avoid talking about the man who was your direct boss for the last three years? You were Frank's protégé, for Christ's sake!'

They reached the cross-street at the bottom of the hill and

stopped, looking around for a taxi. Stella said, 'The mergers game was boring me, anyway.'

It was time for Jack to turn the tables. 'So, Stella,' he said, 'what is it *you* want to do next?'

'Well . . .' she said.

Jack took her gently by the shoulders and turned her around to face him. 'Well?' he said. 'Well, what?'

She lifted her head to look at him. Her eyes sparkled as she said, 'I have a proposition for you.'

Acknowledgements

My thanks to all the friends and family who have supported me during the writing of this novel. Their encouragement and advice has been invaluable.

Particular credit must go to my sister Jeneen, whose unfailing enthusiasm and guidance kept moving me forward towards the final goal. Thanks also to Jeneen's book club, the Blah Blahs, and the other readers who gave me both helpful feedback and vital motivation.

To Kirsten Abbott and Arwen Summers at Penguin, thank you for your strong support and valuable input, and to my editor Jody Lee, many thanks for your tremendous eye for detail and your professionalism.

Finally, it must be acknowledged that there would be no book to read, edit or publish without the love and support of my partner Julia, for which I am forever grateful.

GUARANTEED GREAT READ
or your money back

If you are not completely satisfied with this book, please complete this coupon and return with the book and original proof of purchase to:

Marketing Department

Penguin Group (Australia)

PO Box 701

Hawthorn VIC 3122

Please allow up to eight weeks for your refund. Refunds are only payable if the book and original proof of purchase are provided.

Name: _____

Address: _____

_____

Daytime phone number: _____

Offer expires 31 December 2009

Get closer to your favourite crime authors at

penguinmostwanted.com.au

The Beijing Conspiracy

Adrian d'Hagé

From China's western-most province, near its border with Pakistan, comes the threat of a devastating biological attack and a coded ultimatum. In the White House Situation Room, the President and his cabinet dismiss it.

But CIA agent Curtis O'Connor isn't so sure. The warning comes from Dr Khalid Kadeer, a brilliant Muslim microbiologist. O'Connor, an expert on bioterrorism, knows Kadeer isn't bluffing.

So does Australian-born Kate Braithwaite. She works in a deadly hot-zone laboratory, on the USA's own top-secret biological weapons program, genetically engineering Ebola, Marburg and Smallpox to create a super virus. If the results of Dr Braithwaite's research fall into the wrong hands, millions of people will die.

As Curtis O'Connor and Kate Braithwaite work to unravel the riddles of Kadeer's warning, they being to uncover a threat more sinister than they had imagined – a threat from within, from a man whose lust for power drives him to orchestrate a plan that will devastate the human race. The clock is ticking . . .

The Beijing Conspiracy is a frighteningly real novel showing how a scientist with a cause can hold the world to ransom.

The Omega Scroll

Adrian d'Hagé

A Dead Sea Scroll has lain undisturbed in a cave near Qumran for nearly two thousand years. The Omega Scroll contains both a terrible warning for civilisation and the coded number the Vatican fears most.

The Pope's health is failing and the Cardinal Secretary of State, the ruthless Lorenzo Petroni, has the Keys to St Peter within his grasp. Three things threaten to destroy him: Cardinal Giovanni Donnelli has started an investigation into the Vatican Bank; journalist Tom Schweiker is looking into Petroni's past; and the brilliant Dr Allegra Bassetti is piecing together fragments of the Omega Scroll. While they fight for their lives in a deadly race for the scroll, the Vatican will stop at nothing to keep the prophecy hidden.

At the CIA's headquarters in Virginia, Mike McKinnon suspects a number of missing nuclear suitcase bombs are connected to the warning in the Omega Scroll.

In the Judaean Desert a few more grains of sand trickle from the wall of a cave. The countdown for civilisation has begun.

'A provocative book in which every sort of dogma is questioned and every preconceived idea turned on its head'

SUNDAY MAIL

'A classy action thriller'

SUNDAY TIMES

Dead and Kicking

Geoff McGeachin

When a movie about an Australian war hero takes Alby Murdoch to Vietnam, he discovers that some old soldiers never die and that it's not just the cameras doing the shooting . . .

A job as stills photographer and some top-notch nosh were two good reasons for Alby Murdoch to be in Saigon. The third was that he had to clear out of Sydney and the spy game for a while.

But when Alby snaps a photo of the wrong passing cyclo, suddenly more action is taking place off camera than on. Alongside his old flame, the bootylicious Jezebel Quick – and his new friend, the alluring Inspector Hoang – Alby is thrust into the murky, watch-your-back world of casino crime lords, bent politicians, rogue expats, killer fish and ruthless celebrity chefs.

Dead and Kicking takes us racing through the adrenalin-charged streets of Saigon, Hong Kong and Macau, through Darwin and the Top End and into Canberra's corridors of power. It's Geoff McGeachin at his irreverent, page-turning best.

Sensitive New Age Spy

Geoff McGeachin

All Alby wants is a decent coffee and a day off. But there's a hijacked tanker with a deadly cargo in Sydney Harbour, and bullets are flying on board a US Navy cruiser. Three sailors are dead and a Seahawk chopper is missing.

Who's behind the mayhem? Why is the government intent on shutting down Alby's investigation? What's the connection to the smooth-talking Reverend Priday, spiritual leader to the upwardly mobile? And can Alby trust Lieutenant Kingston, a weapons specialist with the longest legs he's ever seen on a sailor and not a tattoo anywhere on her stunning body? Special agent Alby Murdoch, reluctant hero, is right back in the thick of things in another hilarious, page-turning romp.

'A rip-roaring and sexy spy novel that is unputdownable'
NEWCASTLE HERALD

'Wonderfully entertaining . . . rich with humour,
an abundance of thrills, and a pace that never flags'
SUNDAY TASMANIAN